Moon Child

Lycanthropic Book 6

Steve Morris

This novel is a work of fiction and any resemblance to actual persons living or dead, places, names or events is purely coincidental.

Steve Morris asserts the right under the Copyright, Designs and Patents Act 1988 to be identified as the author of this work.

Published by Landmark Media, a division of Landmark Internet Ltd.

Copyright © 2021 by Steve Morris.
All rights reserved.

stevemorrisbooks.com

ISBN-13: 979-8783873409

The Lycanthropic Series

Acknowledgements

Huge thanks are due to Margarita Morris, James Pailly, Josie Morris, Alex Vines, Mary Van Ede, Marc Mantione and Deborah Thornton for their valuable comments and feedback.

Dedication

For my mother, who, much to my amazement, has become my number-one fan.

Prologue: Two Years Before the Apocalypse

The Carpathian Mountains, Romania, waning moon

The creature wrestled to free itself, snarling menacingly as Leanna Lloyd and the others approached it along the forest path. Fear was evident in the jerky movements of its limbs. It panted rapidly, its long tongue hanging out.

Canis lupus. A wolf. Caught in a trap.

Leanna stood behind Professor Wiseman and her two fellow students, Adam and Samuel, feeling just as frightened as the animal looked.

It must have spent hours there already. Yet despite the beast's obvious exhaustion, its eyes remained alert and cunning, and it returned Leanna's gaze as an equal, searching for an opportunity to escape, and perhaps even to turn the tables on its captors. It rolled its jaws open, showing her its teeth. Paired upper and lower carnassials, ready to tear meat. Wicked canines, protruding like sharpened stakes. She could see where it had tried in vain to chew away the netting that held it. The creature flexed its legs, revealing sharp claws capable of rending the flesh of its victims. It was a predator, easily capable of ending Leanna's life if it were not trapped. Attacks on humans by wolves, bears and lynx in the mountains of Romania were not that uncommon. In winter, wolves sometimes even entered villages to slaughter sheep and other prey.

'Don't be afraid,' said Professor Wiseman, striding confidently up to the net that secured the beast in place. 'Remember what the villagers say. *Do not fear the wolf that walks by light.*'

Leanna understood the meaning of the saying well enough. *The wolf that walks by light is not a werewolf.* This was not the creature they had been hoping to trap. It was just an unfortunate animal in the wrong place at the wrong time. She felt a sadness, and hoped the wolf had not been hurt.

'Let's cut it free,' said Wiseman, producing a hand axe from his kit.

The trap was of a simple design. A net suspended from a tree sapling, with two metal hooks driven into the ground to hold it in place, ready to be triggered by a tripwire if a large animal stepped into it. Smaller variations of this type of trap were traditionally used to catch rabbits, wildcats and other vermin and pests. Wiseman and the team had set the trap on a woodcutter's path leading through the forest, a few miles out of the village.

Setting traps for werewolves wasn't something you learned at medical school. But with practice, they had honed the skill rather effectively. Leanna worried that they might inadvertently catch one of the villagers, or some other unfortunate passer-by. While not technically illegal, setting the trap on a path used by the locals seemed ill-advised to her.

Wiseman had dismissed her concerns in his usual breezy way. 'This is a humane trap. Trust me, it's a lot safer than the snares the locals use. And a hell of a lot safer than what the hunters get up to.'

The sport of hunting had long been popular in Romania, especially of brown bears, wild boar, deer, wolves, lynx, foxes, hares, rabbits and birds. During the Communist era, only Party members had been permitted the privilege of hunting, but that had provided little respite for the wildlife. During those years the country's notorious dictator, Nicolae Ceaușescu and his cronies had massacred almost half of the region's bear population. Now, since the fall of Communism, hunting rights had been restored in full and sometimes hundreds of hunters could be found at work in the mountains, blasting away at beasts and birds with their shotguns and rifles. It was a wonder anything was still alive.

Wiseman lifted his axe aloft and brought it down on the sapling. With two swift chops he cut the rope, and the net that held the wolf sprang loose. The creature bounded free in an instant and dashed off between the trees, sure of its footing and apparently uninjured.

Wiseman watched it go. 'There, you see? No harm done. But I guess we'll have to wait another month before we get our next chance.'

The next full moon. They had been living in the mountains since late spring, and now it was the height of summer. The high Carpathians were stunning in July, flush with wildflowers like jewels. A carpet of clover, lavender and harebells turned the hillsides purple, and up close the blue of cornflower mingled with the crimson of campion, carnations and wild strawberries. The air smelled sweet and pure. The land was an undiscovered Eden.

Here, nature still held sway. The villages were small and isolated, nestling in deeply wooded vales and connected by narrow mountain passes. The forests were cool even in the heat of summer – flickering green worlds of light and shadow beneath a canopy of glittering leaves. Trunks of beeches, oaks and hornbeams marched for mile upon mile in all directions, and if you strayed from the path you could quickly become lost. Beyond the forest, more mountains flanked the horizon, pale blue in the shimmering haze of the sun.

But Wiseman and his team had not come here to enjoy the views. Legends and lore of beasts and monsters abounded in Transylvania, where vampires were believed to walk the forest paths, and a stranger encountered at a crossroads was regarded with suspicion, if not outright fear. If Wiseman was right, then somewhere within this untamed wilderness lurked a creature straight out of myth and fairy-tale. The werewolf, or *vârcolac* in the Romanian tongue.

Not that the locals ever used that word in Leanna's presence. They were cautious, suspicious of strangers. They did not trust the foreign professor, nor his team of students. It was easy to understand why. The Carpathian Mountains were wild still. The vast mountain range crossed many borders, extending into Ukraine in the east, Serbia in the south, Slovakia in the west and Poland in the north. The twenty-first century was only just starting to bring change to the country folk who lived there. Here in Transylvania, in the heart of the mountains, the older people did not care for change and they did not trust outsiders.

Leanna could hardly blame them for being wary of the new arrivals. The mountain range, with its dense forests, winding roads and ancient settlements was filled with mystery. In winter, mountain passes could be blocked by snow and cut off for days. The legend of Vlad the Impaler had originated nearby. Born in the city of Sighişoara and buried in Snagov Monastery, the fearsome ruler, Prince Vlad Tepes, who was rumoured to have drunk human blood, had inspired the *Dracula* story.

There was no doubt that Vlad had been bloodthirsty.

He had slaughtered hundreds of his enemies and left them impaled on spikes. That was a matter of recorded history. The ruins of Poenari Fortress, home to the prince and known popularly as Dracula's Castle, were there for all to see, and many tourists came to do just that. Their tour bus would take them on to eat the exact same meal that Jonathan Harker had eaten at The Golden Crown in Bistrita and to stay at the Castle Dracula Hotel, located on the Borgo Pass.

Truth and superstition were hard to disentangle in the Carpathians, where a *vrăjitoare,* or white witch, lived in every village, and the old folk and the gypsies still whispered incantations to fend off the evil eye. Had Vlad Tepes been merely a cruel ruler, exceptional even for the barbaric times in which he lived, or was he, as the legends claimed, part human, part monster? Professor Wiseman had his suspicions, and he had brought his team to Romania in order to find out.

Leanna recalled when the professor had first broached the idea of the expedition, back in London. He'd done it in a furtive, roundabout way, presenting her initially with a well-thumbed copy of Bram Stoker's *Dracula*. 'Have you ever read this?'

'The original vampire novel? No, I haven't actually.'

'You should. It's a cracking good tale. Bram Stoker based it on traditional Romanian folk beliefs in vampires and werewolves.'

'Werewolves?' queried Leanna, puzzled. 'I thought it was all about vampires.'

Wiseman smiled. 'Vampires and werewolves are relatively modern concepts. In Romanian folklore, such creatures are often indistinguishable. They appear in a wide variety of forms –*strigoi, moroi, pricolici, căpcăun* and *vârcolac.* Read the book and you'll find that Count Dracula has the ability to shapeshift into the form of a bat, a wolf and a large dog. So even in Bram Stoker's story, the division between werewolf and vampire isn't as strict as most people imagine.'

'But why do you want me to read it?' Leanna asked. It wasn't the kind of reading material a professor of medicine normally gave his students.

'Read it first. Then I'll explain.'

Several months later, Leanna and Wiseman's other two students, Adam Knight and Samuel Smalling, had flown to Bucharest, where the maverick professor had picked them up from the airport in his clapped-out old Land Rover. After spending a night at a cheap hostel in the city, they had driven north, first to the medieval walled citadel of Sighişoara, then further into the wilds of Northern Transylvania. Travelling through rural Romania was like returning to a lost time. Here, horses ambled along dirt-track roads, pulling gypsy caravans driven by sullen men and smiling women and packed full of brown-eyed children who looked as wild as their animals.

The roads climbed forever upward, snaking across mountain passes and twisting between dense pine forests, beneath jagged clifftops and across plunging gorges. In the villages, brightly-painted houses lined the roadsides, their roofs sloping steeply like witches' hats. Everywhere, there were people, dogs and horses.

Leanna had quickly fallen in love with this untamed country.

She was getting to know the other students better too. Adam, super-competitive and sporty, and Samuel, big hearted and generous, were two of the brightest graduates in their year. The professor had picked his three helpers astutely. Each had their own personal reason for following him on this mad trip to the back of beyond, following a line of research that any sensible student would have shunned.

'I know why you came here,' said Wiseman the night after they'd arrived in the mountains and had worked their way through half a bottle of his favourite single malt whisky. 'You all came for different reasons. Adam, because you enjoy taking risks. You couldn't resist getting involved in the biggest scientific discovery of the century, even though the chance of my mad idea turning out to be true is a million to one. Samuel, you're here to escape your latest doomed love affair, and to put as many miles as possible between yourself and London. And Leanna' – he looked straight at her – 'you're pursuing your own crazy dream of finding the fountain of youth. Am I right?'

She nodded. Ever since childhood, she'd yearned to find the secret of immortality. Watching her own mother die from a pneumonia infection had been agony. She'd felt the pain of her mother's torment like a spear through her own heart. As an adult, the suffering of all humanity weighed heavily on her shoulders. The monstrous effects of disease; the tragedy of ageing; the unbearable anguish of death. It was too much for her to bear. It had to stop.

That was why she'd chosen to dedicate herself to the study of disease. She'd hoped to apply her skills diligently, making a modest but meaningful contribution to medical science, perhaps pushing back in some small way against one of the many ailments that afflicted humankind. Now here she was, filled with a desperate hope and engaged in a ridiculous pursuit on the strength of legends, myths and fantasy. This might all be a colossal waste of her time. And yet, if Wiseman was right and these creatures were real, they held out the chance not only of defeating disease, but of conquering death itself. If vampires really could claim eternal life by drinking the blood of others, and if werewolves could achieve rebirth through transformation, then even if the hope was as slender as one of her own golden hairs, she had no choice but to pursue it.

It was only fitting that they should come to this modern-day Eden in search of the impossible. For not only had the original garden contained the Tree of the Knowledge of Good and Evil, it had also held the Tree of Life, the source of immortality. As a scientist, Leanna believed that the biblical story was nothing more than fairy-tale and metaphor. But still, it was a powerful one.

Just like Eve, Leanna was tempted. Eve had tasted the fruit of the forbidden tree and gained knowledge of good and evil. God had thrown Adam and Eve from the Garden, and their sons and daughters had wandered the world ever since, seeking to reclaim the lost paradise. Now, this was their chance. Wiseman and his team of scientists had come to this new Eden armed with knowledge, in search of good. They wouldn't make the same mistake as Adam and Eve.

The notion of drinking human blood like a vampire was repulsive to Leanna. Yet if it could be proven to work, there would be no need for her to taste that forbidden fruit herself. With modern medicine they could synthesize the necessary elixir in the laboratory, and inject it directly into the bloodstream, or turn it into tablets that could be swallowed. Nobody need actually drink the blood of others, and nobody had to die to make this work. In fact, if the expedition into the mountains revealed that lycanthropy really existed, then perhaps nobody needed to die ever again.

Leanna would happily tolerate Professor Wiseman's dubious ethics and his reckless quest. For if these creatures were real, she and the others would find them, and the world would never be the same again.

Chapter One

South Downs National Park, waning moon

The Foxhound rumbled noisily along the narrow country road, with Corporal Llewelyn Jones at the wheel, whistling tunelessly as he drove. Police Constable Liz Bailey sat in the passenger seat, gazing out of her side window. It was a perfect July afternoon, the sun floating high with only a light breeze to push the few scattered clouds lazily across the cobalt blue expanse of the sky. Liz wished she could open the window to let some air inside, but the Foxhound's bulletproof windows were bolted firmly shut. The designers of the military vehicle had evidently prioritised defence against roadside bombs over the comfort of its passengers.

In any case, Liz was fooling herself if she imagined she could allow the hot sun to fall against her face. Now she was a vampire, she would never be able to enjoy that feeling again. Even through the toughened glass, the sun's rays pricked at her skin like needles. Without the window's

Lycanthropic

UV protection, her pale skin might burn to a crisp, and if she ever removed her dark sunglasses the bright sunlight would surely blind her. Night was her time now, and she felt dozy in the hot afternoon. She wouldn't become fully alert until after sundown, but it was safer to travel by day. Vampires weren't the only creatures that hunted by night.

Fortunately, the countryside they were driving through was deserted. The crops in the fields were unharvested, and the hedgerows that edged the road grew wild and untamed. If they remained untended they would eventually swallow the road entirely, making it impassable. Already the longest branches reached almost far enough to scrape against the sides of the armoured vehicle. Perhaps that explained why Llewelyn, or "Clue-Ellin" as he had told her to say his name, was driving down the middle of the road.

'You should slow down,' Liz told him. 'What if we meet another vehicle coming in the other direction?'

'Give over, Liz. We haven't met a single vehicle since we left Gatwick.'

'But what if we do?'

'Then I'm sure they'll come out of the encounter a lot worse than us. Unless they also happen to be driving a seven-ton armoured truck.'

'That's not really the point.'

'Well, it is.'

Liz was too sleepy to continue the argument. 'You always have to get the last word, don't you?'

'Always.'

'Even when you're wrong.'

'Especially then.'

She and the Welshman were a proper couple now, or at least Liz thought so. She wasn't sure she would describe their relationship as romantic, given that Jones was the least romantic man she'd ever known. And he had run away from her once, leaving her in danger, but had returned in the nick of time, promising never to leave her again. "Never" was a very long time in Liz's opinion, but she was happy to have him around for as long as they both still wanted each other, even though he could be an irritating bastard at the best of times. But that was what all boyfriends were like, weren't they?

She peered into the side mirror to check that the other vehicles following them were okay. Now that her tribe had grown to include not only herself, Llewelyn, Kevin and Mihai, but also Samantha, Lily and baby Leo, not to mention the motley crew of kids they'd picked up in London, they'd had to requisition a couple more vehicles to carry everyone. Samantha was following closely behind with her own two kids and Mihai in a big Volvo, and Liz's father, Kevin was bringing up the rear of the convoy in a seven-seater Ford Galaxy, in which about ten of the London kids had wedged themselves like sardines.

Kevin had moaned about having to drive them, yet despite his loud complaints, he was beginning to reveal a soft spot for the kids. Perhaps they reminded him a little of himself.

'There are far too many to fit in one car,' Liz protested when they'd first all piled inside the Galaxy. 'It's not safe. There aren't enough seatbelts to go around.'

'They're jammed in so tight I don't think that matters,' said Kevin. 'Anyway, don't worry about health and safety, love. We have bigger problems than car accidents to think about these days.'

'But I do worry, Dad. And I worry that you're not worried. If you worried more, I wouldn't need to worry so much.'

Kevin pulled a face, trying to untangle her logic. 'If you want something to worry about, worry about what will happen if one of these mental kids gets hold of my machine gun.'

'I hope you've locked it safely in the car boot, Dad. And you can't keep calling them mental kids.'

'Why not? They are mental.'

'Even so. Just stop it.'

'What shall I call them, then?'

'They have names.'

'Yeah, but too many to remember. Anyway, the bloody ankle-biters never use my name. They just call me "chief". I think they're taking the mickey.'

'Just be glad that you don't have a nine-year-old boy with a giant sword sitting right behind you,' said Liz.

She was talking about Alfie, one of the London gang, who was riding in the back of the Foxhound, refusing to give up the weapon he carried everywhere. Leah, the gang's leader was also with Liz, along with a few of the older gang members. All of them carried weapons of some kind. Liz had confiscated their firearms, but they were still loaded up with knives, baseball bats and a couple of crossbows. With so much weaponry in the hands of children, Kevin was right that a road accident was the least of their risks.

Still, she worried. How could she not when she shouldered so much responsibility? A year ago, she'd been living alone in her small apartment, without even a cat or dog to look after. Then she'd adopted a Romanian orphan, her father had moved in, Samantha and her family had come to stay, baby Leo had been born, and finally the London gang had joined them. Now she had an extended family of twenty to look after. And they still had nowhere to live. They'd been running ever since escaping from the battle with the werewolves at the southern evacuation camp at Gatwick Airport. Liz feared that she would spend the rest of her life running. But that wouldn't be fair on the kids. It wouldn't be fair on any of them. They needed to find a place to stay, and start to put down roots. Otherwise how could they ever begin to feel safe?

Up ahead a set of wrought iron gates were set back from the road. A tall brick wall marked the boundary of a substantial-looking property.

'Stop!' cried Liz. 'Stop right here!'

The Foxhound screeched to a halt in the middle of the

road, hurling them all forward in their seats and making Liz glad that at least she was wearing a seatbelt.

'Jesus Christmas, Liz,' moaned Llewelyn. 'Give me some warning next time, won't you?'

But Liz was peering out of her side window, trying to see what lay beyond the gates. A long sweeping driveway led into the distance, but the area was too wooded for her to see where it went. 'Let's take a look at this place,' she said. 'It's time for a comfort break anyway.'

'Well, I'm always ready for a little comfort,' said Llewelyn.

They all climbed out of the vehicle to stretch their legs, glad to be out of the hot tin can of the Foxhound. Liz pulled her hat down low to shade her face, and thrust her hands into her pockets. Alfie swung his sword, while the older kids mooched around looking sullen, their hoods pulled over their heads as usual. Behind them, the Volvo and the Ford drew up. Kevin wound his window down. 'Problem?' he enquired.

'Nah,' said Llewelyn. 'Just taking a nose around. Liz fancied a stop.'

The brick pillars that stood to either side of the entranceway were crowned with stone lions bearing shields. A brass sign on each pillar indicated that this was a four-star hotel and spa. Or had been.

'It looks posh,' said Llewelyn, grinning. 'Do you think they'll let us in?'

Liz indicated the metal gates barring entry into the hotel grounds. They were secured with a heavy padlock. 'It's been locked from outside, so I don't think there's likely to be anyone at home.'

'You're thinking we might kip here for the night?'

'I'm thinking we might finally have found ourselves a home,' she said, looking eagerly through the metal bars.

Home. It was what she'd dreamed of her whole life. Her childhood home had been a broken one – less a home, more a repository of painful memories. After her mum had taken her own life and her father had dropped out of being an adult, Liz had fended largely for herself, cooking, cleaning, shopping and making sure that the bills got paid. It had been no life for a teenage girl. Later, although she'd rented her own apartment, it had never felt like home. A home should be a solid edifice: permanent, unchanging and indestructible. And a real home needed children, running everywhere, getting in the way, and enjoying the freedom of a proper childhood. Well, she had children in abundance now. All she needed was somewhere to stash them. Maybe this could be the place.

The gates were securely locked, but with Kevin around, no kind of barrier needed to stay sealed for long. Within minutes he had the lock picked, and the convoy was rolling up the driveway.

'I have a good feeling about this,' said Liz, giving Llewelyn a smile.

'That doesn't happen often,' said the Welshman. 'Let's hope you still have it after we've checked the place out. It might be trashed, or worse.'

The hotel itself came into view as the Foxhound rounded a cluster of trees standing around a small ornamental lake. A red tiled roof over white walls, arranged on three levels. The place might once have been a large country estate. There was more than one building, and in fact, the place resembled a small village. Liz counted at least four separate buildings in addition to the main house itself. One of them appeared to hold an indoor swimming pool. Another looked like an old barn converted into additional accommodation.

Llewelyn swung the Foxhound into the car park and drew to a halt, leaving the vehicle straddling three marked parking places.

'So you're just going to leave it here like this?' asked Liz.

'I don't see anyone else wanting a place. There's no one around.'

He was right. The car park was deserted and the hotel looked abandoned. But it seemed to be in a good state of repair, and plenty big enough for all of them, with extensive grounds for the kids to run wild. There was a lake to provide fresh water, and with Kevin's mechanical ingenuity they would probably be able to rig up a generator to provide electricity. They would be able to grow food here and keep animals too, if they put their minds to it. And the brick wall that surrounded the property would provide a first line of defence. It seemed almost too good to be true, and Liz was nervous about raising her hopes too high. Yet already her mind was racing ahead into the future, and finding cause for optimism.

'So what do you reckon?' she asked tentatively.

Llewelyn pushed open his door and jumped out. 'I reckon we should check out the bar first, and see if they have any beers left.'

Chapter Two

Stonehenge

The great stones of Stonehenge glowed oppressively beneath the late-afternoon sun. All day long the heat had been building as dark clouds pressed in from the south. A storm was brewing, promising violence. Now, as Rose Hallibury placed her hands against the pitted surface of the Slaughter Stone, the strangely-shaped hunk of rock seemed to radiate a malign power from its fissures and crevices. Beyond it, the white ash of the bonfire still smouldered, spending its residual warmth, and a thin wisp of smoke curled into the air before the wind snatched it away. It was here that Rose had taken a life. A man had bled to death at this very spot, spilling his life beneath the solstice moon so that she could be free again.

But freedom feels no different to bondage.

The old man, Rowan, had told her that she was the virgin priestess, destined to lead her people to salvation. What a terrible burden he had placed upon her narrow shoulders, and all so that he could twist her words, using her as a means to impose his own malign vision on those she led. It was only right that he had paid the price with his own blood sacrifice.

Now, beyond the rings of stones, her people gathered, awaiting her decision, their fate in her hands. But how was she to decide what to do? Why had she been singled out to bear such responsibility? If she made the wrong choice, these people would starve, or worse. She wanted to run away, leaving them to make their own decisions and follow their own path. But she knew she couldn't abandon them.

Even Nutmeg knew it. The dog sat dejectedly at her side, twisting her head to gaze up at her mistress. The dog's hazel eyes looked to her for reassurance. Rose squatted down and rubbed Nutmeg's wet nose. 'There, girl, don't worry. We'll be leaving this place soon.'

That much was clear. There was nothing to keep them here. No food. No shelter out on the bleak plain. Only bad memories. Memories of barbarism, of primitive ritual, and of killing.

All around her on the plain stood barrows, stone cairns, burial mounds and tumuli. One vast graveyard dating back millennia. A place of death. A place of execution. A place of worship.

'You are the virgin,' Rowan had told her, countless times. 'Our hopes rest with you, Rose, for you are the prophetess.'

But Rose wasn't sure she believed in prophecies. Her waking visions had been the product of Rowan's herbs; her nightmares brought on by the horrors she had witnessed. Just a natural consequence of post-traumatic stress, according to Chris.

Yet they had seemed so real at the time. She had foreseen the moment of sacrifice, when blood washed over the stones as her curved blade opened Rowan's neck. She had lived it over and over before acting it out for real. *I will lead my people to salvation*, she had declared as the old man lay dying at her feet. Like reading from a script, written long ago by another's hand. Now those vain words sounded hollow. Lead her people where?

The shadows lengthened as the day grew long. Inky fingers reached out for her across the flat grass of the plain, just as black blood had flowed under the firelight.

The blood is on my hands.

Rose studied her fingers, but they were scrubbed clean, pale and slender.

The stain lies on my heart. It will never be washed away.

Another weight that she must bear, alone. One thing she knew: the people had chosen her as their leader. A young girl, a virgin, knowing little of the world. She was their sacrifice now. She must carry their worries on her shoulders, so that they could walk free.

She left the half-buried Slaughter Stone and walked across the grass toward the main circle of standing stones. Huge sarsen stones crowned with lintels rose before her, and she touched the wicker headdress on her forehead in reply. Some of the children had made her the crown. Woven from dried straw and entwined with flowers of buttercups and daisies, it encircled her red hair. Over her dress she wore the multicoloured patchwork cloak that had belonged to Rowan. Its many pockets still held herbs, though not the bitter herb that brought on visions. She was glad to be rid of that.

She passed through the first gateway to the inner ring of bluestones and on to the open horseshoe of sarsen stones before reaching the Altar Stone at the heart of the ancient monument. There she turned back to face the distant Heel Stone where the midsummer sun had risen this very morning.

The place where the earth meets the sky.

She had allowed herself to be led astray by such thoughts. Sky, earth, blood, stone. But she was no nearer to the wisdom Rowan had promised. She needed to focus now on mundane matters. Matters of survival – food, water, shelter. These were what her people needed. Not visions, nor prophecies.

Nutmeg barked as a group of people approached. Chris, Seth, and Ryan. The rest lingered a distance away, too afraid to come closer. She waited for her three friends to arrive.

Of the three, only Seth was in a good state of health. A slight limp betrayed the fact that he had broken his leg on the journey from London and had been carried halfway to Glastonbury. But now the fracture had healed. During that journey his hair had reached shoulder length and his beard had grown too, becoming thick and matted. He flicked his hair aside but it returned immediately, covering half his face. Ryan had been badly beaten by Rowan's men on the night of the solstice and was clearly still in pain. He limped badly on one leg, and his right arm rested in a cotton sling. Chris' nose had been broken when one of Rowan's men punched him. It had turned black and purple, and had swollen to double its normal size. His eyes were ringed red from hay fever, and his skin was blistered and peeling from sunburn. Yet despite the heat, he wore a winter coat to protect himself from insect bites. It was the same coat he had worn since leaving London in February.

Nutmeg ran to them, licking Seth's hand. Rose remembered how terrified Seth had been when they'd first encountered the dog on their way out of London. Now man and dog were best of friends.

The three men said nothing. They knew the burden that had been placed upon her and they had granted her this time to make a decision. Yet still she didn't know what to do for the best. They must leave Stonehenge, but she had no idea which way to go. She had walked so far already, all the way from her home in London, along the Ridgeway, past the White Horse at Uffington, to Glastonbury Tor, and then to Stonehenge. She was so tired, she wished her journey could be at an end.

'I had a vision,' she told them. 'One final vision, last

night, beneath the light of the blood moon.'

'You don't have to tell us about it,' said Ryan. 'Remember what Rowan said. The visions were for your eyes only.'

She shook her red hair. 'Rowan was wrong. About many things. I need to tell you what I saw, because I don't understand what it means.'

'It might not mean anything,' said Chris. 'It was a psychedelic experience brought on by a hallucinogenic plant.'

'Ignore him,' said Seth. 'Tell us what you saw.'

Rose closed her eyes, consulting her memory of what she had been shown. The vision was fading, yet vivid enough to recall when her eyes were firmly shut. 'I was standing on a hilltop. A large, flat-topped space, covered with grass. It was circular in shape, protected by ditches and ramparts. The wind blew my hair, and a bird was calling.'

She had been shown so many things, it was hard to know which details were significant and which were not. They had all felt important at the time.

'At the centre of the hill was another hill, surrounded by a moat and topped by a stone wall. A bridge spanned the moat and steps led up and down, and at its heart was a building of some kind. A castle, or a tower. There were other buildings too, but they were all in ruins. It seemed very old.'

She opened her eyes to find the others staring at her uncertainly.

'My spirit guide told me that it was a lost city.'

'Your spirit guide?' said Ryan.

She nodded. She didn't dare tell them that the spirit who guided her through the vision was another version of herself. Chris was already regarding her as if she had lost her mind.

Only Seth seemed enthusiastic about the vision. 'Well, it seems perfectly simple to me. Your spirit guide was showing you where to go. So let's go there already.'

'But where?' asked Rose. 'I don't know where it is. I've never seen that place before.'

'You haven't?' Seth seemed disappointed. 'Perhaps someone else might know where it is.'

'It isn't a real place,' said Chris. 'How can it be? A lost city! It's just something you imagined.'

Ryan looked dubious too. 'This place you saw might be real, or it might not. But if you don't know where it is, the vision won't help right now. The most important thing is to find food and clean water. I think you should choose a direction to go, and if we find this lost city on the way, then we'll stop there.'

'You must choose our path,' said Seth. 'You are the priestess.'

'I'm not a priestess,' said Rose. 'And I have no idea which way to go. Why does it have to be me who decides?'

Ryan took her hand and turned her to face the crowds of people waiting beyond the stone circle, their tents stretching away across the flat grassland. There must have been hundreds. Men, women and children, some sitting in groups, others standing. 'Because the people here believe in you, Rose. And they will go wherever you command them.'

Chapter Three

The English Channel

It was always windy at sea, even when the waters were calm, and today the waves rose in white fury, driven on by a summer storm. Onboard HMS *Queen Elizabeth*, Colonel Michael Griffin felt thoroughly seasick. On his first visit to the aircraft carrier, Commodore FitzHerbert had asked him whether he had sea legs. Now he knew the answer.

'Damned summer gales,' muttered FitzHerbert as he surveyed his bleak domain through a pair of binoculars. 'They sweep across the Atlantic from the south-west. There'll be more following behind this one, you mark my words.'

The commodore was dressed informally today, in a navy-blue jersey over a white cotton shirt. Only the rank insignia on his shoulder epaulettes revealed that he was the most senior surviving officer in the Royal Navy. Yet as always, he was clean-shaven, and stood straight-backed amid the rolling sea.

In spite of the ship's vast size, the swelling waters were enough to make the carrier pitch like a fairground ride. Rain pelted against the glass windows of the forward tower like a never-ending drumroll, and the gusting wind made steel sing. But the twin carriers *Queen Elizabeth* and *Prince of Wales* were faring far better than their attendant destroyers and frigates. To port side, HMS *Dragon* was being washed by surf every other minute, and HMS *Northumberland*, a Type 23 frigate, was almost invisible amidst the maelstrom, its bow buried by every wave the storm hurled at it.

Better by far, thought Griffin, to be an army soldier, and to know that the ground beneath your feet could be trusted. Looking out over the broken surface of the sea, he wondered why anyone in their right mind would choose to join the navy and subject themselves to this tyranny of constant motion. Even when the weather was fine, the gentle shifting of the deck left him reeling. Since injuring his leg when his helicopter was downed over London, Griffin struggled to walk even on dry land without the aid of his crutches. Here, in the middle of the English Channel, he could barely stand.

The sea was its own kingdom, as changeable as the land was fixed. From blue-green warmth to chilly grey; from gently swelling undulations to white-crested breakers chasing each other in endless discord. Gulls on the wing; the smell of salt; the ever-troubled sky above. Today the clouds flowed in dark and angry ribbons, rolling over the fleet as the waters rushed beneath. Lightning flashed in a sudden fork, freezing the scene for a dreary instant, until thunder broke the spell like the clash of Neptune's trident.

'It's just as well we suspended air ops in advance of the storm,' said Group Captain Bampton, seated next to Griffin. The group captain looked queasy too, and was clearly a lot less comfortable in this watery environment than the commodore. Even though he had once flown fighter planes in low-level combat missions, placing his trust in flimsy wings and aerodynamic theory to stop him plummeting from the sky, the retired pilot was as ill-suited to life onboard ship as Griffin.

Yet regardless of the storm, Griffin was glad to be away from the oppressive surroundings of the Northwood Command Centre. Northwood was where the Prime Minister had first dragged him into this mess, tasking him with the impossible challenge of defeating the werewolf army. He had finally stood against the PM and brought her down, but the job of leading the government forces to victory had not diminished in her absence.

Northwood was also the place where Griffin had faced up to his own injuries and acknowledged that he would never walk again without crutches. Although he had saved himself from bleeding to death at the crash site of his Wildcat helicopter, the broken bone in his leg had never properly healed and the inflammation caused by his malrotated femur refused to leave him in peace. The injury had become infected due to constant abrasion, and his leg was a permanent torment. Sitting in the leather seat of the *Queen Elizabeth*'s command centre as the ship lurched up and down was agony, far worse than the bile sloshing about his insides. But only the ship's doctor knew the full extent of his condition, and he had been sworn to secrecy. It would not do to let others know that their commanding officer was so frail.

'Perhaps a rum would help to soothe your discomfort,' suggested the commodore, cutting through his introspection.

Griffin shook his head, and raised his mug of black coffee. 'I think that this will do just nicely.' He had no desire for alcohol, especially not while he was using morphine to manage his pain. The drug was already making him drowsy, and alcohol would exacerbate the effect. He had begun with two tablets daily, but had been forced to double the dose. He would double it again if necessary, or move to injections, but for now he could cope. He could have allowed the surgeons to perform corrective surgery on his leg, but an operation would leave him incapacitated for weeks, and that was time he could not afford to lose. In any case, he had chosen to endure the pain. As a reminder.

As long as I feel pain, I will never forget her.

Chanita. He had been trying to reach her when his helicopter was blasted out of the sky by the force of a nuclear explosion. He'd spent weeks alone in a forest, nursing his injury and learning to walk again. Then, when he'd finally arrived at the evacuation camp at Stoke Park, he'd found the place abandoned, its buildings burned, its occupants dead or scattered. There was no trace of the woman he loved. It had been so long since he'd seen her face he sometimes forgot quite how she looked. Smooth skin. Shining black hair. Kind dark eyes. And that smile. A smile that could brighten Hell itself.

'Then to business,' continued the commodore. 'From here we command the seas and the air, but the land is another matter. I trust that you have a plan for how you intend to conduct this campaign, Colonel Griffin? Else to what do we owe this visit?'

Griffin put aside all thoughts of pain, seasickness and lost love and turned his mind to the reason he had ventured out to this godforsaken watery wilderness. The campaign against the lycanthropic forces.

A series of battles had been fought, and progress had been made, but the defeats were as great as the successes. After the werewolves' stronghold at Windsor Castle had been located, the *Queen Elizabeth* had deployed its squadron of F-35 Lightnings in a massive air strike. The castle had been utterly destroyed, only for battlefield intelligence to reveal that the enemy had already moved on and escaped before the attack. The Wolf Army had been engaged again at the southern evacuation camp at Gatwick Airport. But at the very last moment Griffin had called off the air attack when a human shield consisting of hundreds of human captives chained to the enemy's vehicles was spotted. With only ground forces at his command, the ensuing battle had been bloody and inconclusive, resulting in heavy losses on both sides.

Now the F-35 Lightnings were stowed safely below deck away from the buffeting winds and even when the weather improved they would not be flying combat missions anytime soon. Millions of pounds' worth of advanced weaponry had been rendered useless by the simplest enemy tactic, and as long as the Wolf Army surrounded itself with hostages, the colonel's greatest asset would not be deployed.

If the Prime Minister were still in charge he knew what she would have said. *Do what is necessary.* But Griffin was no General Ney, ready to engage in total war and defeat the enemy at all cost. No doubt the general would have bombed the werewolves to oblivion already, killing hundreds or even thousands of captured civilians in the process. Not Griffin. Hell, he was supposed to be a doctor.

I joined the army to save lives, not to take them.

But he knew that he could not afford to hold back from fighting indefinitely. Short of wholesale slaughter of the innocent, he must do whatever it took to win this war. To lose was unthinkable.

FitzHerbert and Bampton were eyeing him expectantly.

He cleared his throat. 'Here is the situation as I see it, gentlemen. Our greatest single military asset is this fleet and the combat aircraft operating from it.'

Eight ships in total – hardly a fleet, but it was all that remained of the Royal Navy, not counting the *Vanguard*-class nuclear submarines that made up the country's strategic nuclear deterrent and that Griffin had sworn never to use.

The carrier battle group comprised two aircraft carriers, HMS *Queen Elizabeth* and *Prince of Wales*, two Type 45 destroyers, two Type 23 frigates, and two supply tankers.

Forty-eight F-35B Lightnings were stationed on the carriers, plus a total of fourteen Merlin, eight Wildcat and four Chinook helicopters on the carriers and their supporting ships. The destroyers' long-range radar and surface-to-air and surface-to-surface missiles provided air and sea defence for the carriers, while the role of the frigates was to protect against submarine attack. Combined with the air power provided by the carriers themselves, the battle group was impervious to any threat it was likely to face. A force of two hundred and fifty Royal Marine commandos was also onboard, awaiting deployment. Under Griffin's orders, the fleet had sailed from the Western Approaches of the North Atlantic to its current location in the English Channel, ready for operation.

'As the commodore has said, the carriers give us unopposed control of British territorial waters and airspace. But as you well know, we are unable to make use of aerial firepower as long as the lycanthropes continue to hold human hostages.' He paused to finish his coffee. 'The situation on land is rather different. Following the Battle of Gatwick, our ground forces have been reduced to fewer than two thousand fighting men and women, together with a greatly reduced number of tanks and other armoured vehicles. It is scarcely an army. And yet it is all we have.'

'Indeed,' said FitzHerbert. 'So how do you intend to use it?'

'The answer, I'm bound to say, is with caution. We cannot afford to lose more men, and must take no risks. We may get only one chance to strike at our enemy, and we must choose a time and a place that gives us maximum advantage.'

He hated himself for setting such a cautious tone, and knew that FitzHerbert and Bampton would be disappointed to hear it. But he had no choice. A military commander could neither permit himself the luxury of hope nor indulge in the futility of despair. He must see the world as it was, not as he wished it, and steer a course through the narrow straits that led to victory.

'For now, we will continue to observe the enemy from the air. We will track their movements, monitor their numbers and look for opportunities to strike. But we will take no action until the time is right. Commodore, maintain the fleet's present position. Bampton, I would like you to take charge of air operations. As for myself, my duty lies with my men. On land I can assume overall responsibility for government forces.'

The two men saluted. 'Very good, Colonel,' said the commodore.

Griffin had nothing more to add. He had never asked for this burden of responsibility. He had resisted the Prime Minister's demands, asking instead for permission to go looking for Chanita, even though he didn't know whether she was alive or dead. If the PM were still in command, he could have offered her his resignation, or allowed her to dismiss him. Ironically, he had removed her from office instead, and now that she was gone he had left himself no other choice. He must stay and see it through until the end.

Then, if he was still alive, he would finally go in search of his love. Where he would go, he had no idea. But as long as his heart was beating, he would never give up on her.

Chapter Four

Christmas Common, Oxfordshire

The moon hung low and pale in the indigo sky, seeming to hurtle through gaps in the quickly-fleeting clouds. It was past its peak, little more than a slash in the heavens, yet at each brief reappearance, James Beaumont could feel its pull like a faint but unstoppable force.

When he had first become a werewolf, he had been at the mercy of its power. Even now, a supreme effort was required for him to deny its lure. He wondered how potent that lure would become when the moon reached its fullness in a few weeks' time. It was easy to imagine the strength it would grant him. The ability to tear skin, rend flesh, and grind bones between mighty jaws. He had experienced that dark energy flowing through him many times.

Why even try to resist?

Iron surged in his veins at the thought, and he allowed

the change to take him in its embrace. He stripped off his clothes quickly so as not to ruin them, then slipped away from the house into woodland as fine hair clothed his nakedness. His teeth thrust through the well-worn holes in his gums, and he felt the aching in his fingers as his nails twisted into sharpened talons. His body thickened as his muscles enlarged and his snout reached forward, reshaping his face. Soon he was a wolfman again. He was himself.

Now the moon glinted brighter than ever, tinted yellow in his vision against a backdrop of a million million stars, and the forest came alive with sweet music. Birds nesting in the safety of whispering branches stirred softly. Owls flitted stealthily through the sky, hunters like him, beaks and eyes hungry for prey. Squirrels scurried watchfully across the forest floor. He could even hear the moles treading blindly through their hidden networks of burrows in pursuit of worms to consume. A world of secrets, no longer hidden to him. Behind him stood the house, a home for humans. Ahead lay woods and fields, a place for wolves. He dropped to all fours and slid between the trees, unheard and unseen.

Since returning to Christmas Common he had spent more time in wolf form than in human. It was better to be a wolf, easier to avoid the others, especially Ben who guessed too much. Alone, he followed the forest paths, tracking far and wide in search of prey and watching for danger. So far he had seen none. But it was out there. It was coming.

He emerged from trees into the white space of an open field. It had been dark when he left the house, walking slowly on two feet. Now all was bright, and he was fast and sure-footed. He dashed across the field, slipping noiselessly through tall stalks of flax, their pale blue flowers turned to the moon. Pollen drifted on the still-warm air like cool mist on a winter's morning. Then a new scent filled his nostrils, and his mind emptied of all other concerns. It pulled him on like an invisible rope. His prey was ahead.

He rushed through the field like a hurricane, landing on the hare with his claws outstretched. The animal barely had time to yelp before it was between his jaws and its life was gone. James stopped to devour his meal, stripping the fur with his teeth and spitting it on the ground along with the bones. Everything else he devoured. It was a hungry night.

When he was done he stopped to clean his paws and look around. He was pretty certain Ben hadn't followed him, but it was best to be sure. Ben could move with stealth when he wanted to. But not as stealthily as James. And he didn't know James' secret places.

When he was positive that he was alone, he moved forward again to the edge of the field and into a stream to throw off the scent of his kill. The water was cold and refreshing, and shallow enough for him to splash along its length. Quick water sparkled in the moonlight like diamonds as it gushed over smooth stones and found its way around sodden logs covered in water weeds. A frog stopped mid-hop, startled by his arrival, but James carried on. A wolf did not eat frogs.

When he was confident that he could not be followed, he rushed up the bank on the other side, pushing through a line of trees and onto the road that led away from the village. If he followed the road he would come to a town. But a town was a place for men, and James was not a man. Instead he crossed the road and dived into the undergrowth on the opposite side. A secret way, known only to him. He stopped to sniff the air, testing it for danger, but the way was clear. Through the thick brush he ran, four sure feet pounding along the narrow track, past pungent ferns, around patches of nettles, passing snaking briars clad in thorns. No one knew this path but him. No one knew his lair.

When he reached it he stopped to sift the air once more. There were no tell-tale signs. No Ben. No human. No wolf. The way was clear. He slipped inside, squeezing his slender body through a crack in the rock face, no more than twelve inches wide, concealed by trails of ivy. Deep within the thicket it was invisible to anyone who didn't know it was there. He had discovered it by accident one night while in pursuit of a small deer, a muntjac. He had followed the frightened animal into the cave, and there had feasted on its flesh. But the deer had given him far more than a meal. It had shown him a secure hiding place. Here, screened from discovery and protected from the elements by solid rock, he was safe. He could sleep, or eat his prey, or make plans. And it had become a storage place for the things he would need on his journey. Beside the bones and dirt that covered the floor, a flat ledge jutted out near the back of the cave. There he had laid them all out. A map. A knife. A flashlight. A Bible. A set of dry clothes.

Of all these, the Bible was his most treasured possession. He had brought it back from Joan's house in Virginia Water, where he had taken Ben when he first turned lycanthropic. Ben had tried to kill Melanie then, so James had led him far away until he could be cured of his murderous impulses. Now, with hard physical work and regular wolfsbane tea, Ben was no longer a danger to his loved ones. It was safe to leave him behind. Joan, however, had been less fortunate.

The old woman had known the risks of taking two werewolves into her home, but in the end it wasn't Ben who killed her, but rebel werewolves come for James, wanting him to lead them into battle against Leanna. He had told them he would not fight. But that was not what they had come to hear. In their anger they had taken Joan's life. Now, the Bible was all James had to remember her. He went to it now, struggling to turn the pages with clumsy wolf paws.

He flipped it open and the page fell on Revelation.

It was the book he read most often. The words of St John, written two millennia ago, yet so prescient. He began to read the words automatically, his yellow eyes following chapter and verse in the half-light of the cave, his wolf lips moving silently, the familiar words following well-worn tracks in his mind. The events that St John had foreseen seemed unimaginable, and yet James had witnessed them unfold with his own eyes. He had stood and watched, transfixed in horror as one after another the seven seals of Revelation had proceeded to open and the beasts had stepped forth. First the white horse of Lycanthropy had galloped across the globe, spreading disease wherever it went. The mighty horse of war had followed close on its heels, and then the black horse of famine and the pale horse of death. When the fifth seal shattered, the souls of the martyred cried out as one, and then at midsummer, the sixth seal was broken and the blood moon rose.

Now all that remained was the breaking of the seventh and final seal, which would be opened by the lamb. Then the trumpets would sound and the wrath of God would be poured upon the earth. But that catastrophe could still be averted if just one person was brave enough to offer themselves as a sacrifice, and atone for the sins of the world. To put a stop to the madness, and suffer and die, so that others might live.

That person was him.

God might have turned His back on him, but James had not given up on God.

He already knew what he had to do. Return to Leanna, and give himself to her.

Chapter Five

Peaslake, Surrey

Morning came, and Vijay Singh woke with tears streaming down his cheeks. His beloved grandmother was dead. His parents too. He had loved them all dearly, but it was his grandmother that he wept for most.

He recalled the sound of her knitting needles click-clacking together, her small, quick hands in constant motion. She was so tiny and frail, but bursting with energy and determination. Now that energy was all gone, and he would never hear the sound of her needles again. He burst into fresh tears, though it seemed impossible that he could have any more to shed.

Was it wrong to miss your grandmother more than your mother and father? Probably. But he had given up trying to know what was right and wrong. The Sikh elders at the Gurdwara had taught their lessons and he had listened attentively, but now that the world was burning he could hardly remember anything he had learned. 'Follow your heart,' his grandmother used to say, and she was always right. The heart was the only true guide.

When he was younger, she had tried to teach him how to knit, but he was all thumbs and could never master the dexterity needed to turn yarn into hats and scarfs the way she did. Instead, she had shared with him her love of plants, teaching him to nurture green miracles in the tiny garden at the back of their South London house. There, she had conjured all kinds of exotic specimens from the bare soil. Bitter gourds, looking like spiky cucumbers. Okra plants with their broad green leaves. And his favourite, the amaranth plants with their bright pink flowers that would turn into seeds to be harvested and cooked by his mother.

'They will be ready to pick when the birds come to peck at them,' his grandmother told him. 'How big do you think they will grow? As tall as this?' – indicating his knees – 'Or as tall as this?' – pointing to the top of his head.

'As tall as you, Grandmother,' he said.

She leaned forward to plant a kiss on his forehead. 'One day you will grow as tall as me, Vijay, and taller too. Taller than your father, even. Perhaps as tall as the amaranth plants.'

'When, Grandmother?'

'These things take time. Don't be in such a hurry.'

The amaranth had reached almost six feet tall by summer's end, but it took Vijay some years to match his grandmother's height, and even now he was still not much taller. At school he had always been the smallest boy in his class, but the words of his grandmother that day had never left him. 'It doesn't matter how big you are on the outside, Vijay. What matters is how big you are on the inside. A stout heart and a generous spirit – that is how to judge the true size of a person.'

His grandmother had been the shortest person he knew, but on the inside she was the kindest and most fearless who ever lived. Vijay clutched at the knitting needle she had given him as they made their escape from the evacuation camp at Gatwick Airport. 'This is my sword, and I shall use it,' she had declared, brandishing her own needle high as she turned to face the onslaught of the enemy. 'My cause is just and I do not fear to die.' It was the last time he had ever seen her.

He felt another huge sob rise up inside him. His grandmother and his parents had sacrificed themselves to save him, his sister, Aasha, and his friend, Drake. He would never forget them, and he would never forget his grandmother's final, parting words – 'Do not waste this precious chance. Live life to the full, and never let opportunity slip through your fingers.'

To honour her memory, he must never waste a single chance, and never give up, no matter how difficult the challenges he faced. He would value every second, and never forget the price she had paid so he may live.

And that was why he must never abandon his search for Rose.

He stirred from his makeshift bed and leaned over to rouse Drake and Aasha from their slumber. 'Wake up, it's time for us to go.'

Already the morning sun was peeping in through a crack around the door of the wooden shed they had slept in overnight. The previous night's storm had passed. Birds were singing and the world was in motion. Somewhere the amaranth plants were growing tall, using every drop of precious sunlight to lift them higher so that they could flower and bear seed.

'Another few minutes,' said Aasha, rolling over.

He shook her gently. 'No. We need to get moving. We need to find food.'

They had spent the night in a potting shed in an allotment. It was the kind of place his grandmother would have loved, full of tools, broken pots, thick leather gloves, and packets of seeds. All kinds of plants were growing in the allotments, and thanks to his grandmother's teaching, Vijay knew them all by name. Potatoes, beans, peas, raspberries, strawberries, tomatoes, rocket. They had been planted and tended, and then left abandoned. Now they grew wild and unkempt, the fruit half-eaten by birds, the cabbages and spinach all gone to seed. But among the profusion, there were edible plants if you knew what to look for. While Drake and Aasha readied themselves for the day ahead, Vijay went from row to row with a basket, gathering berries, tender carrots, onions, tomatoes, plums and squash. He washed the root vegetables in a bucket of rainwater and shared them with the others.

Drake's black cat, Shadow, had caught a field mouse during the night, and was still chewing on the remains of his meal.

'This ain't too bad,' said Drake, nibbling hesitantly on a carrot, 'but we should try to find some real food next.'

'What do you mean?' asked Vijay. 'This is real food.'

'No, I mean like something out of a can,' said Drake. 'Like meatballs or sausages. Something filling. We'll just need to find a way to heat it up.'

Vijay wrinkled his nose. 'That's not real food at all.' His mother had never bought canned food, but had cooked from fresh ingredients. But the other two took no notice.

'Where would be the best place to find stuff like that?' Aasha asked Drake. 'In a supermarket?'

'Maybe. But they've probably all been looted already. I reckon we should start looking in people's houses. Then we can sleep in a proper bed, too, instead of places like this old shed.'

'But we mustn't break into houses,' said Vijay. 'And we can't take food from them either. That would be stealing.'

Drake looked at him as if he'd lost his mind. 'Mate, are you having a laugh? Where do you think the food in the evacuation camp came from? The soldiers grabbed it from wherever they could. We're in survival mode now. We have to do whatever it takes, yeah?'

'No,' said Vijay. 'We must always do the right thing. Otherwise, we will dishonour the sacrifice the others made for us.'

Aasha reached out her hand to take his. 'Vijay, listen. I'm missing Mum and Dad and Grandmother just as much as you, but Drake is right. They gave their lives so that we could live. We have to do whatever we can to get through this.'

'No,' Vijay insisted. 'We have to live the right way, just like they always taught us. Nothing has changed, just because of what's happened. These difficulties are sent to test us, but we must prove our worth by rising above them. And that means living honestly, with honourable actions.'

Drake shook his head. 'Mate, honest living is for people with warm, comfortable homes and food on the table. Take a look around. The world's fallen apart. We'll be lucky if we survive at all.'

Chapter Six

Haywards Heath, West Sussex

Lord General Canning sat at his war desk, engrossed in his plans and his maps. He was reminded of his teenage years, spent cooped up in his bedroom, poring over the boards of his beloved wargames, the various fighting units ranged across the playing surface. Infantry, artillery and cavalry, each one lovingly hand-painted, the uniforms correct to every last detail. The books piled high on his bedside locker had held true accounts of the greatest battles of history – Waterloo, Agincourt, Stalingrad – and he had spent countless hours absorbing the tactics and strategies of the military leaders who fought them. Now he was commander of his own army.

He looked up as the flaps of his field tent opened and a messenger approached his desk warily.

'What news?'

The messenger gave him an anxious salute, although

there was really no need for the man to be so nervous. Canning had only ever had one messenger executed, and that had been more than a month ago. 'More arrivals, General Canning. At least a hundred, maybe double that.'

'All of them lycanthropes?'

'Yes, General.'

Fresh recruits were welcome news, especially in such numbers. Canning gave the messenger a reassuring smile. 'Do we have space to accommodate them?'

'Not in the camp. But they say that they don't require shelter. They are happy to sleep rough.'

'Very good. Ensure that they are fed and watered, and tend to any who need medical assistance. I will inspect them later myself.'

He rubbed his hands together in satisfaction as the messenger scurried away to do his bidding. His forces were growing in size with each new day, and Canning could scarcely believe his good fortune. It wasn't long since the debacle at Gatwick, where he'd lost a good many soldiers, not to mention equipment, and had been forced to retreat under fire from the oncoming government forces. It was only the shield of human hostages that had saved the Wolf Army from complete annihilation by the enemy's air power.

That had been a dark day, a humiliating one, and very nearly his last. But Leanna had given him one final chance to prove himself, and the tide was turning steadily in his favour. With every passing day, the balance of power tipped decisively to his advantage.

The new arrivals were coming from the north, drawn by news of a queen, drawn by the lure of a great battle. A battle to end all battles. One that would bring about a decisive victory for werewolves and finally end all human resistance.

The northerners were gruff folk, who showed little respect for authority, and Canning hadn't trusted them at first. He never trusted strangers. Come to think of it, he didn't trust anyone. That was the only reason he was still alive.

The newcomers came from far-off places like Lancashire and Yorkshire, and even as far north as County Durham, which was virtually in the Arctic Circle as far as Canning was concerned. It was certainly not on any of his maps. Canning had no love for the North of England or its inhabitants. In his opinion it was a cold place that bred rough, ill-mannered louts. He had never been there and never wanted to, particularly now that he had learned of the devastation that had been visited upon the cities of the north.

Greater Manchester: three million dead. Leeds, Bradford, and Sheffield: another two million. Liverpool: half a million or more. And those were just the immediate casualties from the nuclear strikes. Countless millions more had perished from the disease, starvation and strife that followed. Radiation sickness was also widespread. According to first-hand accounts from the incomers, the nuclear fallout had been much worse in the north, and no large-scale evacuation had taken place like the one that had moved much of London's populace to the relative safety of the emergency camps at Gatwick, Stoke Park and Stansted. It was said that the rivers and lakes of the north were heavily contaminated and to drink from them was death. The humans and animals who lived there were sick and dying, and there was nothing to eat.

The north was a wasteland, and it was no surprise that any surviving lycanthropes were fleeing south. They were flocking to him in their thousands, swelling his depleted ranks and he intended to use them to his advantage.

He was already coming to appreciate their qualities. They were good fighting men, hardy and tough. And strong fighting women too. Only the meanest and toughest had survived, and they had proved themselves in battle. They had a tongue in their head and weren't afraid to use it. Canning liked that – he knew what they were thinking. It was better that an enemy should declare hostilities openly rather than lie in wait, ready to strike unawares. It was the quiet ones that made him sleep with a pistol at his side and a knife concealed in his boots.

Some of the new arrivals had special talents. Rumours had circulated of a new kind of werewolf, transmuted permanently into wolf form. Some of them were said to be all wolf from muzzle to tail, while others retained their human bodies but their heads had been transformed into wolf heads. Yet others had the head and torso of humans but the hind quarters of a wolf. These half-wolves stood erect, and could use weapons. They were gifted with the powers of wolf-smell, wolf-sight and wolf-speed. And when they fought, they had the strength of wolves too.

Wolfmen, they called themselves. Or wolfwomen – smaller than their menfolk, yet just as fierce.

At first, Canning hadn't believed in the existence of such exotic creatures. In times of war there were always stories, most of them false. But he had seen the new arrivals with his own eyes now. They were real. They were numerous. And when fully equipped and trained in the use of weaponry, they would make his army invincible.

The northerners brought more disturbing stories with them too. Tales of strange bloodsucking creatures that hunted werewolves. Their skin was bone-hard and bone-white, their fingers like twisted knives that could reach inside a man's chest and pluck out his living heart to be devoured. They hunted at night, but drew their power not only from the moon, but from the blood on which they gorged. Canning shuddered at the thought, wondering if he could believe such tall tales. But the wolfmen had turned out to be real, living creatures, and he couldn't afford to ignore the warnings about the bloodsuckers.

The northerners were an unruly lot, prone to picking fights with his own men. The women were as bad, or worse. They were like wild animals, dressing like savages, wearing the bones of their victims as jewellery, mating openly beneath the stars. Canning knew that in order to tame them, he would need to enlist one of their own to lead them. It hadn't taken him long to single out the right candidate.

Although Canning had yet to make his acquaintance, William Hunter was said to be a giant of a man, six foot six inches tall and built like a rock. He was one of the wolfmen, his head permanently fixed in the form of a beast. Those who had seen him reported that his face and neck were clothed in thick chestnut fur, and that his bright piercing eyes flashed like yellow moonlight whenever he was roused to anger, which was said to be often. He hailed from Yorkshire, and had supposedly travelled south on foot, gathering a loyal band of fighting men and women as he went. A dangerous adversary, but a useful friend. Canning knew that it would be a challenge to win this wolfman to his side, but that if he succeeded, the rest of the northerners would follow him until their death.

He summoned one of his lieutenants to his tent.

'Lord Canning?'

'This man called William Hunter,' Canning drawled. 'Find him for me.'

The lieutenant accepted his instruction without a blink. Loyal, this one. Just how Canning liked them. 'Is he to be imprisoned, General? Or killed?'

Not just yet.

'No, he is to be treated with the greatest of courtesy, and invited to parley.'

'Very good, General.' The lieutenant saluted, then went away to deliver his invitation.

If Hunter accepts, I will receive him graciously and discuss terms. If he refuses, I will have him butchered like a pig.

Canning smiled to himself. Either outcome would be perfectly satisfactory.

Chapter Seven

Stonehenge

The sky was huge and filled with fast-moving clouds. Beneath it, the low rolling plain stretched out for miles, carpeted with short, wind-flattened grass and other low-growing plants, all seemingly afraid to poke their noses more than a few inches above the dry, chalky soil. A few trees dotted the landscape, their green canopies swaying gently in the wind. In the distance, low hills squatted against the horizon, forming a huge circle around them.

The breeze carried smells of wild thyme and chalk dust, and bees droned between white daisies and purple orchids in their endless quest for food. Nutmeg dashed ahead through the grass and flowers, chasing butterflies.

Rose had taken the first few steps of her journey, leading her followers to safety. *The first steps are the hardest*, she told herself, although she doubted that were true. She still didn't know where they were heading, or how far they had to go, but she knew she had to put Stonehenge behind her. There was nothing for them in that dead place. The stone circle had witnessed blood and sacrifice, and they must leave it far behind. They had stayed one more night there before leaving early in the morning. Rose led them away from the standing stones, choosing to strike out in a westerly direction. The sun rose at her back, and her shadow walked before her.

The ruined city from her vision may or may not be real. If she saw it, she would know it. First they needed to find food, and water too. All around the grass was yellow and dry, and the drinking water they had brought with them was gone. Already the children were crying, their throats parched beneath the relentless blaze of the sun.

At Rose's side, Chris sneezed loudly. His hay fever was getting worse, and so was his mood. 'My nose hurts.'

'Then don't sneeze so much,' said Seth.

'It doesn't hurt because I'm sneezing. It hurts because it's broken.'

'It's not really broken,' said Ryan. 'It'll get better if you leave it alone.' Ryan's own face was badly bruised from his beating, and his arm and leg were injured, but he wasn't complaining.

'So I'll just stop breathing then, shall I?' said Chris.

'Yeah,' said Seth. 'Why don't you do that?'

The clouds scudded quickly across the sky and Rose watched them with envy. She increased her gait, trying to put some distance between herself and the others. She longed to be free, like Nutmeg, running ahead between tufts of grass. But the others sped up, keeping pace with her.

She slowed back down again. She knew she could never be free like the wind and the clouds, at least not until she had fulfilled her role as leader. She thought of all the people she had lost since setting out on her journey, so many months before in the cold of January on the night of the wolf moon. Her poor brother, Oscar. Her parents.

Vijay. Casting a glance over her shoulder at the long line of people trailing in her wake, she vowed not to lose a single one more.

The going was slow, their progress limited by the children and the old folk. They had to stop frequently for the injured to rest, but by mid-morning they stumbled across a brook. A thin trail just two feet wide and inches deep was all that remained of the stream, but Rose rushed to it gratefully, scooping up cold, muddy water with her hands to drink. Once everyone had satisfied their thirst they filled bottles.

Chris looked around, scratching his head. 'There ought to be more water than this.'

'It's all dried up,' said Seth.

'But if this is a floodplain, there must be a proper river somewhere.'

'Well, this will keep us going for now,' said Ryan. 'Next we need to find food.'

The fields around Stonehenge had been full of cattle when they first arrived. But it hadn't taken long for the hundreds of people to eat their way through a field of cows. Chris had warned everyone not to kill them all, but to keep the cows for milk, rationing their consumption and conserving their resources, but it had been impossible to stop the people from slaughtering the animals and feasting on meat every night. Rowan had encouraged the feasting, but Chris had been proven right.

In fact, Chris seemed surprisingly knowledgeable about agriculture and sustainable farming generally. He had elaborate ideas involving breeding cows, pigs, sheep and chickens, and ploughing the fields so they could grow crops. If prompted, he would talk endlessly about crop rotation, seed banks and nitrogen fixation. He also had ideas about housing and the organization of communities in the post-apocalyptic era. He was talking about rebuilding civilization from the ground up. But that was a huge project. Perhaps it would be better for Rose to put

Chris in charge.

But she knew that would be a disaster. Chris might know what needed to be done, but nobody would ever follow him. To put his ideas into practice, someone must lead. And that was her.

'Where should we look for food now?' she asked him.

Chris had obviously been giving some thought to the question. 'The most obvious place would be a town or a city where we could forage for provisions in supermarkets and houses.'

'Let's do that, then,' said Seth.

'No,' said Chris. 'It would be an easy short-term solution. But it would make us dependent on pre-existing food sources. Besides, cities are dangerous. There will be others in competition for the same supplies as us. We must try to avoid built-up areas if possible.'

'Where then?' asked Ryan.

'We need to start moving towards a long-term programme of food production. That means living off the land, managing livestock and harvesting crops.'

'Don't be daft,' said Seth. 'We're hungry right now. How can we grow crops quickly enough to eat?'

Chris sneered at him, as best he could with a broken nose. 'I didn't say grow crops. I said harvest them. Look around. Where are we?'

Seth shrugged. 'In a field?'

'A field of what?'

'I dunno. Plants?'

Chris sighed. 'It's wheat. This field won't be ready for harvesting until the end of the summer, but there will be other crops that are ready to eat right now if we can find them.'

'Like what?' asked Rose. 'And how do you know all this?'

'Like barley,' said Chris. 'And because I read a lot of books. I'm the only one here who did any preparation for the apocalypse.'

'So we need to find a field of barley?' Rose had no idea what barley looked like. None of what she had been taught at school had prepared her for this. Once again she felt completely daunted by the task ahead.

But Chris seemed confident in his knowledge. It was remarkable how the weedy tech support nerd from her old school had become a survival guru. 'It doesn't have to be barley. It could be some other crop that's ready to eat. Wiltshire is one of the most important farming areas in England. There's loads to eat all around us if we know what to look for.'

'Good,' said Rose. 'So let's start looking.'

She set off again with a new sense of purpose. Despite the lack of food and the growing hunger in her belly, Rose liked it out on the plain. Since leaving London she'd grown very fond of the countryside, and Nutmeg loved it, running freely with the other dogs, sniffing and digging everywhere. Gradually the feeling of oppression that had set in at Stonehenge lifted as the sun rose in the big sky.

The fields they crossed were mostly grass, but some were planted with cereals and other types of food crops. Chris pointed out a leafy green field of sugar beet, and a field of wheat, just beginning to turn yellow. But neither crop would be ready to eat until much later in the season.

They came to a low hedgerow bounding two fields. A metal gate blocked the gap in the hedge and a sign was fixed to the bars. *Military firing range. Way closed. Unauthorised access strictly prohibited.*

Chris leaned over the gate, peering into the yellow field beyond. 'I'm sure that's barley, and it looks ripe enough to eat.'

The field stretched out golden under the sun, the tall stalks of grain waving lazily in the wind. Abandoned by whoever had farmed this land, it was waiting to be harvested.

'And you're sure we can eat it?' Rose asked.

'Yes. You collect the seeds and grind them to make

flour, or boil them in water to make a stew. It's very nutritious.'

'But what about the warning sign?' asked Seth. 'It says it's a firing range.'

Ryan climbed up onto the gate, hoisting his injured leg carefully over the top. 'I don't see any soldiers around. It looks safe enough to me. Come on, let's grab ourselves some food.'

Chapter Eight

Somewhere in England, quarter moon

Warg Daddy was dying. He had been dying since the day he was born, for all men must perish. Young men thought themselves immortal, yet Death stalked them unseen in the shadows, or rode out on his great warhorse, delighting in the carnage of battle and the roar and thunder of the earthquake; watching gleefully as pestilence took hold, spreading plague-infested fingers across the land; revelling as plunging waves swallowed great ships, sucking crew and passengers to a watery grave. Warg Daddy had felt Death's bony fingers rest briefly on his own shoulder once or twice, and had heard his breathless voice whisper gently in his ear. But the sharpened scythe of the reaper had not come for him. Yet.

It surely wouldn't be much longer though. With one arm missing after his duel with Slasher, and a fever burning in what remained of his broken body, Warg Daddy knew that Death was coming. And so he headed east, away from the setting sun, hoping to cheat Death for a little while longer. That was all anyone could hope for. And what other choices did he have? None that he could think of. They had all been taken from him.

As he walked, he stared up at the night-blackened sky that arched above him like a vault, and wondered what course his end might take. It would be horrible, no doubt. Delirium, starvation, madness. The only question was when. The gods already knew, and he could find out easily enough by a toss of a coin. One quick flip, and his fate would be known. Life, or death, decided in a second.

He pulled the coin from his pocket, and fingered it hesitantly. Did he really want to know the answer to that question? If he did, he would be forced to face his own demise, staring knowingly into the jaws of oblivion. But the alternative was to walk on blindly, ignorant of his impending doom, like an animal to the slaughter. No man should live like that.

Up went the grimy disk, seeming to fly forever, struggling to break free of the Earth's pull. Then down it came, landing in his outstretched palm.

Heads.

Life, then. For now, at least.

When dawn broke and daylight reached for him, he crawled beneath the trunk of a fallen oak and took shelter amongst its gnarled and twisted branches. The fiery sun beat down, threatening to burn him to a crisp if he emerged from his hiding place. And so he lay on his back, as the Earth whirled around the sun, and clouds tracked slowly across the sky. The gods in their wisdom had granted him a short reprieve. He would not die today, but he knew that he was doomed.

Time passed, and Warg Daddy waited each day and night for Death to come. But Death seemed to be in no great hurry to claim him. And so he fell into a rhythm, spending the hot days dreaming in the ink-dark shadows of trees, rocks and stone walls, and his nights on foot, stargazing as he walked.

He was no expert on stars, not like his old compatriot Wombat, but knew enough to name the patterns written in the sky. There was Orion the Hunter, his belt marked by three stars in a line. Nearby stood Gemini the Twins and Taurus the Bull, its two horns locked in perpetual battle with the seven sisters of the Pleiades. Aries and Pisces were visible at the edge of the cloud cover, and the red eye of Mars looked on, greedy for war and glory. Venus, the evening star had long since set, her love short-lived and wavering.

As night grew longer, more stars emerged from hiding, revealing themselves to his sensitive eyes as a reward for his patience, or perhaps in compensation for his various afflictions. Thousands of pinpricks of light spanned the velvet backdrop of his world. Millions; billions. Stars, nebulae, comets, asteroids. Maybe even a few leftover tin cans of satellites and space junk. He tried to count them, but the task became impossible as yet more lights appeared against the blackness. He wondered whether the whole sky would eventually turn white if he watched it long enough. He hoped not. It was only the darkness that made sense of the light. Without it there would be no patterns and the vault of heaven would become a meaningless place, just like Earth below.

One thing Warg Daddy knew was that his fate was written up there. If only he could fathom how to read it. But although the stars were vivid and bright, his future remained murky, teasing him with mystery. To answer his question, he would get no help from stargazing.

To live, or to die. That was the big question.

Well, it was one question anyway. But possibly not the best one to dwell on, given the precarious state of his health. And in any case, he already knew the answer. No, it would be more productive to ask a different question. But what?

Questions within questions. No matter how far he

walked or how hard he stared at the celestial sphere, he grew no closer to finding the right question to ask, let alone being able to answer it.

And all the time his body grew weaker.

When had he last eaten? He couldn't remember. When had his dried, cracked lips last tasted blood? It was just another unknown, to add to all the other conundrums. At times, when the pressure inside his skull grew too great, everything became an enigma. When the fever burned hot, he struggled to remember even his own name. His life was slipping away from his grasp, one drop at a time. But he knew he had been master of his own destiny once. He had been leader of the Wolf Brothers. Mounted upon a mighty motorbike, his woman behind him and his Brothers at his side, he had stolen and killed and done as he willed. None had been strong enough to resist him.

Now the sun had set on his glory and he was nothing. He was no longer Leader of the Pack, no longer even a Brother. He had slain two of his former Brothers, and others had died under his command. It wasn't surprising that Slasher had challenged him for leadership, or that Vixen had left him, taking the surviving Brothers with her.

He thought of his fallen comrades: Wombat, Snakebite, Meathook, Slasher, and the others, whose names he had forgotten. They would be waiting for him in Valhalla. He hoped to join them there, feasting and drinking mead until the world ended. Already he could hear their voices calling.

But what were they saying? He strained to catch their words.

'Warg Daddy.' The voice was Wombat's, the first of the Brothers to be killed. He had died at Leanna's hands, but it was Warg Daddy who was to blame. He had led him to the Common that night, in search of a werewolf. The guys had told him it was a dumb idea, but he had insisted. Now Wombat pointed an accusing hand in his direction. 'We trusted you, but you betrayed us.'

'No,' he rasped, his tongue struggling to form words in his parched mouth. 'I never betrayed you. I always did my best for you. You were my Brothers.'

'You murdered your own Brother, man.' This time it was Snakebite's voice. 'You killed me in cold blood.'

Warg Daddy tried to recall the face of the flame-headed giant, but all he could see was the bloody stump that remained after he had blasted his former deputy into oblivion with his shotgun. The ghost of Snakebite leered at him, his red beard the only recognisable feature amid the blood and gore that dripped from his splintered skull.

'I had no choice,' Warg Daddy protested.

'You had choices, but you threw them away,' accused another ghost. Meathook. 'Every time you had a chance to choose, you tossed that stupid coin instead. And that was why I ended up getting killed.' Meathook's ghost was even more badly disfigured than Snakebite's. His entire head had been blown off his shoulders, and he carried it under one arm.

'I didn't kill you!' said Warg Daddy. 'That bishop did it!'

The bishop himself appeared then, his mitre on his head, his golden crozier in his hand. 'I never meant to kill anyone,' he protested. 'You invaded my abbey. You brought death to my doors.'

'I was following the will of the gods,' said Warg Daddy. 'The coin led me along the path.'

'So you claim,' said Slasher. 'But that's just a lame excuse. The truth is, you were too afraid to own your decisions.'

Warg Daddy cowered before the crowding phantoms, unable to resist their combined assault. He knew the truth as well as they did. And what was the point in fighting them, anyway? He was as good as a ghost himself. He hung his head in shame.

Then he raised it once again. Another light had appeared in the firmament above him – a new light, moving quickly. Was it a comet? A meteor? He didn't know. Not a plane, certainly. Not a firework. Then, what? The sparkling light was brighter than any star. It swept across the sky in a long arc. A shooting star. It was a sign of something, but he couldn't guess what. The gods were mocking him again.

'Tell me what to do!' he bellowed into the sky, although his voice was no more than a hoarse whisper.

Silence came back to him. The light in the sky flickered and died. So briefly it had flared, and so brightly. Warg Daddy yearned to be like that star. Like the Viking warriors of old, he longed to spend what little remained of his life in glory, and then to die in battle, a hero. Was it so much to ask?

Yet here he was, a ruin of his former self. He could barely walk, let alone fight. The cruel gods would not allow him even this final wish.

As morning drew near the stars faded one by one. When they were all gone it was difficult to believe that they had ever been there at all. Now day came in their place, spreading faint grey and then a pink glow across the eastern sky before him. He pulled on his Ray-Bans but the sun's hot fingers soon stabbed at his brow. He rolled beneath the shade of a rocky outcrop, knowing that the heat would rise inexorably as the day grew long. As the sun searched for him with its fiery hands he shut his eyes tightly and waited for cool night to return, wondering if he would live to see it.

Chapter Nine

Midhurst, West Sussex

The sun was already high when Liz rose from bed. It was hard for her to sleep at night, especially now that the long days of summer were here, and so she'd adopted late habits, burning the oil until well past midnight and then lying in until midday. After years of working shifts and responding to late-night callouts as a police officer, it was easy to adapt to the body clock of a vampire.

She pulled on dark glasses and rubbed sun cream on her face and bare arms before heading downstairs. Llewelyn and Kevin were at work in the kitchen, where they had teamed up like a pair of zero-star Michelin chefs to serve unclassifiable meals largely out of tins. Llewelyn was wearing a blue-and-white striped apron, and Kevin had found a ridiculous chef's hat. Judging by the smell of cooking, she'd arrived just in time for lunch.

'Morning,' she said. 'What is it today?'

Llewelyn was spooning out servings onto plates. 'Roast pork served with a gourmet bean stew.'

'Sounds delicious.' Liz eyed the food suspiciously. 'It's tinned spam with baked beans again, isn't it?'

'You saw right through our cunning ruse.'

She breathed in the aroma of the food, and found that she was hungry. 'Extra spam for me, please, but go easy on the beans.' Meat was what she craved these days, and the bloodier the better. This tinned meat was far too processed for her taste and there was no blood, just tomato sauce. But she would take whatever was on offer.

Not a single drop of fresh blood had passed her lips since the night of the summer solstice, and perhaps that was for the best. Blood filled her with unimaginable strength, but it fed the darkness inside her too.

'Let's round up the kids and get this food on the table,' said Kevin.

'All right.' Liz helped to carry the plates through to the dining room, while Llewelyn went off to shout at the kids and to tell Samantha that lunch was served. A minute later the kids were at the table, knives and forks scraping, acting like they'd barely eaten in months. Judging by how thin they were, they probably hadn't. Liz dreaded to think what would have happened to them if she hadn't found them and brought them out of London.

At first they'd been a wild mass of tangled hair and tattered clothes, almost indistinguishable from each other with their hooded, scowling faces and unintelligible street talk. Now, one by one, she was getting to know them. She had learned their names and heard their stories. Leah – who talked and acted as tough as a boy because it was the only way she knew to survive. Alfie – who clutched his sword the way other kids his age might hold a soft toy for comfort.

Their lives were similar in many ways to Liz's own childhood, just worse. And their stories were depressingly similar to each other. Fathers gone. Mothers unable to cope. Flotsam and jetsam on the great tide of human tragedy. As a police officer, she had often had to caution or detain kids like that, but had always wished she could take them home and look after them instead. Now she had.

Already they were changing visibly. Leah was taking on the role of a mother, bossing the younger kids around and organizing them into sleeping groups. The quieter ones were gaining in confidence and starting to respond to Liz's questions with more than grunts and monosyllables. And they were exploring the hotel, fascinated by all the facilities on offer. Mihai had joined them, enjoying the company of kids his own age. Being an orphan himself, he had a lot in common with them.

'So what have you guys been up to this morning?' Liz asked.

'Swimming,' said Alfie.

'We went in the pool,' said Leah.

'How was it?'

'Rank,' said Alfie. 'It stinks!'

'And is cold, too,' said Mihai.

'That didn't stop them diving in and splashing round for a full minute before running out again screaming,' said Samantha.

'Maybe I could get it working again,' said Kevin. 'You know, heat the water, change the filter and get the pump running.' He had already rigged up a generator to provide electricity, and coaxed the hotel's heating system into supplying hot water so they could take a shower every day.

'I don't think it's a priority, Dad. We're not short of other jobs to do first. Besides, we need to conserve our heating oil for essential use.'

'I'm sure we can find more oil,' said Kevin.

'Even so, let's not waste any.'

The hotel was everything that Liz had hoped for, and more. The main building held a dozen guest rooms, all individually decorated and each equipped with a king-size bed and an en-suite bathroom. The various outbuildings offered as much accommodation again, and the dining room, lounges and entrance hall were large and furnished in the style of a late Victorian country house with polished wooden floors, Persian rugs, deep sofas and gilt-framed paintings on the walls. It was a luxurious place to live, with more than enough space for them all.

Liz had chosen a bedroom at the front of the hotel for herself and Llewelyn, and Kevin and Mihai had moved into a room overlooking some now rather overgrown grass tennis courts at the back. With Samantha, Lily and Leo installed comfortably in a third room in the main building, that still left plenty of space for Leah, Alfie and the other kids to sleep.

But it was outdoors that the country hotel really came into its own, offering acres of grounds in which the kids could roam freely without supervision. After eating they all rushed off, heading for the tennis courts. The fact that no one had cut the grass in months didn't seem to stop their enjoyment of the game.

Liz watched them go and couldn't prevent a huge grin from spreading over her face. Was this paradise? As good as it got? She hadn't imagined finding her dream home amid a post-apocalyptic landscape, but all the necessary elements seemed to be present, so she guessed it must be.

When lunch was over she went outside and stood by the front door with Llewelyn. The sun was high overhead and she had to fight an urge to retreat back inside to the cool shade. She wanted to see everything for herself, to check that it was real, and not some mirage.

'What are you doing?' Llewelyn asked as she placed her hands against the warm bricks of the building.

'They feel so solid.'

'Bricks usually are. It's why they build houses out of them.'

'I've never lived anywhere that felt as solid as this before.'

Lycanthropic

'Shoddy London builders, eh?'

She took Llewelyn's hands in hers and felt their strength. He was like the bricks himself: a man-mountain hewn from stone, with a granite jaw and arms that would never let her fall. 'Seriously, though,' she said. 'Is this it? Somewhere we can finally put down roots? A place where we can grow old together and die?'

'Don't get heavy with me, Liz. Nobody's dying. At least, not unless that tennis match turns nasty. You never know with those kids.'

'I want to give them the best chance in life. Them and Mihai. And Lily and Leo too. All the children. Do you think we can fix this world for them?'

Llewelyn shrugged. 'We can try. But it'll need a lot of fixing.'

'Yes, but this is a chance to start all over again. Perhaps we can make it right this time. Better, even. No racism, no sexism, no warring religions. We can put all that behind us and make a fresh start.'

'Sure, man. Peace and love, let's all be like John Lennon. Equal rights for werecreatures.'

'I mean it.'

Llewelyn gave the question his consideration. 'I don't know about that, Liz. It seems to me that men have always fought other men, and that life has never been easy. But I know this: we have to try. We have no other choice.'

Chapter Ten

Gatwick Airport, West Sussex

Colonel Griffin sat at his temporary desk beneath canvas in his field HQ. The world as he knew it had come to an end, but somehow paper still made its way to him for signing, just as it always had. Like some kind of zombie lifeform, administration refused to die.

When all human life is finally snuffed out, the paper trails we create will live on. Even when we are perished and resting in our graves, documents will still be waiting to be signed, and letters to be sent.

It seemed impossible to fight a war without them. Wearily, Griffin scratched his name on the latest pages and passed them to an aide to deliver.

He stretched his leg tentatively beneath the desk, turning it a little and feeling the malrotated femur rub against his hip bone. No matter how long he endured it, it never got any easier. It was that constant abrasion that had caused his leg to become reinfected. Yet some regular movement was necessary, otherwise it would stiffen up and be even worse when he eventually did try to walk.

Thank God for morphine.

The tent flaps opened and Griffin looked up. He was startled to see Bampton entering. The group captain must have just returned from the *Queen Elizabeth*. Griffin's spirits rose at the sight of his friend and comrade, then immediately fell. If Bampton had travelled all this way in person, he must be bringing important news. And news these days was rarely welcome.

'Griffin. It's good to see you. No need to stand.'

But Griffin struggled to his feet, unwilling to concede defeat to his wasted leg.

We are not at sea now. And I am not completely incapacitated. Not yet.

He leaned heavily against the desk and stretched out an arm. 'Bampton.' The two men shook hands warmly. The informal greeting was not the military way of doing things, but Griffin made his own rules now.

The only compensation for the burden I must carry.

'All is well at sea, I trust?' he enquired.

'As well as it can ever be inside a floating tin can.'

Griffin grinned, sharing Bampton's feelings for the maritime life. Although, he reminded himself, Bampton's natural environment was in the air. Army, Navy and Air Force – they were almost as distinct from each other as humans from werewolves.

Give me the certainty of ground beneath my feet any day.

'I expect you'd like to stretch your legs after your flight,' he said.

A look of concern flitted across Bampton's face. 'There's no need to walk. I'm happy to sit.'

'No,' said Griffin, reaching for his crutches. 'Fresh air will do me good. We can walk and talk, and it will stop my leg from seizing up.'

'As you wish.' Bampton waited patiently while Griffin manoeuvred himself around the edge of the desk. Every walk was an ordeal now, and every step a challenge, but one that Griffin would not shirk from.

Each stab of pain reminds me of my true purpose. Once all this is over, to find her.

Bampton lifted the tent flaps to let Griffin duck outside. They emerged into daylight, the camp around them teeming with activity. Soldiers went about their duties, cleaning weapons, loading or unloading trucks, carrying out their training. Shouts filled the air and men saluted him as he lurched along, his crutches sinking into the soft turf. The smell of cooking wafted on the breeze. Army food, as deadly as the soldiers who ate it.

Busy people, doing as I asked them. But to what end? Do they simply prepare themselves for their deaths?

Griffin shook the negative thoughts from his mind, and turned to give his full attention to Bampton. 'So, what brings you here?'

Bampton seemed reluctant to talk. 'Let's go somewhere quieter.'

Griffin slowly made his way across the field toward the edge of the camp, step by painful step. It took an age, but when he turned and looked back, he could see that the camp was not so large. With only a thousand men and women located at the field HQ, his entire army was less than a brigade, scarcely a regiment. Not that such distinctions existed anymore. They were a mish-mash of fragmented units, drawn from infantry battalions, armoured divisions and logistics corps. Whatever was left after a string of defeats.

They are all we have now. And they are our finest.

Griffin leaned on his crutches, easing the pressure on his damaged leg. He braced himself for Bampton to break his news, whatever it might be. But he knew that if it was good, the group captain would already have shared it with him.

Bampton turned and gazed back across the field that Griffin had chosen as his temporary base. 'I wish to report the latest from overseas.'

Griffin hadn't expected that. 'Overseas?' As far as he knew, there had been no news from overseas since shortly after General Ney's nuclear attack had rained down on Britain's cities. It had been a precursor to a wave of similar events around the world. Russia, the United States, China and France had all unleashed a barrage of destruction against neighbouring states or long-held enemies. India and Pakistan had been the first to join the frenzy, closely followed by North Korea, unwilling to be left out of the carnage.

Scores had been settled, fear and paranoia had won over common sense, and the world had torn itself apart. The insanity had not lasted long, and had been followed by silence. The world beyond the UK's shores had gone dark.

Griffin waited for Bampton to elaborate, but the group captain's face remained grim. 'It's not good, I'm afraid. But I suppose that it might be worse. After weeks of attempting to make contact, we have succeeded in exchanging messages with several groups of survivors.'

'Where?'

'The US, Spain, and South Africa. But the groups are small and isolated. In every case, the reports are the same – each group is unaware of any other survivors, and they are unable to provide help. We're completely on our own, it would seem.'

Griffin wasn't surprised by the news, but he felt the blow nonetheless. Alone. This conflict he faced was now a fight for humanity's very survival. It was the most important war in human history, and possibly its last. There could be only one victor in the coming battle and it was madness that he was fighting against an enemy clothed in human form.

'We stand alone, then,' he said, hoping he sounded braver than he felt. 'It is as we expected.'

Bampton placed a reassuring hand on his shoulder. 'Not alone, Griffin. Together. Even though we are few.'

'Together,' agreed Griffin, glad to have his friend back at his side, even though he was the bearer of such bad news. 'Come, let's share a drink before you return.'

Chapter Eleven

Salisbury Plain

Chris Crohn had problems, so numerous that they were almost too many to count. Yet despite that, he was determined to itemize each and every one of his grievances.

First there was the fact that, whatever Ryan might say, his nose was still broken. A huge fist in his face from one of Rowan's thugs had mashed it into a purple pulp. At least he assumed it was purple. Without a mirror to view himself he had no way of telling. It felt purple at any rate. The pain when he sneezed was almost unbelievable, and it was a testament to his own fortitude that he could endure it. Even days after sustaining the injury it felt no better. If anything it was worse, and he was worried that infection might be setting in. If that happened, he could die.

Death by nose infection – what a horrendous prospect. Yet no matter how much he drew the attention of Seth and Ryan to his predicament, they didn't seem to care.

Instead, they told him to stop moaning. Didn't they realise that without his knowledge of how to rebuild civilization, they were all doomed?

'I could die,' he kept repeating, to anyone who would listen, and several who wouldn't. 'I nearly died already. The druid wanted to turn me into a human sacrifice.'

He was the only person among all these halfwits who understood the rudiments of survival. Preparation – no one but him had bothered to do any. And did anyone thank him for acquiring this crucial knowledge? No.

'Stop moaning about your nose, Chris,' was all anyone said to him. They hadn't even thanked him after he led them to the field of barley and showed them how to turn it into edible food. No one had said, 'Thanks for saving us from starvation, Chris. That barley stew was really good.' Some of them even had the cheek to grumble about the flavour. Although to be fair, it *had* tasted totally disgusting and vile.

Even his so-called best friend, Seth, had no sympathy. 'Never mind your nose, Chris. I broke my leg thanks to you.'

'Your leg wasn't broken,' said Chris. 'It was just sprained. Anyway, I carried you and your "broken" leg halfway across England. Nobody's offered to help me with my nose.'

'Do you want someone to carry it?' asked Seth with a sarcastic sneer.

Seth was sneering far too much these days. In Chris' opinion, someone as prone to uttering inane drivel as Seth ought not to sneer at others quite so often. It was annoying that with his bushy beard and long hair, Seth now carried the air of a wise man. If he held his tongue, he could pass for a young Merlin or Gandalf. It was only when he opened his mouth that stupidities tumbled out.

'I just want some sympathy,' said Chris. But what he really wanted was painkillers. And a course of antibiotics, to be safe.

Lycanthropic

His nose might be his number-one grievance, but it was far from his only one. On top of that he counted sunburn, hay fever, insect bites, a host of newfound allergies, and a generalized aversion to Nature in all its diabolic forms. He had never before realized that the wilderness was so inhospitable to human life. While he'd understood well enough the challenges presented by desert or polar exploration, none of the survivalist blogs he'd studied back in his apartment in London had really managed to convey just how tough the English countryside in summer could be.

It was all so unfair. He'd been raised and educated to be a cyber dweller, permanently plugged in online, fully expecting to one day upload his mind into a digital substrate and achieve a virtual existence that would enable him to leave the constraints of the physical world far behind. Instead, he was now condemned to spend the rest of his days in a neo-primitive phase of post-history in which everything that was good had been swept aside, and all he had to look forward to was a meaningless life of cold baths, hard labour and a diet of boiled plants.

He had a good mind to turn his back on the others and strike out alone. Except that he'd tried that once, at the beginning of the Ridgeway on Ivinghoe Beacon, and hadn't got further than half a mile before turning back. He knew from his extensive reading that the chances of long-term survival alone were very small, and that humans thrived best in groups, using the power of language to achieve cooperation and the division of labour. Logically, that seemed the best way forward. He, Chris, would use his superior intelligence and knowledge to decide what jobs needed to be done, and to divide the tasks amongst the others. Rose, as designated leader of the tribe, would act as the mouthpiece for his commands. Ryan would be the heavy, in case anyone refused to carry out their allotted tasks. And Seth ... well, Chris would try to think of a use for Seth later.

Right now he had more immediate worries. Up ahead, the dark grey smear of a road had appeared beyond the lip of a low hill. It stretched out before them, perfectly straight from left to right. The road was empty of vehicles, and the only sound was the ceaseless moaning of the wind. It was the first proper road they had encountered in days, and its neat parallel lines invited them to follow it wherever it led.

But Chris didn't trust roads. Roads connected one town or city to another, and towns and cities were no-go zones in the post-apocalyptic age. They were no longer places where you might find offices, convenience stores and high-speed internet connections. Now a city was more likely to harbour outlaws, bandits or even werewolves. Avoiding towns and cities had been Chris' primary objective ever since leaving London.

Predictably, the others saw things differently.

'Great,' said Seth, stroking his exuberant beard. 'Civilization, at last. Let's check out the nearest town.'

Ryan walked over to the road. He was still limping a little on one leg. But he never complained about it, so it can't have hurt that much. He looked up and down the road, staring into the distance in each direction. 'Yeah, but which way should we go?'

'Neither,' said Chris. 'We should keep walking across the fields. Roads are to be feared.'

'That,' said Seth from behind his beard, 'is the dumbest thing you've ever said.'

Chris didn't bother to answer him. Words were wasted on Seth.

'Why, Chris?' asked Ryan. 'Why should we fear roads?'

'Because they lead to towns, and towns are dangerous.'

'We don't know where this road leads.'

'Somewhere bad.'

'But we need to find food,' countered Ryan. 'And a town is the most obvious place to find it.'

'Better than hunting around for turnips in a farmer's

field,' added Seth with a sneer.

'Turnips won't be ready until late autumn,' pointed out Chris, although he wondered why he bothered.

Rose, as usual, was listening carefully to the discussion but saying nothing. She stood still, her feet planted firmly on the warm tarmac of the road, her red hair flowing in the wind like water in a stream. 'We need to eat,' she said at last. 'And Ryan and Seth are right. Going to the nearest town would be the quickest way to find food. We have to follow the road and see where it takes us. If it leads us to a town, we'll search for supplies. As we go, we'll keep looking for any crops or animals that we can eat. And we'll keep a close look out for any signs of danger.'

Chris should have known that no one would do what he said. They never did. Still, he admired Rose's style of leadership. The girl never wasted time in fruitless argument but listened to the views of her advisers and made her decision. She was efficient. She was authoritative. She commanded respect. No wonder everyone did exactly what she said.

People skills, he supposed you might call it. Perhaps he could learn something from her. But what, exactly? The art of persuasion remained a mystery to him. Reluctantly he set off along the road, trudging in the wake of the others, hoping there would be no town at the end of the road, but feeling pretty sure there would.

Chapter Twelve

Christmas Common, Oxfordshire

A week had passed since the summer solstice and the terrors and joys of the night of the blood moon. Melanie Margolis had feared she would die that night, trapped in a darkened cellar by ferocious werewolves. But Ben and James had returned just in time to fight off the attackers, and now she and Ben were reunited for ever. It was like a fairy-tale.

And I have never stopped believing in fairy-tales.

June had turned into July and was rushing headlong toward golden August. Before too long September would be upon them – season of ripened fruits and harvest time.

A good season for a pregnant woman like me.

Already the jeans that she had worn since leaving London had grown uncomfortably tight around her thickening waist.

I am going to burst out of them if I don't move up a size soon.

Chanita laid her hands against Melanie's belly, prodding

and poking in a most unwelcome way. 'The timing is wrong,' she muttered. 'This baby was conceived much earlier than you think. At least twelve weeks, I would say.'

'How could it have been?' asked Melanie. 'Ben wasn't here then. He went away after he turned into a werewolf and didn't return until the night of the summer solstice. That was when it happened.'

Chanita frowned at being contradicted. 'Even so, I can tell. The pregnancy is far too advanced. You are showing all the signs of the second trimester.'

Melanie grunted. Chanita might be a good nurse, but Melanie was the baby's mother. She knew what she knew. Still, pregnancy was agreeing with her nicely. Apart from her waistband, and the fact that she'd been sick once or twice at the beginning, she had quickly settled in and now felt very comfortable. Her hair, already long and thick, had become as glossy as one of those women who advertised outrageously-expensive conditioner back in the days when Melanie had made weekly visits to a hair salon. Back when hair salons were a thing.

'Do you feel any pain at the side of your belly?' asked Chanita.

'Not pain. Just a sensation of getting larger.'

'Headaches? Nosebleeds?'

'No.'

'Dizziness? Feeling hot?'

'A little. I feel dizzy with joy and hot as sin!' Melanie giggled. 'Just ask Ben.'

Chanita gave her a poke. 'Ben's pleased about becoming a father?'

'Ecstatic.'

Chanita completed her examination. 'Well, there's nothing much wrong with you. But you're definitely well into the second trimester.'

Whatever. It was easier just to smile and agree with Chanita's opinion. The baby would come when it was ready. 'It's a girl,' said Melanie. 'I can tell.'

Chanita's face expressed scorn. 'Mothers sometimes think they know the sex of their baby, but without an ultrasound scanner, there's simply no way to tell.'

'A girl,' insisted Melanie. 'I need to think of a name for her.'

'There's plenty of time for that. Another twenty-six weeks to go, I would think. So you're looking at a January birth.'

January. That seemed like a very long way off. Melanie had never been any good at waiting. As a little girl, she had always sneaked downstairs on Christmas Eve to unwrap her presents as soon as they appeared beneath the tree. Perhaps her baby would prove to be just as impatient as her and arrive sooner. Maybe in time for Christmas. A Christmas baby in Christmas Common. That would be just perfect.

She swung her legs off the couch and jumped to her feet. She felt as fit as she ever had. And she had a raging hunger. Eating for two was a lot more fun than the desperately joyless diets she had forced on herself in an effort to squeeze into the latest fashions. But fashion was dead and now she didn't care how big she got. If ever there had been an excuse to indulge her appetite, this was surely it.

'Right,' she said. 'I'm going to start cooking. Then after lunch I want to carry on with repair work on the house.'

The attack on midsummer's night by the marauding werewolves had wreaked destruction on the house and the surrounding grounds. Melanie's home-made defences had proved to be devastatingly effective, but had wrecked half the house, turning the place into a death trap. Now they were making it habitable again, trying to find a balance between liveability and security. The house would never be properly comfortable. It was too old and draughty for that. Yet it had an abundance of charm, or would do, once the repairs were completed. There were so many jobs still to be done – repairing the leaks in the roof, fixing the windows that had been broken during the attack, reinforcing the doors, re-digging the pits and the oil-filled trenches around the perimeter, setting up more booby traps and alarm systems ...

'Melanie,' said Chanita, 'you need to slow down. You're going to make yourself exhausted.'

'No. I feel fine. I want to work, and now that I'm expecting the baby, it's more important than ever that we keep ourselves safe.'

'Ben and James can do the hard work,' insisted Chanita. 'And me and Sarah too.'

'While I stay home like a good little housewife? That's not ever happening.'

Chanita let out a long sigh. 'All right. Just try to apply a little moderation. That's all I'm asking. Let other people take on the heaviest jobs.'

Melanie tossed back her hair. 'Moderation isn't really part of my skill-set. But I'll try.'

She went outside to look for Ben and found him in the back garden, stripped to the waist, splitting logs with an axe. She leaned against the door, admiring his physique and feeling a stirring in her loins. Pregnancy hormones were the best thing ever. Since the very moment of the conception her sex drive had shifted into top gear, but she knew she had to exercise a little restraint. *Some of the time, at least. I can probably wait until the evening.* 'Hey,' she called.

'Hey.' He set aside the axe and came over to give her a kiss. 'What does the nurse say?'

'She says I'm good, but I need to slow up. I need to lie down in a darkened room like a Victorian lady.'

Ben raised an eyebrow in amusement. 'Right. Let me know what you intend to do about that.'

'Chanita says you need to do all the hard work. Like a real man.' She ran her hands across his bare chest.

'Well, I don't mind that. Hard work helps to keep me on the straight and narrow.'

There was a half-smile on his mouth, but Melanie knew

the dark truth he was alluding to. When Ben had first become a werewolf, he had tried to kill her. He had run away with James to stop himself from harming her, and over time had learned to keep his urge to consume human flesh under control. Hard physical labour was part of the cure, as well as regular cups of wolfsbane tea. Together, they enabled him to suppress the harmful side of his nature, but she knew that it would never completely go away. There would always be a wildness in his eyes from time to time, especially around the peak of the moon.

'Where are the others?' she asked. 'James and Sarah, I mean.'

'Out looking for more kerosene. Since you set the village on fire, we need to find a new supply.'

'I didn't set it on fire,' she protested. But her fire traps had taken out half the werewolves, and had proven their worth. They needed to be replenished, and soon.

A frown crept over Ben's face. 'Speaking of James, what do you think about the way he's been behaving lately?'

'What do you mean?'

'Have you noticed anything different about him?'

'Since he returned? Well, he's become stronger during the time he spent away. All that work chopping logs, I suppose. He's grown into a proper man at last.' James had definitely matured in his appearance in the months he'd been away from Christmas Common. He was eighteen now. Tall, with a thick sandy beard, and long blond hair that tumbled to his shoulders. His skin was bronzed from long hours working in the sun, but his green eyes held shadows and secrets. Melanie could no longer tell what he was thinking. Sometimes tears sprang spontaneously from those sad green eyes, perhaps as he recalled his many losses and sorrows. And sometimes she caught a glint of something darker, and feared he was just one step away from violence. Yet it was James who had brought Ben's own violent impulses under control and had returned him to her. Melanie owed James everything. She would trust him with her life, and he had saved it on more than one occasion.

Ben brooded thoughtfully. 'James is a troubled soul. He's lost so much in his short life, and taken on so much responsibility. But it's since we returned that I've noticed the change. He's become withdrawn. Secretive, almost. I think he's planning something.'

'What?'

'I don't know. And that's what worries me most.'

Chapter Thirteen

The Pilgrims' Way

Once, a pilgrims' route had led this way, from Winchester Cathedral to the cathedral at Canterbury, via the towns of Alton, Farnham, Guildford and Rochester. A distance of some hundred and fifty miles. A journey of two weeks on foot. *The Old Road* it was called and the faithful had followed its path for a thousand years. Vijay had learned about it in Religious Studies.

They had studied all kinds of religions at school. Christianity, of course, as well as Islam and Judaism. But also Hinduism, Buddhism and Sikhism. Vijay liked to hear about other people's beliefs. It was wrong to think that one group had all the answers.

'But the pilgrims went east,' he said aloud, as if the others had contradicted him. 'We are walking in the other direction. We're going west.'

'Nobody said anything about pilgrims,' snapped Aasha,

giving him a strange look.

'East, west, whatever,' said Drake. 'We ain't no pilgrims anyway.'

'I'll tell you what I am,' said Aasha. 'I'm hungry, I'm tired, and all my muscles ache from sleeping on the floor. I want a warm bed to sleep in. And some proper food too.'

Vijay glanced at his sister. She was a shadow of what she'd once been. Her long black hair trailed down her back, unwashed and matted, and the pounds had fallen from her, leaving her thin and wretched-looking. They had spent the previous night in a barn, sleeping on bales of straw. They'd had nothing to eat for breakfast, and only a handful of berries during the day. He had tried to eat some of the plants they found growing in the fields, but they tasted bitter and he spat them out quickly, afraid of eating something poisonous.

But it was important to always look on the bright side. 'It wasn't so bad in the barn, not really,' he said, even though the straw had scratched his skin.

'It was,' said Drake. 'It was smelly and full of rats.' Drake had also lost weight, but he looked better for it, and had a hard, wiry look about him. He'd gained an inch or two in height since leaving London, making him tower over Vijay. And his sandy beard was starting to thicken, while his hair, which had once been closely-cropped, now reached almost to his shoulders. His skin was darkening under the summer sun, especially since he was in the habit of stripping off his shirt as they walked along country lanes, clambering over wooden gates and stiles. Vijay caught Aasha staring at his arms and torso as he flexed his muscles. Drake was becoming a man, and a wild-looking one at that. He spat on the ground. 'I've had enough of this.'

'Well, me too,' said Vijay, 'but it doesn't make any difference whether we like it or not. We still have to follow the rules.'

He was tired of the arguments that raged between him

and the other two. His stomach was just as empty as theirs; his heart was empty too. But his resolve to live the right way was as strong as ever. Stronger. He began to list the rules that every Sikh was expected to follow. 'Work hard and honestly. Share with others. Do not steal. Avoid lust, anger and greed –'

'Stop going on about those stupid rules,' said Aasha.

'Who made them, anyway?' asked Drake.

'Guru Nanak, the first Sikh Guru,' replied Vijay. 'And the nine Gurus that followed him.'

'Why can't you just shut up about it?' said Aasha. 'We're free to make our own rules now. We can do whatever we like.'

'People have always been free to do what they liked,' retorted Vijay. 'That's why they get themselves into so much trouble.'

The sacrifice that his parents and grandmother had made had placed a heavy weight of responsibility upon his shoulders. It wasn't enough now simply to survive. He had to demonstrate that he was worth their sacrifice. It was the same with Rose. His goal wasn't only to find her, although that was going to be hard enough. He had to prove to her that he was good enough for her.

'Well, look,' said Drake, 'I don't mind following rules. I mean, I'm not a Sikh or nothing, but I'm happy to do all that stuff you talk about – sharing with others and not stealing and so on. In normal times, at least. But in my book, stealing ain't stealing if someone's gone and left their house behind. They're probably dead anyway. So how can you steal from a dead person? I don't reckon that's stealing at all.'

'We wouldn't know whether or not the owners were dead. They might be coming back.' Vijay hoisted the heavy rucksack on his back and climbed over another stile leading from one field to another. At first he'd enjoyed being out in the countryside, away from the dirty and overcrowded surroundings of the evacuation camp, feeling the warm sun beating down on his face and listening to the songs of the birds, but all these fields were starting to look the same. Stinging his hand on nettles was getting old too.

'Now you're just being pig-headed,' snapped Aasha. 'Is this your way of dealing with Mum and Dad and Grandmother getting killed? Because it's not very helpful. If we carry on like this, we'll end up dead too, and then what would be the point of their sacrifice?'

Vijay felt her rebuke like a slap to his face. *Is there truth in what she says? Am I just being pig-headed?* There must be a germ of truth, or else her words wouldn't have stung so much. It was like when he was being bullied at school – the names the bullies called him hurt more because he had called himself the same. *Coward, midget, wimp.* He was all those things and more. But now was the time to prove he could be brave. He blinked away the fresh tears that filled his eyes. 'We can't just give up on everything we were taught,' he protested. 'Grandmother never stopped doing the right thing, no matter what difficulties she faced. Even when our grandfather died, she didn't lose faith.'

Aasha's voice grew kinder when she saw how much her words had hurt him. 'I'm not saying to give up, just to be practical. The houses we've passed have all been empty. Their owners are long gone. Let's not waste anything they left behind. Waste is wrong too, isn't it?'

'Well, yes, I suppose so.'

Sometimes it was so difficult to find the right path through life. Traps lay on every side. He wanted the way to be clearly signposted so that he could choose to follow the truth. But sometimes it seemed like the truth had been deliberately hidden so that even when he resolved to do right, he ended up doing wrong. Right now he was so confused he didn't know what to think. Perhaps he should just do what the other two wanted. Aasha was right about the houses being deserted. They hadn't encountered a single person in the small villages and farmsteads they'd passed since leaving the camp behind. Perhaps Drake was right too, and their owners were dead already.

'So let's go find the nearest town, yeah?' said Drake. 'There'll be shops there and lots more houses. I hate the countryside anyway. It's too big and empty. And why does everything have to be so green? It ain't natural.'

They came to the end of the path they'd been following along the edge of a field and climbed over a gate. Now they found themselves on a tarmacked road. 'This is more like it,' said Drake enthusiastically. 'Come on.'

'Just be careful,' called Vijay, although he hated to hear the sound of his own voice, always moaning, always whining.

The road led them to a town and before long shops and houses sprang up on either side. Just as they'd expected, there was no one around. A strange hush filled the streets, with none of the usual sounds of civilization like the rumble and roar of traffic, the chattering of voices or the shrieks and shouts of children playing. The town was empty of life and not even birdsong broke the silence.

Their hopes of finding food and shelter were quickly dashed. The shops had all been ransacked and the buildings gutted by fire. Blackened windows of houses, offices and apartment blocks stared down at them like dark eyes, and white ash washed over the road like foam on the sea. Burned-out vehicles stood wherever their owners had abandoned them. One of the houses still had a "For Sale" board on display, but no one would be buying it now.

Apart from Vijay, Drake and Aasha, no living soul walked these streets. But the town was not deserted. It was home to the dead. Corpses littered the roads in isolation and in heaps. Some were half-eaten, though whether by werewolf or animal, it was impossible to say. Some displayed savage wounds where they had been shot or killed with a blade, or even bitten to death. Others looked unharmed, as if they might start walking again if told to rise. But a dreadful stink hung over the town, and black flies crawled everywhere, supping on the decomposing bodies and laying their eggs.

Even Drake seemed shaken by the sight. 'This place is a graveyard,' he whispered.

Chapter Fourteen

Somewhere in England

The sun rose steadily in the sky, reaching down to sear Warg Daddy's cracked and reddened face. No matter which way he turned beneath his rock, it sought him out, as determined as it was cruel. *How many days have I endured this agony? How many days still remain?* He yearned for blood, imagining how sweet it would taste as it trickled down his parched throat, like drops of rain sinking into desert sand. But there was no blood in this place, save for his own, spilled and dried like rust on the ground. And no water either. No life. No hope. Perhaps today would be his last.

The stars were long gone, burned away like morning dew, and the cooling shade of night was far behind him – less a memory, more a dream. He feared he would never see those stars again. Not in this life, at least.

The sun rose higher, rising on a tide of heat, and whichever way he turned beneath his rock it reached for him. Eventually he abandoned all efforts to keep from its grasp, giving himself up to its searing embrace. It was time he stopped hiding. *Take me, then. Let me die a hero.* With one last effort he dragged himself upright and sat with his back pressed against the heat-soaked stump of the rock, feeling its burning touch even through the thick leather skin of his jacket. He set his blistered face against the noonday blaze, wondering what he had done to make an enemy of the sun god.

After a while a dot appeared from out of the layers of dust and hot air that shimmered against the horizon, and grew steadily larger. It was a long way off but as it grew nearer he began to discern a shape. A figure was approaching, riding briskly across the flat plain on horseback. A dark figure, clothed in black robes that swirled around him, billowing like a cloud. The figure carried a long pole over his shoulder, and as it grew closer, Warg Daddy saw that the pole was tipped with a long and deadly blade glinting silver as it caught the light.

The stranger stopped his horse a short distance away. The beast was large yet somewhat skeletal, as if it had not eaten for many days. Its coat was pale, though not exactly white, and its eyes were pink. It turned its head towards Warg Daddy, its nostrils flaring, yet it made no sound of breathing, even after cantering at speed for some distance. Instead a deep hush fell over the world and the wind dropped to nothing. The birds ceased their singing, and the creaking branches of the trees overhead fell quiet. Even the whispering leaves grew still, afraid to break the silence that had descended.

The figure dismounted his horse, which began to crop the dry grass at its feet, its tail swishing noiselessly against the flies. He walked closer until his long shadow fell across Warg Daddy's face, bringing blessed relief from the rays of the sun. Warg Daddy didn't rise to greet him. He didn't have the strength.

The figure was uncannily tall, perhaps eight feet, but

seemed gaunt beneath his flowing robes. His long cloak fell right to the ground, revealing only a glimpse of face and hands. Narrow fingers clutched the tall scythe tightly to his chest. Warg Daddy lifted his gaze to the man's cowl, which clothed his features in shadow. The hooded cloak seemed to repel all scrutiny, but with effort he brought his eyes to rest on the man's face. Immediately he wished he hadn't. In stark contrast to the stranger's black velvet cloak, his face was white as bone. Beneath the cowl, parchment skin, stretched taut, held a translucent quality. Lips, so thin they might not exist, revealed a toothless and mirthless grin. But the worst horror was the eyes. They were like two galaxies, spiralling slowly within hollow orbs. To look into them was to risk madness.

With the greatest effort, Warg Daddy dragged his gaze away.

Still the man said nothing.

'Hey,' said Warg Daddy eventually, his voice seeming to reverberate in the soundless air, 'are you –'

'Do not speak my name,' cautioned the stranger, although his paper-thin lips appeared not to move. 'I have come for you, Warg Daddy. Perhaps you have been expecting me.'

'I have.'

Warg Daddy knew why the stranger was here. There was no point resisting the inevitable. In any case, he could barely stand. He had only one arm and was in no position to flee or fight. He couldn't even remember where he'd left his combat shotgun. And what kind of foe was this anyway? *An image conjured from dust and despair.* The dark figure before him might be no more real than the ghosts that inhabited his head. He wasn't going to waste his last drops of energy struggling against some phantom of his own imagination.

The visitor glided closer, his black cloak fluttering even though there was no wind. Warg Daddy glanced briefly again at that hooded face, but his eyes refused to linger and he quickly turned away. 'You know my name, then?'

'I know the name of every man who walks this earth. And every woman and child. I know the names of the birds that roost in the trees and the worms that burrow blindly through the ground. I have visited every town and country in this land, and every ship that sails upon the ocean. All inhabitants of this world are known to me, and all shall meet me at the appointed hour.'

So this was it, then. The time of his reckoning. 'I was hoping for a little while longer,' said Warg Daddy.

'What for?'

'I hoped to fall in battle. I wanted a good death.'

'You think that death can be good?' mocked the visitor.

'I wanted to die a hero, so the Valkyries would carry me away to feast with the gods.'

'A dead hero. They are always the best kind.' The voice was laced with sarcasm. 'I suppose you hoped for songs to be written about you too.'

'I don't need songs,' said Warg Daddy. 'Just a worthy opponent to slay me.'

'You wished to die like your fallen Brothers, no doubt.'

'You knew them?' Warg Daddy reeled off their names. 'Snakebite and Wombat. Meathook and Slasher.'

'I knew them,' agreed the visitor. 'I ushered them into the next world when it was time. And even though you didn't see me, Warg Daddy, I saw you, for you were present when they fell. I saw what you did.'

An awkward silence followed. 'About that ...' said Warg Daddy. 'I didn't mean to –'

'You killed two of them, it is fruitless to deny it. And the others died because of your reckless negligence. But don't worry, I haven't come to condemn you. That's not my job.'

'Okay.'

'In any case, it was not you who cut their souls from their mortal remains. That was me. For I am the reaper.'

'Sure,' said Warg Daddy. 'Well, I guess my time is up.

Let's get on with it, then.'

'What's the big hurry?'

'Well,' said Warg Daddy, 'aren't your services in high demand?'

'Yes. Mine is an important job, to be sure. I am the reaper of souls; the harvester of mortal lives. I open the doorway to the eternal. Both the good and the wicked I usher to the world beyond. All must meet their fate through me.'

'Exactly. So why aren't you busy doing that right now?'

'You think I am not? You assume I cannot be in two places at once? You think like a mortal.'

'I guess.'

'Who can blame you?' mused Death. 'It is how you were made. Like all men, you were born to die. It's a cruel set-up, but don't blame me, I am not the maker of the system. I am merely here to balance the ledgers.'

'Ledgers?'

'It's a metaphor, of course. You might think of me as an accountant. I match the debits and the credits; the profit and the loss. It's double-entry book-keeping. Without it, things get messy, and no good ever came of that.'

The big warhorse was busy eating, ripping up tufts of grass and chewing them hungrily. But Warg Daddy guessed that no matter how much it ate, it would never grow any fatter. He risked another glance at Death's face, but his companion's dreaded visage remained shrouded beneath his black velvet hood, and even the thin line of his mouth was not visible.

'So, when will I die?' Warg Daddy asked. 'Will you take me today?'

Death shook his head.

'Then tomorrow?'

Another shake.

'When, then?'

Death sighed – a deep rumbling noise that made Warg

Lycanthropic

Daddy's fingers tremble. 'Do not ask me. No man may know the time of his passing. Or the means. You are mortal flesh, carved from dust and dirt, and it is not for mortals to bear such knowledge. It is enough simply to know that all men must die.'

'You're not allowed to tell me?'

A fly buzzed lazily around Death's head before crawling into one of his darkened eye sockets. Death swatted it away in irritation. 'I refuse.'

'But why?' pressed Warg Daddy. 'Do you think I'm too weak to cope with that knowledge?'

'No,' said Death.

'Then, do you think I might try to escape my fate?'

'No.'

'Then, why? What can't I know?'

'Because I enjoy surprises,' said Death. 'Believe me, after doing my job for so long, it's the only thing that makes it worthwhile.'

Warg Daddy pondered the answer. 'Then will you tell me what happens after death? Will I go to Heaven, or Hell? Or perhaps to Asgard? Will I live forever in paradise, or be roasted on a spit, or drink mead with dead heroes?'

'I shall not say,' said Death.

'Why not?'

'Because mortals enjoy surprises too.'

Warg Daddy nodded. It seemed that his companion was a man after his own heart. Adventure and the unknown were the stuff of life. How appropriate that they should also be the stuff of death. And yet it seemed curious that the bringer of destruction should have a taste for fun.

'Do you ever grow lonely?' asked Warg Daddy. 'Doing this job of yours. It seems like lonely work.'

'Lonely? No. I get to meet everyone, you know.'

'But not in the happiest of circumstances. And only once. Do you ever wish you could have a more lasting relationship with someone?'

'What is lasting? I watched the first city rise and fall. When the oldest civilizations were yet young, I was already aged beyond measure. When the last human falls, I will be there to catch them. And afterwards, when all are gone, and the stars in the sky look down upon an empty, lifeless planet, I will still be here, gazing back at them.'

'That's a long time, to be sure,' said Warg Daddy. 'But still, don't you think it would be nice to get to know someone a bit better, even if only for a short while?'

'Do you mean … a friend?'

'Yes.'

'I don't know,' said Death. 'I have never had a friend.'

'Me neither.'

Perhaps Snakebite had been the closest to a real friend Warg Daddy had ever known. He and the flame-haired giant had shared some good times. But a Brother was not the same as a friend, and a Leader could never permit himself to get too close to any of his followers. There was no room for sentimentality at the top. That's why he'd had no choice when Snakebite became a challenger for leadership. The shotgun had been the only solution.

'Would you like to play a game?' asked Death. 'To fill the time, while we await your passing.'

'A game?'

'Unless you had something else planned?'

Warg Daddy wondered if this was a trick of some kind. Although Death was dependable, there was no guarantee that he was trustworthy. 'What kind of game?'

'I've always been quite partial to chess.'

A black-and-white chequered board appeared on the ground between them, arrayed with pieces ready for battle. Kings and queens; bishops and knights; rooks and pawns. Death sank to his creaking knees, drawing his black cloak close around him. He propped his scythe against a nearby tree. 'Would you like to move first?' he enquired.

It had been a while since Warg Daddy had played chess. As Leader of the Pack, games like poker had been more his style. If he'd felt a little livelier, a game of pool in the back room of a pub often followed by a punch-up had helped to while away the hours. But chess ... it had been many years since he'd felt the wooden pieces in his fingers.

In his youth he'd been a keen player. Patterns and strategies long forgotten began to bubble back into his consciousness, feeling fresh as he turned them over in his mind. The King's Gambit, the Sicilian Defence, the Scandinavian. Yes, he could do this.

He turned his attention to the board, studying the splendidly carved figures that adorned it. The white pieces etched in bone, their skeletal limbs clothed in dry, brittle fabric; the black pieces carved from ebony, their faces hooded in black robes that matched their owner's garb. He thought for a moment, then reached out with his one arm and slid a pawn forward two spaces.

'The English opening,' remarked Death. 'A highly flexible move. Fischer used it with devastating effect against Spassky in the 1972 World Championship. But there are traps for the unwary. I hope you don't fall into any of them.'

He lifted a wizened hand and advanced his own pawn forward.

Chapter Fifteen

Guildford, Surrey

The corpses were covered with feasting crows. They rose into the sky as Vijay and the others made their way down the abandoned streets of the town, cawing in annoyance, a cloud of black wings flapping like the wind.

The rancid stench from the rotting bodies was nauseating, and Drake was quickly sick in the middle of the road. Vijay felt queasy too, especially when he saw the guts and entrails that the crows had pulled out for their feast. He ducked in alarm as the birds swooped and dived noisily overhead. 'This is horrible.'

'I'm not staying here overnight,' said Aasha, clutching Drake's arm. 'It gives me the creeps. Let's turn around right now.'

'She's right,' agreed Vijay. 'We don't know who killed these people. Whoever did it might still be here. It's too dangerous to stay.'

'No,' said Drake, after he'd recovered himself. He glanced around the deserted town. 'These people have been dead for a long time. Besides, we came looking for food, and we're not leaving without it.'

Yet even Drake seemed to have changed his mind about staying a moment longer than necessary. There was no more talk of finding somewhere to sleep for the night, or of leaving the countryside behind and staying in the town.

'Let's just find what we need, then go,' said Aasha.

Shadow walked before them, untroubled by the slaughter, sniffing at the corpses with interest, his black tail tall and quivering. The cat had managed to find his own food in the wilds and was the only one of them not looking sad and scrawny.

Vijay risked a closer look at the nearest body and wished he hadn't. The crows had been busy picking the flesh from the faces of the dead. Where eyes should have been, dark pits stared sightlessly back, the putrid hollows filled with maggots. He jerked his head away and didn't look again.

Before long they moved past the charred buildings and came to a part of town that seemed undamaged. The road ahead was mercifully clear of bodies. Drake began to check the doors of the houses, but the first dozen he tried were locked.

'I expect all of them are locked,' said Aasha gloomily.

'No problem,' said Drake. 'A brick through a window will fix that easily enough.' He bent down to scoop up a piece of rubble from one of the front gardens, and stretched out his arm to chuck it.

'No!' said Vijay, grabbing his arm. 'You can't!'

'What? Why not?'

'We can't smash someone's window. What if they come back and find it broken?'

Drake laughed. 'Mate, half the houses here have burned to the ground. What difference does a broken window make?'

Aasha gave a loud sigh. 'No one's coming back here, anyway. Vijay, we already had this talk. You agreed.'

'I agreed we could take anything that people left behind. I didn't say it was okay to smash their houses up.'

'How else are we going to get in?' said Aasha in exasperation.

'I got an idea,' said Drake, looking up.

Vijay followed his friend's gaze. An upstairs window of the nearest house was partly open, its curtains twitching in the breeze. But it was at least twelve feet from the ground to the window sill. 'How are we going to climb up there?'

'You're not,' said Drake. 'I'm gonna do the climbing. You two stay here and keep watch.'

'But –'

Drake dragged a wheelie bin from one of the front driveways into place, then nimbly hopped on top. Seconds later he was reaching up to the open window before hauling himself up and over the sill, his arm muscles flexing, his feet scrabbling against the rough pebbledash wall of the house. He tumbled into the room beyond, then a moment later his face was at the open window. 'Easy!' he called down.

Vijay waited nervously for him to reappear, while Shadow sat in front of the door, licking his paws in the sun. The door soon opened and Drake reappeared. 'Told you it was easy. Come on.'

Shadow hopped over the threshold into the house and Aasha followed the cat inside. Vijay hesitated, then went in too.

The interior of the house had a musty smell, but seemed safe enough. Coats hung in the hallway, and several pairs of shoes stood neatly by the doormat, as if the owners might still be at home. It was tempting to think that they were in the front room watching TV, or upstairs taking a nap. But as Vijay entered the kitchen it was obvious from the stink of rotted meat that whoever lived here had long since fled.

Aasha opened the door of the fridge and quickly closed it again at the sight of mouldy vegetables, cheese and other ancient foods. 'That's gross.'

Drake rifled through the kitchen cupboards, pulling out canned and packaged food. 'Look, there's loads of good stuff here. Meat, fish, beans, rice. See if you can find a tin opener and some knives.'

'If we take a saucepan we'll be able to cook over a fire,' said Aasha, lifting a small pan from a hook.

They filled their rucksacks with food and other gear before moving on to examine the rest of the house. The place was comfortably furnished, although rain had come through the open upstairs window and left a damp patch of mildew on the carpet.

Aasha opened a door and entered another of the bedrooms. Vijay followed her in and found her standing still, staring at the bed, one hand raised to her mouth. On a white sheet with pink pillows, a teddy bear was propped up, its button eyes staring back watchfully. Pinned to the pink walls were a child's drawings, depicting rainbows, ponies, and flowers. Aasha crossed the room to a brightly-coloured painting of two smiling faces. The words "Mummy and Daddy" were scrawled beneath them. She reached out to touch the picture and seemed unable to tear herself away.

'Come on,' said Vijay. 'There's nothing here for us.' He took hold of his sister's hand and led her away.

Drake emerged from the third bedroom carrying a fresh T-shirt. He pulled it on, dumping his old one on the carpet. Vijay had no wish to wear other people's clothes, but he took some clean sheets from the airing cupboard and stuffed them into his backpack. He found the bathroom and tried the shower, but after a short dribble of cold water, nothing more came from it.

When he returned to the ground floor, Aasha was busy examining the shelves in the living room. She had changed clothes, and was wearing a new set of jeans, vest and a hoodie. Vijay cast his eye around the room. Some photos were hanging on the wall, showing a mother and father with their two kids. The girl and boy beamed happily back, dressed in their blue and grey school uniforms, or wearing bathing costumes at the beach. Their faces were frozen in time, mercifully ignorant of what the future would bring. Vijay wondered where they were now, and if they were still alive. Whatever had happened to the family, it was obvious that they hadn't even had time to take the photos with them when they left the house.

Aasha was busy flicking through a collection of CDs next to the hi-fi. She held one up. 'Oh my God, I love this music. Do you remember this one? I've got to have it.'

'You can't take it,' said Vijay, appalled at the way she was intruding into the family's private possessions. 'We must only take things we need, like food and clothing, and leave the rest.'

'Well, I need music. I haven't heard any for months. I'm going nuts without it.'

'There's no way of playing it,' said Drake. He pressed the power button on the hi-fi, but nothing happened.

'There must be somewhere I can listen to it. What about a car? Some cars play CDs, don't they?'

'I guess.'

Vijay glared at them in annoyance. 'But we can't steal a car too.' This was getting out of control, just as he knew it would. When people started breaking the rules, they didn't know when to stop. What had begun as a search for essential food was turning into a free-for-all.

'No one said anything about stealing a car,' said Drake, laughing. 'We're not going to drive anywhere. We don't even know how.'

They went outside and Aasha marched off down the road, clutching the CD. It was her mission now to find a car with a working CD player, and Vijay knew she wouldn't stop until she found one. She tried the doors of every car she came to.

'You have to stop her,' Vijay begged Drake, but his friend shook his head.

'Just let her get it out of her system. She'll be impossible otherwise.'

Vijay knew that Drake was right. When Aasha was in this mood, she was almost unstoppable. But he wished he had the strength and courage to stand up to her for once. He wanted to shake her by the shoulders and make her understand that a thief brought only dishonour and suffering upon themselves. With reluctance and a heavy heart he closed the door of the house behind him and set off after the others.

It didn't take Aasha long to find a car that was unlocked. She cried out in triumph and climbed inside.

Drake turned back to Vijay with a wry smile. 'Don't worry. There probably won't be any keys. Or if there are, the battery will be flat.'

But he was wrong on both counts. The car key was in the ignition, and the lights on the dashboard sprang eagerly to life as soon as Aasha turned it. Drake climbed into the seat next to her and Shadow leaped up onto his lap. Vijay joined them in the back of the car.

'I told you,' said Aasha triumphantly. She removed the CD from its box and slid it into a slot in the dashboard. To her delight and Vijay's alarm, music soon began to blast from the speakers. Aasha turned it up. 'This is what I'm talking about.'

'Turn it down,' said Vijay. 'This is such a bad idea.'

'No,' said Aasha firmly. 'This is the best idea in ages.' She turned the volume up again.

They had reached the opening of the second track when Vijay caught the sound of a dog barking. 'What's that noise? Listen!'

Drake reached for the dashboard and killed the music. A sudden hush descended over the car, and then the sound of more dogs barking split the silence.

Vijay hated aggressive dogs. 'Let's go!' he shouted.

'No,' said Drake. 'We stay in the car.'

And then the pack appeared, bursting from a side street and running down the road, barking and snarling in a frenzy. A dozen dogs, all of them mean, all of them hungry. Some wore collars, but they looked as wild as feral beasts. They ran to the car and barked until Vijay thought his head would explode.

Chapter Sixteen

Gatwick Airport, West Sussex

Griffin stretched out his shortened leg, lifting his foot ever so gently in an effort to keep the joints supple. He grimaced as his knee spasmed, causing hot pain to flash up his thigh. He winced as stinging fire reached his hip, causing his back to arch.

The pain is everywhere now. It has claimed my entire body.

Slowly he lowered his leg to its previous position, flinching as his foot touched the floor.

And what, precisely, did that exercise achieve?

He knew he had to keep movement in his ruined limb, or else it would seize entirely. But every move was an agony. The inflammation was worsening, the infection taking deeper hold. Morphine kept the worst at bay, but he was steadily increasing the dosage, and that could only end badly.

What he needed was rest. But it was the one thing he couldn't afford. The ship's doctor from HMS *Queen*

Elizabeth had warned him that if he carried on this way he risked losing his leg entirely. But he knew what his real choice was.

Lose a leg, or lose a war.

That was no choice at all.

Bampton had returned to sea to supervise flying ops, and Griffin felt more alone than ever, despite being the centre of attention. All day long, junior officers trooped in and out of his command tent, delivering new reports, awaiting fresh orders.

They do whatever I command, yet still the news grows worse with each passing day.

At least his intel reports were first-rate. Regular reconnaissance missions by scouts on the ground, and detailed aerial photographs taken from the sky. But the more he learned, the gloomier he became. The latest reports had revealed just how bad the situation was becoming. He pored over them as one of his intelligence officers waited.

'These numbers,' said Griffin at last, 'how reliable are they?'

The officer, a lieutenant with the Intelligence Corps, was ready with his facts. 'We believe that the latest troop numbers are accurate to within ten percent, sir. In total, the Wolf Army now has between five thousand and six thousand armed combatants. To describe them as trained soldiers would be to overstate their training and discipline, but nevertheless they greatly outnumber us. As for armour, the number of vehicles has been counted precisely from the air.'

Leanna's forces had taken heavy losses at the Battle of Gatwick, as bad or worse than the government side. But while Griffin's troop numbers had remained constant ever since, new recruits were flocking to join the enemy side in droves. The Wolf Army had doubled in size in the past few weeks.

'Where can they be coming from?' he wondered aloud.

The lieutenant shifted uncomfortably. 'We can't say for certain, Colonel. But my own belief is that the most plausible scenario is that they are survivors migrating from northern cities. There are reports –'

'I have read the reports,' snapped Griffin, cutting the officer off mid-flow. He knew what the man was referring to. Strange non-human creatures. Mutants. Monsters. 'I prefer to stick to facts.'

'Yes, sir. Very good, sir.'

He turned to the next report on his desk, detailing the current status of the army's supply chain. Armies had always marched on their stomachs, and it was no less true now. The report made for grim reading. Supplies of all kinds of provisions were drying up, and sourcing fresh inventory was becoming more of a drain with each passing day. As the Wolf Army retreated west, it burned supermarket supply depots and logistics warehouses, slowly strangling Griffin's access to essential foodstuffs.

He closed the report with a sigh. It was hard to think clearly. The morphine was muddling his mind.

'Lieutenant, give me your assessment of the effectiveness of our current strategy.'

'Sir?' The officer looked shocked to be asked such a question.

Griffin hesitated. Was it wrong to reveal his self-doubt to a junior officer? Possibly, but the time for pride was long past. He needed to listen to as many different voices as possible. He softened his voice. 'Lieutenant Hastings. I would like to hear your frank opinion. You're an intelligence analyst. Give me the benefit of your intelligence.'

Hastings nodded. He was a bright young man with a keen mind. Griffin waited to see what he would say.

'The current strategy, sir, as I understand it, is one of containment. We are driving the Wolf Army west, preventing them from splintering into groups and spreading out across the country.'

'Go on,' said Griffin.

'Our key advantage over the enemy is that we possess sea and air power, whereas they have only ground forces. However, their human shield currently prevents us from employing our assets to the full. Therefore, we must wait until an opportunity arises to strike.'

'Correct.'

'The risk, sir, is that if we continue to wait, we may lose the initiative, and our chance to strike will be lost. The Wolf Army may become too strong for us to defeat.'

The bald statement echoed Griffin's own misgivings. No matter how many times he turned the facts over in his mind, the conclusion remained the same. Delay would lead inevitably to defeat. Yet to move too quickly risked catastrophe. All those men, women and children chained to the enemy's vehicles. They would perish in an all-out attack.

'That is the problem,' agreed Griffin. 'So what is the solution?'

Hastings met his gaze square on. 'Sir, to bring forward the attack. To strike while we have the advantage.'

'And the human shield?'

'Collateral damage.'

'Thank you, Hastings,' said Griffin curtly. 'That will be all.'

Chapter Seventeen

Haywards Heath, West Sussex

General Canning inspected the interior of his command tent, keen to create the best possible first impressions on his visitors. William Hunter had accepted his offer of a meeting, and he and his entourage were due to arrive at any moment.

The tent was a good place to entertain guests, full of trappings designed to radiate authority. A selection of his favourite art works were mounted on wooden stands behind the desk. He had rescued the paintings from various National Trust properties and country houses. Masterpieces by Bruegel, Titian, Rubens, Canaletto and Turner. He was particularly fond of the portraits of military leaders, and was considering commissioning a likeness of himself if he could find a suitably talented artist to do the work.

On his desk stood an original marble bust of Marcus Antonius, the Roman general who had played such a key part in bringing about the end of the Roman Republic and establishing the autocratic rule of the Empire. A man that Canning greatly admired.

The rest of his desk was spread with strategic maps, measuring the extent of his rule, and the size of his ambition.

He had arranged for a number of humans to be brought into the tent to serve as slaves. The human shield that he had gathered to dissuade the government forces from launching an air attack against his army was proving useful beyond mere deterrence value. Leanna had selected the strongest humans to be transformed into wolves and join the ranks of the Wolf Army. The weakest were good for food or sport. The rest had been repurposed as slaves, carrying equipment, hauling vehicles from the mud when they became stuck, collapsing and erecting the field tents each day as the convoy moved slowly but relentlessly westwards.

The slaves he'd selected for today's meeting were among the strongest and fittest of the survivors. Five males, stripped naked to ensure they carried no weapons. They were here to demonstrate Canning's power over all he surveyed. If the presence of the slaves didn't impress his guests, then perhaps he would kill a few of them, to show who was boss. He did enjoy theatrics.

He wondered how to position himself for best effect. Seated, behind his desk, like in the old days, when badly-behaved children were sent to his office for punishment? Or standing, his hands clasped behind his back, radiating superiority, as he had done when addressing school assemblies? He tried out each option, and opted for standing. It wouldn't do to place himself at a lower level than his guests.

A lieutenant came in. 'My Lord, William Hunter is here to see you.'

Canning nodded. 'Send him in.'

The lieutenant hesitated. 'General, he insists on

bringing some of his men with him.'

'His men?' Canning hadn't anticipated such a move. And yet perhaps it was not unexpected. His guest must be feeling nervous, not knowing who to trust. Canning decided to show some indulgence toward his visitor. 'All right, they can come too.'

The lieutenant left, and the northerners came in, entering the tent in a tight group, their leader at the front, flanked by six of his henchmen, as if advancing into battle. It was Canning's first chance to appraise his guest in the flesh, and despite being forewarned of his appearance he was taken aback by what he saw.

William Hunter's head was that of a beast, with thickly matted brown fur covering the entirety of his face and neck. His jawline projected forward, the nose extending to form a broad snout, whose whiskers twitched gently at every sound and whose nostrils flared wide with each breath. His wolf eyes were bright yellow with jet black pupils and his ears were drawn back against the sides of his head. The man's jaws were huge, and even when clamped shut, revealed flanks of razor-sharp teeth, the canines nearly an inch in length. As he surveyed the interior of the tent, the wolfman parted his lips and a long pink tongue slipped out to taste the air.

The wolf's head made it impossible to estimate his guest's age, but there was no doubting his size and strength. William Hunter was heavily built and muscular, and Canning was disconcerted to discover that he was even taller than the rumours suggested. He towered at least four inches over Canning, and Canning was not a short man.

In fact, all of the northerners were giants. Four of William's compatriots were also wolfmen. Two bore the heads and necks of wolves like William himself, while two stood tall on wolf's hind legs. They wore no shoes, but padded along the ground on great hairy paws, tipped with iron claws. The remaining two were in human form, but

Canning knew they were not human, but lycanthropes just like himself, ready to transform into wolves at the first kiss of moonlight.

Surveying the new arrivals, Canning began for the first time to entertain doubts about what he had let himself in for. He was outnumbered seven to one by these strangers, and although he had taken the precaution of carrying a concealed gun and a knife, while giving strict instructions that the northerners should be disarmed before being admitted, still he wondered if he had badly miscalculated by arranging to conduct this meeting without any of his own men on hand.

All seven of his guests wore British Army issue combat dress, but whether they were trained soldiers or had stolen their uniforms from defeated foes, Canning did not know. They swept around the tent, their eyes everywhere, searching for danger and treachery.

Wise fellows. It pays to be wary when sitting down to sup with a stranger. Yet treachery is not on today's menu. Not on my part, at least.

'Welcome,' said Canning, stepping forward, doing his very best not to betray the disquiet he felt. He stretched out his hand in greeting, arranging his features into a pleasant smile.

William Hunter did not return his courtesies. He stood with hands on hips, a stance clearly calculated to display maximum rudeness. 'So,' he said in a rough, northern accent, 'you must be the one they call "General".'

Canning inclined his head politely. 'That is the title that has been granted to me by our queen. But you may call me Canning. And how would you like to be addressed?'

The wolfman grunted, making no reply. Instead he eyed Canning up and down suspiciously. His look did not suggest that he was favourably impressed by what he saw. 'I am told that you were a schoolteacher, before the war.'

Canning bristled at the implied slight. 'I was a headmaster, in fact, and well versed in leadership. And I have always been a keen student of military history and strategy. It is I who leads the Wolf Army on behalf of our queen.'

William cast a contemptuous gaze at the five naked slaves lined up against the far wall of the tent, their eyes wide with fear at the sight of the wolfman and his entourage. He spat on the ground. 'If these are the toughest opponents you have fought, forgive me if I refrain from congratulating you.'

He goads me, that is all. I should ignore his provocation.

But Canning hadn't reached his present lofty position by embracing meekness. 'My forces went to battle against the entire British Army at Gatwick,' he declared. 'And achieved victory.'

The northerner remained unimpressed. 'Victory, you say? Is this how victory looks to you, General Canning? A hideout in the woods. A makeshift battle camp. This has the look to me of a war that is not yet won. By either side.'

Canning glared angrily at the wolfman with his one good eye. No one had ever spoken to him this way before. Of if they had, their bones now lay in the dirt, their insolence drained, along with their blood. If one of his own men ever dared to challenge him so blatantly, the full force of his wrath would be unleashed upon them in a heartbeat. But he held his rage in check. He must not allow himself to become like Leanna. Whatever his personal feelings for this uncouth wolfman, he knew that he must win him over without violence.

'This' – Canning cast his arms around the interior of the tent – 'is how the road to victory looks. To the battle-hardened, like you and I, it should look like home. Or do you northern men require greater comfort from your living quarters?'

Fury flashed in Hunter's eyes, but then his mouth twitched, and his great wolf jaws cracked open in a grin. He threw back his giant head and laughed, a sound like thunder rolling in the hills. When he was done, he closed on Canning and grasped his hand, nearly crushing the bones of his fingers with his strength. He pumped his arm vigorously, the smile still on his face, but his eyes not leaving Canning's for a second.

'I don't require comfort,' he said. 'And I'm not one for fancy titles either. So you can call me Will, the same as my men do. Now if we're done with talking, you can take me to see your queen.'

Chapter Eighteen

Guildford, Surrey

Vijay didn't know what kind of breed the dogs were. Rottweilers or Alsatians, or Pit Bulls, he guessed, though he had no real idea what those breeds actually looked like. These dogs looked mean and hungry. Starving, even. They surrounded the car, rising up on their hind legs in their desire to get inside. One headbutted the window next to Vijay and he jumped back in fright. Another opened its jaws so wide that all Vijay could see was a slavering tongue behind a wall of sharp teeth. Eyes rolled in the animals' heads as they threw their weight desperately against the doors and windows. The dogs barked mechanically, loud enough to split an eardrum. Vijay covered his ears but the noise wouldn't stop.

'How are we going to get rid of them?' yelled Aasha.

'We're not,' said Drake. 'We just have to stay here and wait it out. Eventually they'll calm down and leave.'

'What if they don't?' said Aasha. 'What if they wait until

we're desperate and try to make a run for it? Then they'll kill us and eat us.'

'That won't happen. We have food. We can sleep in the car if necessary. The dogs will give up.'

'No they won't,' said Vijay. 'Look how desperate they are.'

'Just shut up, will you?' said Drake. 'I'm trying to think.'

'This is all Aasha's fault!' wailed Vijay. 'I said we mustn't steal. This is our punishment.'

Another sound brought their argument to an end. A metallic whining sound as Aasha turned the key in the ignition. The starter motor spluttered, turning over and over as it strained to kick the cold engine back to life. The dogs paused their relentless barking briefly, but it seemed like the engine was too far gone to ever start. The dogs resumed their cacophony. Then, after a cough, a wheeze and a splutter, a deep-throated hum filled the air.

'The car's started,' said Aasha. 'Cool.'

The dogs began to bark even louder than before, sensing that their prey might be about to get away.

'But how are you gonna drive it?' asked Drake. 'Do you know how?'

'Sure. I went out with Dad once or twice for practice. I was going to take proper lessons, but they were so expensive I never got started.'

'So do you know how to work it?'

Aasha flashed a wide grin. 'Of course.'

'But what if there's no fuel in the tank?' asked Vijay. 'What if the engine breaks down?'

'What about shutting up and letting me drive it, bro?' Aasha was concentrating on the controls, one hand on the gear stick, the other flicking switches and pushing buttons on the dashboard. 'It's a manual. That's the same as Dad's car.'

'Is that good?' asked Vijay.

'No. Manuals are much more difficult to drive. I never managed to get the hang of changing gear. Now, have you all got your seat belts on?' She reached up to adjust her mirror.

'What are you doing?' asked Drake. 'You don't need to look at yourself in the mirror. Just get us out of here already.'

The biggest dog hurled itself against the front door, making the car rock from side to side.

'I'm not looking at myself, stupid. I'm looking at the road behind. Dad always said it's important always to check the mirrors before driving off. Mirror, signal, manoeuvre.'

'That was when there were no wild dogs involved. Just drive!'

'Shut up and watch me.' Aasha pushed her foot down and the engine roared like a beast. She wrestled with the gear stick, shifting it into position with a horrible crunching noise like the sound of metal tearing.

'Ouch!' said Drake. 'You're gonna break it like that.'

'No, I won't. It always does that.' Aasha worked her feet and the tone of the engine dropped an octave, making it purr like a tiger. Vijay felt the engine's power throbbing through the body of the car. The front begin to lift as if the car itself was eager to be off, but still they didn't move. Aasha's brow was furrowed in concentration.

Drake opened his mouth to say something, then obviously thought better of it. Vijay held his breath. Even Shadow looked apprehensive.

Then the car shuddered violently and the engine died.

'Shit!' said Aasha.

'What's wrong? Is it bust?' said Drake.

'No, it's just stalled.' She put the car back into neutral.

Outside, the dogs began hurling themselves against the car in another desperate bid to gain entry.

'Try again,' urged Drake. 'Stay calm.'

Aasha turned her scowling face on him. 'I am calm. So just keep your mouth shut or else you're dog food.'

She checked her mirror again, restarted the engine and

scrunched the car back into gear. The dogs began to bark louder in a rising frenzy. Beads of perspiration appeared on Aasha's forehead. She pressed her foot all the way to the floor, making the engine howl, but still the car stayed motionless.

It's not going to work, thought Vijay. *We'll all be dog food soon*. But he knew better than to voice his thoughts out loud.

Aasha's feet worked feverishly. The rev counter spun up into the red and the engine screamed.

'Why aren't we moving?' yelled Drake.

'Shut up. I don't know!' Aasha began to scream too, pounding the steering wheel with her fists.

Vijay closed his eyes and began to move his lips in silent prayer.

'Handbrake.' Aasha released it, and the pressure that had been building spilled out suddenly like a bursting dam. Vijay opened his eyes in astonishment. Wheels spun, kicking up a storm of dust, and the car lurched forward. One of the dogs went under a front wheel and the car bucked over it with a soft squelch. Another dog was standing on the front bonnet, jaws wide open. Its legs flew from under it and it rolled across the windscreen and into the street yelping. The rest of the pack followed in pursuit of the car, barking in anger as they watched their dinner escaping.

'Go faster!' shouted Drake.

'I don't know how to change gear,' said Aasha. 'I've only ever driven in first.'

The engine was screeching like a banshee and the rev counter was pushed to the max. Aasha drove on, ignoring the protests of car, dogs and Drake alike.

'Where shall I go?' asked Aasha.

'I don't know,' said Drake. 'We can't keep driving like this. It's insane.'

Yet despite being in first gear, the car was slowly gaining speed, steadily leaving the dogs behind. They didn't give up easily, continuing to run as fast as they could, but eventually the last dog abandoned its chase and the road behind was clear.

'I'm going to try to change gear,' said Aasha, her forehead creasing in concentration.

Vijay felt sweat prickle his skin. He braced himself for the worst.

Aasha stamped on a pedal and the car lurched almost to a standstill. The engine shrieked like a toddler throwing a tantrum, hurling Vijay forward against the front seat. A hideous grinding noise followed as Aasha wrenched the gear stick into a new position and the car lurched again. But then the raucous scream of the engine ceased and the vehicle put on a fresh burst of speed.

'Yeah, I got this,' said Aasha, a wide, satisfied grin stretching across her face. She switched the music back on and began nodding her chin up and down to the beat.

'You're pretty good at this,' said Drake.

'Just watch me.' Aasha turned the volume up until Vijay thought his ears would explode. 'This is as good as it gets,' she said. 'I'm going to change up to third next. Nothing can stop us now.'

Vijay pressed his palms to his ears and said nothing. It was too loud to talk in any case. He turned away from the window, where large immovable obstacles were flashing past at dizzying speed, and focussed his gaze on his hands. He just wanted this ride to be over.

Some miles further down the road, his wish came true.

Chapter Nineteen

Midhurst, West Sussex

It was late in the afternoon, and the sun was losing its fiery heat. Liz went outside with Llewelyn to watch the kids at play. Today the gang had invaded the croquet pitch, inventing their own rules for the game and turning the sedate pastime of the English upper classes into a violent contact sport.

Llewelyn pulled up a couple of deck chairs so that he and Liz could watch a match unfold. Soon mallets were swinging and balls were flying across the field at high velocity.

Liz took refuge behind her dark glasses, pretending not to notice the frequent examples of foul play that were taking place in front of her.

'Go on, give it some welly!' yelled the Welshman happily as he supped from a bottle of beer.

'Who's winning?' asked Liz.

'The team with the least injuries, I guess.'

'It's hard to tell which side that is,' said Liz. 'They're all going to walk away with a lot of bruising. Assuming that they're still able to walk.'

But she could hardly complain. After all, this is what she'd wanted – kids running wild and free, enjoying a childhood unrestrained by adult concerns and pressures. 'At least they're not stabbing each other with knives.' Liz had seen plenty of teenage kids go that way during her days as a serving police officer. Perhaps not everything about the apocalypse was bad.

'Maybe,' remarked Llewelyn. 'But they need to know how to use knives. These kids will have to grow up tough. I thought I had a rough childhood, and a dangerous job in the army, but that's nothing to what these kids are going to face.'

Liz didn't dispute it. 'Do you think they'll make it? Or will this be the last generation?'

'I wouldn't worry too much about that, Liz. The way this lot play croquet, I reckon they're tough enough to take on whatever comes their way.'

'I hope so. And if we stay here and lie low, maybe we can avoid the worst of it.'

'Leave others to deal with the end of the world, eh? That sounds good to me.' He finished his can of beer and lay back in the deckchair, his eyes drifting closed.

Liz left him to it. After everything they'd been through, they all deserved a rest. But Llewelyn's words hadn't eased her thoughts. Was that really what she was doing – lying low, while others dealt with the problem of the werewolves?

Well, why not? She had done more than her share of killing. And she had a lot of people to look after now. By keeping them safe she wasn't shirking her duty; she was facing up to it.

It was funny, really. Her father had spent his life doing whatever he could to avoid responsibility, whereas Liz had craved it like a drug. There must be something wrong with her, she supposed. She was damaged goods, broken in some way by Kevin's negligent parenting and by her mother's untimely death. Still, it could have been worse. She might have turned out the same as Kevin, and that would have been unbearable.

Llewelyn opened one pale blue eye. 'Oh, yeah. I forgot to ask you something.'

'What?' She recognised that tone of voice. Something was coming, something unexpected. Something big.

He opened both eyes and pushed himself up out of the chair. 'I'm not sure how best to put this. There's a traditional way to ask the question. The way it's done in the movies. Or I could keep it casual, so there's no pressure.'

Now he really was alarming her.

'Keep what casual?'

'You're not making this easy, Liz. Would you like me to do it the old-fashioned way, with all the trimmings? I can do that if you want.' He dropped to one knee.

'What the hell are you doing?'

He cleared his throat. 'Miss Elizabeth Bailey, would you do me the incredible honour of becoming my lawfully wedded wife?'

'Wife?' She stared at him.

'Now when I say lawful, it might not be. We don't exactly have a vicar to hand. And as for documentation and so on, you can forget about that. But this is the right kind of place for a wedding, isn't it? I reckon they must have married loads of couples here. It's certainly posh enough, so it's probably legit. You don't have to become Mrs Jones. Not unless you want to.'

'You have got to be kidding me.'

'No joking. Not this time. And to be frank, I was hoping for a more positive response. I don't go around proposing to women every day of the week.'

'You want us to get married?'

'That's the idea. We could live –'

'What? Happily ever after?'

'Maybe not that. I'm not saying it would be easy. We'd have to deal with more than the usual set of challenges married couples face.'

'Man-eating monsters, a post-apocalyptic wasteland, my craving for human blood …'

'Yeah, that kind of thing. But think of the upside. There'd be no nine-to-five drudgery. No daily commute. No mortgage repayments. We could be happy together, is all I'm saying.'

'I –'

'Now you're supposed to say yes,' he prompted, 'or no. But an answer one way or the other would be the thing. Hell, Liz, I'm asking you to marry me, not save the universe.'

'I –'

'Take your time. I'm in no hurry.'

'Just shut up, will you?' She took a deep breath and released it slowly. 'Llewelyn Jones, you are without doubt the most annoying man I have ever met. But yes, I would be delighted to become your wife.'

Chapter Twenty
The English Channel

The flight out to *Queen Elizabeth* was excruciating. Griffin had doubled up on his morphine prior to boarding the Merlin helicopter, but even so, the vibration of the engine and the throbbing of the rotor set his leg ablaze. He had hoped to avoid making the journey but the matters he needed to discuss with FitzHerbert and Bampton were too important to conduct over the radio.

At least the weather was fine this time. The most recent storm had blown itself out, ushering in high pressure and clear skies. Fields of green gave way to white cliffs as the Merlin pushed out over a perfect sea, the sun sparkling on its glassy waters. Today its colours were jade and aquamarine, silver and pearl. Yet still the buffeting of the wind as they crossed the English Channel was almost too much to bear. The flight lasted little more than an hour but by the end of it, Griffin felt almost delirious with pain.

When all this is over, I will never board a boat or leave the ground again.

On deck, FitzHerbert was waiting to greet him. 'Griffin.'

Each time he met the commodore, the man seemed to have aged. Whatever trials Griffin faced, the commodore clearly had his own personal demons to battle too. Griffin had never asked what they might be. A man deserved some privacy, and FitzHerbert wasn't the type to share. If there was something Griffin needed to know, he felt sure the commodore would tell him.

FitzHerbert saluted, and Griffin allowed himself to be led below deck. The short journey down the ringing metal steps was traumatic. Griffin leaned heavily on his crutches, grabbing for the narrow handrails, clumsy in the unfamiliar environment. By the time he reached the lower deck, his leg was on fire and his face was bathed in sweat.

Bampton was waiting for him in the commodore's cabin. He jumped to his feet as soon as Griffin hobbled through the door. 'Griffin. It's good to see you again.'

'Bampton.' They shook hands, and Griffin lowered himself carefully into the relative comfort of a leather padded seat.

This time, FitzHerbert poured rum without asking if anyone wanted any. 'Get that down you, Griffin. I can see that your sea legs are no better than when you first visited us.'

Griffin sipped the drink gratefully. 'At least you haven't summoned angry Neptune up from the depths this time,' he joked.

'Believe it or not,' said the commodore, 'on a day like this, the sea is the finest place anyone could hope to be.'

Griffin struggled to fix a half-smile to his lips. 'I believe you, commodore. My leg may need some more convincing.'

When their glasses were empty and they were done with small talk, FitzHerbert set his face into the hard features that Griffin knew best. 'So, I take it you haven't travelled all this way simply to enjoy a pleasure trip and a chat with old friends?'

'No. I need to know how much time we have left.'

'How much time?' FitzHerbert looked puzzled. 'Only the good Lord can tell you that, Griffin.'

'Before we must strike at the enemy.'

'Ah,' said the commodore. 'That's a very good question. We left port with full fuel tanks on all vessels. In the case of the *Queen Elizabeth* that's over a million gallons of diesel for the ship and three quarters of a million gallons of aviation fuel for the aircraft. Enough to give us a range of ten thousand nautical miles, or roughly three trips across the Atlantic and back. That might sound like a lot, but in reality it's only enough for a few months of normal service.'

'But you can refuel at sea? You have tankers in the fleet.'

'RFA *Tidesurge* and *Tideforce*. The good news is that each tanker carries just over four million gallons of fuel – enough for one full refuelling. The bad news is that we've already refuelled once. Those tankers are now empty.'

'Empty? But can't they refill?'

'In principle, yes. We have made attempts to refuel, but so far it has proved to be impossible.'

'Why?'

FitzHerbert's stony face became even more flinty. 'Why? It's not safe for the tankers to return to port. And even if they could, how do you expect them to refuel? Pipelines have been destroyed, refineries have ceased operation, and all commercial shipping stopped some while back. And with the electricity out, there's no way to pump fuel onboard even if we could find any, which I seriously doubt we can. So, Colonel, we have to face facts. We only have a few more weeks available to us before we run out of fuel, a little more if we minimise operations and keep the planes below deck.'

A few weeks. It was even worse than Griffin had

feared. 'You were planning to tell me about this?' he muttered.

'I intended to. But the group captain thought …' FitzHerbert exchanged glances with Bampton.

'I thought you had enough on your plate already,' said Bampton.

'Then,' continued FitzHerbert, 'when I heard that you were coming to visit us, I thought it would be best for you to hear the news in person.'

It would have been better to hear good news, my friend. 'Is there nothing we can do to prolong operations?'

'There is one option, but my guess is that you won't like it. I like it even less, and I hate to say it aloud, but it's my duty to tell you what it is.'

'Go on.'

'Abandon the second carrier, HMS *Prince of Wales*. If we pump all the fuel from her tanks onto the *Queen Elizabeth*, then we can buy ourselves another three weeks. Maybe a month if we're frugal.'

'What about the aircraft currently on board the *Prince of Wales*?'

'We'd be sacrificing them too.'

'And the crew?'

'It's already rather crowded on the *Queen Elizabeth*, but I daresay we can accommodate them onboard without too much trouble.'

Griffin mulled over the commodore's counsel. He could only guess how much the words had cost him. To abandon one of the carriers. No naval commander would ever contemplate the loss of half his fleet unless the circumstances were utterly dire.

Well, they have been dire ever since I took charge.

It was a simple but stark choice: he could have the entire strike capacity of his air and sea forces for a month, or half that capacity for two months. Either way, time was desperately running low.

'So, what would you like to do?' asked FitzHerbert.

'The decision is yours to make.'

Griffin shook his head, knowing that once again he had no real choice. 'We cannot suffer a loss of half our sea and air power. We have precious little advantage as it is. Without the entire fleet at our disposal, the werewolves would gain the upper hand. Defeat would be inevitable.'

I cannot lose this war. The consequences are unthinkable.

'Then the final battle must happen within the next few weeks,' concluded Bampton.

'All or nothing,' agreed FitzHerbert. He reached once more for the bottle of rum and emptied the last of it into the glasses. 'Gentlemen, let us drink to victory!'

Griffin accepted the second drink, clinking his glass against the others', but despite the bullish toast, the three men drank in silence, the mood in the cabin sombre.

Chapter Twenty-One

Salisbury Plain

The English countryside was stunningly beautiful in the summer sun, but devoid of anything to eat. Fertile farmland lay all around, but when Rose sent scouts to investigate the fields of corn, the reports they brought back were invariably the same – the cobs were green and hard and wouldn't ripen for another month at least. Her people were slowly starving, and still there was no sign of a town or any other habitation. She was beginning to despair.

The road they had joined went on and on, holding a straight line for miles on end, and was completely clear of traffic. The grassy verges either side held a few abandoned cars, but they were all out of fuel and refused to start. They crossed a railway bridge, but the rail tracks were as empty and silent as the road itself. Parallel lines of metal track ran off into the distance until they were swallowed by a dip of the land and vanished from view. They saw no one, and passed no houses either. Despite the pleasant green trees and fields all around, the silence of this landscape was fast becoming sinister.

Rose's love affair with the English countryside was dwindling, and she yearned to glimpse a town, or at least a village. Just a few farm buildings would do. She longed to hear a voice or a car engine or any kind of human sound. Anything would be better than this oppressive hush.

Still the road marched on, now flanked by trees so thick that it was impossible to see what lay beyond. According to Chris, roads led to cities and towns. But this road seemed to lead nowhere. More worrying still, warning signs were appearing at the roadside with ever greater frequency. "Military testing" – "No unauthorised access" – "Strictly no entry" and suchlike. "Keep away," seemed to be the common theme. But they had seen no soldiers, and if there really were any military operations in this area they would surely have heard something by now. Yet there had been nothing except the blowing of the wind and the singing of the birds.

Then suddenly the road came to an end. In front of them the way was barred by a heavy metal gate. To either side a barbed-wire fence stretched away into the distance, sealing off the land ahead of them. A guard post stood to one side but the brick building was deserted.

A warning sign was fixed to the gate itself. 'Danger,' read Seth aloud. 'Unexploded military debris. Civilian access strictly forbidden.'

'We should turn around and go back,' said Chris. 'I told you this would happen.'

'No you didn't,' said Seth. 'You said that roads lead to towns.'

'I said they lead to bad places.'

Rose came to a halt before the barricade, feeling the last of her energy and resolution drain from her limbs. She was exhausted and hungry and so were all the others, especially the young and the old. They had walked so far to get here, placing their trust in her, and the prospect of turning back filled her with dismay. Yet she knew she couldn't lead her people into a field with unexploded bombs.

Ryan approached the gate and stepped up onto the lowest bar, leaning over, as if straining to catch a glimpse of any bombs lying in wait there. 'The road carries on across the field. If we keep to it, we ought to be safe.'

'No,' said Chris. 'Read the sign. It says it's dangerous.'

For once, Seth appeared to be in agreement with his friend. 'We can't go into a field full of UXB. That's crazy. We'll have to find another way.'

'No,' insisted Ryan. 'We've come too far to turn around. If we try to send everyone back the way we came, there'll be a mutiny.'

Rose was so tired and hungry, it was impossible for her to think. Her vision had shown her a place of safety, yet all she could find was danger. Perhaps Chris was right and the ruined city was nothing more than a fantasy conjured from her own imagination. She wanted to lie down and go to sleep, but she knew that everyone depended on her. Whatever she told them to do, they would obey. If she told them to walk on through a field planted with bombs, they would do it. If she commanded them to turn around and retrace their steps, they would do that too. Either way might lead to death, or salvation. The responsibility felt like a hundred-pound weight on her shoulders.

Forward or back? She cast her gaze over the long line of people trailing behind. The prospect of telling them to turn around and go back filled her with dismay. Ahead of her, beyond the gate, the grassy expanse beckoned. From this distance it looked perfectly safe. The road pushed straight across the landscape until it disappeared from view. Whatever its destination, the road's builders had been determined to reach it by the shortest possible route. Some crows were strutting along the roadside, pecking at insects or digging for worms. One stretched out its great black wings, flapped them once, cawed loudly, then folded them neatly back into place. Nutmeg eyed the birds eagerly, ready to dash ahead and chase them.

'We have no choice,' said Rose at last. 'We must find food. So we must go on. But warn everyone to stay on the road at all times.'

After a rest, they climbed the gate and carried on down the road, now within the fenced-off restricted zone. Rose put Nutmeg on a short lead and kept her close, even though the dog was desperate to chase the crows. The dark birds stood their ground a few yards away, watching through beady eyes as people clambered one by one over the gate, the strong helping the weak to climb. They squawked in indignation before returning to their hunt for food. Nutmeg glared at them, then followed Rose reluctantly.

Another sign appeared by the roadside, as if giving her a final chance to turn back before it was too late. *Danger – live firing area. Proceed at your own risk.* But still she heard no gunfire or explosions.

'These signs might help to keep other people away from the area,' said Chris. 'If that's the case, we might be safe here after all.'

'As long as we don't step on the bombs,' said Seth.

Ryan's face was grim. 'If we keep to the road, there shouldn't be any danger.'

But Rose knew that she had to do better than simply avoid danger. She had to find food and shelter. Her people couldn't wander around forever. They needed a place they could call home. She had pinned her hopes on finding salvation in a dream, yet with every day that passed, that dream seemed more like a cruel joke. Even if the place she had seen turned out to be real, a barren hillside comprising nothing more than grass and stones didn't seem like a promising place to live. She wondered how far they would have to go before she knew whether she'd made the right choice.

They pushed on for mile after mile, the sun riding slowly across the cloud-swept sky. The ground undulated gently beneath her feet, low but never quite flat, the road dipping in and out of shallow hollows, the wind stirring the grass in incessant, always-changing patterns. Shadows crossed the road as clouds passed overhead in constant flux. The air buzzed with insects and birds, and the sharp smells of chalky turf and of pure oxygenated air filled her nostrils. She began to forget the invisible danger that lay all around. She allowed tiredness to wash over her, and fell gratefully into a trancelike state of perpetual walking, lulled by the rhythmic motion of her limbs, the unwaveringly straight path of the road, and by the soothing layers of scents and sounds that surrounded her.

She was roused from her stupor when Ryan put out an arm to stop her. 'What's that?'

She stumbled to a halt and blinked herself back to reality. At first she could see nothing. Then ahead of her, behind the brow of the next rise, she glimpsed a manmade object. A metal cylinder, perhaps a few feet long, raised in their direction.

Ryan motioned the rest of the group to silence. He crouched down and crept forward, advancing up the gentle slope. Rose followed cautiously, Nutmeg at her side, Chris and Seth close behind.

Ryan reached the brow of the low hill and waved for them to stop, then doubled back. 'It's a tank,' he whispered. 'It's in the next dip of the land.'

'Where did it come from?' asked Rose. 'I didn't hear anything.'

'If it had been moving, we would have heard it. It must have been there already.'

'Is it friendly?' asked Seth.

'There's only one way to find out.'

They walked cautiously up the slope. As they neared the top, the rest of the tank came into view. First the gun, pointing at the sky, then the turret and finally the body of the vehicle. Some way beyond it, two more tanks were visible.

Rose crouched at the lip of the ridge, peering down at the tanks. There was no sound; no movement. Only the continual swishing of the grass and the distant chatter of birdsong. The unbroken calm was as unnerving as gunfire.

'We should go back,' said Chris. 'I said not to follow the road.'

Seth, too, looked terrified.

But to Rose's surprise, Ryan began to laugh. He stood up.

'Get down!' hissed Chris. 'Be quiet!'

'Why?' said Ryan. 'There's nothing to be afraid of. These are old wrecks.'

Rose looked more closely at the nearest tank. Ryan was right. It was a derelict. Its armour was riddled with holes, its metal tracks snarled up, and the wheels that once drove them all buckled. It looked like the army had used it as target practice. No wonder she had heard nothing. It might have been here for years. The other tanks were the same.

As she let her gaze wander into the distance, Rose caught sight of something else beyond the next hill. A church tower, its top just visible above the low horizon. She felt her spirits lift. Despite Chris' warnings, a town or village offered hope. Perhaps they would find food there. At the very least it would be somewhere to shelter for the night. A place of safety, at last.

'Come on,' she said, setting off with renewed vigour.

They passed the three tanks on their way. Close up, it was clear that each one had been blasted by hundreds of explosive shells. Fragments of the shells flecked the ground. Rose recalled the warnings of unexploded debris and held Nutmeg's lead tight.

The land here was grassy scrubland, with no farmed fields. Not surprising, if it was used for artillery practice. And yet the church tower was just beyond the next rise. Rose wondered how it was possible for its inhabitants to live so close to the firing range.

Soon the church came fully into view, nestling in a hollow. It was a small building with arched windows and a square tower. Beyond it were houses, roads and trees. A typical English village. There was even a village pub. All was idyllic and calm.

But something wasn't right. The place stood silent and deserted, the streets completely empty of cars. Like the firing range itself, the village gave the impression of being abandoned for a long time. A low growl came from Nutmeg's throat. The dog felt the strangeness too.

'I don't like it,' muttered Seth.

Then Rose realized what was wrong. Several of the houses were damaged, as if they had been blown up or burned down. There were new buildings too, squat and square and ugly, looking like model houses made by a child. Every one of them was boarded up, their windows blocked. Only the church was as it should be.

'It's a ghost village,' she said.

The road led them into the village past the churchyard. They went slowly, inspecting the houses, the pub and the church itself. Each building had a number painted on it in white. Some of the houses were empty shells, just walls and roof with nothing inside. They had been built simply for target practice. Everywhere, warning signs told them of the dangers of unexploded ordnance and reminded them that the area was strictly off limits to the public. And yet the place was curiously comforting and nostalgic. It was like a toy village built for soldiers to play in. Walking through it was like travelling back in time to an England that never was. It was also a haven for wildflowers and animal life. Birds roosted on blackened rooftops or sang from the trees that overlooked them, indifferent to the damage that had been wreaked on this place.

After exploring the village for half an hour, it became clear that they would find no food here. They stopped to rest in the old churchyard where weathered headstones still poked up between tufts of unkempt grass. Rose's emotions were torn. If she had hoped to find a sanctuary, this village wasn't it. A ghost town was no place for a new beginning, and if the signs were to be believed they were in danger of treading on an unexploded bomb if they lingered long. The army training ground was also a grim reminder of the war they were fleeing.

But the village offered hope too. If a place as strange as this could exist, then perhaps Rose's ruined city might also be real. If so, she was determined to find it and to take her people there. But where might it be? She still had no way of knowing.

Chapter Twenty-Two

Farnham, Surrey

The car rushed headlong into a tree, making the loudest crash Vijay had ever heard. Even though they were only going about twenty miles an hour, the front of the car crumpled like a tin can, and the windscreen turned into a white spiderweb of cracks. Vijay's seatbelt caught his body before he could be turned into roadkill, but Shadow went flying off Drake's lap with a cry and disappeared into the footwell of the car.

The engine died and the music stopped. Only the frightened mewing of the cat and the tick-ticking of the car's metal frame broke the stillness. For a few heartbeats, Vijay sat in dull shock. And then the shouting started.

'What the hell did you do that for?' Drake yelled at Aasha. 'You nearly got us killed!'

'I was turning to avoid the broken-down car in the road.'

'You turned us into a tree instead!'

'Well, driving's a lot harder than it looks. I got us away from the dogs, didn't I?'

'Yeah, but we're not going any further in this wreck.'

'I didn't see you doing anything to help.'

'Well, I'm not the one who's had driving lessons, yeah?'

Vijay couldn't stand it a moment longer. Drake and Aasha were always rowing. It was how they were together. He knew they would kiss and make up again later as if nothing had ever happened, but he'd had enough.

'Stop it!' he shouted. Hot tears of frustration were running down his face and he felt his cheeks burning. He threw open the door and pushed himself out of the car.

Drake and Aasha emerged a few seconds later and regarded him with surprise. 'What's the matter?' asked Aasha.

Vijay said nothing, just looked at the car, which had crumpled to about half its original length. Steam was billowing from the front bonnet.

'It wasn't such a bad crash really,' said Drake, inspecting the damage. 'No one got hurt.' Shadow had reappeared again and seemed none the worse for his mishap. He curled himself around Drake's ankles.

'And we escaped from the dogs, didn't we?' said Aasha.

'Only just,' said Vijay. 'But this car crash could have been much worse. We could all be dead now. We got lucky, that's all that saved us.'

'Well, I think I did pretty well for a first attempt,' said Aasha. 'With practice, I could get better. Why don't we steal another car? I mean borrow one.'

'Sure,' agreed Drake. 'We just need to be more careful next time.'

Vijay began to cry harder. They just didn't get it. 'If we carry on this way, there might not be a next time. We're so bad at this. Look how much we messed up today. The truth is that we're just a bunch of kids. We don't know what we're doing.'

'We're doing our best,' protested Aasha.

'But we need to be so much better,' he countered, 'and quickly, or else we're not going to make it. Anyway, it's not enough to just survive. We need to live a life worth living. We have to prove that we were worth saving.'

A hush greeted his pronouncement. Then Drake nodded. 'Come on, then. Standing here arguing makes us easy targets for whoever – or whatever – is out there. Let's move on.'

He hoisted his bag onto his shoulders and set off along the road. Vijay hurried to catch up with him.

'At least we have food now,' said Aasha after they'd walked some way. 'And new clothes.'

'What we really need,' said Drake, 'is a way to defend ourselves.' He produced a kitchen knife from his bag. 'I've got this. Has anyone else got something they can use as a weapon?'

Aasha reached into her bag and pulled out the metal saucepan she'd taken from the house. She tried an experimental swipe with it. Vijay shrugged. He had only his grandmother's knitting needle, and that would be as much use in deadly combat as Aasha's saucepan. He was about to say that they didn't need weapons, but stopped himself. Drake was right. This was just another indication of how amateurish they were. This wasn't a game. It was life or death; kill or be killed. The dogs would have ripped them to pieces if they'd had a chance, and dogs weren't the most dangerous creatures at large.

'We need to tool up as a priority,' said Drake. 'And we need proper kit. Tents, sleeping bags, and so on. That's what we need to find next.'

They were on the outskirts of another town now, and the evening shadows were lengthening. But after the events of the day, none of them fancied heading into the town for the night. More dogs might be waiting for them, or there could be worse horrors, like the crow-eaten corpses they had encountered earlier. Avoiding built-up areas might be a smart move.

'Come on, then,' said Aasha. 'Let's find a barn or somewhere we can kip for the night.'

It was full dark by the time they came to a promising location. A small group of buildings clustered together in a hamlet, comprising a farmhouse, some cottages and a small commercial development. 'Looks like offices or workshops,' said Vijay.

'Let's see if we can break in,' said Drake.

This time Vijay didn't protest. He'd had enough of climbing in through windows and other kinds of messing about. It was time to start doing this properly.

First they checked the outside of the buildings to make sure no one was around. Then Drake tried each door, but all were locked and the workshops appeared deserted. No barking or other animal sounds came to them, apart from the distant hooting of a pair of owls.

'All right,' said Drake. 'Stand back.' He picked up a concrete breezeblock from the yard and lobbed it through the nearest window. The smashing of glass was deafening in the still night, and the three of them froze. But no sound came to answer it, and after a while Drake continued with his break-in. After knocking away the shards of broken glass from the frame, he lifted himself up and climbed in. 'You stand guard,' he said, but Aasha hauled herself in after him. After a moment's hesitation, Vijay followed. Shadow jumped in too.

The inside of the building was dark, but Vijay's eyesight soon adjusted and he found he could see well enough. Shadow lived up to his name, blending into the pools of blackness, although his eyes were wide green lamps in the dark. The cat jumped up lightly onto some kind of work surface.

Vijay examined the shelves along the wall of the workshop and discovered a useful collection of tools that might once have been used for gardening. He picked up a small axe and felt its heft in his hand. It would be good for chopping logs, but just as useful in self-defence. The others were busy too. Drake found a pitchfork that was light enough to carry over one shoulder. Aasha grabbed a small coil of rope, some netting and an evil-looking metal hook. She whipped it from side to side, swiping its curved blade through the air. Shadow hopped to the floor in alarm.

'Let's grab as much stuff as we can carry,' said Drake.

In the back of the building they discovered a roll of waterproof tarpaulin and a handful of cushions and took those too. Now they had a better chance of survival.

'Shall we stay here for the night?' asked Aasha.

'It's as good as anywhere,' said Drake. 'No point going outside again.'

They lit some candles and opened some of the tinned fish they'd found earlier. Shadow looked hungrily at the provisions, but Drake shooed the cat out of the window. 'You can fend for yourself,' he told the animal. 'We have to make our food last.' Shadow looked miffed, but vanished into the night without turning back.

As they ate they talked about what they would do next. 'You still want to look for Rose?' asked Drake.

'Of course,' said Vijay.

'Even though we don't know where she's gone, or even if she's still alive?'

'What else are we going to do? Have you got any better ideas?'

'No. Just checking to see if you've changed your mind.'

Vijay shook his head. 'I'll never change my mind. I won't stop looking until I find her.'

Aasha took his hand in hers. 'Don't worry, little bro. We won't stop either.'

Chapter Twenty-Three

Haywards Heath, West Sussex

'Bring in the prisoner.' Leanna Lloyd stood in the royal tent, her retinue of courtiers arrayed before her. Her castle at Windsor may have been destroyed in the air assault by government forces, and her throne lost during the fighting at Gatwick, but she retained her crown, and her authority. None dared defy her wishes.

She watched as a human female was hauled into the tent, a steel band around her neck, pulled by an iron chain. The woman was dragged onto her knees. A wretched specimen: her limbs thin, her hair unkempt and long. It trailed over her face, but Leanna didn't need to see the woman's eyes to know that they were filled with terror.

Pathetic. This was what all humans were like without Leanna's gift. Weak, frail, doomed to a life of misery. The sight of the woman disgusted Leanna. And her smell was even worse. The raw stench of fear leached from every pore of her skin. Well, Leanna would soon put an end to that.

Humans were not entirely useless. Leanna had developed a taste for their organs, particularly the liver. Freshly killed, its flavour and texture were exquisite. Saliva dripped from her tongue in anticipation of the delicacy that awaited her. She rose from her throne, readying herself for the kill.

But before she could act a herald entered. He was one of Canning's men, a living embodiment of her general's military fantasies. The man was dressed in a ridiculous medieval costume, a brightly-coloured tabard bearing golden lions and red dragons over black stockings. He knelt before her. 'Lord General Canning begs an audience with the Queen.'

Leanna growled. 'I do not take kindly to those who interrupt my meals.'

The man paled. 'I beg pardon, your majesty. Lord Canning brings urgent news.'

'Good or bad?'

'I ... I do not know.'

Leanna considered having the herald killed. The liver of a werewolf would taste as fine as any human meat. But she had lost rather too many of her followers in the recent battle. She couldn't afford to be careless. Besides, news might be welcome ... if it was good. And Canning was not so stupid that he would bring her bad news in person.

She seated herself in her replacement throne and made herself comfortable while she considered her response to Canning's request for an audience. There was no need to hurry. She liked to keep her general waiting, and the human female would benefit from having her torment lengthened.

Her new throne wasn't a throne as such, just a big chair, but if the queen named it a throne, no one would dare question her. And Leanna Lloyd was unquestionably queen of all she surveyed.

She was the most powerful woman in the land and had

fulfilled her life's ambition by conquering disease through the transforming power of lycanthropy. Moreover, she had succeeded in eradicating weakness from humanity by the simple expedient of slaughtering the weak. She was surrounded by servants, who brought her everything she asked for.

And yet happiness had proved to be strangely elusive. Who was to blame? It was the traitors.

The treachery had begun with Professor Wiseman, and the list of those who had betrayed her along the way had grown long.

Wiseman was the first to seek to frustrate her goal, even though it was he who had given her the means to achieve it. She would never forget those dark days in Romania when he had kept her a prisoner, tied to her own bedframe in their cabin in the forest, in a desperate bid to save his own skin. But she had tricked him into freeing her, and he had provided her first taste of human flesh.

Leanna's hand drifted involuntarily to the red scars across her cheek where Doctor Helen Eastgate had thrown acid into her face. Helen was dead now, too.

And then there was Warg Daddy, who had led her army before Canning's arrival, and who had been her lover. But Warg Daddy had taken another into his bed. Leanna had bade her farewells to him with a parting gift of poisoned pills.

Three traitors dealt with. But others remained at large.

Top of her list was James Beaumont, the boy werewolf. His crime was the most unforgivable, as he had betrayed his own kind, choosing instead to save human lives. And then there were James' two minions, Melanie and Ben, who had fought alongside him and robbed Leanna of the chance to kill him. Melanie had even dared to strike her with steel. Leanna rubbed at her lower back where the metal bar had pummelled her. That bitch! She was almost as bad as James himself. Then there was Vixen, one-time leader of the Wolf Sisters. If it had not been for that scheming whore, Warg Daddy would never have turned against her, and she would not be saddled with Canning now.

Canning. He was the greatest thorn in her flesh these days. So full of words, but always short on results. He had twice led her army to the brink of defeat, first at Windsor, and then at Gatwick. And he had failed to bring her any of the traitors, even though she had told him to make it his first priority, even ahead of defeating the government forces.

Leanna had three questions to ask herself about Canning. Could she trust him? That was the easiest one to answer – not one inch. Could she replace him? The truth of this was harder to accept, but no, she couldn't, at least for the moment, for which of her fawning fools and sycophants might she put in his place? The third question was the hardest of all and was this – if she needed him, but couldn't trust him, how could she control him?

The answer was fear, to ensure that he lived in permanent dread.

'Tell the General he may enter,' she commanded the herald, and watched him bow low and scurry away to fetch his master.

Canning. What news did he bring? None of Leanna's own spies had told her anything interesting in recent days apart from the welcome arrival of the new recruits from the north. Was that all that Canning had to offer her? If he imagined that stale news would please her, she would have some hard lessons to teach him.

The general swaggered into the tent, his black patch over one eye, his silver hair combed back over his high forehead. He seemed self-assured, but then he always did. She'd allowed that veneer to fool her at first, until she'd discovered just how empty his promises could be. Why did she tolerate him? Because she had no better option.

Her general was followed by seven ruffians, and Leanna sat up in alarm. What fool had permitted these strangers to enter her royal tent? She would ensure that whoever was responsible would pay for such a stupid breach of security.

She gasped. The man behind Canning was a giant with the head of a wolf. At his shoulders stood two more wolfmen, their huge beast heads fixed to human bodies.

Leanna rose from her throne. 'What manner of monsters are these?'

The first and largest of the wolfmen stepped forward, forcing Canning to one side. Two of her courtiers rushed to intercept him, but he grabbed them by the collar and hurled them to the floor as if they were dolls. An insolent grin spread across the stranger's face and he stood before her, his hands on his hips.

'Why, your majesty, by all accounts we are your children and have you to thank for our monstrous appearance.' His voice was rough, his accent northern. There was an impudence to his speech, which both repelled and attracted her.

'How dare you!' she shouted. 'I have killed people for less.'

The wolfman threw back his head and laughed. 'Kill me then, if it pleases you. But I would rather you kissed me.'

'Kiss you?' Leanna had not encountered such insolence since … she didn't think she had ever experienced such loutish behaviour. And yet something about the stranger was alluring. Her heart beat quicker, and not just with anger. 'I shall have you whipped, at the very least.'

The grin spread further across his hairy face, revealing pointed teeth as bright as the silvery moon. 'Whip me? Aye, if you will. If it is done by your own hand, I will accept a beating gladly.' He reached out a hand as huge as a ham. 'My name is William Hunter. I have travelled all the way from York to gaze on your beauty.' He winked lewdly. 'I have to say, it was worth the walk.'

Leanna was at a loss for how to deal with this

interloper. Kill him? Kiss him? She wanted to do both. 'So you have seen me,' she answered. 'What now?'

'That is up to you, your majesty. I can teach your soldiers to fight like northern men. I can lead them into battle. I can bring you the victory that your general has failed to deliver.' He cast a backward glance at Canning, whose face was purple with rage.

William Hunter was growing on Leanna with every word he spoke. Might he be the answer to her prayers? But she was no lovestruck fool. This wolfman gave off the scent of danger even more strongly than the grovelling woman on the floor revealed her terror.

I fell for a man once. Warg Daddy. And he repaid me with betrayal. I will not fall a second time.

The wolfman strode across the floor, closing the remaining distance between them. This time no one stepped forward to intercept him. As he grew near, she felt the hairs on her neck tingle in anticipation.

He is more man than all the others here.

He drew to a halt before her, then leaned in and whispered in her ear. 'Take me to your bedchamber and I will show you what else I can do.'

Chapter Twenty-Four
Imber Village, Salisbury Plain

The houses might have been fake, but the shelter they offered against the cool of the night was real enough. Rose found a small house at the edge of the village, and with the help of Chris and Seth was able to pull away the wooden boards that blocked the entrance door. Inside, the building was nothing more than a shell, with no internal walls or upstairs floor, just blank boarded-up windows. It was like being on a film set and she felt more than ever like an actor playing a role that had been thrust upon her. She had never auditioned for this part, had never wanted to be anyone other than herself, but the Rose she had once been was almost lost to her now. That shy South London schoolgirl seemed less real than what she had become. A virgin priestess. A prophet. A leader.

I must play the part a little longer, until I have led my people to safety.

She just wished she knew what lines she was supposed

to speak, and longed for a glimpse of the script she was following.

Ryan returned after an hour. 'I've been making sure that everyone has a place to sleep for the night,' he told her. 'I don't think it's going to rain, but everyone seems to want to stay indoors for a change.'

Rose felt the same desire. After living among fields and hedgerows and beneath the huge, oppressive sky for so long, if felt good to be around bricks and mortar again. 'It gives them a sense of security,' she said.

'I guess.'

But she knew that this security was as flimsy and fake as the houses themselves.

Rose had eaten nothing all day and feared that the gnawing emptiness in her belly would keep her awake, but she fell quickly into a deep sleep, her limbs grateful for rest after so many miles of walking. When she awoke, hours later, it was pitch black and she had trouble remembering where she was and what she was doing. In her dreams, she was not the virgin priestess carrying the weight of the world. She was Rose Hallibury, a teenage girl with all the promise of life ahead of her. Her brother, Oscar, was still alive, always smiling, and her Mum and Dad were there to take care of her. A bell rang gently in her ears, calling her from afar.

Shaking away the soft tendrils of sleep, she sat up straight. The clanging of bells was close and urgent. They rang wildly, calling out in the night. It took her a moment to realise what they were.

'The church bells. Someone's ringing them.'

Nutmeg yelped, frightened by the commotion, and Rose held her tight.

A shadow moved beside her. Ryan was on his feet. He shook Chris and Seth awake. 'Come on! Get up! We have to move.'

'What is it?' murmured Seth.

'I don't know,' said Ryan. 'But we need to be ready for

whatever it is.'

The open doorway cut a paler shade of grey against the obsidian black inside the house. Rose stumbled toward it and emerged into the night. Outside, the wild peals of the bells were louder, shaking the still, cool air alive.

'It's a warning,' said Ryan. 'Someone's ringing the bells to sound the alarm.'

Others were emerging from nearby houses. On everyone's lips, the question was the same. 'What's happening?'

Nutmeg barked. Rose listened and heard another noise – a deep rumbling beneath the tenor notes of the bells. The engines of moving vehicles.

'Quickly.' To Rose's relief, Ryan was taking control of the situation. He ushered people from the nearest houses and gathered them into a group. 'Everyone be quiet!'

They listened together, as the bells rang ever more frantically and the sound of vehicles drew closer. The topmost section of the church tower was dimly visible above the tree line, standing grey against black and crowned with pinnacles and battlements. The bells rang out from behind the slatted windows. And then they began to slow, dying out gradually, and finally ceasing altogether. A loud crack punctuated the silence, and then another. The engines revved again, and lights cut through the darkness, as startlingly bright as the bells had been loud.

A voice shouted, 'Werewolves! We're under attack!'

There was no full moon tonight. No moon visible at all. But that meant that the attacking werewolves must be in human form, just as dangerous as any other human, but stronger, and with night senses. And it sounded like they were armed.

'That was gunfire,' said Ryan. 'Come on, run!' He herded the people away from the church and out of the village toward the surrounding plain. Rose heard shouts and screams from all around, and more gunshots. The white beams of headlights swept across the fronts of the houses, casting monstrous moving shadows. The intruders were coming closer.

In the confusion, it was impossible to know what was happening. People were running everywhere, but Ryan ushered them away from the village as best he could. Some followed, some ran back into the houses. Still others fled in different directions. For once, Rose was willing to follow, and let someone else give orders. She ran where Ryan told her and reached the edge of the village. Beyond was nothing but the grassy plain, swallowed by the darkness. She felt as if she were standing on the edge of the world.

'What about the bombs?' wailed Seth. 'We're heading into a minefield.'

But there was no alternative. Behind them, the relentless noise of gunshots and screams continued above the roar of the engines. The bells had ceased their clamour now, and Rose dreaded to think what had happened to whoever had rung them to raise the alarm. She fixed Nutmeg's lead to the dog's collar and stepped out into the unknown. 'Come on. Follow me. And be quiet.'

She hurried as best she could across the rough ground, taking care not to stumble or trip. From time to time the beam of a headlamp crossed her path, showing her what lay ahead. At other times she was almost blind. Seth followed, then Chris and the others. She had no idea what had happened to Ryan, or the rest of the people.

After walking for a few minutes she turned and stared back in the direction of the village. The sight was like a vision of Hell. The werewolves had begun to torch buildings, sending fierce flames licking up the sides of the box houses. The shrieks of those trapped inside were as bad as any Rose had heard during her months of nightmares. But she was relieved to see that many had got away and were following her in a line across the fields. If they could keep going they would escape.

But then the first of the invading vehicles came into

view. A military car of some kind, perhaps a Land Rover. It turned, shining its lights directly into her eyes and she blinked them shut. When she opened them again, her worst fear was realised. The Land Rover's engine roared as it began to accelerate, chasing them across the plain. Two more vehicles emerged and joined the first in pursuit. The hard crackle of automatic gunfire punched through the air and was met by more screams.

Rose quickened her pace, Nutmeg bounding in front. Every step she took might set off a buried shell or unexploded grenade but there was no time to think about where to place her feet. The sweeping glare of the headlamps lit her way now, and the terrible sounds drove her on. Once again she was leader of her people, although how many of them still survived she had no way of knowing. She hoped they had scattered to evade the attack and that most were still alive, hiding or running for their lives.

The sound of the Land Rovers grew louder, the lights more blinding as they swung in her direction. The grass before her turned ice white under their glare and her shadow ran before her like a phantom, its black limbs pumping wildly. Something whickered overhead and she realised with a gasp that it was a bullet. The hunters were drawing closer and there was no way she could outrun them.

Then suddenly the night grew light as day.

An explosion ripped across the field. White, orange, and yellow strobed the ground, as bright as a flare. An enormous boom followed a fraction of a second later. Rose turned, shielding her eyes against the glare. Fire had engulfed the lead Land Rover and thick curtains of smoke rolled up into the sky, glowing orange from below. From beneath the upturned vehicle, a dark silhouette looking like a demon from the underworld struggled frantically to free itself from the blaze. The lone survivor of the explosion crawled away from the burning wreck, but the flames went with him, outlining him in fire. He writhed on the ground, clutching to life for a few brief seconds, before falling still.

Behind the wreckage, the two other Land Rovers ground to a halt then turned slowly in an arc. The timbre of their engines dropped as they sped away, leaving the area still again. Now only the gentle roar of the flames broke the silence. The leaping fire cast an orange glow across the scene, revealing bodies lying where they had fallen. Old men. Children. A woman with a baby clutched to her breast.

Rose cast her gaze across the devastation and wept.

Chapter Twenty-Five

Somewhere in England

Inky shadows slid like snakes across the chess board as the day grew long. The ache in Warg Daddy's skull, which had receded as he became engrossed in the game, slowly returned and he rubbed at his head with one large thumb, surveying his position with dismay.

The game had started out well enough, with Death matching each of Warg Daddy's moves until both sides' knights and bishops were in play and the kings safely castled. But then the game had taken a turn for the worse. Death moved to the attack, capturing first a pawn and then a knight. Warg Daddy did his best to fight back but Death continued with a series of moves that confounded him, leaving his pawns trapped and his bishops and remaining knight exposed to attack. He couldn't understand how it had happened. When Death's bishop swooped down from out of nowhere and captured his queen, he began to suspect that some kind of black magic was at work.

'You cheated!' Warg Daddy accused, as Death reached out with long bony fingers to snatch the white queen from the board.

His opponent appeared offended by the charge. 'I did not. Prove it.'

Warg Daddy couldn't be sure exactly *how* the cheating had been done, but he knew he'd been hoodwinked *somehow*. He'd played cards against Weasel often enough in The Tarnished Spoon to spot a swindle at a hundred paces. 'Prove that you didn't,' he retorted.

'Now you're being silly,' said Death. 'Why don't you just concede defeat gracefully?'

'Concede defeat?' Warg Daddy had never conceded defeat in his life. You didn't get to be Leader of the Pack by giving up when the going got tough. Although, he recalled, he was no longer Leader of the Pack. The Brothers had abandoned him, choosing Vixen in his place. Had he, in fact, conceded defeat in allowing her to take them with her?

I fought valiantly when Slasher challenged me, he reminded himself. *I won the duel even though I lost my arm. I didn't give in.*

And yet the Brothers were all gone and Vixen had even taken his motorbike with her. He had lost everything including his dignity without even knowing how. He eyed Death suspiciously, unable to meet his hooded gaze. 'What happens if I lose the game?'

'Good question. I don't recall agreeing the stakes. Perhaps we should discuss them now.'

'No. That's not fair!' protested Warg Daddy. 'You can't agree the stakes halfway through the game.'

Death regarded him with what he guessed was a look of amusement, although it was hard to tell whether any real emotion had ever flickered across that stone-white countenance. 'Where in the rulebook does it say that life must be fair?'

Warg Daddy knew then that he had been well and truly deceived. All that talk of friendship had been nothing more than a ploy. This was no mere game to pass the time. He was locked in a deadly duel, playing for the ultimate prize. He switched his attention back to the game, moving his knight to threaten black's queen, but Death responded immediately with a move to check. It looked like there was no way out.

'This was all just a mean trick,' complained Warg Daddy. 'Why didn't you just take me when you first arrived? Why all this charade?'

'The time was not right. Besides, I enjoy a game of chess. It's your move, by the way.'

Warg Daddy blocked the check, then played a desperado move, sacrificing his rook to avoid defeat.

'Hmm,' said Death, stroking his grinning skull face with one bony finger. 'You intend to play on to the bitter end?'

'To the end.'

'Very well.'

It took only three more moves for the game to end in checkmate. Warg Daddy stared at his trapped king in dismay, but there was no way for him to save it. 'So is this it?' he asked. If his demise had finally come, he would face it like a hero. Perhaps this was what he had yearned for after all – to fall in battle to a worthy foe, even one who cheated like the worst kind of scoundrel. The chess board wasn't the battlefield he'd imagined, but he had fought his best, avoided the temptation to concede defeat, and soldiered on until the bitter end.

'Will you take me now?'

But Death made no move to gather his scythe. Instead his thin lips twitched into a ghost of a smile. 'I told you before, no spoilers.'

'Then what? Are you going to keep me here forever, just waiting to die? Why don't you take my soul now, so I can die a hero?' Anger bubbled up inside him. He deserved better than this. A hero ought to be treated with respect, especially at the hour of his passing. He should not be swindled and mocked and kept waiting.

Warg Daddy knew he hadn't lived his life as a good man. He had never claimed to. Life hadn't presented him with good choices. But he had always faced his challenges, never backing down, never taking the easy way out. He had stood as Leader and gathered the Brothers to his side, scooping them out of the gutter and making men of them. They had looked up to him and he had given them their pride. That must count for something, surely.

Death regarded him disdainfully, saying nothing. But Warg Daddy no longer cared. He knew he had lived life on his own terms. He had, as the song went, done it his way. So, yes, he had no regrets.

'Take me now!' he roared. 'My time is done! I demand that you do your job and allow me to pass on to the next place, wherever it may be!'

But when he looked next, Death had vanished. The entire world had gone. There was no longer a chess board on the ground. The rock he had made his home was no more. Instead he was in a narrow, darkened tunnel. He rose slowly to his feet. Ahead of him, a long way in the distance, a tiny pale light twinkled like a lone star in the firmament. It beckoned to him and he took one shaky step forward, then another. The going was slow, his limbs weighed like lead, but he continued to stagger toward the light as if it were the last sight he would ever behold. Perhaps it was. Slowly it grew until its brightness filled the world.

And now he could make out sounds. The voices of angels, or devils, or fallen heroes, he knew not which.

'Hey, just leave him,' said the first voice. 'He's trouble. Look at him.'

'No. We can't leave him.'

'Why not?'

Warg Daddy stumbled toward the voices and the light, determined to leave the tunnel behind. The light grew blindingly bright and he shielded his eyes from the searing pain, but didn't stop walking. Eventually he broke free of the tunnel and blinked his eyes slowly open.

He stood in a strange land filled with rocky boulders. Was this Hell? It certainly didn't look like the halls of Valhalla. There was no mead, no meat, and no feasting. And these weren't fallen warriors before him. They looked like kids.

'Am I dead?' he demanded, before adding, 'And who the fuck are you?'

Then he collapsed to the ground, exhausted.

Chapter Twenty-Six

The Pilgrims' Way

They found the stranger on a dusty path that led across a dry, yellow field. He was terrifying to look at, dressed in black leathers with a white wolf stencilled on his back, and built like a bear, a wall of solid muscle. In the old days, Vijay would have run a mile from a man like this, but he was a lot braver than he used to be. Besides, it was obvious even from a distance that the guy was badly wounded. He had lost an arm, and a lot of blood, and seemed to be drifting in and out of consciousness. Sometimes he sat still, with his back to a rock and his eyes firmly closed. At other times he ranted and raved like a madman. Who he was talking to was anyone's guess.

They watched him from behind a low stone wall.

'What shall we do?' whispered Aasha.

'Keep well out of his way,' said Drake. 'Obviously.'

'Hush,' said Vijay. 'He's moving again.'

The man's eyes opened and he blinked like a mole emerging from its dark tunnels. He was evidently stronger than Vijay had realised, because he lurched suddenly to his feet using his one huge hand to push himself up. Standing tall, he surged forward purposefully in their direction. But he still seemed unaware that he had company.

'What shall we do now?' asked Aasha.

'Run,' said Drake.

'No,' said Vijay. 'Let's stay here and watch for a bit longer.' An idea was forming in his mind. Crazy, perhaps, but one he couldn't easily ignore.

They crouched down behind the safety of the wall.

The man staggered along the path, shielding his eyes from the sunlight with his arm. Beads of sweat stood out across his massive forehead, and his mouth moved silently, forming soundless words.

Vijay weighed up his options, then made his decision. 'We must go and help him.'

'What?'

'No! That's mad!'

'Yes.' Vijay rose from his hiding place and the man lurched toward him. Up close, he towered over all three of them and Vijay began to doubt the wisdom of what he was about to do. But then he thought of his grandmother, and steeled himself to act.

The man came closer, his heavy brow darkened in fury, his one hand clenched into a fist.

Aasha grabbed hold of Vijay's arm. 'Hey, just leave him. He's trouble. Look at him.'

'No. We can't leave him,' said Vijay.

'Why not?'

The giant came to a juddering halt before them and looked around as if he had no idea where he was or how he had come to be there. Then his eyes came into focus and rested on Vijay.

Vijay stared back, taking in the stranger's bulging forehead and thick bull neck. His legs began to tremble, but he stood his ground.

The giant's eyes widened. 'Am I dead?' he demanded, before adding, 'And who the fuck are you?' Then he dropped to his knees and toppled forward, planting his face firmly into the ground.

Vijay crouched beside him.

'Vijay, this is mad.' Drake kneeled down too, glaring at the stranger, his eyes filled with mistrust. 'We can't help this guy. He looks ready to die.'

'But that's exactly why we have to help him. He needs us. If we leave him here alone, he'll die for certain.'

'No,' said Aasha. 'Drake's right. If we stop to help, we could end up as dead as him. He might even kill us himself. Look at him. He's rough.'

'Just help me turn him over,' said Vijay.

Between the three of them, they managed to roll the man onto his back. He lay there, unconscious but still breathing. Shadow hissed at him and drew back.

Aasha was right about the man's appearance. He was certainly no beauty. His large bulbous nose rose beneath the dome of a perfectly bald head. His face bristled with a vast beard that was as black as his leather jacket and looked like it was infested with bugs. He'd obviously been in a fight, and his hand and face were caked in blood, either his or someone else's. But how dangerous could a man in his condition be? One of his arms was missing, and he was barely strong enough to stand. Besides, they were armed with weapons now – Vijay an axe, Drake a knife and pitchfork, and Aasha her metal hook.

But still Aasha wasn't convinced. 'What were you telling us about keeping safe? Now you want to put us in danger again. We can't risk it. Not to help a stranger.'

'But if we turn away and refuse to help a stranger, why should we ever expect anyone to help us?'

'We don't need anyone's help.'

'Maybe not right now, but we did back in town when those dogs attacked us. And we'll probably get into trouble again. Everyone needs help sometimes.'

'But just look at this guy.'

Vijay looked, and his knees trembled. But he recalled the words of the Sikh Gurus. 'It doesn't matter how he looks. We don't get to choose the people who come to us for help. The only choice we get is how to respond to them.'

Aasha was about to make some retort when Drake whistled. He had walked over to the rock where the man had been sitting when they first spotted him.

Aasha looked up. 'What have you found? Oh my God, is that a gun?'

A black metal object lay on the ground near the rock. It was definitely a gun, and a big one at that – about three feet long. Did it belong to the man, or had it been used to shoot him? And what kind of man carried a weapon like that, anyway? It looked like the kind of gun that the soldiers had used back in the evacuation camp. But this stranger was no soldier.

Drake picked it up gingerly. 'It's a combat shotgun, like they use in the army.'

'Be careful where you point it.'

'Duh, obviously.' Drake was examining the weapon, turning the deadly-looking object over in his hands. 'This beats a pitchfork any day.'

'Do you know how to use it?' asked Aasha.

'I can work it out.' Drake returned, carrying the gun with him, its barrel pointed down at the ground. 'Or perhaps we can ask him.' He gestured at the stranger, and they all turned back to look at him.

The giant's eyes were half open, blinking slowly in the sunshine. His mouth stirred and a single word fell out. It sounded like, 'Shades.'

Vijay knelt next to him and spike slowly and clearly. 'My name is Vijay Singh. This is my sister, Aasha, and my friend, Drake. What happened to you?'

The man's head turned a fraction. 'Light,' he rasped.

'Too bright. Need shades.'

Drake moved so that his shadow fell across the stranger's face. 'He's asking for his glasses.' A pair of sunglasses were clasped in the man's hand. Drake prised them free of his thick fingers and placed them over the stranger's eyes. It seemed to bring him some relief.

'We can help you,' said Vijay. 'Would you like some water?'

The man rubbed at his forehead with his thumb, making it squeak. 'Food,' he growled. 'Need food.'

Vijay heaved his rucksack from his shoulders and pulled out a can of vegetable soup. 'Would you like this? We can warm it for you if you like.'

The man wrinkled his great nose in disgust. 'Meat. Need meat.'

'I've got a tin of corned beef,' said Drake, reaching inside his own rucksack. He opened it with the ring pull and passed it to Vijay.

Vijay took a small piece of the meat and offered it to the man. 'Here,' he said, placing it between the stranger's lips. 'Eat this.'

The man's huge jaws began to work at the beef, chewing it and swallowing it down. Vijay offered him some more.

The man accepted it, but the food didn't stay down for long. He retched, bringing it back up in a pool of yellow bile. With surprising strength his huge hand reached out and gripped Vijay's arm. 'Prey,' he whispered. 'Must eat prey.'

Vijay tried to pull away but the man's fingers held him in an iron grip.

'You look tasty,' he mumbled.

'Oh my God,' said Aasha. 'He's a werewolf!' She stamped her foot, bringing her heel down full square on the man's face. There was a loud crunch and Vijay felt the giant's fingers go limp. He jerked his arm back to safety.

The man roared in pain as blood streamed from his

nose. He gazed hungrily up at them, his cracked lips parted, revealing pearl-white teeth and a fleshy pink tongue. The tongue slid out to lick at the blood from his own wound, and his mouth twisted into a contented smile. 'Mmm,' he murmured. 'Tastes good.'

A wave of nausea rose up from Vijay's stomach.

'All right,' said Drake. 'Are you satisfied now? This guy's a werewolf and he wants to eat us. Come on, let's get out of here.'

But Vijay made no move to leave. He knew he ought to be fleeing for his life, but even though the stranger was terrifying, he still needed their help.

'What are you doing now?' asked Aasha. 'Why aren't we gone already?'

'Because we have to help him, even though he's a werewolf.' This test was much harder than anything Vijay had expected to face. But tests were meant to be … well, testing. If they weren't, they wouldn't really be tests. And he knew that if he failed it, he would spend the rest of his life in shame.

'You must be joking,' said Aasha. 'Tell me you're not serious. What Guru ever talked about helping evil man-eating monsters?'

Vijay was already thinking about what they could do to help. The stranger needed meat. Prey, he called it. Obviously they weren't going to allow him to feed off human flesh, but perhaps they could find an animal to give him. Shadow was always catching birds and other creatures and bringing them back. They could give him one of the dead animals to eat.

Aasha crouched down next to Vijay, her sharp hook in her hands. She rested it against the man's neck. 'We should kill him, not help him. That would be the best thing. I'll do it if you don't want to. I could slit his throat with this, or stick the pitchfork in him.'

'Or shoot him with his own shotgun,' suggested Drake, who was still gripping the weapon he had found.

'Because that would be easy, wouldn't it?' said Vijay angrily. 'So much easier than showing compassion. You could just kill him and walk away, and try to forget about what we did. But I don't want to spend the rest of my life walking away from people who need my help.'

'We don't need a lecture from you, Vijay,' said Aasha, her dark eyes flashing. 'Creatures like this killed our mum and dad, and our grandmother. Have you forgotten?'

'Of course I haven't. But this man didn't kill them. And he's not a creature, he's a person suffering from a horrible disease. He's a victim.'

'We don't even know his name,' said Drake.

Aasha stood up and dug her shoe into the stranger's side. 'Hey, monster, what's your name?'

The man ignored her. His eyes had closed again, and his lips were making the shape of silent words, as if in conversation with some imaginary person.

'I said, what's your name?'

The eyes opened once more and the giant turned his huge bald head to look at her. 'My name? I used to have a name. I was Leader of the Pack. People called me Warg Daddy.'

'What kind of name is that?' said Drake.

'A stupid one,' said Aasha. 'I'm not wasting my time on someone with such a stupid name.'

A slow grin crept across Warg Daddy's ugly face. 'I like this girl. She's fierce.'

Aasha turned away. 'Come on. Let's go.'

'No.' Now that the stranger had a name, Vijay was even more certain he had made the right decision. This was exactly the kind of question he'd spent hours debating at the Gurdwara, yet this was no abstract moral debate. Warg Daddy was a real person with a real life. He had hopes and dreams and feelings just like everyone else. Saving this man would be a huge challenge, but it was only by serving others and by seeing the divine order even in people like this that it was possible to get closer to God.

Drake gestured with the barrel of the shotgun. 'Vijay, even if we could save him, he'd probably just go off and kill someone. That's what werewolves do, yeah?'

'He might kill us,' said Aasha.

'No,' said Vijay, sure of himself now. 'We can never know the future consequences of our actions. We just have to do what we know to be right at the time.'

Drake shook his head. 'Mate, that's mad talk. He's a werewolf. It's his nature to kill people.'

'But if we show him kindness, perhaps he can change. Everyone deserves a second chance. God can be found inside even the most wicked person.'

Drake shrugged, but seemed to have no counter-argument. Instead, it was Warg Daddy who spoke up. He was studying the three of them, Vijay especially. 'I've seen you before.'

'No,' said Vijay. 'I don't think so. I would have remembered.'

'Yes,' insisted the man with surprising vigour. 'In London. On New Year's Eve.'

Vijay cast his mind back to the events that had unfolded at the year's end. He and Drake had gone out with Rose that evening to keep an eye on Aasha and her friends. They'd got caught up in the fighting at Battersea and ended up getting cornered by a gang of thugs in a back alley behind a pub. A huge black werewolf had appeared, bounding down the alleyway, its yellow eyes blazing in the night. Vijay had faced the beast alone, protecting Rose from danger.

'I tried to eat you,' said Warg Daddy.

Vijay would never forget the huge jaws and devil's teeth of that terrible creature. He studied the man in front of him. He was broken and weak now, but still powerfully built. Though completely bald, his thick beard was as black as coal, just like the wolf that had almost killed him that night.

'Was that you?'

'You were with the girl. The one with red hair.'

'Rose?'

'You stopped me from killing her.'

'I did.'

Incredibly, it seemed that Warg Daddy was telling the truth. 'I saw her again,' he rumbled.

'What?' said Vijay in astonishment. 'You saw Rose? Where? When?'

But the patient was drifting away again.

Vijay shook him by the shoulders. 'Where did you see her? You have to tell me!'

But Warg Daddy no longer seemed to hear. His eyes rolled closed and his lips began to move. 'Bishop to e5,' he muttered. 'Knight to f3.' His huge head slumped back.

'He's dying,' said Aasha.

'He needs food,' said Drake.

'Then, come on,' said Vijay, getting to his feet. 'Let's fetch him some. Let's find him some prey.'

Chapter Twenty-Seven
Imber Village, Salisbury Plain

There were tears for the dead, but no tools to dig graves for their bodies. Rose walked among the survivors, doing her best to comfort them, while Ryan organized a team of men to recover the bodies of the fallen and carry them to the churchyard. There, grieving relatives claimed their loved ones and wept over them.

It was the morning after the werewolf attack, and no one had slept since being awoken by the ringing of the church bells during the night. Now the final count had been completed, Rose contemplated the bad news. Twenty-four dead out of more than three hundred people. It had been a senseless attack, the werewolves opening fire on their victims for no reason other than to kill as many as they could. They hadn't even stopped to feast on the bodies.

Small mercies.

But at least the explosion of the buried shell had

frightened away the rest of the werewolves. For now. In the danger zone beyond the village the wreckage of the Land Rover still burned, and the charred carcasses of the werewolves could be seen from the edge of the churchyard.

'The others will be back,' warned Ryan, once he had completed his grim task of reuniting the dead with the living. 'And they might bring reinforcements this time. We have to get out of here long before nightfall.'

Rose knew what she had to do next, but breaking the news to the mourning relatives would be one of the hardest things she had ever done. She didn't flinch from it, though. She had failed her people once. She wouldn't fail them again.

'I know that you want to bury your loved ones and give them a proper funeral,' she began, 'but there is no time. We have no spades for digging, and the werewolves may return again tonight. Instead we will burn the bodies using wood taken from the houses. We will do this now and leave the village immediately afterwards. I hope you will understand the need for urgency.'

A woman wailed, but others nodded or bowed their heads, accepting what she said.

'Go and collect firewood,' Rose told Ryan. 'I want this done within the hour.'

A new hardness had entered her thoughts. Before the massacre, she had yearned to be relieved of her heavy burden and for others to take responsibility. Now she understood the truth. She must bear this weight alone, and embrace it without question.

The girl who dreamed of her lost home and family is dead. She died last night. Now only the virgin priestess remains. She is the sacrifice. She will do what her people require, and they will do what she commands.

Her order was obeyed to the letter, and soon fresh flames were billowing in the morning sky, kindling wood ripped from the door and window frames of the houses.

Black smoke twisted high above the church tower as the bells rang out once more, not in warning this time but in mourning. Solemn words were spoken as the dead turned to ash, and the survivors made what peace they could.

When the unflinching fire had finished its purifying work, Rose gathered the people around her. 'You chose me as your leader, and placed your trust in me. But I have let you down. I will not fail you a second time. As long as there is strength in my arms, I swear I will not let any harm come to you again.'

The promise was an empty one, but it was all she could offer. She knew she must rally the people to her cause. To give in to despair would be to sign their death warrant. There was no room for dissent, no space for doubt.

'We will leave now, and walk until we find food and shelter.'

Her voice sounded small and scared to her own ears, but the people listened in rapt attention. They did not see a shy teenage girl, struggling to overcome her own fears and doubts. They saw their saviour.

A voice called out, 'Have you seen this in your visions?'

Another cried, 'Tell us you have seen a place of safety.'

Rose swallowed. 'I have seen it. And I will lead you there. Come.'

She turned from the pyre and stepped out from the graveyard, Nutmeg trotting alongside. She didn't look back, but heard the others follow. Away from the church she walked, and soon the village was behind her and she was back on the open road, heading into the unknown. The road led on, picking a straight path through the firing range. Clouds raced across the huge sky, showing her the way, yet she kept her eyes on the tarmac, searching for bombs, grenades or other dangers.

Ryan kept pace with her. His leg had healed now and he no longer limped. His mood was sombre and he said nothing. Even Chris had stopped complaining about his nose. The dangers they faced were greater than ever, and their needs more urgent. Food. Safety. Shelter. If they kept on walking, they would surely find all three. But how long it would take and where they would end up, she couldn't say. How many more would perish along the way? *None*, she vowed.

She stopped once to allow a rest, but kept the break short. Nutmeg gazed up at her with pleading eyes, and she rubbed the dog's head to soothe her. 'I know what you want, girl, but there is no food.'

In the early afternoon they finally emerged from the firing range, through a gate and sentry post much like the one they had used to enter it. The road led away from the danger zone and soon the barbed wire fence and warning signs were all behind them.

Open grassland gave way to farmers' fields, but there was still nothing to eat. The land rolled on, green with unripened crops, and trees now covering the low hilltops. A giant white horse cut a great scar into the chalk slope, much like the one she had seen at Uffington while walking the Ridgeway. Perhaps as much as two hundred feet from head to tail, it was visible for miles across the plain. She walked on past it, not deviating from the direction she had chosen.

If we keep on going, we must reach safety.

They stopped to make camp at night, then continued for another day. That morning they found a field with French beans and onions. The onions were covered in dirt and already starting to sprout and turn soft, but they tasted like nectar after days without food. They set off again, even though the youngest and the oldest struggled to keep up. Friends and family helped them along the path.

Afternoon turned to evening and the sun dipped low behind Rose's back, but still she drove her people on. The green of the land grew deeper and the sky turned salmon pink. A line of telegraph poles rose ahead like dark sentinels and she passed beneath them. Then, just as the sun met the horizon and became a ball of flame, the land dipped away as she crossed the brow of a wooded ridge. She heard herself gasp with delight.

No more than a mile distant, a green hill ringed by trees rose above the surrounding landscape like an upturned bowl. It was almost perfectly round, perhaps a mile in circumference. Within the outer circle a second layer rose higher, and inside that a third and even taller mound stood at its very heart. It was an ancient hill fort.

Seth's mouth dropped open in amazement. 'The lost city. It's real.'

Ryan's hand rested on her shoulder. 'You did it, Rose. You brought us here.'

'I did.' Suddenly the strength that had propelled her across the plain fled from her, and the hunger, fear and exhaustion she had carried for so long overwhelmed her. Her legs began to shake and buckle at the knees. She reached out but there was nothing to grab hold of. She fell to the ground and into the embrace of the hard, yellow turf. It was a relief to feel its solid support beneath her. Rolling onto her back she saw nothing but sky overhead. Then a long wet tongue licked her cheek. Grabbing Nutmeg, she pulled her close and felt the dog's warm breath against her skin.

'It's all right, girl,' she murmured. 'Everything's going to be all right.'

Chapter Twenty-Eight

Gatwick Airport, West Sussex, crescent moon

'Sir, there's someone to see you. A civilian.'

Griffin glanced up with irritation from his desk. He could tolerate no distractions now. He had given his orders to FitzHerbert, and final preparations for battle were underway. One last roll of the dice. If this operation failed, the war would be lost.

The timing had already been taken out of his hands and he could not afford to lose control of any other aspect of the operation. Even though his forces had supremacy at air and sea, the numbers on land were firmly against him. The real battle would take place on solid ground, and it would be a desperate fight for every square foot.

A brutal, bloody slaughter.

'He won't take no for an answer, sir.'

The flaps of Griffin's tent opened and a newcomer made his way inside. He was a tall, middle-aged man bearing a heavy load around his middle, but his muscular arms had not yet gone to fat. His face was weather-beaten, his hair grey and drawn back into a ponytail. His beard was long and black, and his neck was inked with the image of a rose. He wore combat trousers and a khaki shirt – a hotchpotch of a uniform that looked like it had been scavenged from an army surplus store.

He bowed low in exaggerated greeting, sweeping a green beret from his head. '*Saludos*, my friend. My greetings to you. My name is Johnny Perez and I am a businessman of a very special kind. I have a unique proposition to offer you.' He winked conspiratorially.

Griffin allowed a yawn to escape him. His leg had kept him awake for most of the night. He was dog-tired and had no time for foolishness. 'I'm a very busy man, Mr Perez. Forgive me if I don't rise to greet you.'

'Of course, Colonel, of course. I understand that. I am a busy man myself. I am not here to waste your time, nor my own, I assure you.' He pulled a cigar from his shirt pocket and offered it to Griffin, who shook his head. Smiling, he unwrapped it and placed it between his teeth.

'So what can I do for you, Mr Perez?'

'It is more a question of what I can do for you, Colonel. And you must call me Johnny, if we are to be friends. What should I call you in return?'

'Let's stick with Colonel Griffin, shall we?'

Perez accepted the implied rebuff in his stride. 'As you wish, Colonel. It is always wise to reserve judgement of a man until he has had an opportunity to prove his worth. Is that not so?' He struck a match and lit the end of his cigar, puffing at it until it caught. He drew in a deep lungful of smoke and exhaled with satisfaction. 'So, to the point, I bring you an offer. One that you won't want to refuse, I think. Let me see. Am I correct in thinking that you are in search of fighting men?'

Griffin wafted away the plume of smoke. 'You are correct.'

'Then I'm sure I won't be wasting your time. In fact, I think my proposition will be of immense interest to you.'

Griffin sighed. 'Yes? What precisely are you offering?'

'Two hundred fighting men, to complement your own forces.' He waggled his large fingers, several of which were ringed with gold. 'I say two hundred, perhaps it is a few more than that. Let us say two hundred and ten, two hundred and twenty, something like that. You could use that number of men?'

Griffin regarded his strange guest cautiously, not knowing what to think. 'Two hundred? I could use ten times that number. But these are civilians?'

'Civilians, soldiers ... sometimes the distinction is not so easy to make. They are experienced fighting men, familiar with a variety of weapons. In former times, they found employment in alternative sectors of the economy. My own field of expertise is in import and export, if you catch my drift?' He puffed at the cigar and blew smoke toward the ceiling.

'Are you telling me that you run some kind of criminal gang?'

The man's lips curved into a smile. 'My men are entrepreneurs, every one of them. They are men of action. Hard men, unafraid to kill ... or be killed. *Mercenarios*, you might call them. Yes, I think that is a very good word.' He puffed at the cigar, sucking in his cheeks with a look of satisfaction.

Griffin's eyes narrowed. 'Mercenaries? You have come to me for money?'

The cigar smoke blew out in a long stream. 'Payment will be required, of course. Not for myself, but for my men. No man can work for nothing. Think of it as a means of covering their expenses and compensating them for their time. Yes, that would be a very good way to describe my proposition to you, I think.'

Griffin allowed the anger he felt to colour his reply. 'Payment? Look around you, Mr Perez. My men and women aren't fighting for money. They're fighting for freedom. They're fighting for the very survival of the species!'

Perez remained unperturbed by Griffin's outburst. 'A noble cause, and all that, et cetera, et cetera, Colonel. I salute their bravery. But my men will not risk their lives for nothing, not even in support of such great causes as you describe. As I mentioned, they are businessmen. But if I may correct a small misunderstanding, I didn't say anything about money. No, my men will be wanting gold.'

At that, Griffin laughed out loud. 'Gold? What use is gold to you now?'

Perez spat on the ground. 'A darn sight more useful than those funny pieces of paper that the good old Bank of England used to print by the trillion. The only thing those notes are useful for these days is wiping your arse. And to be blunt, they're not much good for that. They're *no bueno*, you understand me? No, gold's the only true store of value in uncertain times. Apart from weapons, that is. Guns never go out of fashion. But don't worry. We can supply those ourselves.'

'Naturally.' Griffin eyed him warily. 'What makes you think I'm willing to give you what you ask for? What makes you think I can even lay my hands on gold?'

Perez's face split into a grin. 'We're negotiating now, eh, Colonel? Good. So, this is how we'll play it. My men and I will be back here in three days. If you've got the gold, we're good to fight and lay down our lives for the greater good, et cetera, et cetera. If not, then *adiós amigo*, we'll take our services elsewhere. No regrets, no hard feelings.'

'What do you mean "elsewhere"?' demanded Griffin. 'You'd sell your services to the enemy? To the werewolves?'

The man pasted a frown across his face. 'I didn't say that, now, did I, Colonel? That would be a little reckless, I think, working for those werewolves. My men love the shine of gold, they certainly do, but they also like the feeling of waking up in the morning with the blood still flowing in their veins. Strikes me that if we were to partner up with our friends in wolf's clothing, we might not get to experience that particular feeling for much longer.' The grin reappeared on his face, carving out a crooked curve. 'But there's always someone willing to pay for the rare skills my men can offer. I'm giving you first refusal, Colonel. I feel it's my patriotic duty, et cetera, et cetera, but if you don't want to strike a deal, we'll be looking elsewhere for honest employment. My men aren't monkeys, and they don't work for peanuts.'

'Let's take a look at your men, then. Are they here?'

'Of course. Naturally. We are a band of brothers. We always stick together. Come, they are waiting outside.'

Griffin hauled himself laboriously out of his seat and lifted himself up, one crutch underneath each arm.

Perez regarded him with some sympathy. 'A nasty injury you have there, Colonel. I see that you have already paid a hefty price for your duty to crown and country, et cetera, et cetera.'

Griffin sucked at his teeth and lurched forward. 'Let's just get this over with, shall we?'

He followed Perez out of the tent to inspect his men. They were gathered at the edge of the encampment, safely out of harm's way, and watched over by Griffin's own soldiers. Two hundred men, or thereabouts. Perez had not been lying about the numbers. Griffin hobbled awkwardly over to them, eager to get a feel for their quality.

Up close, they made a motley group of thugs, dressed like extras for some bad-ass movie – shaven headed, tattooed, clad in leather and denim and steel-capped boots and the mismatched uniforms of a dozen different armies. Insolent smiles and scowling grimaces adorned their rough faces, and metal studded their ears or looped their necks in heavy chains. They were as unlikely a band of rogues as he had ever set eyes on, and he had visited some dubious bars and nightclubs during his postings abroad.

But they looked tough. And they were well armed, with a variety of weapons on display. They may not have real combat experience, but Griffin was willing to bet they'd clocked up a fair few fights between them. Or unfair fights, in all likelihood. In his current predicament, he could hardly afford to turn away assistance of any kind.

But where to find gold? That was the question.

Chapter Twenty-Nine

Christmas Common, Oxfordshire

'Are you sure about this?' called Chanita from below.
'Yes.' Sarah Margolis looked down and saw Chanita's anxious face peering up. The ground seemed to sway a little and she switched her gaze quickly back to the horizontal. 'Just make sure you keep a firm hold of that ladder.'

'Don't worry. I'm not going anywhere.'

Sarah had climbed about twenty feet off the ground and was looking out across the roof of one of the oldest houses in the village. It was a dilapidated affair, made from loose stones held together by thick clumps of moss and other plants rooting in the cracks and gaps. A red brick chimney teetered above her like a tower ready to collapse. It seemed to be swaying gently in the wind, or was that just Sarah's imagination? Since it had stood for hundreds of years already, she decided that the chance of it collapsing right now were extremely low. Pretty low, anyway. And that was good enough these days.

Despite the height of her vantage point she couldn't see too far for all the trees that crowded in around her, gently rustling their leaves. She felt like one of the doves perched on the nearby branches, level with the rooftop but just out of her reach. The birds had taken flight when the ladder was first manoeuvred into position. Now, as Sarah hollered down to Chanita, they rose once more into the sky, with an indignant cooing and flapping of wings.

Sarah apologized to them. 'Sorry, guys. I'll be out of your feathers before too long.'

The village was small and she had come to know it like the back of her hand, but there were still a few houses she hadn't properly explored. A collection of new-builds stood at the edge of the village, there was a hotel down the road, and another village was located close by. One by one they were breaking into every house and outbuilding within miles, plundering them for essentials and carrying their spoils back to the ramshackle old building they now called home.

The house they had chosen to live in was just as ancient as the one Sarah was now stripping of its roof tiles. It dated back several centuries and had already been badly in need of repair when they first moved in. The werewolf attack had left it in even worse condition, and it would perhaps have been wiser to move on somewhere new, but they had invested so much work in doing the place up that the idea of moving hadn't even been discussed. Instead they had all pitched in harder than ever to make the necessary repairs. Today, Sarah was hoping to return with the tiles she needed to fix the leaks in the roof.

'Who are you talking to up there?' shouted Chanita.

'The birds.' Sarah leaned over the rickety roof and began prising a stone tile loose with her wrecking bar. The tiles were heavy, but held loosely in place with mortar that was crumbly to the touch. It didn't take her long to loosen and remove the first one. She slid it into her rucksack and proceeded to help herself to more tiles. Behind her, the birds returned to their perch again and sat watching her in a line. 'Maybe you can make your nest in this hole,' said Sarah. 'We all need a place to live.' The doves watched her carefully, but kept their opinion to themselves.

She returned to the ground with her booty, and handed it over to Chanita.

'It looks like you've discovered your true passion,' said Chanita as she loaded the stones carefully into a wheelbarrow.

Sarah laughed. 'Being a handyman? Maybe. I used to think I was destined to be a nurse, but maybe fixing up old houses is my true calling.'

'Well, I think we all need to learn as many skills as we can.'

'True enough.' When Sarah had lived in London with Melanie and Grandpa, she had wondered if she could ever have a real purpose in life. She had educated herself on medical matters and nursed Grandpa each day, but there had been nothing to look forward to, no goal to work towards. The future seemed dark and frightening. Now life was full of possibilities, and there was no limit to the range of new tasks she could apply herself to.

'Why don't we take a break before you go back up the ladder?' suggested Chanita.

'Sure, if you like.' Sarah had no need of a rest just yet. They had hardly started. But perhaps Chanita wanted to talk. In the old days, Sarah wouldn't have been able to hold a conversation, but now words came easily. At least with friends. She took a seat on the ground and pulled the ring off a can of lemonade. Already the morning sun was making her sweat. Climbing ladders was hard work. It would be good to cool off in the shade for a while.

Chanita sat next to her, but didn't join her in a drink. There was definitely something on her mind. Sarah waited patiently, knowing that Chanita didn't like to be rushed.

'You're looking thinner these days,' said Chanita.

Sarah hadn't been expecting that, but she was flattered by the comment. Had anyone ever said such a thing to her before? She didn't think so. She seemed to have spent her entire life getting steadily larger. But since leaving London she had slimmed down a lot. The Apocalypse Diet, it was all the rage these days.

'It's all the physical work, I guess. Or perhaps Melanie's awful cooking is to blame.' That was something else that was new. Cracking a joke. The old Sarah had barely smiled. It was always Melanie who made the wisecracks and snarky remarks – often at Sarah's expense. No, she didn't miss the old days one bit.

Chanita's serious look didn't change. 'You've gained in confidence too. You were incredibly shy when I first met you.'

So this was going to be a discussion about Sarah. Well, as long as the compliments continued to flow, Sarah was happy to go along with that. After years of her self-imposed isolation from the outside world, subject to Melanie's frequent caustic put-downs, she was due some flattery.

'It wasn't shyness,' she told Chanita. 'It was a pathology. When I lived in Richmond I couldn't speak to anyone. I couldn't even leave the house. Dealing with the postman would leave me traumatized for hours. An Amazon delivery? Forget it!'

Chanita raised one dark eyebrow. 'Well, you've certainly managed to overcome that now.'

'We've all had to step up, right? It's either that or die.'

'Life's become brutal, for sure.'

'Yes,' said Sarah, 'but it's actually been really good for me. It jumpstarted my life. Before I left London, I used to have very dark thoughts. I spent too much time alone, brooding. I would have carried on that way if it hadn't been for the world getting turned on its head.'

Chanita took her hand. 'If you ever have any dark

thoughts, Sarah, you know you can always talk to me?'

'Of course. But really I'm much better now.'

Chanita nodded. 'So from the way you describe things, I guess there was never anyone special in your life?'

'Only Melanie and Grandpa. They were always special to me. But that's not what you're asking.'

'No. But perhaps there might be one day?'

'Yeah, right,' said Sarah laughing. 'Because there are so many suitable men available in Christmas Common.'

Chanita smiled. 'You never know. Life's full of surprises.'

'What about you?'

'Me?' A shadow passed over Chanita's face like a rain cloud. 'There was someone, once. But …'

'I'm sorry,' said Sarah quickly. 'I shouldn't have asked.'

'It's all right. We weren't really a proper couple. We had only just got involved, there was never any time for us to really get together, and then … the last I heard of him was that his helicopter had gone down over London. It was at the time of the nuclear attack. I waited, but I never heard anything from him. So I have to face the facts …'

Sarah squeezed Chanita's hand. 'I'm sorry.'

They sat together quietly for a while, the doves cooing soothingly overhead, the sun growing stronger in the clear morning sky.

'What about Melanie?' asked Chanita. 'How has she been changed by everything that's happened?'

'Well, in a peculiar way, I think this catastrophe has been good for her too. She's still just as stubborn and argumentative as she always was, but she's had to give up on being so self-absorbed. The world isn't all about her anymore. She's part of a team. Ben's been good for her too, and perhaps the baby …'

Chanita nodded eagerly and Sarah realized that this was the real focus of their talk. All that buttering up had just been to get onto the subject of Melanie. Well, Sarah was used to playing second fiddle to her sister.

'You think she'll make a good mother?' asked Chanita.

Sarah chose her answer carefully. 'She thinks she will. She certainly wants to.'

'But she refuses to take my advice and slow down.'

Sarah chuckled. 'Melanie take someone else's advice? Trust me, that won't ever happen.'

'Motherhood can change people.'

'Not Mel. She'll never change. Not in that way. She'll always be a fighter.'

Chanita pursed her lips. 'Fighting's all well and good, but if she's not careful, she might have no choice. She might have to start changing.'

So now they were getting to the heart of Chanita's concerns. 'You're worried about the pregnancy? Is that it?'

Chanita sighed. 'No, not exactly. There's certainly nothing wrong with Melanie's health. Far from it. It's just that …'

'What?'

'I'm probably just being silly.'

'About what?' asked Sarah.

'Well, the pregnancy is already quite advanced. Second trimester, by my reckoning.'

'Okay,' said Sarah uncertainly. She had no experience of looking after pregnant women, but she knew that the second trimester was the middle three months of pregnancy. She did a quick calculation in her head, but the dates didn't make any sense. By that reckoning, the child must have been conceived while Ben had been away with James. Sarah looked expectantly to Chanita for an explanation.

'I know what you're thinking,' said Chanita. 'I must be wrong. But I know I'm not.'

'Well, there must be a rational explanation. Perhaps the pregnancy is even more advanced than you think. She might have got pregnant before Ben went away.'

'Melanie insists that the baby was conceived the night Ben came back. But that was only a few weeks ago.'

'How can she be so certain?' asked Sarah.

'She says that's when her bleeding stopped.'

'But if she conceived then, the pregnancy wouldn't even be showing yet, would it?'

'No,' said Chanita. 'So something's not right.'

'Well she must simply be wrong about the dates.'

'That's what I told her.'

They settled into quiet reflection for a minute, letting the sun's rays bathe them in warmth. Sarah swallowed the last of her lemonade. It was going to be a thirsty day. 'I'd better get back up on that roof. Those tiles aren't going to steal themselves.'

'Sure,' said Chanita absently. 'It's just that…'

'What?'

Chanita turned her dark eyes directly on her. 'If Melanie's right, and she really did conceive the baby when she thinks, then…'

'What? Say it!'

'The only logical conclusion is that the pregnancy is proceeding at an unnaturally fast rate.'

Sarah frowned. 'How is that possible?'

'It isn't. Not in humans. But the gestation period for a wolf is a little over two months.'

Chapter Thirty

Midhurst, West Sussex, waxing moon

The pond was green and murky but Kevin Bailey knew there were fish in it somewhere, even though the little buggers were good at hiding. There had to be, it stood to reason. Fish lived in ponds – even a city dweller like him knew that. He wondered what kind lived in this one. Salmon? Trout? Carp? He'd find out soon enough.

He cast his line as far as he could into the still water. To do it right was a lot harder than it looked. The first few times his hook got tangled in the reeds growing around the bank and he had to fix the bait back on before continuing. He'd finally got the hang of that, but still couldn't catch any damn fish. He began to wonder if this was the wrong sort of pond.

He'd found the fishing gear stashed in the back of the Ford Galaxy he'd picked up when they made their escape from Gatwick. A couple of rods together with reels, hooks, floats, nets and buckets. There'd even been a book explaining how to fish, but Kevin didn't like to read books.

'Fishing can't be that difficult, can it?' he said to Mihai. 'It's not like fish are smart. They're not cunning like foxes.'

'No, chief.'

Kevin frowned. 'Don't call me that.' The Romanian boy had begun to copy the street kids that Liz had brought back from London. They were a bad influence, that lot. Kevin didn't want Mihai to grow up to be like them. It was one of the reasons he'd brought the kid fishing, to get him away from the others. They'd found this pond a few miles away from the hotel, where it was nice and peaceful. Just the two of them together, like in the old days. 'You should call me Grandpa Kevin, like you used to, kid.'

'Then don't call me kid,' said Mihai sullenly. 'Am not kid anymore.'

'All right,' Kevin agreed.

The kid was right, he supposed. He was certainly growing up fast. Already he was ten – or was it eleven now? Kevin had never been much good with dates. But he remembered well enough when he'd been that age himself. Already he'd been helping his old man in the butcher's shop at weekends and during school holidays. From the age of twelve he was preparing cuts of meat to sell to customers and had started making sausages even younger. When he turned thirteen, his father told him he was a man and allowed him to bone his first carcass. That was one of the proudest days of his life. He'd never bothered with school much after that. The school of life had been enough, and the army had taught him a lot too, even though he'd hated all that stomping about and shouting, 'Yes, sir!'

Now it was Kevin's job to teach Mihai how to be a man.

'You need to learn things,' he told the kid. 'Knowing how to do things will keep you alive.' He wished he'd understood that when he was young. Maybe then he'd have paid more attention and learned more. But that was the thing about knowing. You didn't know what you didn't know.

So far he'd shown the kid how to sharpen knives, pick locks, tie knots, build a fire and use a gun – although he'd made damn sure that Liz was well out of the way before he let Mihai shoot some rounds. He'd even tried to teach the boy to drive a car. Trouble was, his legs were too short to reach the pedals, even with a cushion jammed under his arse. But there would be plenty of time for driving when he grew a bit bigger. Right now, catching fish was the challenge and Kevin was beginning to wonder if he ought to have read that fishing book after all. They'd been here an hour and still not a nibble. But how hard could it be? Not so hard that he needed to read a bloody book.

'Practical skills, that's what you need in life,' he said to Mihai. 'Not stuff out of books.' That had always been true, and even more so now that shit had hit the fan in bucketloads.

The float at the end of Mihai's line began to waggle.

'Hey,' said Mihai excitedly. 'Fish is biting!'

'Really?' Kevin couldn't help feeling miffed that the boy had beaten him to it. But there was no doubt about it. The float disappeared beneath the surface, then bobbed back up. The kid really did seem to have something on the end of his line. Maybe just an old boot.

'Reel it in slowly,' said Kevin, trying to sound knowledgeable. Not that he'd ever been fishing before in his life. When he was growing up, there'd been nowhere for him to go. Back in those days the Thames was as black as pitch, more like an open sewer than a river. Factories had spewed toxic sludge straight into the water and the only fish in it then had been dead ones, drifting along the surface.

The float was moving now, making ripples in the water. Mihai began to wind it in and Kevin reached for the net. Soon a silver shape appeared, thrashing vigorously just beneath the surface. Kevin scooped it up and dropped it into the bucket.

'Well done,' he said, slapping Mihai on the back. 'That's carp, I reckon. Or maybe a catfish. Or … or …'

'We can eat it?' asked Mihai.

'Sure, kid.'

'Is not kid.'

'Yeah, okay. Let's –' A sudden rumble in the distance made Kevin stop. 'Get down!' he hissed. 'Quick! Out of sight!'

Soon the rumble became a growl. Kevin knew that sound. Motorbikes. They were approaching along the main road. He was glad he'd parked the Galaxy off the tarmac behind some big bushes. With luck the vehicle would be out of sight from the road. A lucky break like that could mean the difference between life and death. Although, come to think of it, Kevin had never done very well when it came to luck.

'Keep quiet, kid,' he whispered. 'Let's see who's coming.'

'Am not kid!'

Kevin wrapped a hand over the boy's mouth to shut him up. He still couldn't see the bikes, but their booming engines were growing to a full-throated roar. An arrhythmic phut-phut sound that seemed to fill his ears. They were coming straight for him.

'Bugger,' he whispered. He lay flat, pushing Mihai down too.

The bikes came closer and seemed to be slowing down. Kevin heard them ride off the road and onto the smooth grass that led down to the pond. The first rider came into view a few seconds later – a woman, clad all in black. A white wolf reared across the back of her leather jacket and she wore black wraparound shades beneath her long hair. She was a skinny sliver of a thing, dwarfed by her huge bike. She stopped at the edge of the pond and cut her engine.

A second biker followed, and then a third and a fourth. Men this time, with black wolves tattooed on their necks. Huge, muscular bastards, all wearing matching leathers emblazoned with the white wolf design. Kevin counted six riders including the girl. After they killed their engines a hush descended. Kevin motioned for Mihai to stay still, but that was hardly necessary. The kid was no fool. The two of them pressed their bodies to the ground behind a low rise.

The biker gang was no more than thirty feet away. 'We'll stop here and wait for nightfall,' said the girl. 'Bloodbath, you keep watch. The rest of us will get some sleep.'

Kevin eyed them anxiously. He'd hoped they were stopping just briefly for some water. Nightfall was hours away and he didn't fancy waiting for them to leave. But there was no chance that he and Mihai would be able to drive off in the Galaxy without waking them from their slumber, especially if one of them stayed on guard. And there was something about the gang that gave Kevin a creeping feeling of dread. Was it the wolves on their backs, or something else?

Still, he had an ace up his sleeve. Or slung over his shoulder, to be more accurate. An L110A1 5.56mm light machine gun, to give it its proper name. Jones had given it to him after the rest of the Welsh Guards were massacred on the rooftop back at Gatwick, and Kevin carried it everywhere, even when he went to bed.

Speaking of which, the bikers were settling down under the shade of a tree for some kip. They'd left their bikes a short distance away, and the big hairy geezer called Bloodbath was keeping watch.

Kevin watched him closely. As long as the lookout stayed awake, they were trapped. But it was a hot, sunny day. If the sentry nodded off …

It took nearly an hour, but eventually Kevin grew pretty sure that the guy had closed his eyes. He waited a minute, then tossed a small stone into the pond, making a soft splash. Nothing. The bikers didn't move.

He motioned to Mihai, trying to explain his plan with just hand signals. The kid was bright and seemed to get the idea quickly enough. He didn't look too happy about it though.

Never mind. Kevin had learned always to grab hold of opportunities when they came along, and an opportunity this good wasn't likely to come his way again. He'd always fancied a bike just like the one this girl was riding. The Galaxy was a practical family car, but it had no style.

Slowly, silently, with the kid following in his wake, Kevin began to creep toward the sleeping bikers, the machine gun cradled in his arms.

Chapter Thirty-One

The Pilgrims' Way

Breakfast was a protein bar; lunch a can of soup. Day after day passed, and only the flavours changed. After a while they all began to taste the same. Vijay almost envied Warg Daddy his bloody meals. At least the werewolf had variety. Some days a field mouse, others a pigeon or a blackbird; sometimes dead, but often still struggling desperately for life. Vijay offered the terrified creatures to him, then turned away in disgust as he bit off their heads, or snapped their necks before gobbling them down, fur, feathers, bones and all. His appetite for blood and freshly-killed meat seemed boundless.

'This is sick,' said Aasha. 'I can't believe we're doing this.'

Neither could Vijay, but he would do anything to learn the truth about Rose. Warg Daddy hadn't yet revealed any more about her. He had hardly said anything comprehensible since the day they'd found him. He was still too weak. Infection from his severed arm had spread through his body, and his fever had grown ever more consuming. Vijay had feared he would die without speaking another word, but his temperature had reached a crescendo, peaking three nights after they'd first stumbled upon him, and he had begun to show signs of improvement. A weaker man would have succumbed to death long ago, but Warg Daddy was strong, anyone could see that. Vijay feared what he might do when he fully regained his strength.

'Let's tie him to a tree,' said Aasha. 'It might not hold him forever, but it will slow him down if he tries to break free.'

Drake had done it, looping a rope around the man's thick wrist, neck and legs, allowing him some limited movement, but keeping him tethered to a stout trunk. With only one hand, it would be impossible for him to untie the knots, and even with superhuman strength the rope would be hard to break. As long as their visitor remained weak, he would be going nowhere.

Not that he showed any desire to leave. At night Warg Daddy lay on his back, staring up at the stars, seeming to glimpse objects that were too faint and distant for normal eyes to see. In his hand he held a dirty old coin, turning it relentlessly over and over between his thumb and forefinger. Heads, tails, heads, tails, in an endless meaningless dance. During the days he curled into a ball beneath his tree, his dark glasses clamped firmly over his eyes, hiding from the sun.

They had set up camp next to him, building a homemade shelter out of a sheet of tarpaulin strung over ropes suspended from nearby trees, making themselves comfortable on the stony ground with the help of cushions they had taken from the farmhouse and outbuildings where they'd stopped to shelter after crashing the car. It wasn't much of a life, and their progress on the road had ground to a halt. But until Warg Daddy revealed what he knew about Rose, there was no point going anywhere.

He refused all offers of shelter or water or company, accepting only the prey Vijay brought for him. Sometimes he babbled, mumbling half-heard words to people who were not present. At other times he lay still. He refused to answer any questions, or was perhaps not even aware they were directed at him.

But he was slowly returning to health, rebuilding his strength.

At the end of the tenth day, as twilight was settling andced the first stars winked into life, he finally began to speak lucidly.

'Why did you help me?' he whispered.

Vijay was sitting cross-legged on the ground next to the tent, watching the flames from the cookfire slowly die away. The embers burned a hot red against the deepening blue of the sky, and the charred logs crackled gently to themselves. Drake and Aasha were off somewhere, and Shadow had long since slunk away to hunt.

Drake had taken the shotgun with him but Vijay had his hand axe if he needed to defend himself. He reached for it now, even though Warg Daddy was securely tied and had not made any movement. Then he turned to look at his patient, not sure if Warg Daddy was addressing him or one of his imaginary friends – not that he showed a lot of love for the people he spoke to. A good half of the characters he addressed seemed to be enemies rather than friends.

'I was dead,' said Warg Daddy, gazing at the stars. 'You brought me back to life. Why?'

Vijay gave the answer he knew to be most simple and true. 'Because all life is precious.'

Warg Daddy chuckled nastily – a deep sound rumbling up from his chest. He rolled over to face Vijay. 'Even mine?'

'Sikhs believe in the brotherhood of man. Guru Nanak taught that it is not for us to judge others, and that we should leave that to God.' Vijay felt his cheeks growing warm in the cooling air. It seemed like a rather pompous speech to be making. 'Also, I wanted to hear what you know about Rose.'

Warg Daddy rolled onto his back again. 'The girl with the red hair.'

'Yes. You said you saw her again.'

'Why does it matter?'

'Because I care for her.'

'Care?' Warg Daddy turned the word over as if it were strange to him, and then fell silent. Vijay wondered if the conversation was finished. The big man had turned to the starry heavens once more and was studying something up there as if it was the most interesting sight he had ever set eyes on. The tiny pinpricks of light were multiplying as the vault that held them grew darker. They burned brightly, like tiny windows into infinity, each one sparkling with the pure light of God. But Vijay didn't need to look to the heavens to see the divine. God was all around him – in the grass, in the trees, in the smouldering fire – even in the dark heart of the man before him.

'Where did you see Rose?' he prompted.

Warg Daddy continued to stare at the sky, but he resumed his speaking. 'It was at Glastonbury, on the night of the moon. We came from the north, in search of adventure.' His gaze was distant, as if he were seeing the events he talked about play out in the lights in the sky.

Vijay glanced up, but all he could see was stars. He wanted to ask a hundred questions all at once, but he was afraid of interrupting Warg Daddy's flow now that he finally seemed to be talking.

'All the Brothers were there,' continued Warg Daddy. 'Vixen, Slasher, Bloodbath, Meathook ... and the rest.'

Vijay guessed these were the names of Warg Daddy's friends and associates. He shuddered at the bloodthirsty images they conjured, and clutched the axe tightly, steeling himself to continue listening. There would be violence and butchery in this story, he had no doubt, but he needed to hear it for himself.

'From a distance, we saw the fire on top of the Tor, and knew what it meant,' continued Warg Daddy. 'Prey. Meat. Food.'

'Was Rose on the Tor?' Vijay had heard of Glastonbury Tor – the strange mound that stood watch over the ancient town. 'What was she doing there?'

'She was with some guys.'

'What guys?'

Warg Daddy shrugged. 'Just guys. They'd lit a fire on the hilltop. Stupid. Bad things happen to stupid people. When we got there, the killing began.'

Vijay shuddered, his worst fears realized. 'Killing?' he whispered.

Warg Daddy turned once more to face him. 'The coin told me what to do. Who to kill and who to save.' His fingers were fumbling with the coin right now. Turning it over and over and over again. Heads, tails, heads, tails, heads, tails. The metal glimmered in the red glow of the smouldering fire. 'It was fate,' he muttered. 'I had no choice.'

Vijay gripped the axe ever more tightly, feeling his anger rise. 'Who did you kill?' he demanded. 'Did you kill Rose?'

The coin continued to turn. Heads, tails, heads, tails. 'I had no choice,' repeated Warg Daddy. 'The gods decided.'

Vijay sprang to his feet, holding the axe ready to strike. 'We always have a choice!' he yelled. 'Do you think it was fate that led me to save you?'

Warg Daddy said nothing, just turned the coin.

'It was my choice!' shouted Vijay. 'Do you think it was your destiny to be saved? I chose to save you! Now I wish I hadn't. Give me that stupid coin!'

He snatched the grubby metal disk out of Warg Daddy's surprised fingers and threw it to the ground, stamping it into the turf. Then he raised the axe. 'I should kill you!'

Warg Daddy shrugged.

'I should kill you now!' said Vijay.

Warg Daddy turned away, looking bored. 'I didn't kill her. I let her go. And her friends too. The coin told me what to do.'

Vijay lowered the axe. 'She's alive? Then where did she go? What happened to her?'

'I don't know,' said Warg Daddy. 'No more questions. I'm too tired.'

Chapter Thirty-Two

Midhurst, West Sussex

Liz had never been this happy. It felt strange to call herself Liz Jones, but she'd decided that if she had to be lumbered with any man's surname, then she would rather choose Llewelyn's than be stuck with the one her father had bequeathed her.

She and Llewelyn had got married in one of the hotel's small lounges. They had devised their own ceremony, with Lily as bridesmaid, and Kevin giving Liz away and also acting as Llewelyn's best man. With no one officially sanctioned to conduct the service, Liz and Llewelyn had spoken their own vows to each other.

'We make our own rules now,' Llewelyn told her.

'No,' said Liz, laughing. 'I make the rules.'

'All right then,' he conceded. 'As long as I have the final word.'

'You can have the final word,' she promised him, 'as long as that word is always "yes".'

A reception had taken place afterwards in the dining room. Samantha had organised the affair, assigning jobs to Kevin and the kids, and managing to produce a three-course dinner with tables adorned with freshly-cut flowers from the hotel's grounds.

Afterwards, Llewelyn had led her to a private cottage nestled in the grounds of the estate, and their honeymoon had begun. She hoped it would never stop.

She felt guilty about taking time off, but Kevin and Samantha had reassured her they had everything under control and could manage perfectly well without her for a few days. Still, Liz insisted on continuing to help out with the chores around the hotel. But now, she and Llewelyn were taking a break and watching the kids play on the bowling green at the side of the hotel.

Outdoor bowls wasn't the same as the indoor bowling that Liz was familiar with. She didn't really understand how to play, and by the looks of it, neither did any of the kids. But that didn't dampen their enthusiasm. Balls flew over the long grass as long evening shadows crept across the green, giving Liz some welcome respite from the sun. She was looking forward to another night with her husband.

The hum of an approaching vehicle roused her from her contented haze. 'Is that Kevin coming back?' she asked.

'No. That's a motorbike engine.' Llewelyn scooped up the SA80 assault rifle that he carried with him whenever he was outside, and shouted to the kids. 'Everyone inside! Now!'

Liz was on her feet in an instant, her heart beating fast. This was her worst nightmare. Strangers coming to the hotel to disrupt their peace. She rounded the kids up, making sure that none were left behind. Llewelyn was already sprinting towards the front of the hotel, the gun in his hands. The sound of the motorbike grew louder. 'Hurry!' shouted Liz.

'What is it?' asked Alfie.

'Strangers.'

The sense of bliss that had carried her these past days had vanished, to be replaced by a hard lump in her throat and a tight knot in her stomach. How quickly it had gone.

Yet somehow she had been expecting this all along. Even as Llewelyn had proposed to her, an anxiety had festered within her, taking root deep down. She had tried to deny it, but a part of her had always known that the hotel wasn't really a place where she could spend the rest of her days in peace, but no more than a temporary refuge from the war that raged beyond the gates. And now it had come to her door.

The motorbike appeared, barrelling up the gravel driveway at speed. Llewelyn took aim, but Liz grabbed the gun from him and thrust it down. 'Stop! It's Kevin and Mihai!'

The bike drew nearer and skidded to a halt before them. Kevin and Mihai leapt off. But any sense of relief at seeing them was short-lived. Mihai's eyes were filled with terror, and even Kevin looked scared.

'What's happened?' asked Liz. 'Where did you get this bike?'

'I nicked it,' said Kevin.

'From who?'

Mihai answered her. 'From gang of bikers. They come after us.'

Liz stared at her father in incredulity. 'You stole one of their bikes? You didn't think they might notice?'

'I shot out the fuel tanks of the other bikes,' said Kevin. 'But they followed us in the Galaxy.'

'They're coming now?' shouted Liz. 'Why did you leave the keys in the car? Why did you lead them back here? Why didn't you lure them away?'

'Oh yeah,' said Kevin. 'Good points. I didn't think of that. I don't suppose –'

But it was too late. The sound of the Galaxy's engine

was already audible as it turned off the main road and approached the hotel.

Llewelyn readied himself with his assault rifle. 'Kevin, get ready with your machine gun. Liz, get your Glock.'

Liz's hand reached for her automatic pistol. She had used it once, to kill Major Hall, the vampire at the evacuation camp, and had hoped never to use it again. But that had been a foolish wish. She grasped Mihai by the shoulder and pushed him behind her. 'Go inside,' she told him.

'How many bikers are there?' asked Llewelyn.

'Six,' said Kevin.

'Armed?'

Kevin nodded glumly. 'There's something else you ought to know about them. I think they might be werewolves.'

'What?'

'Just from the way they talked, like. And the way they looked. I might be wrong.'

'Dad,' said Liz, 'you've really screwed up this time.'

The Galaxy screeched to a halt at the end of the driveway behind the cover of some trees. The doors swung open and its black-clothed occupants jumped out. Even from this distance, Liz could see that they were armed with assault rifles and combat shotguns, and seemed to know how to use them.

'You think if we give them their bike back they might go away?' asked Kevin.

'I think they might want more than that,' said Llewelyn through gritted teeth.

Liz sniffed the air. When she was in vampire form she could easily smell werewolves, but now, at this range, she could smell nothing. She glanced at the sky. The moon was up, already rising above the roof of the hotel, but it wasn't yet full, and its milky light was tempered by the fiery evening sun. It was far too weak to power her transformation. Whatever happened next, she would have to face it in human form.

She didn't have to wait long for the fight to begin. The bikers spread out across the terrain, keeping under cover. Then at a sign from one of them, a woman, they opened fire.

Chapter Thirty-Three

A low semi-circular wall stood in front of the hotel and Liz dived for cover behind its solid brickwork. Llewelyn, Kevin and Mihai took up position next to her as bullets flew overhead. Liz turned to Mihai. 'I told you to go inside the hotel,' she hissed.

'Is no time.'

'Well, stay down out of sight. Lie flat on the ground.'

The bikers had spread out, taking up positions behind trees, hedges and stone pillars. They covered each other, maintaining a barrage of gunfire as they crept forward.

'We're surrounded,' said Liz. 'And outnumbered six to three. If they get around the side of the hotel they'll be able to break in through a window and take Samantha and the kids hostage. Our only chance is to negotiate a truce.'

'You think they'll be willing to talk?' asked Llewelyn.

'We have to try. We have no choice.'

She peered over the lip of the wall, but a gunshot

showered her face with brick dust and she ducked back. 'Stop your fire!' she shouted. 'We want to negotiate!'

The enemy gunfire came to a halt.

A young woman's voice called out. 'Throw down your weapons!'

'No, Liz,' whispered Kevin. 'They'll kill us.'

'Kevin's right,' said Llewelyn. 'If we give up our weapons, we'll have no bargaining chips.'

'We have none now,' said Liz. She called out, 'I'm going to show myself. Hold your fire!'

Llewelyn grabbed at her arm, but she shook him off. 'I have to do this. It's the only way.' She laid down her pistol and rose to her feet, her hands in the air.

Silence. No shots rang out.

The woman who had spoken stepped out from behind some shrubs, an assault rifle in her hands, aimed at Liz. She was barely a woman, more a girl. 'Step into the open where I can see you,' she commanded.

Liz did as she said.

'Take off your hat.'

Liz glanced nervously up at the sun. It was low on the horizon and had lost much of its strength, but when she removed her hat, its harsh rays pricked her skin, making her feel weaker.

'Stop!' The girl tasted the air, sticking out her tongue, lifting her face to the sky, her nose furrowed. She sniffed, turning this way and that.

She can smell me.

The girl finished sniffing and pointed at Liz. 'Watch that one, she's dangerous. The others, they're just meat.'

One of the bikers took a step forward, a shotgun cradled in his muscular arms. A wicked-looking blade was sheathed at his waist. 'Let me have them,' he muttered. 'Let me have them.'

'I'm not meat, biker boy,' shouted Llewelyn from his hiding place. 'So take a step back, unless you want a bullet in your brain.'

'Don't shoot!' shouted Liz. 'We'll give you whatever you want.'

The girl beckoned her closer. 'What can you give us that we can't take ourselves by force?'

'We'll give you back your bike, and any other vehicles that you want. No one needs to get hurt.'

The girl cast her gaze around the vehicles parked in front of the hotel. As well as the bike, the Foxhound stood next to the Volvo. Her eyes locked greedily on the armoured vehicle. 'That one.'

Llewelyn must have seen what she was looking at. 'No way, not the Foxhound,' he bellowed from behind the wall.

But Liz had seen a way to end the impasse peacefully, and she wasn't going to allow Llewelyn's obstinacy to scupper the deal. Besides, what did they need with the Foxhound now that they had the hotel as their refuge?

'Agreed,' she told the girl. 'You take the Foxhound, and you leave us in peace. I'm Liz, by the way. What shall I call you?'

The girl considered the offer before nodding her curt agreement. 'Vixen. It's a deal.' She lowered her rifle and addressed her fellow bikers. 'No one shoot. We grab the patrol vehicle and we get out of here. Bloodbath, take the wheel. Get that thing fired up.'

The biker with the shotgun scowled briefly at being ordered around, but seemed to brighten up at the prospect of driving the Foxhound. He skulked over to the vehicle, swung open the door and clambered inside. After a moment, the diesel engine roared into life, spluttering smoky fumes through its exhaust.

Liz wouldn't be too sorry to see the back of the old monster. It was a dirty, noisy, uncomfortable ride, and brought back too many memories of death and destruction. To give it up in exchange for an end to hostilities sounded like a good deal to her.

But it seemed that Llewelyn wasn't willing to let the

first love of his life go without a fight. He jumped up, the SA80 levelled at Vixen. 'Stop!' All eyes swivelled to him. 'I won't let you take it. You can have the Volvo and the Galaxy. Anything else. But not the Foxhound.'

'Llewelyn,' pleaded Liz. 'It's just a piece of metal.'

But that was the wrong thing to say.

He strode forward, marching toward the vehicle, where Bloodbath sat in the open cockpit. He pointed his rifle at the biker. 'Now, unless you want to start a bloodbath yourself, switch off the ignition and get out of there right now.'

In response, the engine of the Foxhound revved harder.

'I'm warning you,' said Llewelyn.

Vixen's rifle swung toward him.

'No!' screamed Liz.

From behind her, a stream of automatic fire burst forth as Kevin let rip with the machine gun. One of the bikers went down, his body riddled with holes. Llewelyn opened fire too, but Bloodbath ducked behind the wheel of the Foxhound, dodging the bullets.

Liz felt a rush as the scent of fresh blood from the dead biker filled her nostrils, but smell alone wasn't enough to overcome the weakness brought on by daylight. She was too slow to react, and she had left her Glock behind the low wall.

One of the bikers had perished in the first few seconds of combat, but now the others joined the battle, their guns blazing in fury. Bloodbath let off his shotgun from inside the Foxhound, the noise deafening inside the steel cockpit. Vixen screamed as she squeezed her trigger, and a hail of lead and steel sprayed out across the driveway. The other three stepped out into the open, two with automatic rifles, the third with a shotgun.

Liz ducked back, using the Foxhound as a protective barrier, and Kevin dropped down behind the cover of the wall. But Llewelyn stood in full view of enemy fire. A slug caught his lower leg and he stumbled onto one knee.

He raised his rifle to return fire, but before he could squeeze the trigger, a shotgun blast caught him fully in the chest. His body rocked under the onslaught of lead and he collapsed onto his back.

'No!' Liz was running before she knew what had happened. She skidded to a halt and dropped to Llewelyn's side. Around her she was dimly aware of more gunfire.

Her husband's body was broken and bloody and she cradled him gently in her arms. The strength had gone from him, and he felt like dead weight. He opened his eyes and cracked a half-smile for her. 'Happy ever after didn't last so long, eh, Liz?'

'Don't die on me!' she pleaded.

The Welshman coughed, his entire body jerking, and he spat out a mouthful of blood. 'I don't think I have much choice. Life's a bummer, eh? Just when you think everything's running smoothly, something comes back to bite you.' He coughed again, spattering blood across her face. 'Goodbye, Liz. Take care.'

His eyes rolled back into his head.

'No!' Salty tears stung Liz's eyes, and the smell of blood was overpowering. More shots echoed in her head as the gun battle raged around her. When she eventually lifted her eyes from Llewelyn's dead form, she saw that Kevin had killed the biker who had shot him, and had stopped to reload. Of the six werewolves, two were dead and one was injured. The girl, Vixen, had run to the motorbike and was kicking it into life. Bloodbath and the other two survivors looked ready to join her.

A high-pitched cry of rage rang out from behind Liz. Mihai. He was running toward the motorbike, Liz's Glock in his outstretched hand.

No.

But her voice was frozen. She watched helplessly as the boy took aim at the girl werewolf and fired a round. The gun jumped in his hand and the bullet went wide.

Leave her, mouthed Liz silently.

The other bikers piled into the Galaxy and set its engine roaring. The car screeched across the driveway, wheels spinning in the gravel. Vixen followed on her bike, but as she left the grounds of the hotel, she turned and let off a parting burst of gunfire.

'No!' screamed Liz. She watched as bullets danced across Mihai's skinny form, ripping into him and making him jerk like a rag doll.

Kevin was back on his feet, chasing after the departing bikers, the machine gun lurching in his arms. But the gang had already gone. And Llewelyn and Mihai lay still on the ground.

Chapter Thirty-Four

Haywards Heath, West Sussex

Suddenly, William Hunter was everywhere that Canning cared to look. At Leanna's side. Overseeing the northern men and women. Even engaged in whispered conversations with Canning's own spies and servants. Everyone seemed to like him, despite his loathsome swaggering and breath-taking arrogance. Perhaps because of that.

Fools! They are all fools!

Canning had quickly come to despise this strutting, pompous oaf. And yet, who could he blame for the northerner's meteoric rise to favour other than himself? He had sought him out and delivered him to Leanna in person.

You are the true fool, Canning! The biggest damned fool of all!

There was no fool worse than one who so eagerly brought about his own demise.

Now the northerner had taken over the training of the

Wolf Army, dismissing Canning's own efforts with a wave of his huge hand. 'These soldiers need proper training. You are not actually a military man, are you, General?'

'I have more experience of running a military campaign than you,' retorted Canning.

Hunter brushed away his protestations with a shrug. 'You know nothing of my background, or my experience.'

That was certainly true. The northerner had appeared out of nowhere and Canning's spies had proven useless at finding out much about him. There were rumours that he had been a soldier. Perhaps a commando, perhaps a regular infantryman. Some said he served with special forces, others that he had been a mere cook with no combat experience at all. Yet others whispered that his background was in the criminal underworld, a ruthless drugs baron who had ruled the cities of the north with an iron fist. Whoever he was, he had become Canning's number-one enemy.

Hunter poured scorn on Canning's maps and battle plans. The only tactic he approved of was Canning's use of human hostages to deter government airstrikes.

'You are cruel and ruthless, General,' he remarked on learning the reason the prisoners were chained to the tanks and armoured vehicles. 'I like that in a man.' He clapped Canning on the back in that over-familiar way that was so irritating. Then he leaned in close and whispered in Canning's ear. 'But you are pompous and ridiculous too. Take these absurd clothes that you wear.' He gestured at Canning's military uniform. 'You realise that your men laugh at you behind your back?'

Canning's lower lip curled down. The clothing he wore had been taken from Windsor Castle, and was the ceremonial uniform of the military knights of Windsor. Canning had selected it for its crimson tailcoat with gold epaulettes, not to mention its cocked hat complete with plume, and ceremonial sword at his belt. 'This uniform demonstrates my position of eminence,' he said. 'Contrary to what you claim, my soldiers respect me.'

If any did not, my spies would report them back to me. Surely, they would. Wouldn't they?

Hunter leered at him. 'Of course, General. I must have mistaken their respect for insolence.'

'At least Leanna still holds me in the highest regard,' countered Canning. 'I see that you have not been made commander of her army.'

'Not yet,' conceded Hunter. 'Just keep watching your back.'

Oh yes, I never stop. And I hope that you watch yours too, young William, or one of these days you may find a blade sticking out of it. Perhaps even this blade that I wear by my side.

Hunter obviously guessed what he was thinking. He pushed his horrible wolf's head into Canning's face. 'Let's hope nothing happens to me, eh? You realize that if anyone should cut my throat, Leanna would surely cut yours in return, whether or not your hand was holding the hilt of the knife. So it's in your best interest to ensure I stay alive.'

'Of course,' said Canning. 'The wind blows in your favour.'

For the moment. But the wind can quickly change direction.

Chapter Thirty-Five

Gatwick Airport, West Sussex

'So, the bulk of the UK's gold reserves are stored in the Bank of England.'

'In London?' queried Griffin.

'On Threadneedle Street, in the City of London. The depository is second only in size to the United States Federal Reserve in New York.'

Lieutenant Hastings had clearly done his homework, and was giving Griffin a detailed briefing on the situation regarding potential sources of gold. Bampton had flown in from the *Queen Elizabeth* to provide input on the military aspects of the operation.

Assuming that some kind of operation is even remotely feasible, thought Griffin. *Most likely this is a lost cause. A waste of valuable time.*

But remarkably, since being presented with Johnny Perez's greedy bargain, the nagging pain from Griffin's leg had dulled.

Hope is as powerful a narcotic as morphine.

It was a slender hope. But hope nonetheless. An adventure, and the prospect had lifted Griffin's spirits. Two hundred men might not be enough to win a war, but perhaps they could tip the balance in his favour.

'The gold is kept in a series of vaults below ground,' continued Hastings. 'In total, some four hundred thousand bars are stored there, each worth around half a million pounds. At least, that's what they were worth when money still held any value.'

Griffin allowed a whistle to escape from his lips. 'That ought to be enough to satisfy even our avaricious friends. The problem is how to get our hands on it.'

'I imagine that might not be a straightforward matter,' said Bampton.

'Fortunately,' said Hastings, 'although much of London is now under water, the City itself lies on higher ground and has not been flooded. With luck, the vaults will still be intact.'

'So we just have to get inside them.'

'That's right.'

'Any suggestions?' asked Griffin.

The intelligence officer nodded crisply. 'I think that high explosives are likely to be involved in some manner. I've been speaking to our experts. One of the main problems is our level of ignorance. We know that there are nine separate vaults arranged over two floors, but we don't really know how deep these go, or how much protection they have. You can understand why the Bank didn't make this information public. But the vaults were originally constructed in the 1930s so they may not be as well fortified as you think.'

Griffin raised one questioning eyebrow.

'Obviously they come equipped with solid steel blast-proof doors as standard.'

'Obviously.'

'There are a host of electronic security layers too, but

fortunately none of those will be operating now that the power grid is down. The vaults are encased by thick layers of concrete, but the Bank is built on soft London clay and there are sewers running beneath, dating back to the nineteenth century. These may well weaken the overall structure. It may not be entirely resistant to a well-placed bunker-busting bomb.'

Bampton leaned forward enthusiastically in his seat. 'So we carry out an aerial bombardment? Now you're talking!'

'It sounds indiscriminate, sir. But I believe it's the best chance we have. If we can score a direct hit on a vault, then our hope is that either the subfloor will collapse into the sewer network below, or else the ceiling of one or more vaults will cave in, exposing the gold to the surface.'

'More likely,' said Griffin, 'we'll simply bury the whole lot beneath a mound of rubble.'

'I'd say there's a fifty-fifty chance.'

'Do we have any better ideas?' asked Griffin.

'Well,' said Bampton, 'given that this Johnny Perez, with his band of hundreds of Britain's most wanted, can't think of a better way to do it, I'd say no.'

Griffin laughed and clapped his hands together. 'So the criminals have come to us for help in robbing our own bank. All right. I can't believe I'm sanctioning this, but let's do it. Let's try our best to pull off the world's biggest bank heist.'

Chapter Thirty-Six

Midhurst, West Sussex

Llewelyn was dead and there was nothing Liz could do to bring him back. But Mihai, although badly injured, was still alive. He was unconscious but his narrow chest rose and fell and Liz could hear his heart beating fast.

'Fetch the med kit from the Foxhound!' she ordered.

Kevin ran off while Liz stripped Mihai's shirt away to examine his wounds. Two bullets had entered the boy's abdomen and he was losing blood rapidly. She could bind the wounds with bandages and that might slow the bleeding, but to stop it completely she would need to remove any bullets lodged inside.

Kevin returned, the med kit in his hand. Liz took it and opened it, examining its contents. A pair of scissors and some tweezers. Rolls of bandages and cotton wool padding. Plastic gloves; some antibacterial gel; some painkillers and a length of plastic tube.

Kevin gave her an uneasy look. 'Can you save him?'

'I've just lost my husband. I'm damned if I'm going to lose my son too.' She snapped the gloves on and removed the tweezers. 'Hold him steady for me.' She knew she could rely on her father not to faint at the sight of blood.

Samantha appeared by her side. She must have seen everything from inside the hotel. 'What can I do to help?'

'We need clean sheets,' said Liz. 'There aren't enough bandages to stop the bleeding. We'll need to wrap him up tightly.'

Samantha went off, always calm in a crisis. Liz just hoped that she could remain calm herself. She pushed aside all thoughts of Llewelyn for now. Grief would have to wait.

With Kevin's help she rolled Mihai over onto his side and examined his back. One of the bullets had gone clean through, leaving a bloody exit wound, and she bound that first. Then, gripping the tweezers, she pushed their tips into the second wound, feeling for the bullet within.

The metal had fragmented, which had stopped it penetrating too deeply. She pulled out the first of the fragments, then felt for more. The smell of the boy's blood was pungent as it flooded out, the rich, life-sustaining elixir leaking into the ground. Mihai's heart beat furiously as it tried to compensate for the loss. The boy's chest rose as his fragile lungs filled with air, clinging desperately to life. Liz continued to draw shrapnel from the wound, feeling around until she was confident she had removed them all. When she was done, she bound the wounds as best she could, wrapping cotton sheets around to stop the bleeding.

'Will he live?' asked Kevin.

Liz could see the worry etched in his face and didn't know what to tell him. 'He's lost a lot of blood already.' She examined the sheets and saw that they were already stained red, particularly around the exit wound at the back. Blood continued to flow, even where she had tied the sheets. The white cotton was turning red before her eyes.

Unless she could stop it, he would surely bleed out. Yet what could she do with such basic medical supplies?

She made a snap decision. 'Bring me the body of one of the werewolves.'

'Liz?' Her father stared at her uncomprehendingly.

'Just do it. There's no time to waste.'

While Kevin went off to fetch a body, Liz grasped the scissors from the med kit. She lifted Mihai's hand and carefully cut a slice across his wrist using one blade of the scissors. Blood began to seep from a vein, but it quickly dried up. Too much blood had already been lost and the boy's blood pressure was falling. Liz could sense his heart begin to labour and falter as it struggled to keep him alive. He might only have minutes remaining. She punctured an artery in her own arm, and inserted one end of the plastic tubing into the incision. Blood immediately began to flow through the tube.

She passed the other end to Samantha. 'Can you insert this into Mihai's vein?'

Samantha grasped the gist of Liz's plan immediately. She crouched down, taking gentle hold of the tubing and doing as Liz requested. Then she tore off two lengths of cotton sheet and used them to bind the tube to the wrist.

It seemed to work. Blood flowed from donor to recipient under the power of Liz's beating heart. Vampire blood had healed her own wounds once before – perhaps it could heal another. It was a crazy risk, but she would grasp at any chance to save the Romanian boy's life.

Kevin returned, dragging the body of the werewolf called Bloodbath along the ground. 'Where shall I put it?'

'Bring it up close to me.'

He did as instructed, depositing the corpse right next to her. Then he took in what she was doing. 'You're giving the kid your blood?'

'Yes. But he's lost a lot. I'll need to replenish my own.'

She could already feel herself weakening. The blood continued to flow. Artery to vein; vampire to human;

mother to child.

Liz pressed her lips to the neck of the dead werewolf. She drew them back to expose her fangs, and bit into the dead flesh, finding the carotid artery nestling in the shadow of the man's spine. The liquid was still hot, fully oxygenated, and strong with the taste of lycanthropy. She sucked, drawing it into her mouth and swallowing it down. She could feel it inside her, passing its energy to her, and in turn to Mihai. The boy stirred, his heart rate slowly increasing, his lips parting as his lungs filled with air.

Above her the moon was growing bright as the sun relinquished its hold, and Liz felt her strength recover. She fed her power to Mihai, her vigour coursing into his veins.

Heal him. Make him live. It's all I ask.

Her heart beat steadily. Drop by drop, the lifeblood flowed from her body into his, reaching into every corner of his being, conveying its restorative energy wherever it was needed. This was the greatest gift Liz could give – finer than rubies or gold, more precious even than a mother's love. Her nostrils flared at its sweet scent. She continued to sup from the corpse at her side, draining it until it was nothing more than a dried-out husk. Meanwhile, her skin drank in the moonlight, turning its cold silver into a dark and terrible power.

Mihai's heart fluttered. It quickened, then began to race out of control. Liz could feel the pressure building in his veins, pushing back against her own lifeblood. His eyelids flickered. His arms convulsed. His breathing turned to a breathless pant.

'What's happening?' asked Kevin. 'Is he waking up?'

The boy's chest swelled as he gulped down more and more air, his heart now pounding at impossible speed. Blood rushed through his veins like a river.

Then his heart shuddered suddenly to a halt.

Liz placed her hand against his breast, feeling for life, but there was no further movement of the diaphragm. She listened, but the pumping of his heart and the rhythmic opening and closing of his lungs had ceased. 'No,' she muttered. 'Not now. Not after all this.'

Her blood should have saved him. Vampire blood; full of healing power. She had given him all she could. So why had it failed?

With her free arm, she placed a hand to his chest and began to pump. She pushed down hard and felt his diaphragm rise in response. She tried again. And again.

Still nothing. A minute passed, with no result.

'You did your best, love,' said Kevin, his voice catching. 'No one could have tried harder.'

'It's not over yet,' she cried. But there was nothing more she could do. Mihai's heart lay still, his lungs deflated. The flow of blood from arm to arm had ceased. The boy's veins were filled to bursting. So why had he died?

An explosive anger was building inside Liz and she could feel the change coming on. Her skin was crackling, her teeth pushing through, her fingernails twisting into corkscrew claws as sharp as razor blades. She ripped away the plastic tube that linked her to the boy like an umbilical cord, hurling it to the ground in frustration.

No longer tethered, she rose to her feet and roared at the night. To lose the two people she cared for most in one day – it was too much to bear. The darkness swept through her like cold fire, turning her thoughts as black as tar. If she could not have life, she would have death. No one would be safe from her wrath this time. Especially not her father, who had brought this disaster to their door. Kevin had gone too far this time. She would make sure he never did again.

Both Kevin and Samantha drew back, noticing the change; sensing the danger. Liz roared with rage, splitting the night with her anger.

Then Mihai's body arched in a sudden spasm. His mouth opened wide as he stole a breath of air from the night. His lungs inflated and his heart rushed back into motion, beating once, twice, three times, before settling into a regular rhythm. Liz could hear it pounding, as loud to her ears as a ticking clock.

'The kid's alive,' gasped Kevin. 'You bloody well brought him back from the dead.'

Liz gaped at the boy. Of course. A vampire must die before being reborn into the ranks of the undead. Just as Liz herself had died. Now Mihai had become like her. She dropped to her knees at his side.

'Forgive me,' she whispered to him. 'I had no choice. It was the only way to save you.'

If she had regrets at what she had done they were overwhelmed by the sense of relief that flooded her. The wound in the boy's arm where she had poured her own blood into him had already healed. The holes where the bullets had torn his flesh were knitting themselves closed as she watched. In seconds his youthful body was whole again, and perfect. She held her face over his, letting hot tears course down her cheeks, giving thanks to the silver moon that shone down from on high.

Mihai's eyelids quivered. His hands jerked. Then his eyes shot open, as bright as the moon above and the colour of liquid gold. He opened his mouth, showing her rows of pearly white teeth.

'Is back,' he said with a grin.

Chapter Thirty-Seven

The Pilgrims' Way

The sun ruled the sky, and no relief came from its dreadful gaze. The air shimmered with heat, and dust blew across the parched land on dry winds. Yet little by little, Warg Daddy felt his strength returning.

Each day the kids brought him food – field mice, birds, once a rabbit. Finger food, really. More snacks than meals. But it was the first he'd eaten since ... he didn't know how long it had been. *A lifetime ago. I was another man when last I ate. I was Leader of the Pack. Now I am nothing. I am these children's pet monster.*

They had bound him with ropes around his wrist and neck and tethered him to a tree. The girl had insisted. *And with good reason.* He would have torn them limb from limb if he had the strength. That girl was a smart one – smarter than the boy with skinny arms and glasses, who clutched his little axe to his chest like a teddy bear.

I am his teddy bear now; a larger-than-life tame creature to feed and talk to.

Warg Daddy chuckled to himself. He didn't mind being a pet, for a short while at least. It was a novelty having someone to look after him. He had always looked after himself, ever since fleeing from his father's kicks and punches as a boy. But he was no longer strong enough to be self-reliant.

I am weak. I lost an arm, and worse, my pride.

But he would not remain weak forever. The sun might rule the day, but at night the moon was waxing, gaining in power with every passing night. When the full moon rose, his strength would come flooding back, as mighty as a spring tide.

When I am strong, these kids will be my pets, rope or no rope. And there will be no more snacks and treats. I will sup their blood and swallow their flesh.

Or perhaps he would permit them to live. He didn't know. He didn't know anything. The boy had snatched his coin from him and stamped it into the dirt. He could see it, sticking in the ground like half-buried treasure, glinting when it caught the sun. Tantalising him, just out of reach. No matter. It would be safe there until he was strong enough to reclaim it.

When the moon comes. When I am strong again.

Then the coin would decide. A quick flip, and all would be known.

Heads: butcher them. Slaughter them, and pull out their entrails. Feast on their flesh and scrape meat from their bones.

Tails: show kindness, and let them go.

Kindness. That was a novel thought. In the old days, it would never have crossed his mind. What good was kindness? Kindness was for weaklings. He hadn't become Leader of the Pack by being kind to anyone – not to his friends, and especially not to his enemies.

Kindness. That's what these kids had shown him. No one had ever done that before. All his own father had shown him was the back of his hand and the toe of his boot. Perhaps he could show the kids some kindness in return.

The skinny child, Vijay, was big on kindness. And compassion. Forgiveness too. That kid could talk forever about being nice to other people. Warg Daddy might eat him just to shut him up, except that there was so little meat on him it would hardly be worth the bother. The other boy, Drake, would make more of a meal. But the sister, Aasha, looked tastiest. And of the three she trusted him the least. *Clever girl. She deserves to live.* Warg Daddy liked her. He'd always had a soft spot for insolent chicks.

The others, too. A strange and unfamiliar idea entered his head. *I am growing fond of them.* If life had been different, he might have had children of his own.

I never found the right woman. I never looked.

Leanna wasn't the maternal type, nor Vixen. Anyway, Leanna and Vixen had made their own choices, selecting a future for themselves that didn't include him. Every woman he'd ever known had betrayed him eventually. *Apart from the ones I betrayed myself.* That had happened quite often, now he came to think of it.

What to do, then? That was the question. That was always the question.

He dragged himself across the ground, pulling the rope that bound him into a taut line, and stretched out his one arm as far as he could. His fingers grasped first at empty air, then burrowed into dry soil, but the coin remained tantalisingly out of reach.

He retreated again from the burning sun, taking refuge in the cool shadow of his tree. As long as the coin remained buried, so would the answers to his questions. But that didn't stop him from asking them.

Should he eat the kids?

Heads: eat them. Tails: don't eat them.

Simple.

But was that even the right question? His head began

to throb at the thought. If he didn't know what question to ask, there was no hope for him. He would be stuck here forever in a state of not knowing. Eventually the kids would grow bored of their pet and move on. Even the skinny kid would surely exhaust his supply of kindness in the end. Then Death, that low-life swindler, would return with his pale horse and his chess board, eager to cheat him again.

So he needed to find the right question, or else he would perish.

Here was a better one, then. A question that only the coin could decide: which kid would he eat first?

Chapter Thirty-Eight

Christmas Common, Oxfordshire

There was only a pale moon tonight, softly silvering the clouds, and a splash of bright stars splayed like tiny lanterns across the midnight blue of the heavens. But to Ben's wolf eyes the lay of the land was clear enough. The dip of a scarp to one side, leading down into the hollow of the old chalk pits. To the other, the steady rise of Watlington Hill, inked deep in tree shadow. On the road behind, the town he and James had just left. It was a part of their regular patrol, though usually Ben took day duty while James went out alone at night. But on this occasion Ben had insisted on joining his young protégé.

'I don't need you,' James had protested. 'It's better if we go alone. If you come with me at night, who will do the day patrol tomorrow?'

'I'll manage both,' said Ben. 'I'd like to join you for a change. We never get to talk these days. We're like ships that pass in the night.'

'What do you want to talk about?' asked James.

Sharp suspicion was etched into his features, confirming the worst of Ben's fears. James was definitely up to something. It wasn't simply that he had become withdrawn and solitary. He was hiding some secret, and Ben was determined to find out what.

'Nothing in particular,' he said. 'Just a catch-up.'

'All right,' said James with a shrug. 'If you want to. But I really don't need any help.'

'I know that. This is just to chat. Two old friends on the road together. Like when you took me to Joan's house.'

James flinched at the mention of Joan's name, and Ben immediately regretted it. James and the old woman had shared a close bond.

'It's not your fault that she's dead,' said Ben. 'It's Leanna's fault.'

'It was the fault of the wolves who killed her,' said James. 'And they paid for it with their lives.'

Ben nodded. The three werewolves who came to Joan's house at Virginia Water had been turned with James' own blood, and shared his power to transform at will. They had come to make him their leader, to mount a rebellion against Leanna, the mad queen. James had rejected their offer, but not before being tempted. The lure of becoming ruler of all werewolves and bringing an end to the war with humans had been a strong enticement. But the rebel werewolves had not come with peace in mind. They wanted James to lead them into war. They had yearned for slaughter.

Joan had given it to them, taking down two of the wolves with her shotgun, and Ben had killed the third, jumping to Joan's defence while James stood powerless to one side, caught in dreams and yearnings. But Joan herself had been mortally wounded in the fight. The old woman died in James' arms.

Ben knew that James' failure that day had left a scar on

his heart that time hadn't healed. Instead it had festered. Ben ought to have intervened sooner. He ought to have been there when his friend needed him most. Instead he had been bound up with Melanie and her pregnancy. Well, it was time to put that right now.

James bounded along the road that led from the town. As usual they had encountered no one on their patrol. That was just how Ben liked it. But not James. As he ran ahead, his sandy fur dark beneath the cloudless sky, Ben could tell that there was a hunger in the boy's limbs. A desire for savagery.

'Slow down,' called Ben. 'I'm too old to keep up with you. Let's take a breather.'

James slowed reluctantly, then stopped and squatted on his haunches, waiting for Ben to catch up.

Ben came and lay beside him, front paws stretched out on the warm surface of the road, still full of the day's heat, his chest heaving from the exertion. He hadn't been lying about struggling to keep up. James had grown into a strong young man, broad-chested and tall. The skinny boy he had once been had all but vanished, and in wolf form he was truly formidable.

'So,' said James, without turning his head, 'what did you want to talk about?'

Ben parted his jaws wide in a grin. 'I'm that obvious, huh?'

'You are.' At last, a hint of a smile crept across James' face. A glimpse of the boy he had once been. Ben wished he could have met him before all this happened, before James had been bitten, before Samuel had been taken from him, before Leanna had killed his parents. Before all the damage was done. How could one man endure so much tragedy and not be overwhelmed by it? Perhaps they couldn't. It was clear that something within James was badly broken.

'I may as well come out and say it,' said Ben, 'since I'm so transparent.'

'Say what?'

'Say that I'm worried about you.'

'There's no need to be.'

'Well, I disagree.' Ben sat up and scratched his side with his paw, enjoying the cooling night breeze against his sweating flank. 'We've spent a lot of time together, and I like to think that we're good friends.' He sat back, waiting for James to acknowledge it.

'We are good friends.' James turned to look at him at last. 'You know we are.'

'Good. So you know that you can share anything with me, don't you? If there was something worrying you, for instance.'

'There's nothing worrying me.'

'Honestly?'

'Honestly.'

'Well then, since we're being direct, let me say what's bothering me.'

'Okay,' said James.

'I'm concerned that you're not drinking your wolfsbane tea.'

A silence greeted him and Ben knew that he'd hit home. He and James had discovered the properties of wolfsbane tea while at Joan's house. Regular drinking of tea made from the plant's leaves had the power to bring a werewolf's most violent urges under control. The plant was literally a lifesaver. When Ben had first turned, he had tried to bite Melanie. Now, with his daily dose of herbal tea, the impulse to taste human flesh was entirely gone. He was back in control. If James had stopped drinking his, he was a danger both to himself and to the others.

'You –' began Ben.

But James interrupted him, raising one paw. 'Shh!' He rose to all fours and lifted his nose to the air. His nostrils flared as he took a long sniff. 'Do you smell that?'

Ben sniffed too, straining to catch whatever it was that James had sensed. It didn't take long for him to smell it too. A faint trace, far off and carried by the summer breeze. But unmistakeable in its acrid bitterness. Smoke. 'It's coming from the village.'

'Someone's lit a fire. Come on, up the hill.' James bolted away immediately up the steep, wooded slope.

Once they were through the trees the ground became open scrubland and Ben could see further, but they were the wrong side of the hill to see what was happening in Christmas Common. Instead Ben filled the void with his own terrible imaginings, picturing the house in flames, the women dead. And it was all his fault. If he had stayed behind as he was supposed to, he would have been there when the attackers came. But here he was. Far away, and far too late.

He bounded desperately after James, almost catching up with him as they crested the hill. There they stopped to take in the reality of the scene.

Christmas Common lay directly before them, half a mile away across open fields. Three houses were on fire, black smoke billowing up into the still air before drifting gently toward them on the breeze.

'Come on,' said Ben. He ran down the hillside taking the straightest, shortest route. The ground was rough, with long untamed grass, but it was quicker than going the long way by road. James ran behind him, catching up as they neared the edge of the village.

Close up it was impossible to see much apart from tongues of fire between the trees. The roar of the flames grew louder, as did the stench of the smoke. And then too, the cries of men going about their evil business. Ben's blood pounded in his ears, and not just from the exertion of the run. No matter how much the wolfsbane may calm him, if someone hurt Melanie he would tear their body into scraps.

He and James burst out together onto the road that ran through the village. Immediately before them stood a house, a single-storey dwelling converted from an old barn. The wooden structure of the building was all that remained, standing black against orange incandescence. Already the fire had taken the windows, and the door too. Now the rafters of the roof were immersed in flame and looked ready to collapse at any second. Sparks and cinders flew into the air and it was impossible to get closer because of the heat.

Ben turned away from the fire and ran farther along the road, passing another inferno on his right. This building too was well on its way to total destruction and nothing could save it from its doom. But that wasn't Ben's main concern. His own home lay just around the next bend. Melanie's home.

When he reached it he breathed a sigh of relief. The house was still there, with no sign of fire. But his relief was short-lived. A Ford Transit van was parked on the road and a group of dark figures stood in front. The men were dressed in black clothing with hoods pulled low over their faces. Ben counted six – four carrying plastic removal crates filled with the trophies from their looting spree, one with a jerry can of petrol, and one with a shotgun.

'Looters,' he whispered to James, motioning for them to draw back into the safety of the shrubs at the roadside. 'They haven't seen us. Let's wait and watch.'

The men unloaded their loot into the back of the van and slammed the door shut. But they weren't finished yet. They looked up and down the road, sizing up the houses and considering their next target.

At Ben's side, James gave a low growl. Ben touched him lightly, but the growl became a snarl.

'What's that noise?' said one of the raiders.

'A dog?'

'I fucking hate dogs.'

The man with the shotgun approached them. 'I'll get rid of the bastard.'

James' snarl became a roar.

'What the fuck?'

Lycanthropic

James stood up, showing himself to the thieves.

The shotgun blasted, as loud as a firecracker at close range, but James had already moved. Ben dodged the opposite way, and they closed in on the man as he spun his gun round wildly. The shotgun cracked again, discharging the second barrel, but the man's leg was already between James' teeth and the shot went wide overhead. Ben left James to it and threw himself at the second man.

The thief struck out with his plastic tray, but that made a useless weapon against a wolf. Ben dashed the flimsy carton aside and closed his jaws around his victim's neck, spraying hot blood as red as the dancing firelight.

The rest of the looters fled for the van, two in back and two in front. One was slow and James took him before he could reach safety. His three compatriots had only their own skins in mind and slammed the doors closed as their friend lay dying.

Ben stood to watch them go, but James hadn't finished. He hurled himself at the front windscreen, falling on it with his full weight and breaking the glass like ice cracking on a frozen pond. Two terrified faces greeted his arrival in the front seats of the Transit, and in seconds the inside of the van was as bloody as a butcher's block.

The final member of the gang made a bid for freedom through the back doors. But Ben was waiting for him. An image of Melanie loomed up in his mind as the man's face twisted into horror, and he lunged at his victim's throat, ripping it out without mercy.

When it was done, the bodies lying in the road, the burning houses behind, Ben and James turned to grasp each other. They hugged, brothers united in blood once again. The danger was over, but Ben would never rest easy knowing how close he had come to losing everything.

Chapter Thirty-Nine

Midhurst, West Sussex

They buried Llewelyn at first light, at the start of the day before the sun grew too strong for Liz to handle. She had stayed beside his body since he had been killed, refusing to leave her husband's side until he was properly buried. She would sleep after the funeral, if she could. Samantha had tried to lead her inside, but she refused to go. When Dean had been killed by werewolves back in London, Liz had intended to give his body a proper burial, but then the nuclear strike had erased London from the map.

Kevin had dug a grave six feet deep. 'I could try to make a coffin,' he said, 'but I'm not sure I could do a good job.'

'No matter,' said Liz. 'Llewelyn was never big on ceremony or custom. He'll be happy enough being put in the ground just as he is.'

She stroked Llewelyn's waxen face, doing her best to

absorb a picture of how he looked. He was no longer quite the man she remembered, and she knew that her memory of his face would dim further as time passed. She could sometimes hardly picture how her own mother had looked. The likeness of her police partners, Dave Morgan and Dean Arnold were already beginning to merge in her mind, taking on a single heroic aspect – solid, strong, and dependable. One day her remembrance of Llewelyn's boyish face would soften and fade, just as his flesh decayed in the ground, and she would be left with just a faint recollection of how he had once been. She ran a finger across his thick brow, trying to absorb the feel of his strangely cold skin, touching his fine golden-red hair, his fair eyebrows, his short, stubby nose. Her hand caressed his flinty jaw and tender lips, buried amid a field of flaxen stubble. More than anything, she longed to look once more into those pale blue eyes, and catch a glint of humour there as he teased her. But she could not.

His voice hadn't gone, though. It was still with her, inside.

Did you really think I'd let you have the last word, Liz?

'No,' she mouthed to his still form, gripping his fingers tightly and splashing bitter tears across his chest. 'I never thought that.'

After the sun had risen and Kevin had finished his digging, Samantha came to fetch her. 'It's time,' she said.

Liz stood up, letting Samantha's hand close around hers. Two widows together. If anyone could understand what she was going through, it was Samantha. But Samantha said nothing more to try to comfort her. Perhaps she knew that words meant nothing now.

Liz was glad of the dark glasses that hid her bloodshot eyes from the sun and from the others. They had all gathered. Kevin, Mihai, Leah, Alfie and the other kids. She had never seen them so subdued. They clustered together, a short distance away from Llewelyn's body, not knowing what to do.

Nobody knows what to do.
There were no rules anymore.
We make our own rules now.

In the immediate aftermath, Liz had felt hot anger toward Kevin, who had inadvertently brought about her husband's death through his usual stupidity. But she had put that aside. Llewelyn had never harboured grudges, and had always been quick to forgive. Now that he was gone, Liz needed all the family she could get. And Kevin was clearly full of remorse. His night-long digging of Llewelyn's grave was perhaps just the start of his attempts to make amends for what he'd done.

Now he cleared his throat and began to speak. 'Llewelyn Jones was a giant among men. Brave and fearless. A soldier. A husband. A friend.'

Liz stared at her father in astonishment. He had never made a speech before in his life.

'He gave his life protecting the ones he loved,' Kevin continued. 'He didn't deserve to die.' He cleared his throat then ground to a halt, apparently out of words.

'He was a good man,' said Samantha, picking up where Kevin had stopped and giving Liz's hand a squeeze. 'We will never forget him.'

'Never,' said Alfie. 'He was a boss.'

Liz wondered about saying something herself, but there seemed no need.

I can still talk to you whenever I want, can't I?
I'll be here, Liz. You know where to find me.

No one seemed to know what to do next. Llewelyn's body needed to go into the hole, but how it was going to get there was anyone's guess. Liz released Samantha's hand and squatted down at Llewelyn's shoulders. 'Take his feet,' she told her father. Together they shifted the body over to the grave, and lowered it in.

Not very dignified this, Liz?
It would be a lot easier if you weren't so damn heavy.
Fair point.

When it was done, she tossed a handful of earth into the hole. It scattered across his face, obscuring the features she had come to know and love so well. The dirt clumped hideously over his mouth and nose, and she had to resist an urge to reach down and brush it away. But she knew it wasn't Llewelyn they were about to bury beneath clods of cold, dark soil. The man himself had fled his mortal cage and had lodged himself inside her head.

There's room for me in here, Liz?
There's room. Even for your enormous ego.

She stood at the graveside, watching the shadows within slowly retreat as the sun rose higher. The back of her neck was beginning to burn under its growing strength.

So, what next?

Llewelyn's death had crystallised a fear that had been building in Liz's heart ever since they'd arrived at the hotel. A knowledge that nowhere was safe and that the greatest danger was seeking false security. They had tried to barricade themselves away, but just like the people huddling inside the evacuation camps, the enemy had come for them eventually.

'Ashes to ashes, dust to dust,' mumbled Kevin. Words that had been spoken so many times and by so many before. *Birth, life, death.* That was the inevitable cycle. Over and over and over again.

Liz had seen enough of death and had buried far too many of her loved ones. She was sick of fighting. But sometimes fighting was the only choice you had. You had to protect what mattered most. Llewelyn was dead, but Mihai, Samantha and the others depended on her and she wouldn't let them down. If she made the wrong choice now they would die too, and Liz wasn't ever going to let that happen.

'Come on,' she said to Kevin. 'Let's get this hole filled. Then we can talk about where to go.'

'We're moving on, then?' asked Kevin.

'We're moving. We have to.'

Duty. It had always been the force that drove her. Perhaps it was a cushion. A comforter. Without Llewelyn at her side, she needed it more than ever.

Pull yourself together Liz. Don't fall apart on me now.

'Just don't leave me,' she whispered. 'Promise me you won't leave me on my own.'

All right, Liz. I'm still here. Just try to man up a bit. This is no time for crying like a girl.

'I wasn't crying,' she said, ignoring the worried look Kevin was giving her. But there was no point lying. Especially to a voice inside her own head. She let the tears cascade freely down her cheeks like streams in a Welsh mountain valley.

Chapter Forty

Haywards Heath, West Sussex

The first rays of the morning sun reached into Leanna's bedchamber, casting gentle shadows across the satin sheets and warming her face with their soft caress. She rolled in her bed and took in the sleeping form of Will Hunter, stretched out next to her.

The wolfman lay on his chest, his arms splayed out across the sheets in the carefree abandon of sleep. His chest was broad and hard, his brawny arms set as thick as trunks. Her gaze roamed over his bare back, taking in its sculpted shape, ridged and taut and dappled by sunlight.

The skin on his arms was red and mottled in places, a result of the radiation burns that were common among the northerners. Unconsciously her hand brushed her own scarred face where the acid thrown by Helen Eastgate had burned her. Will had asked her about those scars the first time she had taken him to her bed, but she had rebuked him firmly.

'Do not ask me where they came from, William Hunter. If you wish to live, never refer to them again!'

He hadn't asked a second time.

His musclebound form undulated as his lungs slowly filled and emptied. She allowed her eyes to linger over the buff cheeks of his bum, before turning her attention to his wolf's head.

The sight of it nestling on the pillow at her side still had the power to unsettle her. Like her, Will was part human, part beast, yet unlike her he bore his animal nature on permanent display. A coat of black hair spread over much of his body, thickening into a carpet over his chest, before flowing up his bull neck and covering his entire face and head with fur. He wore it long at the back, reaching down to his shoulders, but over his face it grew fine and short. Leanna reached out and stroked it.

His snout wrinkled, and he turned in his sleep, bringing his huge face close to hers.

She stared at it, marvelling at the broad muzzle and jaws, parted to reveal a hint of sharp fangs and a long, muscular tongue. She remembered that tongue from the night before and smiled at what it was capable of. It lolled out of Will's mouth now, leaving a trail of drool on the sheets.

Her new bed-mate disgusted her, yet he was curiously and compellingly attractive too.

Grotesque? Yes. Unnatural? Without a doubt. Yet what was natural anyway? A virus – not some man-made biological experiment gone wrong – had cursed, or blessed this man with his freakish form. Anyone who believed that Nature was good and that everything artificial was bad was a halfwit.

As a biologist, Leanna knew better.

There was nothing cosy or comforting about Nature. The natural world punished failure relentlessly, thereby nurturing and rewarding the most ruthless, cunning, resilient and dangerous lifeforms possible.

Predators. Parasites. Pathogens.

Every creature that walked the earth lived by consuming others, whether animal or plant. Every ecological niche was waiting to be exploited and occupied by some invading organism. Every animal that lived would one day die, to be replaced by another, even more finely adapted to exploiting its habitat. And every species on the planet existed under constant threat of extinction, as rival species competed for the same resources. The only real choice in life was whether to kill or be killed. And if you lacked the strength or ability to kill, then to be killed was your fate.

Extinction would soon come to humans, as lycanthropes superseded them. Already they existed only as food. Their sole purpose – to be eaten.

Hunter stirred in his sleep, his arms shifting as he rolled.

Is your fate to live or die, my sweet?

The choice was not his to make. It was hers, and she had not yet decided.

On one hand, he pleased her at night, and she had not yet tired of him. He also maintained the northerners under some semblance of control. And he served as a counterweight to Canning, keeping her general in check and reminding him that he too was expendable.

But Will was not without his faults.

He had talents, but intelligence wasn't one of them. He acted boastfully – disparaging and mocking Canning, sometimes to his face. It wouldn't do to allow him to undermine her general's authority. Regrettably she still needed Canning. And there were signs that Hunter was growing in his arrogance, and might even harbour designs on her throne. If she ever suspected him of treason, she would slit his throat in a second.

She reached across the bed and drew a sharp fingernail across his back, leaving a line of red droplets on his skin in the wake of her touch.

He snuffled, his head turning. His eyelids flickered open, revealing golden orbs sunk in dark rims. Stiff whiskers twitched and his blackened lips parted in what she took to be a smile. But it was hard to tell when a wolf was smiling. It might have been a sneer. 'Leanna. My love.'

She sifted his words for signs of duplicity, but couldn't be sure whether he was being insincere or not. She brought her fingers to her lips and licked them clean of salty blood, studying his face to see how he would react.

A frown compressed his features and he pushed his hand to his back. It came away smeared with blood. He rolled onto his side to face her. 'What have you done?'

'Just a gentle scratch, my love. A trickle of blood to whet my appetite.'

'You feed from me now? You take too much for granted, my queen.'

'Do I?' She swung her leg across him, forcing him onto his back, and sat astride him, her thighs gripping his. He was twice her size and strong in flesh, but she possessed an inner steel, born of lycanthropy, that none could match, not even the mighty Will Hunter. 'Don't ever forget that you are my property and I can do whatever I want with you,' she told him.

Rebellion flashed across those burnished eyes, but it was quenched a second later as he remembered his place. He nodded in submission. 'And what do you require from me this morning, my queen?'

She smiled and brought her lips to his. One day she would surely have to rid herself of him, just as she had ridded herself of other tools that outgrew their usefulness. But not today. For now he was still hers.

She moved her body against his, feeling his flesh respond. 'I think you know what I want.'

Chapter Forty-One

Christmas Common, Oxfordshire, full moon

The morning after the attack, nothing remained of the burned houses but blackened stumps. A few pieces of charred furniture stood amidst the debris, and here and there some personal item. A child's toy, some kind of animal, distorted beyond recognition. A photo frame, the smiling faces it had once contained now nothing but curled ash. Memories of the people who had lived there, all gone, just like the owners themselves.

The heat from the smoking ruins kept Melanie from getting any closer.

I've already seen as much as I need to. One burned-out house looks much like another. Ours would look the same if someone poured on petrol and threw on a lighted match.

She allowed her gaze to wander over the rubble and wreckage a little longer before turning to business. Ben, James, Sarah and Chanita were wandering aimlessly around, looking like they didn't know what to do. But

Melanie knew exactly what needed to be done.

'We need to get ourselves better protection,' she said to Ben. 'We can't rely on you and James to keep us safe.'

Ben looked abashed. 'Look, I know it was my fault. I'm sorry. I shouldn't have gone out with James last night. One of us should always remain in the village. I won't make that mistake again.'

James nodded his agreement. 'If Ben had been here, he would never have allowed those men to do so much damage.'

'And no real harm was done,' added Chanita. She glanced sideways in the direction of the dead men. 'Apart from to the looters, I mean.'

Melanie shook her head. 'No. It's not good enough for us women to be dependent on you men to keep us safe. We need to be able to defend ourselves.'

'What did you have in mind?' asked Ben.

Ben Harvey, you can be a dimwit at times. What do you think I mean?

'Proper weapons.' All they had at the moment was a wrought iron poker and a cricket bat. Melanie brandished the shotgun they had seized from the looters. 'This will do for a start. But we need more.'

And something that isn't normally used for taking potshots at rabbits and clay pigeons.

She could tell that Ben wasn't happy at the suggestion. He had always been squeamish around guns. 'Where are we going to find them?'

'James can take us to that military base he knows.'

'RAF Benson?'

'If that's its name, yes.'

James had reported his discovery of the abandoned air base some months earlier. It was a place he passed on his night-time patrols. Melanie had never walked far enough from the village to see it herself, but an old RAF base sounded like a likely place to start looking for weapons.

'I can take you there,' said James. 'But the place is

abandoned. I don't think we'll find anything.'

'Even so,' said Melanie. 'Unless you have any better ideas, we'll take a look around.'

'All right,' said Ben, throwing up his hands in submission. 'James and I will go and check it out. If there are guns, we'll bring them back. But Melanie, in your condition, I don't want you coming with us. You should stay here.'

Why, thank you for referring to my "condition" for about the fortieth time.

'You must be kidding, Ben Harvey. And how dare you refer to "my condition". What century do you think this is?'

'Ben is right,' said Chanita. 'You can't ignore the fact that you're pregnant. It would be better if you rested. I'll stay with you.'

'No way. How safe do you think you and I are going to be all alone in the house unarmed? This is all about making ourselves safe. And the way to do that is through action, not waiting around to get killed.'

I did enough of that last night, looking out of the upstairs windows of the house and watching as first one, then another and another building was set ablaze. The next time I see that happen, my finger will be curled around a trigger.

'And I'll tell you another thing. Being pregnant gets old pretty quickly.'

It was inevitable that she would get her way. She always did. And in this case, she knew she was right. Within the hour they were on their way to the RAF base, James leading them, Ben following behind the three women.

Boys playing at being soldiers, again. Well, sometimes girls want to play that game too.

Melanie had used a gun before, when werewolves had attacked the refugee centre at Stoke Park. She had taken a life to defend herself then and she wouldn't be afraid to take more if looters or werewolves – or anyone else – came to the village again.

I'll take as many lives as I need to. I have a baby to think about now.

Not that there was any chance she would be allowed to forget that.

The RAF base was about eight miles away by road. James was used to travelling there cross-country, but Melanie wasn't about to climb through hedges and tramp across farmers' fields when there were perfectly good roads to walk on. She wasn't willing to admit it to the others, but being pregnant definitely made the journey into a slog. That extra weight didn't carry itself, and she was quick to break out into a sweat as they marched up the hills. But she wasn't giving up, and she wasn't going to complain either. She had got what she wanted – a chance to tool up and to get herself a gun.

It felt strange to be out in the open after months spent in Christmas Common, rarely venturing far from the house. Her world had become smaller, her horizons limited to the treetops around the village. Here, as she marched up and down the hills of South Oxfordshire, she had time to glimpse a larger world. But it was still tiny compared with the freedoms she had once enjoyed. Long-haul flights had made even the most exotic destination feel routine, shrinking the planet to a collection of beaches, hotels and restaurants arranged for her convenience. Now, even a journey of a few miles seemed like a great expedition into the unknown.

When they eventually reached it, their destination was hard to miss. RAF Benson cut a huge swathe through the surrounding countryside, dwarfing the town it was named after. Through the perimeter fence, Melanie cast her gaze across the flat grassland of the air base, bisected by two long runways making a cross on the ground.

X marks the spot.

From the air it would be visible from many miles away.

She was keen to get inside. 'Where are the – you know – the hangars, or whatever they have here?' she asked

James.

'The hangars are where they keep the aircraft,' remarked Ben. 'We won't find handguns there. But I expect there's an armoury over by the main buildings near the entrance.'

Melanie looked to where he was pointing. She could just make out a cluster of low-level brick buildings halfway across the airfield. 'Duh. Well, let's go there already.'

She strode forward, determined not to be a straggler even with her bump weighing her down. Before long they reached the main gate of the base and peered inside.

There was no sign of life within. The base was surrounded by a chain-link fence on concrete posts. Barbed wire ran along the top. It didn't look very secure, although she didn't think that she'd be able to scale it in "her condition." The main entrance, by contrast, was protected by nothing more than a white metal barrier across the road with an old World War II Spitfire standing to one side as gate guardian.

'It doesn't look very well protected,' she remarked.

'I expect they used to have soldiers stationed at the gate when it was operating,' said Ben.

'Well, there's no one here now.' The base had clearly been abandoned by the military, and Melanie realised that they had heard no noise from aircraft manoeuvres in all the time they had been living at Christmas Common. On the face of it, that didn't bode well for their chances of finding weapons and ammunition inside. But having walked so far to get here, she wasn't about to give up without looking. 'Come on, let's go inside.'

Chapter Forty-Two

Old Sarum, Wiltshire

Rose was standing on the roof of the world. From her vantage point atop the central keep of her fortress, she could see nothing but the enormous sky and the tops of trees growing up to meet it. Wind filled her hair and threw it across her face like coils of red rope. Her robes danced wildly and the wind threatened to pluck her wicker crown from her head and toss it over the edge of the rampart into the steep-sided ditch some hundred feet or more below. Pushing back against the raging wind as it tugged at her slender body, she felt a sense of strength and exhilaration. She spread her arms wide, welcoming fresh air into her lungs. A bird of prey flew overhead, gliding effortlessly on outstretched wings. Nutmeg sat at her feet, her long tongue flapping in the wind like a flag.

'Come on, girl. Let's walk.'

The rampart that girded the innermost core of the fortress made a raised walkway, peeking above the tallest treetops. Rose set off around it, looking out across the nested defences of the massive hill fort. The inner bailey of the keep was encircled by a deep ditch spanned by a wooden bridge that led out to a much larger outer bailey. This, in turn, was enclosed by another rampart and ditch, and finally by a third concentric set of defences.

The ruined citadel had a name. Old Sarum. It was the site of the original city of Salisbury, one of the most ancient cities of England. Chris had appointed himself as resident expert, studying the guide books he had found in a small ticket office at the entrance to the fort. It was weird to think that until recently this place had been nothing more than an archaeological site, a place where tourists and schoolchildren came to learn history. Now it was back to its original use. A place of refuge.

Dating back to the Iron Age, the hilltop fortress had been built as one vast defensive settlement. The Romans had occupied it, strengthening its fortifications and turning it into a military garrison before abandoning it to Saxon raiders. After the Norman invasion of England, it became a royal castle. Here, William the Conqueror called together all his barons and landholders. He made them bow to him and swear an oath of fealty. The gigantic earthworks of the fortress and the stone castle that crowned it had made this place a seat of great power. But Rose didn't want power. Power was the last thing she wanted.

Freedom is all I ask for.

But the only freedom she could taste was when the wind tugged wildly at her hair and the birds flew high above.

The Norman castle had long since fallen into ruin, and only the gatehouse remained. In its place, the inner bailey of the keep was now home to several hundred people, their colourful tents dotted amongst the rough flint cores of stone towers and halls. If space ran out, the outer bailey could be put to use, housing thousands more. In time, this could grow to be a great city once again.

A place of safety, at last.

Old Sarum lay at the centre of a cherry bowl, with distant hills making a ring all around. Beyond the outer ramparts of the fort, Rose could see for miles across the surrounding countryside in every direction. To the north, trees gathered along the crests of hills, like ranks of spears raised for battle. To the south lay the modern city of Salisbury, or at least what remained of it. Most of the city had been gutted by fire and only the cathedral spire stood intact. From atop the rampart, the remnants of the modern world looked small and insignificant, already in the past, and this ancient hill fort now claimed the future.

That is what the vision showed me. The future is mine to mould.

By the time she completed her circular tour and returned to her starting point near the gatehouse, a group of people was entering the outer bailey through the narrow gap in the outermost defences. Ryan had been leading search parties to forage for supplies in the ruins of Salisbury. She watched the tiny figures grow steadily larger as they approached the keep, then descended the stone stairs from the rampart to greet them.

Ryan's face was grim when he met her, and the rucksack on his back looked light. 'We didn't find much today. There's hardly anything left. Apart from the cathedral, almost every building's been burned to the ground. And there's no food to be found inside a cathedral.'

The news was no surprise to Rose. Ryan's previous expeditions had brought dwindling success. At first they had found plenty of food to keep everyone well fed, but as the days had passed, it had become clear that they would have to find a new source.

'We have to face facts,' continued Ryan. 'This place can't sustain us. We need to move on to another town or city. Somewhere that hasn't been so badly damaged.'

'No,' said Rose. 'We will remain here. This is the place I was shown.'

A frown creased Ryan's forehead. 'But, Rose —'

'I have already made my decision. And I've been speaking to Chris. The fields around here are fertile land, already planted with growing crops. In the weeks to come we'll be able to harvest them. We'll have cereals, potatoes, all kinds of vegetables, as well as grass for animals. And there are cattle, sheep, pigs and poultry. The land here can support thousands of people if necessary. We just have to learn how to use it.'

'That's not as simple as it sounds.'

'I didn't say it would be easy. I said it was the path I have chosen.'

'Rose —'

'My decision is made.'

The more decisions she took, the easier they became. And telling her followers what to do had also become easier. Difficult choices lay ahead, but she had already made the greatest one. Old Sarum was her home now. She would stay here, come what may. And so would her people, as long as they still wanted her as their leader.

'I have called for a feast tonight,' she told Ryan. 'We will gather together at the old cathedral and we will celebrate all that we have achieved. I have sent men to gather firewood and to bring back cattle.'

I did not ask for power, but now I have been given it, I will wield it to the best of my ability.

Her power was strong, and it was growing stronger. This feast would secure it once and for all, and make her position as unassailable as her fortress.

Chapter Forty-Three

RAF Benson, Oxfordshire

James was up to something; Ben could sense it. Hell, he could even smell it. He wondered that the others didn't seem to notice anything odd about James' behaviour, but of course they only possessed human senses. They could only see with their eyes and hear with their ears. And then only a little. When it came to smell, humans knew nothing of the sensory world around them. It was like they had no noses.

He tried to recall what it had been like to have nose blindness, but he was now so used to relying on his sense of smell, it was hard to remember clearly what it had been like before. Even now, if he'd been asked to describe the smell of duplicity, he wouldn't know where to begin. But James reeked of it. He was planning something.

'You feeling all right, James?' Ben asked. 'Nothing wrong?'

James visibly flinched at the challenge. 'Yes, sure. Why

do you ask?'

'You seem ... a little jumpy.'

James looked around. 'It's just that I've never been inside this air base before. It might be dangerous. Don't you think?'

'Sure,' said Ben. 'We should keep our wits about us.'

'Damn right,' said Melanie, her eyes on the barrier that blocked the entrance to the base to vehicles. 'Of course we will.'

Sarah and Chanita were also looking ahead, unaware of James' off behaviour.

'You guys go ahead,' said Ben, gesturing to James. 'I'll stay at the back and keep watch.'

He waited for them to reach the barrier, James and Melanie in the lead, then followed after them. He couldn't believe that James had any bad intentions toward them, but even so, he wasn't going to let him out of his sight.

They ducked beneath the barrier and entered the base, the metal bar presenting little obstacle to them. But Ben noted how Melanie struggled to bend beneath it. She had been trying to hide her exertions all the way here, panting and sweating, especially up any kind of gradient, but with her gaze fixed firmly on the horizon as if the walk was an easy stroll. Ben wasn't fooled by that. The pregnancy was taking its toll on her, and if she wasn't careful she would end up overdoing it. He needed to keep a watchful eye on her as well as James.

He ducked easily beneath the barrier and caught up with the others as they stopped to assess the route ahead. The air base was laid out in blocks, each one occupied by a large single- or two-storey building set well back from the road. Some looked like admin buildings, others might have been messes or barracks. The largest were clearly aircraft hangars and were painted green, presumably to camouflage them from the air. Ben wondered what kind of planes had flown from here.

They walked along the main road for a way, coming to

a halt as they neared the apron of the airfield. Now the reason for the base's abandonment became clear. The runway had been bombed, and was pocked with a series of craters making it look like a lunar surface. A burned-out helicopter stood at one end of the runway: a twin-engined Chinook. The gigantic craft must have been struck by a bomb or a missile, because its fuselage had broken in two and debris lay scattered about. The Chinook's frame was blackened by fire, and its rotor blades had twisted out of shape, like train tracks after an earthquake. One of the hangars had also been hit, and the roof had collapsed, revealing more broken helicopters buried beneath the roof panels. At least now he knew what kind of base this was. Helicopter squadrons had been stationed here. But none of the aircraft looked airworthy now.

In the distance, beyond the hangars and runway, dark clouds brooded on the horizon. A storm was on its way. Perhaps it would break tonight, covering the moon with thick clouds. Or maybe the wind would steer it away from them. Ben could feel the wind swelling, growing stronger as the day progressed. It swept across the open field of the base, making the place feel even more bleak and unloved than it already did.

Melanie turned away from the runway, heading toward a small squat building that stood to one side. The brick structure had few windows and was surrounded by its own fence. Unlike the main entrance to the base, access to this building was via a locked metal gate. She stopped in front of it, looking up at the razor wire running across the top of the eight-foot wire mesh. She kicked at the gate in irritation. It rang with a clang, but refused to budge. 'Well, they obviously don't want anyone getting inside here, so I think we'll try this first.'

There was logic to her thinking, and the fact that the building was still secure boded well for finding weapons inside. Ben knew that he and James would have no problem scaling the fence, but the others would stand little chance of climbing over. He didn't think that Melanie would be happy to wait outside, but she might not have a choice. 'James and I will try to get inside,' he said.

'And then open the gate for us?' Melanie asked hopefully.

'I don't think we'll be able to,' said Ben. 'Unless they've left a key lying around.' Melanie scowled. 'Listen,' he told her, 'here's what we'll do. You three wait here. James and I will climb the fence and see if we can get inside the building. If we can, we'll search for guns and ammo and bring anything we find back out. It doesn't matter who fetches the guns, does it, as long as someone does?'

Melanie's dark face suggested she thought otherwise, but she nodded reluctantly. 'All right, then. Get on with it.'

With a nod from Ben, James was first over the fence. He clambered up it with ease, his feet finding purchase against the wire mesh, and hauled himself over the top, carefully avoiding the barbs of the razor wire. He landed gracefully on his feet on the other side. Ben followed, jumping down next to him.

From outside the fence, Melanie watched their easy movements with irritation. She folded her arms across her bump.

Ben turned his attention to the next challenge. The building was built from red brick, and its windows were barred by criss-cross metal screens. They would have little chance of gaining entry that way. He moved instead to examine the main entrance and felt his last hopes dashed. The door was a high-security model, made from steel. He tried the handle, but it was firmly locked.

'Can you open it?' called Melanie.

'I don't think so. James?'

James shrugged. 'It seems solid. I don't think we can get in without a key. And the windows look secure too.'

Ben turned back to Melanie. 'We'll have to try the other buildings instead.'

Melanie's dark eyes bored into his. 'If they've made this

one so secure, they obviously have something important inside. Can you see anything through the windows?'

Ben moved to the side of the building and brought his face up close to the security screen that covered the nearest window. The room beyond was dark, but he could see shelving stacked against one wall. Ranks of dark green objects were arranged along the shelves. It was hard to tell, but they might easily be guns.

But how could they possibly get inside?

Chapter Forty-Four

The City of London

The building rose from the rubble like a Roman temple or a Greek acropolis. An altar to the god of gold.

A Neoclassical façade sat atop a stone plinth resting on a dozen Corinthian-style columns. Behind it soared the wreckage of a modern skyscraper, its glass windows cracked and shattered, the steel substructure that lifted it up already rusting now that it was exposed to the elements. A cathedral of commerce, now desecrated and abandoned. Griffin leaned on his crutches, shaking his head in disbelief and wonder. The view was like a fantastical dream, but it was real.

The Bank of England had been established as the bank of the English government in 1694 in order to finance war against France. Now it would fund an altogether different type of military venture. The Bank had been relocated to its present site on Threadneedle Street a century after its founding, and had greatly expanded between the two World Wars to accommodate the ever-growing role of central banking in the affairs of nations. Seven storeys above ground and three below. Griffin's engineers had scoped out the layout of the building and in conjunction with the munitions experts had devised a plan to bring it toppling down.

A single Paveway bomb, weighing five hundred pounds, equipped with a penetration warhead, and precision-guided to its target by laser, would be dropped by an F-35 Lightning from HMS *Queen Elizabeth*. If the calculations — back-of-the-envelope and quickly-made as they were — were correct, the resulting explosion would open up one or more of the vaults to the surface for plunder. The streets of London may not have been paved with gold, but there was gold beneath them. Hundreds of billions of pounds of the precious metal.

Griffin felt like a gangster about to pull off the biggest bank job of all time. He shifted nervously, seized with a sudden fear that someone might have tipped off the authorities.

Get a grip, Griffin. We are the authorities, and the gold belongs to us.

Still, no amount of rational reasoning could quench his last-minute nerves. Nor the growing sense of excitement at the prospect of success, however slim.

If this works, my name will go down in history. If it doesn't, there may be no more history to write.

It was very strange returning to London after all that had happened. Griffin had been flying over the southern fringe of the city when his helicopter was swatted from the sky by the nuclear blasts. He had watched the great mushroom clouds spread their sinister shadows across the sky as the city beneath them burned. He had been hoping to return to Chanita that night, and instead had woken to find himself lying in the smoking ruins of his downed copter, a metal rod impaled in his thigh.

This is where I lost her. And nearly lost my life.

He winced as he recalled the desperate operation he had been forced to carry out to save his own broken and bleeding leg. A dog's dinner of a procedure, carried out amid the mangled wreckage of the helicopter as it lay on its side on the forest floor. No wonder he had made such a mess of it.

Now he was back in the very heart of the capital.

Did I wake, or am I still dreaming?

Although he had delegated the planning of the bullion heist to Hastings and Bampton, he had chosen to observe it at close quarters from the rooftop of a nearby building. He wouldn't get a chance to witness such an event again. No one had ever succeeded in stealing gold from the Bank of England. Would he be the first?

It was hard to believe that it was safe to be standing so close to what had been the hub of the nation – within eye view of its beating financial heart. Surely this whole area should have been a radioactive wasteland. He expected to see men in hazmat suits wielding Geiger counters emerging from the ruins at any moment. But the experts had assured him that radiation contamination in the city was now indistinguishable from background levels.

Indeed, although many of the capital's tallest buildings had been brought down to size, and some of its most famous icons – the London Eye, Buckingham Palace, the Palace of Westminster – were damaged beyond repair, much of Central London was surprisingly intact. General Ney had planned his operation meticulously, deploying his warheads to ensure maximum casualties, while minimizing the radioactive fallout and damage to buildings. *What a clever psychopath you were, General.* Yet still the devastation was mind-numbing. Whole swathes of the capital had been turned to dust; vast areas were flooded. No part had completely escaped damage. And yet remarkably, there had been survivors. The Prime Minister, in her blast-hardened bunker. A few terrified citizens, lucky enough to find themselves below ground when the blasts erupted two kilometres overhead, turning the night sky to day. Everyone else had been wiped out, either by the initial shockwave from the blasts themselves, or by the firestorms that followed in their wake. Now it was a city of ghosts.

A low whisper became audible – the aircraft approaching. Seconds later Griffin saw it in the distance, flying in low over the broken skyline. A silver dot, burnished by the sun.

His radio crackled beside him. 'Daylight One incoming.' Not the most imaginative name for a combat mission, but Bampton and the wits in 617 Squadron hadn't been able to come up with anything better at short notice. *Operation Daylight Robbery*. Well, with no police around to arrest them, why wait until nightfall?

We might as well stroll right up to the front door and blow our way in.

He raised his binoculars and watched the jet close in, the sound of its single engine rising like the roaring of the wind as it drew nearer. He could make out its short, stubby wings and twin tailfins.

The plane was low and coming in fast. In a matter of seconds it was too close for binoculars and he lowered them to watch with his naked eyes. An awesome sight, both exhilarating and terrifying. The plane released its bomb and accelerated away, metal screaming through the sky, its exhaust an orange burn, the noise from its engine now an ear-splitting roll of thunder as if the very air that bore it were on fire. It rolled once in acknowledgement of mission completion, and tore away over the River Thames into the distance.

Griffin turned to watch the bomb descend.

The Paveway IV swooped out of the sky, looking like an airborne torpedo with its small wings outstretched. A three-metre metal cylinder packed with high explosives, smart enough to pick out and glide to its designated target.

But "glide" wasn't a word that did the weapon justice. The bomb flew like a dart, ever faster and with deadly accuracy straight for the bank. It struck the building and Griffin braced himself for the explosion. For a heartbeat nothing happened. Then, after piercing the outer walls, the bomb detonated, delivering the full brunt of its explosive force to the underground vaults themselves.

Exactly according to plan.

A hot flash of fire filled Griffin's vision before quickly being erased by a cloud of black smoke erupting out. A sound like the gates of Hell tearing free from their hinges crashed against him and he raised his hands to cover his eardrums. The ground beneath him quaked, and the building on which he stood shook from its very foundations. Griffin lurched and stumbled on his crutches as he struggled to steady himself. An officer by his side reached out one helping hand.

Thick as mud, the black smoke from the explosion rolled upward, forming crests in a dark crown. It engulfed the Bank before filling the sky and snuffing out the sun. A deep shadow fell, as if all light were gone from the world forever. Across the street, panes of glass dropped out of their frames to the road below.

When the movement had ceased and the noise died down, Griffin raised his binoculars again. Black plumes now billowed out from the target site, and grey rain began to fall as dust filled the air all around. He coughed, covering his mouth to avoid choking. Soon the streets for an entire block around were draped in a thin layer of white. The world was winter.

After the dust had finally settled and the smoke dispersed, the sun returned, as hot as before. One side of the Bank was now completely gone, its elegant architecture reduced to a hill of broken stone, like so many of the classical temples on which it was modelled. In its midst, the ground was splintered, leaving a yawning gap some ten feet in breadth. The vault had been torn asunder. If luck was with him, the gold was ready for the taking. He imagined it lying there, stacked in ordered rows, unperturbed by the devastation all around, indestructible and untarnished and waiting for its new owners to claim it. But all he could see right now was debris and destruction. For all he knew, the wealth of a nation was lost beneath a mound of rubble.

'I've seen enough,' said Griffin. 'Take me back to HQ.'

He could do no more here. It was down to the ground crew now. Most likely he wouldn't know until the following day whether or not the mission had been a success. If it had, he would win over a couple of hundred desperados to his side. If not, it was he who would be the desperado.

He struggled across the rooftop to the waiting helicopter and clambered inside, stowing his crutches away and donning his ear defenders, then signalled to the pilot to take them up. On the ground, the bulldozers had already begun to move in.

Chapter Forty-Five

Haywards Heath, West Sussex

The men were stripped to their waists, their torsos shiny with sweat. Werewolves and wolfmen, side by side in hand-to-hand combat. Women too – Wolf Sisters, clad in combat gear or in their black leather uniforms, fighting alongside the men.

Fists, claws, knives, teeth. The wolf-heads had the advantage of savage strength, but those in human form had speed on their side. Knives flashed in their palms, striking out and stealing blood from their opponents. William Hunter clearly believed that practice sessions should retain all the danger of a real fight.

Canning observed from the side-lines as Hunter inspected his troops and gave out orders. 'You two!' he bellowed at a pair of combatants. 'Begin!'

The two were mixed – a man with the head of a wolf, armed with a baseball bat studded in nails; the second a woman, her arms clothed in fur from the elbows down, wicked claws at the end of each finger. A hideous menagerie of creatures, and a lethal-looking assortment of weapons. Canning watched with interest as the opponents sized each other up.

On the face of it the wolfman held all the advantages – superior strength, greater reach with his weapon, and a fierce array of teeth. But the woman stood her ground, undaunted, her razor-sharp claws capable of delivering a deadly blow if she could outmanoeuvre her opponent.

The man moved first, striding forward, his club raised high. He swung it in a wide arc, aiming for his opponent's head.

Canning grimaced, waiting for the sound of wood caving in the woman's skull, but she moved quickly, dodging aside with blinding speed. Her head was no longer in the way of the bat, which continued to swing, momentum dragging it along its preordained arc. By the time the wolfman had it under control, her claws were scratching at his skin, raking bloody furrows in his chest.

'Good, good!' shouted Hunter from behind.

The wolfman dropped his weapon, grabbing at his foe with his huge hands. He grasped her arms, holding the deadly claws at bay. Now the advantage switched to him. The woman struggled to free herself, the points of her long nails useless in his grip. He lunged with his jaws, sharp teeth ready to draw blood.

But again he was thwarted. Too slow, his teeth closed on empty air as the woman ducked low and rolled into a backflip, pivoting in his grip and using his own arms as a fulcrum. She spun vertically, kicking out with her feet. They connected with his lower jaw, tipping his head back with a crack. He roared in agony and let her go.

Canning watched as she landed gracefully on her feet, then rushed in for the kill, her claws primed to tear flesh from her stunned adversary.

'Stop!' bellowed Hunter. 'Enough!'

The woman's eyes flashed with a desire for violence,

but she obeyed the command.

This is real for her, Canning realized. *Hunter trains his troops as if every day were a struggle to live. I wonder how many have perished on his training grounds.*

The defeated wolfman slumped in despondency, panting from the exertion, while the woman looked on, just as tired, but flushed with the vigour of victory. Hunter went to them, slapping each on the back. 'Well fought. What did you learn here?'

'That speed defeats strength, when used well,' said the woman.

'That strength breeds complacency,' offered the man, his wolf's head down.

'Learn this lesson,' said Hunter, 'and learn it well. Each of us has unique strengths and weaknesses, and we must make the best of what we have. The outcome of any fight is never certain. We cannot rest until the battle is over. Now, fight again. Better, this time.'

He turned away as the man reclaimed his dropped weapon and the woman readied herself once more for battle. Hunter looked across at Canning, grinning his infuriating grin. Canning returned his gaze nonchalantly, his mind spinning with the implications of what he had just seen.

He builds a fighting machine far more effective than anything I have been capable of. In that regard, he cannot be matched. If his talent for strategic planning reaches the same level of proficiency, then I am doomed. Leanna will toss me aside like flotsam on the flood.

There were two wars here – one against human enemies, another against his arch-rival. The first was going well, the second not so much.

But all was not lost. The key to winning the first war was to harness Hunter's skills to best advantage. And to win the second, Canning need only find a way to turn those same strengths against him.

Speed defeats strength. Strength breeds complacency.

Just like Hunter said, each one of us had a unique set of

talents at their disposal. Canning had no doubt where his own particular skills lay.

Deceit. Duplicity. Cunning.

To achieve victory, it was necessary only to deploy them to maximum advantage. He smiled at Hunter, the cogs in his mind continuing to whirr.

Chapter Forty-Six

RAF Benson, Oxfordshire

James' breathing was coming in thick, irregular gasps. He felt like he was underwater. His skin was bathed in a sheen of sweat, and he could smell his own fear dripping from him like cold water. He felt the moon calling, invisible behind a veil of clouds, but undeniable. He felt it in his beating heart, in the blood that pulsed through his arteries, in the very marrow of his bones. He wondered that the others hadn't noticed anything wrong with him, but only Ben seemed aware of his intense emotions.

The arrival of the looters in the village the previous night had brought home to him the urgency of his task, and the killing of those intruders had awakened a dread feeling of impending doom.

He had spent too long in Christmas Common already. It was time for him to be off. He must leave this very day, and begin his long and lonely journey. It was a matter of the utmost urgency.

Only the Seventh Seal remains to be broken.

He couldn't delay another minute. But he couldn't just abandon his friends and leave them to their fate. Melanie was right – they needed weapons to defend themselves. And this armoury was the only place they were likely to find any. While Ben rattled the door and peered through the darkened windows of the building, James turned his attention to the roof. The building was only one storey tall, and made of rough brick. It would be simple to climb, especially in wolf form.

Even without realising it, he had begun to change. He stripped off his clothes and sandals as the silken cloth of gold that was his own fur folded itself across his body, covering his nakedness.

I will wear this new clothing for the rest of my days. I will turn my back on human habits, living henceforth as wolf. The burden is mine to bear, alone.

It took only seconds for the transformation to complete. Now he was his true self. He need not pretend anymore. Standing on his hind legs, he raised his front paws to the wall and began to climb. With the help of a window ledge and a downpipe, he scaled the wall in seconds. The roof was low with a shallow pitch, and his paws were sure in their grip.

'James?' called Melanie. 'What can you see?'

He ignored her voice and focussed instead on the problem facing him. How to get inside? The builders of this place had secured it with steel and stone, and even a wolf could not gain entry. But the roof was made of clay tiles, and tiles, like bones, could be broken.

They stretched in grey lines, parallel in military order, each one lapped by two above it. He flexed his claws and slid them beneath the lowest row of tiles. He tried to lever one up, but it was stuck fast. He wailed in frustration.

I need to be gone from here.

It was already late into the afternoon and the strength

of the sun was beginning to fade, although the tiles themselves had soaked up its heat and were hot to the touch. A dark rage filled his mind at the delay and he thrust his claws deeper under the tile. This time it broke loose, falling to the ground and shattering into shards.

He prised away a second and tossed it aside.

'Hey!' called Ben from below. 'Be careful where you throw those!'

But James was done with care. He scrabbled frantically at the thick tiles, loosening them, stripping them away and hurling them to the ground. Before long he had removed enough to gain access to the under-roof. Beneath the wooden batons that held the tiles in place, he found a layer of felt. Sharp claws ripped quickly through the soft material, and a few hard punches to the wooden struts broke a hole just large enough for him to squeeze his shoulders through. He slipped inside, lowering himself into darkness.

Chapter Forty-Seven

A manic energy had taken hold of James. Ben ducked for safety as a barrage of roof tiles rained down from overhead. He shouted a warning, but James took no notice. A heavy clay tile hit the ground just inches away and shattered into sharp fragments. Ben pushed himself against the wall of the building, pressing his back to the rough bricks.

Beyond the fence, Melanie, Sarah and Chanita watched from a safe distance.

The barrage of tiles ceased eventually and Ben stepped out to see what was happening. Where James had been crouched just a moment earlier, a man-sized hole now gaped in the roof, giving access to a dark void. James had got inside.

The door to the building swung open to reveal James in wolf form, panting breathlessly. He looked up at Ben, then turned and ducked away. Ben followed him inside.

Lycanthropic

The interior of the building was bathed in shadow. It consisted of just two rooms – an office and an armoury. Entering the latter, Ben took in the view of the wall of shelving he had spied through the window. He had been right about the guns. Racked up against the wall of the armoury was weapon after weapon. Handguns, rifles, machine guns, and a stockpile of ammunition to go with them. It was more than he could have hoped for.

James paced the floor restlessly, a low growl coming from his throat.

'James? What's the matter?'

James was still panting from his exertions on the rooftop. But his hyperventilation was due to more than simple fatigue. His yellow eyes were rolling. A steady froth of spit dripped from his loose jaws.

Ben dropped back, keeping a safe distance. 'James, calm down. You're making me nervous.'

The wolf turned his head in Ben's direction. 'Stand aside, Ben. I need to go.'

'What do you mean? Go where?'

The wolf head swung from side to side. 'It's better if you don't know. I have to go alone.'

'I don't understand.'

The wolf advanced. 'I have to go now. Get out of my way.'

Ben closed the door behind him. 'I'm not letting you go anywhere until you explain what you're planning.'

A louder growl greeted him. The wolf padded forward.

'James, stop! Just calm down and talk to me. I'm your friend, Ben!'

But the look in the wolf's eyes was that of a stranger. The creature's jaws opened wide, revealing ranks of sharp teeth within. It hissed a warning: 'Open the door. I won't ask again.'

Chapter Forty-Eight

Old Sarum, Wiltshire

Only the footprint of the original cathedral of Old Sarum had survived the centuries. But Rose had no need for stone walls. The open air would be her place of worship, the star-painted sky her vaulted ceiling. The trees that bent and rustled in the growing wind would be the pillars that held it high. Already the first logs of the bonfire were being piled ready to burn. A cow was being led to the slaughter. Two hundred and fifty men, women and children would gather here tonight, to feast and to celebrate at this once-sacred site.

The old cathedral was one of the strangest features of Old Sarum. It had been built in the eleventh century, but survived for less than a hundred years before its stonework was dismantled and work began on a new cathedral in nearby Salisbury, or New Sarum. According to Chris, the construction of the new cathedral and the city that it spawned led quickly to the demolition of the hilltop castle and the abandonment of Old Sarum entirely. For five hundred years it had lain deserted, an insubstantial ghost overlooking the modern city which grew steadily in wealth and influence. Now, old and new had reversed their roles. New Sarum was gone, and Old Sarum would rise from its ashes.

The foundation stones of the cathedral were located in the grassed enclosure of the vast outer bailey. Chris was supervising the building of the bonfire, telling his work team to separate the wood into logs, kindling and tinder. He seemed to understand the theory of fire-making well enough, even if his approach to giving orders lacked tact. But perhaps even Chris could learn to improve his management skills. Rose would have a quiet talk with him later.

He turned a mournful gaze on her as she approached. 'You mean to go ahead with this feast? You know what I think. We shouldn't kill the cattle. I already told you that. We should preserve the livestock so they can be eaten in winter when food is at its scarcest, and so that more can be bred for next year and the years to come.'

'I know that, Chris. But the people deserve a feast. They've suffered so much and made so many sacrifices, I want to hold a celebration to mark the end of our journey.'

At that, Chris looked more hopeful. 'So you plan for us to stay here? Permanently? And we can all become farmers, like I said?'

'Just like you said.'

'Good.'

Rose was glad that she had Chris' support for her decision to stay. She was used to Chris disagreeing with her, so it was nice for him to have her back for a change. And he had plenty of ideas about how they could become self-sufficient, and make Old Sarum a permanent home for all the people who had come to live there.

'In fact, I want you to become my chief adviser.'

Chris beamed at the news. 'Instead of Ryan?'

'As well as Ryan. Ryan will be responsible for day-to-day issues. I want you to focus on strategy and long-term survival.'

'And what about Seth?'

'What about him?'

'Is he going to be responsible for anything?'

'I haven't decided yet.'

'Okay. Just don't give him anything important to do.' Chris turned his attention back to the building of the bonfire. He strode over to where the firewood was being piled high. 'No, stop! Not like that. I told you to save the biggest logs for last. You have to start with the twigs and dry leaves that will catch fire easily. Look, let me show you.'

Rose left him to it, and went to find Ryan. He was supervising the slaughter of the animal for the feast.

The slaughterman, a trained butcher, was busy sharpening his knife. He acknowledged Rose with a smile. 'One heifer should be more than enough for the number of people here. This young lady's a beauty. Between eighteen and twenty-four months old, I reckon, and grain-fed.'

Rose nodded. She knew little about cows, and nothing about how they were slaughtered. But she didn't flinch as the butcher made a single slash at the animal's throat, cutting through the windpipe, veins and arteries of its neck. Blood gushed out like water, and the parched earth drank it thirstily. The beast's eyes rolled as it staggered and lurched from side to side against its restraining ropes, before collapsing to the ground, where it continued to moan as the life force slowly drained away from it.

'It seems a cruel way to kill an animal,' said Ryan after the blood had slowed to a trickle. 'But we don't have access to modern humane slaughter methods. This is how they did it in the old days.'

The old days. We are living in the old days now. And I must harden myself to them.

Rose took Ryan to one side. 'I would like you to pick out the strongest fighters. Choose as many as you need.' She raised her arms to indicate the vast earthworks that surrounded them. 'This place is well built, but a castle is only as strong as its defenders.'

'You mean to defend this place against a werewolf attack?'

'From werewolves, or anyone else. We saw on Salisbury Plain how vulnerable we are to attack. I won't allow anything like that to happen again. Find weapons. Post sentries at night. Secure the entrance against intruders. Do whatever it takes to make this place impregnable.' She softened her voice. 'I trust you, Ryan. You know that. Of all the people here, you are the one I can depend on most.'

'And yet you've been taking Chris' advice if you think we can stay here and become farmers and hunters.'

'Chris knows a lot. He isn't always right, but in this case he is. I know you want us to keep moving, but we have to think about surviving beyond just today and the next day and the next month. We have to put down roots and work out how to live and prosper in the years ahead. For the sake of generations not yet born.'

Before them, the cow had ceased to moan, and the butcher was beginning to remove the head of the carcass. He wielded his knife expertly, cutting all around the animal's neck. A young lad, no older than Rose, was there to help him. 'My son,' explained the butcher. 'It's high time he learned a trade. What they taught him at school's no use to him now.'

'We will all have to learn new trades,' said Rose. 'We have to rediscover the old ways.'

'All right,' said Ryan. 'You're the boss. We'll do what Chris says and learn to become survivalists.' He gave her a grin to show he harboured no bitterness at being overruled.

In return she hugged him close. What had her spirit guide told her in her final vision? *You are not alone, Rose. You will never be alone.*

It sometimes felt that way, though. What else had the guide said?

Now you lead a vast multitude, an army that will continue to grow. An army that will fight, if you command it.

Rose never wanted to give that command. She had seen enough of fighting and killing. Peace was the only future she wanted to be a part of. She returned to the inner bailey and climbed the stone steps up to the highest rampart. Looking out, she surveyed her new domain. Already this place felt like home. Below her, the crowds were gathering in preparation for the evening's feast. After months of suffering, they deserved some respite. But this night was to be more than revelry.

When the sun had set, she descended from the keep, crossing the wooden bridge that spanned the innermost moat, and made her way to where the crowds had gathered around the old cathedral. The bonfire was ablaze, moving long shadows across the ground where the people danced and swayed. The notes of Seth's flute flew high above the murmur of voices.

The stone foundations of the cathedral were laid out in traditional cruciform shape. Rose followed them to the far end where the altar had once stood in the apse. A memory of the Altar Stone at Stonehenge came back to her, and she shuddered at the bloody ceremonies Rowan had forced her to preside over within that stone circle. They had culminated in human sacrifice, though of Rowan, not his intended victim.

No human lives would be taken at Rose's altar. Only animals would be killed at Old Sarum. And for food, not superstitious belief.

But still, Rowan had taught her the power of ritual and of mystery.

This feast tonight, with its burning fire and ceremonial slaughter would secure her power and bind the people to her cause just as surely as the great lords and barons had sworn their allegiance to William the Conqueror a thousand years earlier.

As Rose stepped into the firelight, the crowds parted and the hubbub died away until the only voice was the roar and crackle of the bonfire. Rose stood before it, feeling the heat of the flames against her face.

She knew what her people saw when they beheld her, shimmering in the night. A young girl, pure and innocent, her red hair crowned with wicker. Emerald eyes and ruby lips set against creamy freckled skin. The virgin priestess. The prophetess. Her long cloak flapping soundlessly in the breeze.

Whatever she told them now, they would believe.

Whatever she commanded, they would obey.

Chapter Forty-Nine

The Pilgrims' Way

The nights grew hotter, and the days hotter still. Warg Daddy took his sleep while the ghosts slept – in daylight, when the sun rode high on its fiery chariot, banishing the voices from his head. At night, the inside of his skull was way too crowded for any sleeping to be done. Besides, he hated the sun and the way it hurt his brain. The night was cooler and gentler, and filled with stars, moon and mystery, and Warg Daddy loved it best.

Now, finally, the night he had been waiting for had almost come – the night of the full moon.

But the omens boded ill.

All day long the sun burned down, so hot that he could find no shade cool enough to sleep. As evening fell, black clouds piled up against the horizon then flooded in to fill the sky with dark foreboding. An ominous silence fell, and the birds grew still, as the whole land waited breathlessly for the violence that was brewing.

Night came, and the kids retreated inside their tent, leaving him alone beneath his tree. As the air cooled, a wind blew up, making the leaves whisper, and bending the branches to its will, making them duck and dive like waves upon the ocean. The storm grew in power, whipping him like a lash as he sat tied to his trunk. The ghosts awoke, murmuring to him, telling him their lies and their secrets, but he took no notice of them, turning his eyes to the boiling skies above.

When the clouds finally broke and the first raindrops fell, it was like stepping beneath a waterfall. A cool river washed over his face, dripping down his nose into his waiting mouth. Warg Daddy had never tasted anything so good. The water ran across his tongue, sweeter even than blood.

He drank it down, feeling strength fill his limbs once again.

I am weak no longer.

The night of the full moon had come at last. But looking up, he saw only swirling darkness and pouring rain. Lightning flashed, illuminating the vast churning underbelly of the rainclouds. The storm hid the moon behind its thick mass. But he wouldn't allow it to steal his chance at freedom. Moon or no moon, he was going to break free.

He rose to his feet, feeling them slide in the mud as rivulets of rain washed over the ground. Water slithered down his spine like a cold snake, and heavy drops hammered at his skull, rousing the ghosts to anger.

'Free us!' they bellowed. 'The time has come!'

He shook his head to silence them, and seized hold of the rope that bound him.

It was thick, and tied fast, coiling itself around his wrist, neck and legs. He had struggled with it before, and his skin bore the chafing and scars of those battles. Now was the time to claim victory from defeat. He gripped the rope with his one hand, and pulled at the end that looped the tree. The tall boy, Drake, had wrapped it three times around the trunk, and tied it with a knot he couldn't unpick single-handedly. But a rope could be broken if the desire was strong, and Warg Daddy had never desired anything so much. He jerked at the rope, tugging it left, then right, rubbing its twisted cords against the rough bark of the tree. It tightened as he pulled it, but the tighter it drew, the harder the tree scratched against it.

To the left, then to the right, then all the way around he dragged it, heaving with his whole body, teasing the thick rope apart, one tiny thread at a time.

'Hurry!' called the ghosts, but he took his time. He had all night.

Still the cooling water fell on him, breaking over his head, filling his eyes with rain and his ears with the roaring of the wind, and washing away everything except him, the rope and the tree.

And little by little the rope frayed.

When it finally snapped, he fell backward, landing on his arse in the slippery mud. He sat there for a while, laughing with joy, as the ghosts cheered him on. Then he slid from his bonds and cast the rope aside.

Free again.

The time had come for answers. But when he looked down at his feet, searching for the coin, all he could see was slithering mud. Rivulets of water ran across the ground, turning all they touched to liquid. Lightning forked overhead as he scanned the ground in desperation, casting around for a glint of gold, but all he saw was black and white.

No.

He dropped to his knees and began trawling through the mud, burrowing his hands into the soft ooze, searching frantically for the lost coin. Cold water poured over him, and his fingers dug deep as worms, but still there was nothing.

It cannot be gone.

Lycanthropic

And then, suddenly, his thumb struck something hard. He scooped it out, cradling the priceless coin, and held it beneath the splashing rain. Water ran across its surface, cold and clear, washing away uncertainty, scattering doubt. It had been tarnished when last he held it, dirtied by the touch of a hundred greasy palms and a dozen dubious transactions. Now, after a good rinsing, it looked cleaner than it ever had. A flick of his wrist and it was in flight, battling against the elements to deliver its message.

The wind blew hard and the raindrops battered against it with all their strength, but no matter how hard they fought to push it off course, the coin would always win. Heads or tails, there was no other possibility.

Warg Daddy caught it in his palm and held it there, hidden from view. In his excitement, he had forgotten to ask a question. But now the time had come, the question he needed to ask was obvious – kill the kids, or let them live?

Heads: *kill them*. Tails: *let them live*.

Head or tails. It was fate, pure and simple.

He unfolded his fingers to reveal the result.

Chapter Fifty
RAF Benson, Oxfordshire

Rain began to fall, cooling at first, but promising to grow cold and hard as the approaching storm broke. Melanie stood with growing impatience outside the fence that protected the armoury, waiting for Ben and James to show themselves again.

James' behaviour had been alarming. The way he had turned into wolf form and scrabbled onto the roof had been like nothing she'd seen before. She was used to his transformations, but this had been much faster than usual, and he had acted with a wild recklessness, hurling heavy roof tiles with abandon in every direction while Ben cowered below.

Ben had been right about James' behaviour. She should have listened to him. Now both Ben and James had vanished inside the building and she had no idea what was happening.

'I don't like this,' she told Sarah. 'What's up with

James?'

'He did seem a bit mad, didn't he?'

'I've been watching him,' said Chanita. 'He's been acting strange.'

'Yes.' Melanie could have kicked herself. Everyone had noticed James' oddness, but she had refused to think about it. She had been so wrapped up in herself, and the pregnancy. She had taken James for granted. But she ought to have known better. James had always been wild and unpredictable, especially in wolf form. The very first time she had met him he had almost killed her. He had come close to savaging her a second time, when the full moon claimed him just as they were leaving London, and he had run away to stop himself from taking her life. James the man was as gentle as anyone she had known, but James the wolf was another matter entirely. And the two were just a quick metamorphosis apart.

'Here he comes now,' said Sarah.

Melanie looked and saw a wolf bounding toward them. With smooth sandy fur it was unmistakably James. But there was a savagery in those yellow eyes. The creature leaped over the fence, and launched itself into flight above the sharp lines of razor wire.

'Look out!' Ben's face appeared in the doorway of the building, fear engraved in lines across his brow. 'James has gone berserk!'

The others ducked back as James landed on the ground, but Melanie stood her ground. Berserk or not, the creature that prowled around her was still her friend. 'James,' she said, as calmly as she could, 'It's me, Melanie.'

Yellow eyes gazed back, intense and feral. She saw desolation in those eyes, and pity, and regret. But also determination.

'What are you doing, James? Talk to me.'

The wolf bared its fangs, but then James' soft voice emerged from its lips. 'I'm sorry, Melanie. I have to leave you. But you'll be safe now. You have guns.'

'What are you talking about? Where do you have to go?'

The wolf shook its great head, as if trying to silence voices it alone could hear. 'I can't tell you. But I'm going. Alone. I won't be coming back.'

'No,' said Melanie. 'You can't just leave without an explanation.'

The wolf stared at her a moment longer, then turned and fled. Powerful legs propelled it forward, speeding it away toward the main gates of the base.

She heard the sound of the fence rattling behind her. She turned and saw Ben dropping to the ground, still in human form.

'Will someone explain to me what is going on?' she demanded. 'Where on earth is James going?'

Ben looked grim. 'I don't know exactly. But he talked about making a final sacrifice. I think he's lost his mind.'

Melanie gripped his arm. 'You have to go after him and persuade him to come back. We can talk this through, knock some sense into him.'

'I don't think so, Melanie. It's like I feared, he's stopped taking his wolfsbane. He's no longer rational.'

'Then you must go with him.' Melanie stared at Ben, studying the care-worn lines on his face. She had lost him once, and had sworn never to part from him again, but she knew with all her heart that she no longer had that luxury. 'James can't go alone.'

Ben looked doubtful. 'You want me to join him on his madcap journey? I don't even know what he intends to do.'

'It doesn't matter. We have to trust him.' Melanie felt sharp tears sting her face. 'I love you, Ben, but I can't let James run away on his own. Go with him, for however long it takes, and bring him back.'

Ben stared into her eyes a moment longer, then nodded. He had long since learned that saying no to her was useless. 'If that's what you want, then I will.'

She gathered him in her arms and kissed his mouth. 'Go,' she said, 'but promise me one thing. You'll come back to me safe and sound.' She patted her round belly. 'Come back to both of us.'

'I will,' he promised, 'and while I'm away –'

She put a finger to his lips. 'Don't you dare mention my "condition", Ben Harvey. Don't worry, I'll be sensible. Now get out of my sight before I start crying. Hurry, now, don't lose him.'

Chapter Fifty-One

The Pilgrims' Way

Heads: kill them.

The coin had sealed Warg Daddy's fate, and those of the three kids.

Kill them.

A simple coin flip had answered his question, and there was nothing to do except get on with the killing.

Killing is best done quickly, before the blood has time to cool. Before the brain has time to think. Before the hand has time to pause.

Thunder crashed overhead, and the ghosts urged him on to savagery, but he stayed rooted beside the tree, suddenly plagued by doubt.

This wasn't how it worked. He had done this all wrong. He had been too quick. He ought to have asked his question before flipping the coin. How could the gods be expected to give an answer to a question he hadn't yet asked? It was hardly reasonable to expect that, even from gods. If Warg Daddy had been a god, that kind of thoughtless behaviour would invoke his displeasure, and divine retribution wasn't something to be taken lightly.

He fingered the coin, turning it over in his hand. Heads, tails. Head, tails. Best to give it another shot, to make sure. If it was destiny, then the answer would surely be the same.

Up went the coin with a flick of his wrist. Wildly it spun in the buffeting rain. Lightning forked in the angry sky, and the wind did its best to steal the coin away.

But destiny would not be thwarted. The coin landed neatly in his palm and he squinted at it to check the result.

Heads, said the coin: *kill them.*

There was no room for uncertainty this time. 'Kill them!' roared the ghosts, and he took a step forward, his foot squelching in the mud.

Yet his doubts bubbled back up, and he halted again. The kids had shown him kindness, especially the skinny one with the thick glasses and the earnest voice. They had risked their lives to save him.

They deserve to live.

But in this world, no one got what they deserved, and kindness got you killed. He should kill them anyway, just to teach them the lesson. 'They stole your shotgun,' the ghosts reminded him. 'They humiliated you and tied you to a tree. They made you their prisoner.'

They deserve to die.

But still, they had saved his life. It was only fair to save theirs in return.

And yet life wasn't fair. No one knew that better than him.

He froze, trapped in indecision. He had thought the coin would free him, but it had caught him in a fresh web of doubts.

I have to make my own choice.

'Impossible!' raged the ghosts. 'The coin told you what to do. *Kill the children. Eat them!* The word of the coin is destiny.'

But what if he defied the coin? What if he could change his destiny?

He remembered what the skinny kid had said to him. *I chose to save you. We always have a choice.* Could that be true?

Did he hold the power to defy the will of the gods?

Thunder rolled over him, as if to rebuke him for his insolence. But there was only one way to find out for sure. He marched across to the tent and ripped it open, dragging away the heavy tarpaulin and letting rain flood over the three kids who cowered beneath it. Lightning flashed again, painting their faces white with terror, and inside his head the ghosts roared their anger, louder even than the thunder that clapped overhead.

Chapter Fifty-Two

The storm was terrible, all crashing thunder and pouring rain. The wind whipped at the tarpaulin, threatening to rip the tent out of the ground and send it soaring away into the night sky. Rainwater ran beneath the fabric walls, trickling across the groundsheet and seeping into Vijay's clothes, chilling him to the bone.

But worse than all of that was the voice of the prisoner, raging and bellowing over the claps of thunder and roar of the rain.

'He's escaped,' whispered Aasha. 'Now he's coming for us. I told you we should have killed him when we had the chance.'

'But I tied him up well and good,' said Drake. 'He can't have escaped.'

The next flash of lightning put paid to any doubts. The wall of the tent turned white, and Vijay saw for himself the black silhouette of a monster raging against the storm, just a few metres beyond the tent. 'Should we run?' he asked.

'It's too late for that,' said Aasha. 'It's time to fight.' She already had the metal hook in her hands, its wicked points looking terribly dangerous inside the cramped space of the tent.

Drake took hold of the shotgun and trained it on the entrance.

Gingerly, Vijay picked up the hand axe he had so far used only for chopping firewood. He tested the edge of the blade against the palm of his hand. It wasn't sharp enough to draw blood, but he had seen the way it split logs. He could scarcely imagine what it might do against flesh and bone.

'Perhaps he'll just go away,' he whispered hopefully. 'There's no reason for him to want to harm us. We helped him.'

'Just keep hoping that, bro,' said Aasha scornfully.

Vijay's hope didn't last long. Seconds later there was a tearing sound as the tent was ripped from the ground and uprooted like a tree. Warg Daddy roared as he hurled it aside, and lightning flashed, freezing him against the night sky before darkness returned and thunder cracked like a rifle shot, drowning even the noise of the rain and the wind.

Shadow drew back, hissing loudly. Rainwater washed over Vijay's face and soaked into every part of him that wasn't already wet, and the wind tugged at his turban. He was too terrified to move, but Drake rose to his feet, holding the shotgun aloft. 'I'll shoot you!' he cried. 'I'm not afraid to shoot!'

Warg Daddy took a step forward, then another.

'Don't come any closer!' shouted Drake.

'Shoot him!' screamed Aasha.

But Warg Daddy came on until he was towering over Drake. His hand shot out and grasped the barrel of the shotgun, holding it tight. He pulled it closer until it was touching his bald head. 'Have you ever killed, boy?' he growled.

Drake shook his head mutely.

'It's not the killing that's hard,' said Warg Daddy. 'It's living with the ghosts of your victims. It will drive you mad if you let it.' He snatched the gun from Drake's hands and spun it around. Now it was pointing at Drake's head. 'Next time, don't hesitate,' said Warg Daddy. 'Pull the trigger. Take the shot. And don't be afraid of ghosts. It's better to live with ghosts than to become one yourself.'

'Are you going to kill us?' stammered Vijay.

Warg Daddy swept his yellow gaze toward him. The gun moved too, and Warg Daddy's finger caressed the trigger, as if he were engaged in some kind of internal debate. Eventually he lowered the gun. 'No. I came to thank you. You saved my life.'

Gratitude was the last thing Vijay had expected from this strange man, and yet he knew instantly how to respond. 'And you saved mine.'

Warg Daddy's eyes narrowed. 'I did. How?'

'I was lost, and confused, and didn't know what to do. But you proved to me that it's always right to help a stranger in need.'

'Even if that stranger is a killer?'

'The past doesn't determine who we are. We are free to make our own choices, and to choose a better future.'

'Are we?' Again, Warg Daddy seemed conflicted, as if unsure of his own mind. Perhaps he really was deranged, just like Aasha said. 'What about fate?' he asked. 'What about destiny? What if the future is already fixed?'

It seemed a strange moment to be debating moral philosophy, but Vijay sensed a genuine curiosity in the man's questions. 'Karma determines what happens to us,' he answered carefully, 'but we always have the freedom to choose our response.'

'Freedom is a heavy burden,' said Warg Daddy. 'What if I choose to kill again?'

'Then karma will –'

'Enough with the philosophy!' said Aasha. She stood up, rain running down her long shiny hair, the metal hook in her hand. 'What are you going to do now?' she asked Warg Daddy.

'I'm going to leave. And what about you?'

'We'll carry on searching for Rose,' said Vijay. 'Thanks to you we know she's still alive.'

'Probably still alive,' said Drake. Vijay looked at him crossly.

'Where will you go?' Aasha asked Warg Daddy.

The giant reached into his pocket and pulled out the coin that Vijay had taken from him and thrown on the ground. He must have picked it up again when he escaped. He turned it over in his hand before replying. 'I still have to decide. But I'll make my own choice this time.' He turned to leave.

'Wait!' said Vijay. 'What is it with that coin? Why is it so important to you?'

Warg Daddy held it up for all of them to see. The storm raged all around, but he lowered his voice and Vijay had to strain to catch his words. 'When things started to go wrong, I lost my courage. Then I lost my self-belief, and my ability to lead. Instead of making decisions, I flipped the coin.' He flipped it now, idly catching it in his great palm. 'But I don't need it anymore. I can make my own decisions again. You showed me how.'

He held out the coin, offering it to Vijay. It glimmered softly in the darkness.

Vijay considered it for a moment, then shook his head. 'Thanks, but keep it anyway. Perhaps it will bring you luck.'

'Luck?' Warg Daddy grumbled, pocketing the coin. 'There's no such thing.'

Chapter Fifty-Three

Old Sarum, Wiltshire, waning moon

Since leaving London, Chris Crohn had found himself increasingly immersed in prehistory. Whether it was stone circles, burial grounds or strange hill carvings, the ancient artifacts that had been left behind on the landscape were deeply mysterious. Nevertheless, lessons could be learned from them, and not just about the distant past, but about the future ahead. Once the last remnants of technology had fallen into disrepair, been lost or else forgotten, the survivors of this cataclysm would know nothing more than their distant ancestors. Perhaps even less, since much of the knowledge of those ancient people was lost to their twenty-first century descendants.

It was exactly like when the Romans left Britain and the country descended into the Dark Ages. A new Dark Age was coming, and the very survival of the human race would fall to people like Chris.

Ruined stumps were all that remained of the mighty

towers and halls that had once graced Old Sarum. Chris wrestled a chunk of rock from the crumbling mortar of a stone wall and examined it closely. Flint. The dark stone was everywhere in this part of the world, almost as common as the white chalk. In fact, flint was a crystalline form of limestone, so chalk and flint occurred naturally together.

The stone had a distinctive appearance, as shiny as a seashell, almost as if it had been polished. Milky clouds swirled across its glassy surface making a decorative pattern. But flint wasn't just ornamental. It could be struck against steel to make sparks for starting fires. And when broken it split naturally into sharply edged fragments. The piece Chris held in his hand now was still sharp, even though it was just a piece of building material, and hundreds of years old. He wondered what he might be able to make of it if he tried to shape it.

He tried an experimental tap against the stone wall. The flint was brittle and chipped easily, producing slim flakes with even sharper edges than the original stone. An idea began to form in his mind.

Seth sloped over to inspect his activity, his beard now so long he was in danger of tripping over it. He flicked his shaggy hair uselessly to one side. 'What are you doing with those rocks?'

'Making tools,' said Chris, not looking up.

Seth laughed. 'Out of rocks?'

'Out of flint.' Chris wondered why he even bothered to explain his actions. It was a waste of energy. He focussed instead on the flint. If he struck the edge of the stone just so ...

'I thought Rose said you were supposed to be coming up with some big ideas,' said Seth.

'I am.' Chris pulled a larger chunk of flint away from the wall and tried to shape it using another rock. Both pieces immediately shattered and fell apart in his hands.

Seth sniggered loudly.

Chris ignored him and tried again with a fresh piece of flint. How hard could it be? Early humans had managed to produce a wide variety of edged and pointed tools using nothing more than – well – Stone Age technology, so it was surely just a question of trial and error.

He struck the new piece against the wall and gathered up the fragments that resulted, turning them over. Gradually, ideas presented themselves to him. This piece looked rather like an axe head. That one could work as a knife. Those small chips could serve as arrow heads …

Chris' thoughts flowed logically, as surely as one step led to another. The mastery of stone back in early prehistory had marked the decisive split of the genus *Homo* from the rest of the hominins, those hairy apelike creatures from which modern humans were descended, propelling mankind down the road to world domination. In fact, those first flint tools had been so successful that humans had continued to produce them in exactly the same way for over two million years before someone had come up with the startling idea that making stuff out of bronze might be cool for a change.

In the books Chris had read as a child, Stone Age people had usually been pictured as hairy ape-like creatures. But that was factually incorrect. Early *Homo sapiens* had been anatomically the same as modern humans, with smooth, mostly hairless skin. Chris tried to imagine the momentous moment when one primitive human had succeeded in making the very first flint tool. It was probably all down to someone rather like himself. Some guy who wasn't as muscular as the rest of the tribe, who perhaps caught the sun a little too easily and had an aversion to biting insects. Maybe a hay fever sufferer to boot. While the rest of the tribe was out hunting sabre-toothed tigers and woolly mammoths with – what? sticks? what a bunch of numskulls! – that nerdy guy was hanging out back at the cave, knocking some stones around, an idea beginning to form in his head before its physical realization came together in his hands. No doubt his peers had ridiculed him. Some guy with a beard had probably poked fun at his stone-making, telling him he was wasting his time. Of course, every man would have had a beard back in those days. They had no way of shaving.

And then – eureka – the first tool. That nerdy guy had been proven right. He had made history. Now that guy was him.

Seth was still watching him as he worked the stone. 'What's that?'

'A flint knife.'

Seth laughed mockingly. 'Wow, awesome, dude. You've reinvented the Stone Age. You've just taken us back a million years.'

'No,' said Chris, holding his prize aloft. 'Don't you see? I've taken us into the future.'

'How come?'

'Modern tools will only remain useful for as long as we can maintain them. Eventually they'll break down or wear out, and they'll become useless. Long term, we can only use what we know how to make ourselves.'

'Stone tools. Wow.'

'Yes, wow. And you know what? You and I are going to do something amazing together.'

Seth regarded him suspiciously. 'What?'

'Come over here.'

'Why?'

'I'll show you.'

Hesitantly, Seth approached.

'Sit down.'

Seth sat on the low wall, eyeing the flint knife warily. 'What are you going to do with that?'

'This.' Chris seized hold of his friend's head, locking one arm firmly around his neck to hold him in place. Seth squirmed, but couldn't escape. 'I'm going to shave your beard,' Chris told him.

'With a rock?'

'With a knife.'

He seized hold of Seth's chin and began to slice away at the annoying forest of hair. Seth wailed, but bit by bit, his baby-smooth face began to reappear after months of concealment. Eventually, Gandalf was gone, and the village idiot was back.

'Next I'm going to give you a haircut,' said Chris. 'Who knows? If you can see the world properly for once, you might start to pay more attention to what's going on.'

Chapter Fifty-Four

Christmas Common, Oxfordshire

The day was hot and the work was hard, but Chanita was glad to be outside, busy doing something useful. She picked up a plank of wood and carried it over to where Sarah was directing operations.

'Set it down here with the others,' said Sarah. 'I'll fix them together, then we'll fill them with fresh soil and compost.'

Chanita did as she was told. Sarah was like a whirlwind these days, constantly organizing and planning and giving orders. It was easiest just do to what she said. Besides, Sarah's ideas were good ones. This raised bed would make an excellent place to grow vegetables. Melanie, too, was busily engaged, fetching water from the well. No doubt the work was helping her to cope with Ben's absence.

It was a week since Ben and James had left, and there had been no word from them. Chanita wondered how Melanie could have sent Ben away so easily. Whatever her faults, Melanie was a strong woman, there was no denying the fact. Both sisters were strong, and Chanita felt glad that she had come to know them. There was no one else in the world she could still count as friends, apart from Ben and James of course. But they could be anywhere now. They might even be dead.

Inevitably, her thoughts turned back to Michael Griffin. She never ceased to wonder at how she had allowed the Colonel to leave her so easily. She had waved goodbye, fully expecting to see him walk back into her life very soon, and that was the last she had ever seen of him.

No one could ever see into the future. You might delude yourself into believing that you knew what was coming, and that life was predictable, but the truth was that calamity and disaster waited around every corner, ready to spring out at the least opportune moment. No one understood that better than Chanita. As a teenager, she had watched in terrified awe as the Soufrière Hills volcano erupted, hurling fire and devastation across her island home of Montserrat, and driving her halfway across the world to Britain. More recently, she had watched as an unknown disease erupted just as suddenly, bringing an end to all civilization and leaving nowhere for her to run.

Yet still she fell for the same old delusion of certainty. She remembered so clearly the last time she had seen Griffin. It had been a momentous occasion. He had announced that he was going away and had put her in charge of running the evacuation camp at Stoke Park. And then they had kissed for the first time. At that moment, Chanita had thought herself to be at the very beginning of a lifelong relationship. She could never have known that she was at its end.

If she could go back in time and change one thing about that day, what would she do differently? Beg Griffin to stay with her? It would have been futile. The Colonel was a man of duty, and would never have allowed personal considerations to stand before the safety of the thousands of people whose lives he had been entrusted with. But knowing what she knew now, she would still have tried.

Melanie had sent Ben away in full knowledge that he would be gone for some time. Knowing even that he may never return. Now that was truly brave. Chanita could only marvel at her sacrifice.

Melanie returned from the well, a bucket full of water sloshing gently from side to side in her arms. She lowered it to the ground next to the raised bed and straightened herself up, pushing her hands against her lower back. Despite Mel's protestations to the contrary, Chanita could see that the pregnancy was becoming more physically burdensome with every passing day.

'Good,' said Sarah. 'Can you bring the compost over next? Let's see if we can get this bed all planted up today. It's not too late to sow cabbage and winter greens.'

Chanita admired Sarah's capacity for practicalities and planning. After James ran off and Ben went after him, it had been Sarah who had worked out a way to climb over the fence into the armoury at RAF Benson and retrieve the guns and weapons they had gone searching for. Now at least they had a small arsenal at their disposal. If any more looters came to Christmas Common, the interlopers would find themselves seriously outgunned.

Chanita had been a good organiser herself once, in her role of nurse at the quarantine hospital in London, and then later at Stoke Park. These days she was happy to let Sarah give the orders. Sarah was becoming good at it. It was because she still held the delusion that she could control the future. Once that illusion was shattered, it was no longer possible to make plans. Chanita certainly had none of her own.

Together with Sarah's sense of direction and Melanie's raw determination to survive, they were building a future. But what kind of future would it be? Would the three of them – or four, once Melanie's baby was born – live here growing old together? All Chanita could see was day after empty day, each one filled with bustling activity, yet all without Griffin. Time was supposed to be the healer, but how could she begin to heal when she hadn't yet been able to grieve? Without seeing his body, without hearing confirmation of his death, without having any certainty about what had happened to him, she was trapped in a state of limbo. There were five stages of grief. She was stuck at the very first: denial.

When they finished planting the bed, they sat together in the shade of an old oak tree, eating out of tin cans and watching the bees go about their business. Everyone seemed so busy these days. It was all quite exhausting.

'Soon we'll be eating our own fresh vegetables,' said Sarah.

'Soon?' said Melanie. 'I thought you said these would be ready to pick in winter.'

'Winter will come around soon enough,' said Sarah. 'Just you wait and see.'

'God, I hope not,' said Melanie. 'Everything's happening so fast. A year ago, things were normal. I was living my old life in London. You were looking after Grandpa. Chanita was working at the hospital. Ben was teaching. James was still at school. Now look at us! Look at the world. How did this ever happen?'

'Change always happens,' said Chanita. 'It can be good as well as bad.' She brushed her lips with her finger, recalling the touch of Griffin's lips against hers. The past year had brought her unimaginable loss and tragedy, but it had also brought Griffin into her life, if all too briefly. Her gaze lingered on the honeybees collecting pollen from the flowers. There was no space in their short lives for brooding and regret. 'The secret is to recognize the good and embrace it. And once it's gone, to hold on to the memories.'

Perhaps this was the true lesson of her life. Not to cling to the past, filled with regrets, but simply to let life flow and learn to enjoy each passing moment, savouring it while it lasted. Griffin had come, she had loved him for a short while, and now he was gone. Whether dead or missing, she might never know. Perhaps she didn't need to know. One day he might return, or perhaps life would bring her new and unexpected joys instead. One thing she knew for certain – living in the past was no way to live at all.

She rose to her feet. 'All right, then. That's enough of a break for me. These bees aren't resting. They know to make the most of the good weather. So let's do the same.'

Chapter Fifty-Five

Gatwick Airport, West Sussex

Griffin's desk was strewn with papers. Lists of regiments and battalions and divisions. Maps at various scales, covered in red lines and handwritten annotations. Endless reports and analyses. Lieutenant Hastings and his team in the Intelligence Corps had been hard at work.

Bampton stood at Griffin's shoulder, staring at the same reports. Together, they had studied these documents more times than the colonel cared to remember, and yet no amount of staring at them could change the brutal arithmetic of war.

'We will lose this battle unless we bring the fleet into play,' said Griffin. 'Our ground forces cannot win alone.'

He had begun his command of the government forces with two thousand men at his disposal, more than fifty Challenger 2 tanks, dozens of Warrior infantry fighting vehicles and other armoured units, a small naval fleet, and two carriers' worth of F-35 combat aircraft. Since the fighting at Gatwick airport, his ground forces were heavily depleted, and he now had just a small number of combat vehicles and a fraction of the soldiers he needed to win a battle. The Royal Marines onboard the ships were ready to be deployed, and after months at sea they were more than keen to taste some fighting. Yet even with the marines swelling his numbers, he still had barely fifteen hundred men and women available to him. He had no artillery or guided missile units, and because of the human shield employed by the enemy, the air force was still confined to reconnaissance flights and had been unable to carry out a single combat mission.

Meanwhile the Wolf Army had more than doubled in size, gaining recruits from the north and turning captive humans into werewolves, trained to fight. The enemy might lack professionalism, but it had greater numbers and superior strength on its side. Even the rumours of wolfmen had turned out to be true, and no one yet knew what they were capable of.

Always it came back to the same stumbling block. The human shield. But the latest aerial photographs of the enemy positions changed everything. Griffin shuffled them around the desktop, suppressing a shudder at what they implied.

'The captives are nearly all gone. Dead, or else turned into werewolves and trained to fight against us.'

He had held back from launching an air attack because of those human captives. The Prime Minister had urged him to bomb the enemy into oblivion when he had the chance, even though she knew that hundreds of innocent civilians would perish. Griffin had called her a monster; had thrown her into jail for suggesting such an outrageous course of action. Now he feared that she had been right all along. He had gained nothing from his display of mercy.

A pointless show of compassion. And for whose benefit?

Had his unwillingness to abandon the moral high

ground been simply to absolve his own conscience? The men, women and children he had refrained from killing were now all dead, or worse. All he had achieved was delay. And thanks to that, the success of the entire operation was in jeopardy.

I was weak. I was wrong. I must not fail again.

He felt a sudden urge to release the Prime Minister from her prison back at Northwood. She may not have an understanding of military strategy, but she had the balls to do what was required. But he knew that was cowardice speaking, and there was no more room for that.

'Then we must seize this opportunity,' said Bampton. 'The weather is likely to remain poor for a few days, but better flying conditions are bound to come soon.'

Griffin lifted a report from his desk. 'According to the Intelligence Corps, the next full moon will be a supermoon, a time when the moon's influence is unusually powerful. Dare we risk an attack when the werewolves may be at their strongest?'

'The fleet has only enough fuel to last another three weeks,' Bampton reminded him. 'We must commit our forces in that time or the chance will be lost forever.'

'I know. And we will only get one chance to strike.'

'Then let us strike as soon as the weather changes,' said Bampton. 'Hit the enemy with all we have. Hit them hard and wipe them out.'

They both knew it could never be as simple as that. War was not a game, with pieces moved around a board. Even with an air attack, the fighting on the ground would be fierce. Massive casualties would result. But the alternative was unthinkable.

We cannot lose this war. If we lose, we lose everything. And if I delay, we may lose our advantage. One way or another, the blood will be on my hands.

Griffin shuffled the maps and photographs together. 'Let us do it, then. Send word to the commodore. Order the fleet to move into position.'

Both Griffin and Bampton knew the plan by heart. The Wolf Army was being steadily driven west and south. Already the enemy had strayed too close to the coast, unaware of the danger they had placed themselves in. The 4.5-inch guns of the navy's Type 45 destroyers had a firing range of almost thirty kilometres. HMS *Dragon* and *Defender* were currently stationed with the rest of the fleet out in the English Channel beyond the Isle of Wight. They were just a day's sailing from the Solent and their home port of Southampton. From there, they would be capable of carrying out a heavy and sustained bombardment of the werewolves' position. That would mark the opening salvo of the final battle.

The campaign would proceed with an air assault from the F-35s onboard *Queen Elizabeth* and *Prince of Wales*, coupled with the firing of guided missiles from the destroyers. When as much damage as possible had been inflicted from a distance, the ground assault would begin. The remaining infantry would engage the degraded enemy forces, in conjunction with the Royal Marines from the carrier group. If all went as expected, victory would be assured.

Detailed plans, carefully made. And yet …

'What's wrong, Griffin?' asked Bampton. 'We've talked this through a hundred times.'

'Talking's easy. If this goes wrong, no one will blame you.'

The group captain placed a comforting arm around Griffin's shoulders. 'If this goes wrong, there will be no one left to assign blame to you or to anyone else. So don't worry about it. You know that this is the best option.'

Griffin managed to flash a wry grin at his friend. 'The least worst, you mean.'

The tent door opened and a junior officer entered. 'Colonel? Mr Perez is here to see you.'

Griffin raised a bleak smile. 'Show him in.' He turned to Bampton. 'At least that son of a bitch has returned as he said he would. But he may not like what I have to tell him.'

'Try not to upset him,' said Bampton. 'The time for choosing our allies is long past. Now we need anyone we can find.'

Perez entered the tent with a swagger and a flourish of his ring-encrusted hand. 'Good day to you, gentlemen. I have returned as promised. I trust that you have kept your side of the bargain.'

'Of course,' said Griffin.

'You have the gold?'

'Yes.'

A crooked smile broke out on Perez's weathered face. 'May I see it?'

'I'll show it to you, but you won't be taking any away with you today.'

The smile faltered as quickly as it had appeared. 'We had a deal, Colonel. Our services for your gold.'

'The deal still stands. The gold will be yours, but only after the defeat of the Wolf Army. For now, we will keep it safe for you. Such a lot of gold. I'm sure you wouldn't want anything to happen to it during the heat of battle.'

The man said nothing. His face might have been carved from granite. Then the smile returned like sun emerging from a stormy sky. 'You are a wily one, Colonel. A keen player. Yes, indeed. I ought to have made my terms crystal clear in advance of us shaking hands. Well, I believe you are a man of your word. I am inclined to trust you on this matter. But if I may just see it for myself …'

'Follow me.'

Griffin jerked himself to his feet, using his crutches to bear his weight. His knee spasmed and his leg screamed with pain as he walked, but he kept on, keen to show Perez the fruits of the operation.

It made quite a sight. In all, two helicopter loads full of bullion had been recovered from the vaults. Each bar weighed in at around twelve kilos, and there were over five hundred bars in total.

Perez seemed impressed that it had been snatched out of the Bank of England. 'So now you are villains, too,' he chuckled.

Griffin ignored the jibe. 'Will this be sufficient to satisfy your men's needs?'

Perez reached out and lifted one of the golden bars in both hands. He turned it over, studying the serial number stamped on it. His dark eyes twinkled with pleasure. 'They look genuine.'

'They are. My experts tell me that this little lot is worth around three hundred million pounds.'

'Why so little?'

'So little?' said Griffin incredulously. This man was infuriating. 'Do you have any idea how difficult it was to get hold of this? If it's not good enough for you, you can take your men and —'

'No need to be hasty, Colonel,' said Perez soothingly. 'It is quite sufficient for our needs. I merely wondered why you had left the rest underground.'

Griffin laughed grimly. 'I don't think that gold will be going anywhere soon, Mr Perez. And frankly, I don't really care if it does. If we want it, we can go back and recover the rest of it later. Right now, we have a war to fight. So, are you with us?'

The man cracked another of his crooked smiles. 'We are with you, Colonel, and ready to do our patriotic duty, et cetera, et cetera. Bring on the fighting! Let's go kill ourselves some wolves.'

Chapter Fifty-Six

The Pilgrims' Way

The storm had gone, and so had Warg Daddy, almost as suddenly as he had entered Vijay's life. So, too, had the tarpaulin sheet they had used as a tent, and the shotgun that Drake had claimed for himself. On balance, Vijay didn't really miss any of them. The shotgun had frightened him, even when it was in Drake's hands, and the tent had leaked whenever rain fell. As for Warg Daddy, Vijay was pleased that he'd been able to help the man get back on his feet, but even more relieved that he had gone away.

'You realize that you unleashed a monster back into the world, don't you?' Aasha chided him as they walked along a narrow path that led through some fields. 'That brute is probably on a killing spree right now.'

But Vijay's conscience on the matter was untroubled. 'It's enough for each of us to account for our own actions,' he lectured Aasha. 'We can't be held responsible for what others choose to do. Whatever Warg Daddy does next is on him.' Vijay knew that he had acted as required – by helping a stranger in need – and that was all that counted.

'Whatever,' said Aasha.

'Well,' said Drake. 'Now we've lost our tent. We've lost our best weapon. And we still don't know where Rose is, or even if she's still alive.'

'She's alive,' said Vijay. 'I know she is. Warg Daddy saw her at Glastonbury. So, we continue to head west.'

'Glastonbury is a long way,' said Aasha. 'It would be quicker by car.'

Vijay levelled a sharp gaze at her. 'There is no way I am ever getting inside a car again. Especially not with you at the wheel.'

She shrugged. 'Suit yourself. I'm just saying that walking's no way to find someone who might be hundreds of miles away by now.'

'Perhaps there's another way,' said Drake. 'Look!'

Up ahead, to the side of the path was an old barn, and leaning against its outside wall were three bicycles. They walked up to the barn, looking out for movement and listening for sounds, but the place seemed deserted. The bikes were mountain bikes – good quality and unlocked. It seemed like a gift from God. Could this be karma rewarding them for their act of charity? Whatever it was, it was too good to ignore.

A low wooden fence separated the barn from the path. Drake quickly scrambled over it and went to examine the bikes. He grabbed hold of the largest one and hoisted himself onto the saddle. 'Cool,' he said, and cycled around the barn, testing the bike for roadworthiness. 'It's a bit rusty, but it works okay.'

One by one, he lifted the bikes over the fence, passing them to Aasha, before climbing back over. He scooped a surprised Shadow off the ground and deposited the cat unceremoniously into his rucksack, before getting back onto the first bike. Aasha took the second one.

Vijay hesitated. 'What if these bikes belong to someone?' he asked. 'We mustn't steal.'

Aasha gave him a dark look. 'Bro, if you want to walk all the way to Glastonbury, go ahead. But I swear you're not getting me off this bike.'

Vijay had doubts. They had saved a man's life, but that didn't now make it okay to steal whatever they fancied. Karma was a ledger, and the debits would quickly erode the credits if you didn't watch out for the small deeds. But Drake and Aasha were already cycling off down the path, and if he wanted to keep up with them, he didn't have much choice. 'Forgive me,' he muttered, then mounted the bike and wobbled off along the dirt track.

They had only cycled a few miles before the law of karma struck back. Aasha came to a sudden halt, and climbed off her bike. 'I've got a puncture!' She threw her bike to the ground in disgust.

'Can't you just ride it anyway?' said Drake.

'No. It wobbles all over the place.'

Vijay wasn't too surprised at the turn of events. Every wrongdoing would come back to you for retribution sooner or later. But he refrained from pointing that out to Aasha. Besides, it was getting late in the day and they needed to find shelter now that they had lost their tent.

Shadow also seemed very glad that the short bike ride was over. He hopped out of Drake's backpack, shook some dignity back into his tail and slunk away into the undergrowth.

They had come to a halt at a staggered road junction with signs pointing in all directions to places Vijay had never heard of. The roadside hedges were overgrown and it was hard to see which way was best. The only guide was the sun itself, slowly sinking toward the horizon. Wherever it set was west, and that was where he would find Rose.

But before they could start moving that way, they heard voices, coming from the opposite direction.

'Get off the road!' hissed Drake. 'Quickly! Hide in the

scrub!'

Vijay dashed to the roadside and tried to conceal himself in the undergrowth. The hedge that bounded the side of the road was thick and spiky, and a long thorn stuck in his hand when he tried to push himself into it. He bit his lip to stop himself from crying out. Then he pressed himself down into the long grass that sprung up at the base of the hedge. Drake and Aasha did the same.

The travellers soon came into view – a middle-aged woman with two teenage boys. They were walking down the middle of the road and stopped when they spotted the abandoned bikes. 'Look, Mum,' said one of the boys. 'Bikes!' He picked one up, and tried to ride it, but he soon gave up. 'It's got a puncture,' he said. 'We can't ride these.'

His mother sighed. 'We'll just have to keep going on foot. We've come this far. We can't give up now.' They set off down the road once more.

Vijay watched them go. Then, before they had time to vanish, he rose to his feet, leaving his hiding place behind. 'Wait!' he called. 'Stop!'

Behind him, Aasha nearly freaked out. 'What are you doing, you idiot? Don't you ever learn?'

The three strangers turned to face him, looking alarmed.

'Don't be frightened!' called Vijay. 'We mean no harm. It's just me and my sister and my friend.'

The woman gathered the two boys to her side. She was wearing a floaty, floral dress, and looked poorly equipped for surviving the apocalypse. 'What do you want?' she asked suspiciously.

'Just to talk. We're heading in the same direction as you, looking for a friend. We need a place to stay for the night. Do you know of anywhere near here?'

The woman nodded, taking in Vijay's appearance and seeming to draw some relief from it. 'We were planning to stop in the next village, if we can find a house to shelter in.'

Drake and Aasha appeared too, Shadow at Drake's ankles. 'Where are you headed?' called Aasha.

The woman studied them carefully, before seeming to make a decision. 'You three children are alone?' she asked.

'Yes,' said Vijay. 'My parents are dead. It's just the three of us and our cat now.' A tear appeared in the corner of his eye and he brushed it away crossly. 'My name is Vijay.'

'I'm Kate. And these are my two boys, Tom and Harry. We're travelling to a place near Salisbury. We've heard that it's safe. People are gathering there because of a young girl with mystic powers. They call her a priestess. She has the gift of prophecy, or so people say. She can cast healing spells, and grant wishes to the virtuous.'

Aasha looked sceptical. 'Do you believe that?' she asked.

'I don't know,' admitted Kate. 'I don't know what to believe anymore. But if people are gathering there, it must be a good place. We have nowhere better to go, anyway. Everything we had is lost.'

Aasha lowered her voice. 'I don't believe in any of that voodoo. Do you?'

But Vijay had already made up his mind. 'If people are gathering to see this girl,' he said, 'then we should go there too.'

'You believe in this witch, then?' asked Aasha.

'I didn't say I did. But if people are flocking to Salisbury to see her, then perhaps we'll find Rose there too.'

'We'd be better off staying well clear, if you ask me,' said Drake. 'This magical stuff sounds like trouble.'

'But where else are we going to go?' said Vijay.

Drake shrugged.

Vijay glared at Aasha, but she said nothing, just glared back. 'That's settled then,' he said. 'We'll go to Salisbury with Kate, and look for Rose there. Then, if we don't find her, we'll just keep on searching.'

Whatever it took, however long he had to keep on

looking, he would never give up. He knew that if he couldn't find Rose, or if she turned out to be dead, then there would be nothing left to live for.

But it was best not to think of that. That was weak thinking, and if Rose had taught him anything, it was to be strong.

Aasha's eyes flashed. 'Okay, then, we'll go to Salisbury. But if this priestess turns out to be a fake, then you and I are going to have a serious talk.'

Chapter Fifty-Seven

Camberley, Surrey

An empty shipping container didn't make the most comfortable place to bed down, but at least it was dry. Ben lay on his belly, his head nestling between his front paws. The relentless drumming of raindrops against the metal roof didn't make sleep come easily though, and with each gust of wind outside the structure creaked ominously. Ben stared into the darkness, hoping the rain would ease, but finding himself none too hopeful. Just because it was the height of summer, in England that didn't mean it couldn't rain all day and all night. And then a bit longer for good measure.

The interior of the container was a steel cavern, hollow and echoing. Shadows reached into the farthest corners, pooling there like black liquid. Someone had spray-painted graffiti against one of the corrugated walls, like a kind of modern cave art. But at least Ben had persuaded James to take cover rather than to stay outside in the wet.

'Wolves don't need houses,' James had protested obstinately.

'Maybe not,' said Ben, 'but real wolves sleep in dens or under trees when it rains. And we're not real wolves, whatever you might think.'

James may have been unhappy with Ben's decision to take shelter from the rain, but he had reluctantly agreed. It was a small concession. Since leaving Christmas Common, James had turned feral, remaining permanently in wolf form, and Ben was obliged to join him. It was the only way he could match the younger man's pace. Besides, having shed his clothes, Ben had no wish to transform back into a naked man. Fur clothed him now, and kept him warm at night.

They had left behind their supply of wolfsbane too, and Ben had found none on their travels. The leaves of the plant had enabled him to overcome his darkest desires, and he feared that without it he would revert to a wild state, like when he had first turned. He watched himself closely for signs of growing hunger for human flesh, for sudden urges to kill. So far he had felt none of the bloodlust that had fuelled his early days as a werewolf.

He knew it would come though, as the effects of the herb wore off. The memory of how it had felt haunted him at night. In his dreams, he was still a monster. Perhaps that was another reason why he was unable to sleep. He shifted his head and turned his thoughts instead to Melanie. He had abandoned her again, although this time it was at her own request. With luck, he would complete his journey and return to her long before the wolf blood claimed him.

James stirred beside him, also unable to find sleep. As far as Ben could make out, James hadn't slept properly since they had left Christmas Common. He was hardly eating either, and seemed to have entered some kind of state beyond normal bodily needs. But that couldn't last forever, and Ben was glad he had joined James on his journey. Alone, who knew what might become of him.

He heard James' voice in the darkness. 'Last time we travelled together, I was following you. Now, you have become my shadow.'

Ben grinned to himself. It was good to hear his friend's voice again. James had turned in on himself, scarcely engaging in more than a few words of speech at a time. 'We make a good team, right?'

James didn't reply to that. Like so often now, he seemed to be alone, even when Ben was with him. It was rare for him to reveal much of what he was thinking.

Ben filled the silence with his own thoughts. 'When I first became a werewolf and ran away from Melanie, I didn't have any plan, other than to get as far away from her as I could, and never come back. Without you, James, I don't know what would have happened to me. I might still be out there now, wandering the world on my own.'

'I have a plan,' said James. 'And I'm not afraid to go alone.'

'We talked about this, James. I'm not going to let you go alone.'

When Ben had first caught up with James, not far from RAF Benson, and insisted on going with him, he had persuaded James to reveal his plan: to find Leanna and negotiate a truce. If a temporary end to hostilities could be agreed with the government forces, James had argued, then perhaps there was a way to end the war and bring lasting peace.

It was a commendable idea, but from the little Ben knew about Leanna, it didn't seem likely that she was one to compromise. But James insisted that he had to try, and with his ability to shape-change between human and wolf forms at will, he was perhaps uniquely placed to act as a go-between.

'You know that it's a crazy plan, don't you?' Ben continued now. 'I mean, we don't even know where Leanna is.'

'She's at the centre of everything,' said James. 'Like a spider in her web.'

'Nice metaphor. But where is the centre of this web? So far, we haven't even found any strands of silk. We're just wandering at random, hoping to stumble on the Wolf Army.'

'When we find Leanna, we'll know.'

'We certainly will. Let's hope she doesn't catch us like flies.'

The rain continued to pelt down on the steel roof, making Ben feel trapped inside the container. He wanted nothing more than to leave and return to Melanie, but he had promised her he would stay with James and keep him safe. But how long would this peace mission last? If they weren't able to find Leanna, and if James couldn't be persuaded to give up his futile quest, when would they ever return to Christmas Common? Melanie's pregnancy was already quite advanced. The thought that Ben would miss the birth of his son or daughter was unbearable.

Besides, there was something else gnawing at Ben, beyond the discomfort of travel, beyond the separation from Melanie, beyond the overwhelming odds against success. There was James' brooding silence, his secrecy, his unwillingness to share his thoughts. They had taken on the form of an almost physical barrier, like a mountain looming over this whole enterprise. Ben wondered whether James had other intentions – some secret agenda that he had not revealed. There was definitely something that James wasn't telling him.

'So what are you going to say to Leanna?' Ben asked. 'The last time you two met, I seem to recall that she tried to kill you.' It had been back in London, the night of the wolf moon. Ben and Melanie had fought off Leanna, alongside James. The memory left a cold feeling in his gut, adding to his misgivings about the wisdom of this quest.

'True,' admitted James. 'But if I can demonstrate that I have forgiven her, then I can win her trust.'

'And then what?'

'Leanna wants power. But not at any price. She's not irrational. She must know that an end to the fighting is now in everyone's best interest. I can be the bridge to peace.'

It was hard to imagine peace after such devastating destruction and such bitter conflict. But James was certainly right when he said that peace was in everyone's interest. So much had been lost, so many lives ruined. If there was a chance at bringing this war to an end, it was surely worth taking. James had worked a miracle already, saving Ben from himself and enabling him to return to Melanie's arms after he'd thought he would never see her again. Perhaps he could do the impossible again.

The rain was beginning to ease now, and the pale bloom of dawn edged the doors of the container in grey. Pale drops clung to the top of the metal frame, hanging milky in the growing light. Ben sat up, lifting his paws from the hard floor, and stretched out his limbs. He would get no sleep now, and it was better to be on their way. He had no desire to spend a second night in this oversized tin can.

'Come on, then,' he said to James. 'Let's get going. Leanna's got to be out there somewhere. The sooner we leave, the sooner we'll find her.'

Chapter Fifty-Eight

Haywards Heath, West Sussex

They arrived with a rumble of engines, stirring dust clouds into the sky and filling the air with a deafening roar and a choke of burned oil. The bikes pulled to a halt and Canning appraised them with curiosity.

Four motorbikes and four riders, each clad in black leather, emblazoned with a white wolf. *Werewolves.* Canning could smell their scent even over the suffocating stink of exhaust fumes. New arrivals were always welcome, but these were no ordinary recruits. Their leader jumped nimbly from her bike and dragged the helmet from her head to reveal the pretty features of a young woman.

Canning knew her face at once. *Vixen, the Wolf Sister.* He had assumed her to be dead. But now he chided himself for his elementary error. *Never assume anything.*

He narrowed his gaze, scanning the other riders. Three men, powerfully built, with the look of battle-hardened warriors. Who else but the Wolf Brothers? They had been twelve originally, but that was before war had ravaged the land, claiming the lives of so many. At least the one he feared to find among them was not here. *That is something.* But what were they doing here? And, more to the point, how could he use their unexpected arrival to his advantage?

He bowed courteously to his new guests. 'Welcome. Vixen, is it? And you must be the Wolf Brothers. I am Lord General Canning. How may I be of service to you?' *Obsequious words.* Always so irritating on the lips of others, and yet they seemed to pour quite effortlessly from his own. *I have had so much practice at being a sycophant.*

If Vixen was surprised that he knew her by name, her face showed no trace of it. Her features remained expressionless, her mouth unmoving, her eyes dead. She said nothing, just turned that cold look on him, drinking him in, as if she were somehow absorbing his very soul.

Canning's mouth turned down with displeasure. He had heard about this woman back in London. A ruthless killer. A silent psychopath. He rarely knew fear, but now he felt a sudden urge to turn away from that dead, all-seeing gaze. A desire to run fast and far.

But he held his ground and pasted a smile back onto his lips. 'Perhaps you are tired after your journey? Come. I will take you to see Leanna.' *Set the cat among the pigeons. Or more likely, feed the pigeons to the cat.* 'But first, if you wouldn't mind removing your weapons?'

He half expected the Wolf Sister to protest, or to shoot him dead where he stood, but instead she nodded to the others and they began to remove an assortment of guns, knives, crossbows, and other lethal-looking items. One of the men had an injured arm. A gunshot wound. But he waved away Canning's offer of medical assistance with annoyance.

When they had divested themselves of their armoury, Canning gestured for them to accompany him. 'Our queen will be pleased to see you,' he continued brightly. 'Of that I have no doubt.'

And just as pleased with me, when I bring her one of the traitors she has sought for so long.

The thought of the reward he might receive for bringing Vixen to the queen was enough to placate the feel of the girl's eyes on his back as he walked. She had still said nothing.

Let her die wordless, then. She is nothing to me.

He led the way to Leanna's tent, pleased to find that his guests followed him, all nice and docile. A ruthless band of killers they may be, but it seemed that they hadn't come to kill him. Hopefully he wouldn't have long to wait to discover exactly why they had come.

He swept open the flap to the royal tent with a theatrical flourish. 'Your majesty, I bring you unexpected visitors.'

Leanna was seated on her throne as usual, Will Hunter fawning by her side. She glanced up at Canning's interruption. But the look of annoyance slid from her face at the sight of Vixen, to be replaced by one of cold fury. She was on her feet in an instant. 'What is this?'

'Vixen and the Wolf Brothers,' intoned Canning unnecessarily, but enjoying being master of ceremonies. 'I brought them to you. I was sure you would be pleased to see them.' He stepped aside and ushered his guests forward.

Vixen slid inside the tent, moving with catlike grace. The Brothers muscled their way behind her, no finesse in their movements, only brutish bulk. They fanned out, seeming to fill the tent. The courtiers in Leanna's attendance fell back.

Vixen took a step toward the throne and Canning wondered if she would rush to the attack. But instead the girl curtsied politely to Leanna. 'Your majesty. We have returned to your service. Please forgive us for our absence, and allow us to repay our debts with our loyalty.' She kneeled before the throne, waiting for Leanna's response.

Canning pushed a hand over his face to conceal a smile. So this was it? The girl who had stolen Warg Daddy away from Leanna had returned seeking forgiveness? Canning had never witnessed his queen forgive the slightest transgression amongst her subjects. *Although it is true that she has given me more than one second chance.* He swept that thought aside, and watched.

Leanna crept forward as Vixen continued to kneel, her head bowed. 'You returned to me after so long. Why?'

'Your majesty, I bring you news. Warg Daddy is dead.'

'Dead?' Leanna's face betrayed puzzlement. 'I know this already. He is dead by my own hand. I poisoned him.'

Vixen's head quivered gently on her shoulders. 'No, your majesty. Warg Daddy did not die then. He lived on. But now he is surely dead. We left him mortally injured, one arm torn from his body.'

Leanna reached out a hand and lifted Vixen's chin. Her voice, when she spoke, was like ice. '*Surely* dead? You did not see him die?'

'No. But we left him for dead. No man could survive such injuries.'

Will Hunter took a step towards his queen. 'Your majesty, perhaps –'

Leanna's voice lashed at him like a whip. 'Be silent! Unless you wish to die too!'

Canning covered his face, unable to stop himself from grinning like a Cheshire cat.

Leanna spoke again to Vixen. 'So now Warg Daddy is dead, and you wish to pledge your allegiance to me? Is that right, girl?'

'Yes,' said Vixen.

'And so, you expect that you can betray me, seduce Warg Daddy, run away with him, and then return and receive my forgiveness?'

A tremor of doubt entered Vixen's voice for the first time. 'No, your majesty. I do not ask your forgiveness. I ask only to serve you.'

'Serve me,' sneered Leanna. 'Lord Canning, tell me, what quality do I require first and foremost from my followers?'

Canning was ready with his answer. It required no great thought. 'Loyalty, your majesty.'

'Loyalty,' echoed Leanna. 'Exactly. Unwavering loyalty. Loyalty that doesn't switch sides whenever it's convenient. Girl, do you understand what loyalty is?'

'Yes, your majesty.'

'And do you understand what treachery is?'

Vixen didn't answer the question. Perhaps at last she had realized her error in returning to Leanna.

'Treachery,' said Leanna, 'is the opposite of loyalty. And someone who is guilty of treachery is called a traitor. Do you know how treachery is punished, traitor?'

Vixen began to rise to her feet.

Leanna reached out and struck her across the face with a resounding slap. 'Treachery is punished by death.'

Chapter Fifty-Nine

Christmas Common, Oxfordshire

It was evening, Melanie's favourite time. Back in the old days, she would have been getting ready to go out, applying her makeup, choosing her clothes, anticipating the pleasures to come. Now she sat miserably on her bed, anticipating no pleasure, tonight or anytime soon.

Ben had been gone for almost two weeks now. Or was it longer? Melanie's timekeeping wasn't quite up to scratch. In fact her ability to think clearly was in sharp decline. Her brain just didn't seem to be working right anymore. Maybe the pregnancy was using up all her blood supply, cutting off oxygen to unnecessary parts of the body.

Who needs brains, anyway? Melanie had always managed quite well with just her looks. But now her supple figure was also a distant memory. Since Ben and James had gone away – however many days that had been – she had moved up first one jeans size, and then another, and then had abandoned jeans altogether. A flowing skirt was far more practical, however frumpy it might make her feel. She studied her rounded profile in the bedroom mirror.

What do I look like? Like the Victorian lady that Chanita thinks I am.

She ran her hands over the curve of her belly, feeling the weight of the pregnancy pressing against her skin.

I look just as fat as my sister.

Yet that wasn't fair, or true. Sarah was no longer the pudgy woman she used to be. Since leaving London she had lost a lot of weight. She was slimmer than Melanie now. For every pound that Melanie gained, Sarah lost one. And she was gaining in confidence too.

She is turning into me. Then am I becoming her?

No. That would never happen. However similar the two sisters' appearances might become, they would always be two very different people. Melanie would never lock herself away from human contact like Sarah had done. And she would never be as practical as her sister either. Nor as selfless.

I am trying my best to help, but this pregnancy turns even simple household tasks into a challenge. And it's so hard to keep my spirits up now that Ben has gone. Oh, please come back soon, Ben Harvey!

Her thoughts lingered a while longer on Ben and James, the two most precious men in her life. She wondered where they were now, and what they were doing, and she hoped that they were still together, and safe. But there was nothing she could do to speed their return, and the realization of her helplessness spurred her into action.

She made her ungainly way downstairs, swaying as she shifted the weight of her bump from one foot to the next. *Waddling.* There was no other word for it.

She was glad to make it downstairs, then immediately regretted it. Chanita was in the parlour, folding clothes from the washing line. Her eyes went immediately to Melanie's bump, and rested there.

'It's rude to stare,' said Melanie.

'Sorry,' said Chanita. 'It's just that –'

'I know. It rather catches the eye, doesn't it?' The descent of the stairs had left Melanie breathless. *I almost feel faint. How tedious.* 'I think I might just sit down for a minute,' she said. 'Get my breath back.'

This damn pregnancy. I wish it was done already.

Chanita took a seat next to her as she recuperated from her exertion. 'If it's any comfort, I think this part will be over quite soon.'

'Oh, really? I thought I would be ages like this. And didn't you tell me that the second trimester is the easiest?'

'It is,' said Chanita. 'But if I'm correct, you've reached the third trimester now.'

Melanie frowned in consternation. First, second, third. She wished that Chanita would make up her mind. 'I thought that would take months to arrive.'

'Normally, yes. It would be the final three months of pregnancy.'

'You were talking about a January birth. That's ages away. It's only August.' Melanie tried to do the sums, but her brain was too full of fog. It was enough to endure each passing week and month. Counting them was too much.

'I think,' said Chanita, 'that you were right about conceiving the baby on the night of the summer solstice. Normally that would mean that we'd be expecting a birth next spring. But all the indications are that you'll be ready to give birth in the next few weeks.'

Melanie felt her mouth drop open. 'Weeks?'

'That's right. The entire gestation will have lasted about eight weeks. Two lunar cycles.'

Melanie stared, appalled. 'I don't understand.'

'This is no ordinary pregnancy.'

Melanie's hands moved back to her belly, and she felt a movement inside. Something stirred – or kicked. 'Then – my God! What kind of creature is this baby?'

Chanita's eyes were filled with the compassion of a

nurse.

Melanie stood up. 'Don't look at me like that!'

'Like what?'

'Like you have some terrible news to tell me. Like someone has died.' Her legs began to shake and she sat back down quickly to hide it. 'It's because Ben's the father, isn't it? He's planted some kind of monster inside me.'

'Don't say that, Melanie.'

'But it's true.'

A creature is growing inside me, feeding off my food, its heart beating with the blood of a werewolf. Are its tiny teeth hungry to devour me from the inside out? Does it lie there, dreaming of the taste of my blood? What manner of creature is it?

'Melanie, stop it. There's no reason to think the worst. But it would be wise to prepare yourself for any eventuality. I think it's fair to say that these are uncharted waters.' Chanita closed her hand over Melanie's. 'But I'll be by your side. We'll navigate this together.'

Nautical metaphors are never very reassuring. Watery graves spring to mind. And worse things happen at sea.

'Look on the bright side,' said Chanita. 'If I'm correct, there really isn't very much more of this for you to endure.'

'Right,' said Melanie glumly. *Like a sinking ship, then. Ready to go down.* 'Typical of me to rush this, eh?'

Chanita smiled. 'You certainly like to get things done quickly.'

Chapter Sixty

Haywards Heath, West Sussex

Vixen was nothing more than a wisp of a girl, her arms as slender as sticks. Could this really be the feared slayer, about whom so many stories were told? Had she really led the Wolf Sisters into battle and slaughtered her enemies with her bare hands? Canning found it hard to believe.

And yet ... there was something about the way she held herself. As upright as Leanna, her stance relaxed and calm even though she faced a certain death, Vixen was silent, dignified. Almost regal. Her eyes betrayed no fear, only serenity. They were fathomless, like the depthless waters of a still lake.

Canning found his gaze transfixed to this legendary killer with the lithe, frail body of a waif.

Before her stood Leanna, cold fury pasted across her features, her sapphire eyes hungry for vengeance. It was all the queen had talked of since Canning had known her. At last she had the chance to kill one of the traitors herself.

Canning had seen Leanna rip grown men limb from limb. She had sliced off heads, wrestled opponents twice her size to the ground before rending them like straw dolls and devouring their flesh. Surely this girl, Vixen, would not last seconds.

And yet … Leanna's victory was not assured. The queen risked much in fighting woman-to-woman. If this went badly for her, Canning stood ready to seize his chance. He touched the hilt of the ceremonial sword at his waistband and fingered the automatic pistol concealed beneath his uniform. Vixen's victory alone would not be enough to ensure Canning's ascent to the throne.

If Leanna dies here tonight, Will Hunter must follow her to the grave.

His mind continued to whir in overdrive. If Vixen won the contest, would she leave, or would she expect to rule in Leanna's place? Canning would not stand idly back, watching as one queen replaced another.

If necessary, both queens must die.

That was a lot of killing to be done, but he knew he would never get a better chance. His fingers curled firmly around the grip of his gun.

A small number of spectators had been invited to witness the combat within the royal tent. Beside Canning and Will Hunter stood a few of the wolfman's henchmen, together with the queen's most favoured courtiers. The three surviving Wolf Brothers had also been allowed to watch. The audience made a ring, within which Leanna faced her opponent. Canning had imagined she would choose to fight bare-handed, but the queen had selected a pair of hunting knives with which to do combat. Will Hunter entered the ring, the knives in his hand. He offered them to Leanna, who chose her weapon, lifting it to her chest where its edge caught the light, blazing like fire.

Vixen accepted the other knife from Hunter, who took up position between the two women. 'This fight will be to the death,' he announced. 'Let the best woman win.' He flashed a smile at Leanna, but she ignored him. Her face was set as hard as stone, and her eyes were fixed on her enemy. If raw hate could kill, Vixen would be dead already.

Vixen, for her part, betrayed no emotion. Neither fear, nor hatred, nor anger. Canning had never seen a face so calm before battle.

Could he really be about to witness Leanna's demise? He had never thought it might come so easily. He held his breath as queen and traitor began to circle each other.

He was reminded of two scorpions, locked in combat, each armed with a deadly array of pincers, stingers and jaws, sizing each other up before moving to the attack. The knives the women carried, though sharp and deadly, were merely the most visible of the weaponry the women bore. Less obvious, yet perhaps just as effective, were their nails and teeth – the killing implements of a werewolf. Leanna's teeth were on full view as she circled her foe. Vixen's mouth, by contrast, remained closed.

Leanna had a mad anger on her side, while Vixen had serenity. Canning had no idea which quality might prevail.

'Your death will not be quick,' declared Leanna. 'I shall rip you limb from limb, and make you suffer, just as I have suffered from your betrayal.'

Vixen made no response. The knife in her palm remained still, as she moved from dainty foot to dainty foot, stepping sideways around the tent.

'You will beg for mercy,' continued Leanna, advancing slowly, 'but you shall receive none.'

Yet still her opponent had no words to say.

It is not words that kill. It is action.

Vixen's attack came so quickly that Canning hardly saw her move. She struck with blinding speed, closing the distance with Leanna, the blade flashing in her fingers. She cut the air with the knife, just an inch from Leanna's face.

The queen ducked away, her hair flying as she spun aside, but Vixen leapt at her again, slashing left then right, drawing blood first from the queen's shoulder, and then from her hand.

Leanna screamed and lunged forward, slashing with her own knife at Vixen's throat. But the girl was already rolling sideways, spinning head over heels as she evaded the attack. She returned to her feet at the other side of the tent, only a slight rise and fall of the breast giving any indication of her exertion.

Canning's hand was glued to the handle of his pistol. The possibility of Leanna's imminent death was growing, and with it the chance that his own moment had come. If it happened, he wouldn't hesitate. A bullet to Hunter's chest and another to his head would finish the wolfman before he even knew what was coming his way. And no matter how fast Vixen might move, she wouldn't expect to be gunned down in the wake of her victory. Then it would be a matter of dealing with Hunter's henchmen, and perhaps the Wolf Brothers … Canning was outnumbered ten to one, but he had men he could rely on too. Men well briefed, and ready for action. His rise to power might be just minutes away, and he could barely keep the grin from his face, even as Leanna panted and sweated, reassessing her opponent's capabilities.

There was no talk now in the arena, only hard breathing and quick movement, as first Leanna and then Vixen made cuts and thrusts with their knives. Parries and countermoves followed, each woman seeking to evade the other's swipes and to launch attacks of their own.

They were well-matched, two werewolves at the height of their powers. Vixen was younger, faster and more agile, but Leanna was stronger and taller. She had reach, and soon one of her thrusts struck home, the edge of her blade caressing Vixen's face and drawing a line of sweet crimson across her cold features.

Vixen spun, pivoting to one side, then whirling back with a counterthrust at Leanna's chest. Leanna dropped low, then rose up, her foot lashing out and connecting with Vixen's chin. The girl's head snapped back, but she moved into a backflip, landing with both feet on the ground as surely as any cat.

Leanna paused, brushing hair from her eyes, and in that second Vixen was on the offensive again, the knife switching almost unseen to her other hand. She came forward in a blur, one hand in a feint, the other concealing the knife close to her chest.

Leanna moved the wrong way, deceived by the bluff, and Canning heard himself gasp. She had left her side vulnerable, and he watched as Vixen's knife hand plunged toward its open target to deliver a killer blow.

But at the last moment, Leanna twisted, bringing her own knife round to parry. She lunged forward with her fingers, driving long nails into Vixen's face, plunging through one eye and deep into the socket beyond.

Canning winced, feeling the ghost of his own lost eyeball writhe in sympathetic agony.

The duel was over as quickly as it had begun. Vixen quivered, then her lifeless body dropped to the floor, the space where her eye had been now dripping blood and jelly and nameless gore.

Leanna fell on her prey with glee, sinking to her knees next to Vixen's still corpse. With the tip of her knife, she opened up the girl's abdomen, cutting through flesh, as fresh blood sprayed her face. Then, with delicate fingers, she reached inside her victim's body and plucked out her liver.

Canning watched, appalled, as his queen withdrew the dark organ. She held it in her hands, gloved wrist-deep in blood before devouring it, cramming it into her greedy mouth and tearing off hunks with her teeth. Even Will Hunter looked on with something approaching revulsion on his wolf's features.

But Leanna was oblivious to her audience. Her hands cradled the plum-coloured offal, and she licked blood from her fingers as she chewed, a look of immense satisfaction on her face.

Canning's hand left the grip of his pistol and returned to his side. It would be far too risky to try to take down Leanna now. If he had imagined that Vixen might do his work for him, that hope had been decisively dashed. Now Leanna was stronger and madder than ever, and the road ahead had become doubly dangerous.

He joined in the cheers and applause as Leanna continued her bloody feast, doing his utmost to make the ends of his mouth turn up in a mockery of pleasure.

Chapter Sixty-One

Old Sarum, Wiltshire, new moon

The sheep were coming into the field, dashing through the open gate as if their lives depended on it, and behind them the dogs barked as if this was the most fun they had ever had. The three men and one woman who Chris had designated as "shepherds" were directing the dogs, and were well on track to achieving their primary objective – moving the flock from field A to field B without loss or casualties. Operation *Swift Fleece* was proceeding surprisingly well.

Chris had a feeling, a feeling that he hadn't experienced for a long time. He was reluctant to put a name to it, because he had never been very good with feelings. They were always so imprecise, so nebulous, and so transient. Emotions weren't things you could grab hold of and pin down. You couldn't put them in a display cabinet for others to see, or examine them under a microscope. You just had to guess what they might be, and Chris hated guessing.

But he began to form a tentative hypothesis about this latest sensation. There was a distinct possibility that this was happiness.

On the face of it, it seemed unlikely. Illogical, even. Here he was, reliving the Stone Age with a bunch of people he barely knew and mostly disliked, with no prospect of ever sitting in front of a computer screen or holding a smartphone again. His life, basically, was over. And yet that feeling wouldn't go away.

He supposed it might be because of the new role that Rose had given him. As the person charged with responsibility for long-term survival, he now had status within the tribe. Not that he was interested in petty social hierarchies, but this status allowed him to spend time doing what he enjoyed most – thinking deep thoughts and telling other people how to live their lives. His nose had healed too, and his hay fever was easing as the season progressed.

So the notion that he was happy wasn't entirely out of the question. He would mull it over a bit longer before deciding what to call it. For the present, he would provisionally label it "contentment" unless any further compelling evidence presented itself.

Right now, he needed to focus on the sheep.

The situation on the ground was changing. The designated shepherds were moving about the field, flapping their arms and shouting at the dogs. Although most of the sheep had now entered field B and were proceeding with their allotted tasks of munching grass and baaing, a few stragglers remained in field A. They were clearly bent on troublemaking. Chris watched as the shepherds attempted to bring their dogs back into play in order to finish the job. The shepherds were keen, and the dogs enthusiastic. But the shepherds lacked experience and the dogs had not been trained. Dogs, it seemed, did not instinctively possess the ability to round up a flock of sheep. The operation was rapidly coming undone.

The fleeting feeling that Chris had grasped so briefly began to dissipate into a cloud of something altogether more familiar – disappointment. He turned away from the unfolding disaster and trudged back across the muddy pastures to the refuge of the hill fort.

Ryan and Seth were waiting for him. He knew they had been watching. He could tell by the anxious look in Ryan's eyes and the smirk on Seth's cleanshaven face.

'Lamb chops tonight?' asked Seth.

Chris knew that the best way to respond to trolls like Seth was to ignore them. But sometimes the provocation was too much. 'We're not going to eat the sheep. I already explained that. We're going to breed them, so we can make more.'

'Make?'

'You know what I mean.' Chris didn't find the matter of sexual reproduction a comfortable topic of conversation, not even with his oldest friend. It was enough to know that there would be more sheep at the end of the process than at the beginning. 'But we can also milk them and shear their wool for making clothes.'

'How do you even shear a sheep?' wondered Seth.

Chris didn't bother to look his way. 'With shears.'

'Seth tells me that you've been making stone tools,' said Ryan.

'I can show you if you like.' Chris led them to his workshop, where he'd been experimenting with different designs. The workshop was really just a tent, but as far as he knew, nobody had ever come up with a world-changing invention in a tent. It was important to name things properly. He showed Ryan his best axe head, a couple of knives that he was working on, and a handful of arrowheads.

Ryan whistled. 'Do they work?'

In reply, Chris indicated Seth's lack of a beard. 'I've proven the basic concept. Now we need to scale up production. And then we need to learn how to weaponize the tools.'

'What do you mean?' asked Ryan.

'I mean turn them into weapons.'

'I know what weaponize means.'

'With wooden handles, we can turn the axe heads into battle axes. With poles we can use the knives to make spears. And with sticks we can manufacture arrows.'

'You're serious?'

'How else are we going to defend ourselves against werewolves and other aggressors?'

'We haven't seen any werewolves since that night on the firing range,' said Seth.

'We've been lucky. But we can't trust to luck, or we'll end up dead. We should have learned that lesson by now.'

Ryan gave the proposal due consideration. 'I looked for guns when we were on the firing range, but there were only spent cartridges and shells. I've had teams out searching for weapons in the military bases nearby, but they've all been picked clean.'

Chris shook his head. 'Modern weapons aren't the solution. Once we've run out of ammunition, rifles and handguns become useless. We can only depend on what we can make ourselves.'

He could tell that Ryan was taking him seriously. In fact, Ryan wasn't half as stupid as Chris had originally thought. It was possible that upper body strength, tattoos and a shaven head didn't necessarily correlate with low intelligence after all. Chris would have to reconsider the way he classified such people in the future.

'All right,' said Ryan. 'Let's start collecting flint and wood. You and I can work on the designs together. As soon as we know what we're doing, we'll start full-scale production and training. But don't say anything to Rose. She has enough to worry about already. I don't think she wants to hear about war and fighting.'

Chapter Sixty-Two

Froxfield Green, Hampshire

The Wolf Army proceeded slowly but inexorably across the open ground, a pair of giant Challenger 2 battle tanks leading the way. The metal tracks of the tanks turned relentlessly under the power of their monstrous 26-litre turbocharged engines, making short work of any obstacles that came their way, flattening the undergrowth and clearing a path for the vehicles that followed. Their turrets swivelled to the left and the right, their 55-calibre guns ready to open fire on enemy activity the instant it was spotted.

Tracked infantry support units rumbled behind them, their short stubby guns deceptively small – the turret-mounted cannons were capable of taking out enemy armour at a range of one mile. Each patrol vehicle carried a crew of ten. Stormer missile launchers followed, scanning the skies for threats, ready to deploy their arsenal of rockets in close air defence. Then came Army Land

Rovers, bumping along in the wake of the tracked vehicles. More tanks brought up the rear.

Engines growled. Wheels turned. Mud splashed.

A long column of wolf warriors walked alongside the vehicles, lugging rifles, grenade launchers and other small arms. Hundreds upon hundreds of fighting men and women, some in human form, some wolf-heads and other mutants. All of them trained to kill. Each one of them hungry for action.

From his vantage point in the middle of the convoy, Canning could see them all.

The northmen had added an assortment of scavenged civilian vehicles to the military convoy. A BMW X6 had become Canning's personal mode of transport. Behind it came a couple of Range Rovers. A bunch of Toyota Land Cruisers followed. All had been stripped down and repurposed for combat. Satellite navigation, air conditioning and other comforts had been removed, and roof-mounted heavy machine guns fitted in their place.

The Wolf Army had blossomed into the most powerful fighting force in the land. According to Canning's latest intelligence, his infantry greatly outnumbered the government forces even though the enemy claimed more vehicles and weapons.

And then there was the human shield.

Not so many of the captured slaves remained now. Most had perished, and those few still alive were growing weaker with each passing day. Soon they would be good for nothing but food, and there would be precious little meat to scrape from their bones when the time came. Still, they had served their purpose, preventing the government forces from launching an air strike on the convoy.

Soon there would be no further need for that shield. The threat from the air would be gone forever, for Canning had devised a scheme of genius. *A masterpiece even by my own lofty standards.* If his meticulous planning bore fruit, he would neutralize the government's greatest asset in one deadly manoeuvre. *Sometimes I amaze even myself with my brilliance.*

With the enemy's air power gone, the Wolf Army would be free to move against ground forces in overwhelming numbers. Wolves versus humans. The final battle would be a massacre.

Canning had also put in motion a stratagem to deal with Leanna and Will Hunter. The time had almost come for the happy couple to meet a sad and unfortunate end.

In war, regrettably, there are always so many casualties. And so many different ways to die. A stray bullet in the back, for instance. Or in the back of the skull at point blank range, to make absolutely certain of the outcome. In the thick of battle, who could say with certainty who might have fired it?

Yes. A terrible tragedy could befall anyone, even a queen and her consort.

And should my plans go awry and my assassins fail to kill their targets, I shall deny all knowledge. Nothing can be proven against me.

But his plans wouldn't fail. He had prepared them too carefully.

Soon my enemies will be vanquished and I shall be king and ruler of the entire world.

It was hard to stop an enormous grin from spreading across his face like an idiot.

'General Canning!' A messenger rode up on a motorbike, keeping pace alongside Canning's command vehicle.

'Yes? What is it?'

'A report from our scouts. An enemy camp has been spotted ahead.'

'A military camp?'

'No, General. Initial reports say that it is a civilian encampment, located close to the city of Salisbury.'

'Salisbury, eh?'

Canning had visited the city once, dragging a diabolical rabble of children there on a school trip. A pleasant enough place, with a well-touristed cathedral close. It boasted the tallest church spire in England, as he recalled, as well as one of the four original copies of *Magna Carta*. Facts that had bored his unruly pupils to death.

'How large an encampment?' he asked.

'Hundreds. Possibly thousands.'

'And all civilians, you say?' Canning stroked his chin thoughtfully. More slaves, ready for the taking. More food, ready for a victory feast. Sometimes, every last detail just seemed to fall into place. It was enough to fool a man into thinking that fortune was on his side. 'You are certain that they are unarmed?'

'No military activity of any kind was observed, General.'

Salisbury. The final confrontation had to take place somewhere. His carefully-crafted plans were all ready to unfold, and there was nothing more to be gained by prolonging this marching from one place to another. Salisbury was as fine a city as any in which to meet his enemies on the field of battle.

'If we join the A30,' said the messenger, 'the road will lead us directly into the city.'

Canning slapped the roof of the BMW with one hand. 'Then let us go to Salisbury!'

Chapter Sixty-Three

Royal Portbury Dock, Avonmouth, waxing moon

They had fallen into a new rhythm, driving in the early morning and late evening, sleeping or dozing in the middle of the day when the sun was fierce and Liz was at her weakest. She came alive at night, and spent the hours of darkness patrolling the camp, searching for danger, and making sure that the others were safe in their sleep.

She was keeping a particularly watchful eye on Mihai. Although the boy had made a full physical recovery from his gunshot wounds, that wasn't what concerned her most.

I changed him, forever. I made him a vampire. What right did I have to do that?

You had no choice, Liz. You did the right thing.

Are you sure?

You gave him the gift of life.

I gave him the curse of undeath.

The boy was more withdrawn than before, but perhaps they all were. The werewolves' attack and its aftermath had left them reeling. Even Alfie, Leah and the other kids were noticeably subdued. And as for Kevin – he would never get over the horrors he had brought to their door.

Every day they moved on, as if by running they could escape the past. The hotel was far behind them, but the events that had unfolded there could never be undone. Liz drove the Foxhound, occupying the seat that had once been Llewelyn's. Kevin had replaced the stolen Galaxy with a Renault Espace, and Samantha was at the wheel of the Volvo. Liz had no idea where they were going. It hardly seemed to matter. Everywhere they went the scenery was unchanging – burned-out buildings, abandoned cars, and unburied corpses making feasts for crows. A wasteland, and a monument to all that was lost. They drove through cities, towns and open country, following major and minor roads, but it was all the same to her. Sometimes they saw signs of life – roads cleared of debris, or else blocked deliberately to keep out strangers – but took care to avoid them. They were a self-sufficient unit, finding all they needed along the way. The kids were resourceful scavengers and could locate food and supplies in the most unlikely of places. And there seemed to be no shortage of fuel, even though it had been in such scarce supply earlier in the year when drivers had waited for hours at the pumps, and everything had been rationed. Now all you needed was a siphoning tube and you could get as much as you wanted out of other vehicles. It would run out eventually, Liz supposed, but *eventually* sounded like a long way off.

That's right, Liz. Focus on the day ahead. The future will take care of itself.

Wise words from a man whose future ended when he got himself shot to pieces in a stupid gunfight.

That shut Llewelyn up for once.

Although they had no plan, they were steadily heading

west, away from the mounds of rubble that had once been London, away from the past, away from all the bad memories. If they carried on this way they would come to Wales, homeland of the late Llewelyn Jones, a mysterious place of mists and dragons and poetry, at least in Liz's mind. Llewelyn had sometimes talked of green mountains scarred by abandoned coal shafts, of relentless rain and voices of choirs raised in song. But she had no idea what the place might look like in reality, except that it was probably very different to London. She wasn't sure she wanted to go there. Still, if they continued on their present path they would either find themselves in Wales, or else run into the sea, and Mihai claimed that vampires were afraid of running water.

The boy had changed fully into his new vampiric form now, with sharp fangs, claw-like fingernails and a pale complexion. Unlike her own transition, which had taken months to come into full effect, his had been almost instant thanks to Liz's blood flowing in his veins. But she was still taken off-guard whenever she saw those dark chestnut eyes glinting yellow in the dark.

His craving for blood was overwhelming, but he was catching wild animals and birds, and showed no signs of wanting to take a bite out of his fellow travelling companions. In fact, Liz was relieved to discover that he was still very much the boy he had always been. It seemed that a descent into evil and depravity wasn't inevitable upon becoming a vampire.

Nothing's inevitable, Liz. We all have choices.
Choices, yes. And the regrets that go with them.
You can't run from your regrets, Liz. They follow you around.
Just like you, Llewelyn Jones. Don't you ever shut up?
Do you want me to?
No. Never. Except when I tell you to. Like now.

The road they were following crossed over a river. The land here was low and she could see for miles. To the left lay the city they had passed the previous day. To the right, a thin sliver of silver. The sea. A mile later they turned off the main road and headed toward it. The coastline vanished as it approached, hidden behind fences and warehouses and row upon row of parked container trucks. A sign announced that they had arrived at Royal Portbury Dock. The set of metal gates that barred entry to the dock had been smashed open, and she drove the Foxhound into the industrial area beyond.

The place was vast, filled with the relics of a bygone era when cargo ships had ploughed across the oceans, bringing all kinds of exotic goods from far-off lands. Now no ships sailed the seas, and the cranes that had handled their consignments rusted silently overhead, casting long shadows beneath the evening sun. It seemed impossible that those luxury items Liz had taken for granted – foods, electronics, consumer products – could ever have been real. As for the far-off lands, who knew what had happened to them? They might as well not exist.

The sun was sinking ever lower, bleeding red into the western sky. The moon was high, pale in the last light, and far from full. But Liz could still feel its draw, like a string tugging endlessly at her soul.

She continued on to the very edge of the docks. The sight that greeted her there was a sorry one. The water in the dock had drained away, leaving great ships lying on their sides, their loads of containers spilled overboard, their hulls half-buried in the grey mudflats. Gulls flew low overhead, shrieking loudly to each other. But that was the only sound, and the only evidence of life in this godforsaken place. The smell was of brine, of sulphur, and the rotting stink of seaweed. It was the end of the earth, and nothing lay beyond but the cold waters of the Atlantic.

Liz wondered what she'd been hoping for. Some sign that the rest of the world was still open for business? That civilization persisted, somewhere across the ocean? That perhaps what had happened here was an anomaly and that even now a great rescue mission was being undertaken to send help from other countries, or other continents? Any such hopes she had secretly entertained were dashed.

There was nothing here, and never would be. Beyond the dock, far out across the open waters of the sea, the sun touched the horizon and set the sky on fire.

A flicker of movement caught her eye and she switched her attention back to her immediate surroundings. Shadows were moving near the warehouses as figures detached themselves from pools of darkness. Gaunt creatures, clothed in hoods that hid their faces. They swept forward at blinding speed, converging on the Foxhound and the other vehicles in the convoy.

Get out of here, Liz.

Thanks for your advice.

Her foot was already pushed to the floor, the engine of the armoured car screaming as it shifted down a gear. The attackers were nearly upon them. As they grew close, Liz caught a glimpse of the features beneath their hoods — yellow eyes burning in bone-white sockets, desiccated skin pulled tight over skulls. Their lips were blood red, their hands like hooks, and as they clambered over the vehicles, they opened their mouths to let loose an ear-splitting screech.

Chapter Sixty-Four

The Foxhound swung into a sharp spin as Liz struggled to throw the attackers off. But her manoeuvring seemed to have little effect. The dark figures clambered on top of the Renault and the Volvo too, as Kevin and Samantha attempted similar evasive measures.

A grinning skull appeared at Liz's windscreen, blocking her view of the road. White teeth protruded from blackened gums. Iron claws scratched at the glass. Liz slipped the gearstick into reverse, hoping to see the figure slide away across the front of the vehicle, but the clawed hands clung on grimly, the leering mouth widening into a triumphant grin. She slammed the gear into drive and gave the accelerator pedal all she could, but the creature dashed nimbly onto the roof, leaving gouges in the toughened glass of the windscreen. Now she heard it above her, tearing at the metal.

The other vehicles were faring no better. One of the creatures punched a fist through a side window of the Volvo, shattering glass and reaching a long arm inside to pluck out the passengers. Leah thrust at it with a spear. Samantha slammed on the brakes in an effort to throw the attackers from the car, but the hooded figures gripped the roof and doors as tightly as the barnacles glued to the bottom of the ships in the dock.

Kevin brought the Renault to a screeching halt and reached for his assault rifle. Liz guessed what was in his mind and shouted, 'No!' But it was no use. He aimed the rifle up and held the trigger, releasing a barrage of rounds that punctured the roof of the car, leaving the metal riddled with more gaping holes than a cheese grater. The figures on the rooftop went into overdrive, scrabbling about so quickly they were just a blur. In seconds they were punching their way through the glass at the front and back of the car, pulling the doors wide open. The driver's door flew out so hard it came off its hinges, crashing to the ground.

In no time the rifle was out of Kevin's hand and pointed at his head. He raised his hands in surrender.

Liz brought the Foxhound to a halt and flung open her own door. 'Don't shoot! Please!'

A shrouded figure appeared from nowhere, standing tall between her and her father.

'Take off your hood,' she commanded. 'Let me see you!'

To her amazement, the ghoul did as she requested. The cowl was thrown back to reveal the grinning skull she had seen before, and with it came the putrid smell of death and decay. Bone-white skin stretched like parchment over the skull, and the figure's eyes glowed golden in the fading light. Its fingers were the ashen grey of death, its long nails extruded into sharp splinters of bone.

Now she understood. The creature's face was a dark mirror that showed her own reflection. It was the face of a vampire.

'Stop!' The creature's voice cut across all other sounds, like an unholy commandment that was impossible to resist. All activity ceased.

The voice was a man's, Liz could tell that much. A cold, ruthless voice, that sanctioned no dissent. Even Liz felt herself yielding to the man's command.

The raging battle that had threatened to claim its first victim halted abruptly.

'Get out of your cars,' ordered the vampire. 'Now!'

'Do it!' called Liz.

He waited until everyone had complied. 'Now, tell me who are you, and what you are doing here.'

The voice was compelling, and Liz couldn't have resisted, even if she had wanted to. 'My name is Liz Jones. And we mean you no harm.'

'Harm?' The skull's grin widened. The creature cast its yellow gaze around the gathering and lingered over Mihai before returning to stare at Liz. 'You are a vampire; this boy too. Who are the others? Your prisoners?'

'No! This man is –'

The vampire raised a finger into the air. 'He is your father. His scent is the same as yours. Almost.'

In Liz's opinion, Kevin smelled nothing like her, but now wasn't the time to argue the point.

A long bony finger pointed at Mihai. 'The boy is not your child.'

'He's my adopted son. His name is Mihai. He comes from Romania.'

The vampire's thin lips twisted, displaying a line of razor sharp but perfectly regular teeth. 'A Romanian vampire. How wonderful.' He turned to address Mihai directly. 'Did you live in an old stone castle, boy vampire? High in the Carpathian Mountains above the deep forests?'

'No. In apartment in București.'

'Bucharest? Then you are a city vampire.' He turned to Samantha and the children. 'And these?'

'They're my friends. We travelled here together from London. These people are under my care. And what about you?'

The man – if Liz could call him that – shrugged. 'We came from all walks of life. My name is Eric. I was a doctor once – a heart surgeon. So I know a thing or two about blood.' He grinned, but then the smile faded. 'We came here from the north. That place is desolate now.'

Eric. The vampire was becoming more human to Liz with every word he spoke. With every fact he revealed about himself. A doctor. He was no monster, but a person just like Liz, with a life and perhaps a family. 'What are you doing here?' she asked him. 'Where are you heading?' An idea was beginning to form in her mind.

'We are travelling south, hunting werewolves as we go.'

Liz could hardly keep the surprise from her voice. 'You hunt them?'

'Their blood tastes sweet to us.'

'And do you kill only werewolves?'

'These are lean times. We must make do with whatever comes our way.'

'If you want to join our group,' said Liz sternly, 'you must swear not to harm these children, and you must promise never to drink blood from any humans.'

Eric threw back his head and laughed. 'Now you are giving the orders. You have spirit, I grant you that.'

Kevin tugged at her sleeve. 'Liz? What are you saying? These vampires can't join us. We can't trust them.'

Eric's eyebrow was raised in amusement. 'What makes you think we would want to join your group?'

'Why are you speaking to us, otherwise?'

'Perhaps we want just you and the boy to join us, and under rules that we make. Perhaps we have no interest in joining these humans who walk with you. Perhaps we would prefer to drain their blood.'

'No.' Liz shook her head. 'If you'd wanted to kill them, you could have done so already. But you're talking, so that means that you want something from us. I'm offering to let you join us, but you must promise not to harm any of these people, nor any other humans.'

'A promise?' The eyes in the sockets of the skull glinted yellow. 'Would you trust the word of a vampire?'

'You will have to earn my trust. But I don't prejudge anyone, whether they are vampire, human or werewolf.'

Eric clapped his hands together. 'You're a straight talker, Liz Jones. I like that, and I think we can help each other. You can join us, or we can join you. Let's not argue the point. These are just different words that mean the same. And let me share a truth with you. None of us has tasted human blood since the day we turned. When we cannot find werewolf blood to drink, we sup from animals instead. You may not believe me, but I was a doctor and spent my whole career preserving human life – why would I now seek to take it?' He paused. 'But I have not been entirely straight with you. We are not simply travellers seeking survival. We have dedicated ourselves to a cause. When you hear what it is, you may not wish to have anything to do with us.'

'Go on.'

'We march to war. A battle is brewing – one that may end the werewolf threat once and for all, or else lead to the extinction of humans as a species. We intend to be at the heart of that battle. I see that you are a fighter yourself, and that your father and these children are all armed with weapons. In the battle to come, every man, woman and child will count. Will you join us?'

Chapter Sixty-Five

Four Marks, East Hampshire

James peered out above the rocky outcrops that marked the scarp of the hill. From this high vantage point he could see far into the valley below. A column of tanks and other armoured vehicles was rumbling along the road, heading west. A Union Jack flag fluttered from the leading tank, but that could mean anything. Were these government forces, or Leanna's Wolf Army?

'What do you think?' asked Ben, voicing the question in James' own mind. 'Humans or werewolves?'

James sniffed the air, but the only scents that came to him were those of the natural world. From up here on the hill, even the stink of diesel fumes were too faint to smell. 'There's no way of telling from this distance.'

'Then do you want to get closer?'

'I think we should keep away for now. Let's watch them and try to work out which side they're on.'

'Good thinking. Perhaps when they stop tonight it will

become apparent.'

They watched as the convoy continued to creep along the road below. There were hundreds of soldiers, perhaps even thousands, and whichever side they were on, it was clear that they were marching to war. They were fools if they thought they could win it. Whether these were humans or werewolves, and whichever side might hold the military advantage, they were marching to their doom. When the seventh seal broke, all the terrors of Hell itself would be unleashed upon the world.

James and Ben followed the army along the valley. When it stopped for the night, they advanced a little way down the hillside, keeping low and out of sight.

'I think they're human,' said Ben. 'Just from the way they're behaving.'

'I can't see any sign of Leanna,' agreed James. 'So that means that the Wolf Army must be in front of them. If we run on ahead, we can try to catch up with her before the two armies meet. If we go right now, we can get a night's travel in before they start moving again.'

There was still time to stop this war. And that meant there was still hope. James had lost his hope once, and he had lost his faith. He ought to have known better. It was when all the odds were against you and everything looked desperate that faith mattered most. Stronger than optimism; more rational than blind hope; faith was the pillar on which you could depend when all else was gone.

'What's that?' said Ben, turning his head. 'Do you smell something?'

James lifted his nose to the wind, sifting the scents that blew across the ragged hillside. Not the sharp exhaust from the vehicles, nor the sweet smell of the wildflowers that scattered the ground like jewels, but something else. Something unmistakeable. 'Humans,' he hissed.

A sound came to him then – the snapping of bracken being crushed underfoot.

He turned and saw shapes moving in the falling light.

Men approaching from all sides. Soldiers, armed with rifles. It was time to run, but there was nowhere to go. The men came on quickly, their guns pointed at him and Ben. It was too late to escape, and now he could only pray.

He waited for a bullet to come. Instead, a rope went around him, tangling his legs and binding him tight. By his side, Ben struggled to resist, but was treated to a rifle butt around the back of his head.

The soldiers had surrounded them, and now a net dropped over James' head and was quickly drawn tight. There was no point in struggling, and he allowed himself to be trussed up like a goose, ready for the oven.

A man strode out of the rough undergrowth that covered the side of the valley. A tall man, older than the rest, and with an air of command. Yet he didn't look like an army officer. He wore a khaki vest with a black skull printed on it, and had long grey hair pulled into a ponytail. Up close, he stank of stale whisky and sweat.

'Well, well,' he said. 'Look what we've found here. *Dos lobos*. A pair of wolves.'

'Don't kill us, begged James. 'Please. We're on a peace mission.'

'A peace mission, eh?' said the man with an amused grin. 'Tell that to the Colonel. He'll be all ears.'

Chapter Sixty-Six

Royal Portbury Dock, Avonmouth

A change had come over Eric since Liz had started talking to him. His yellow eyes were dimming. The deathly pallor of his face had warmed. The long corkscrew stakes at the tip of each finger were slowly unwinding, retreating back to normal fingernails. He was becoming human again. Before long, an ordinary man stood before Liz. A little taller than average, perhaps, and still trim for his fifty-odd years. Grey haired, with a neat beard and blue eyes. He had a kind, intelligent face, and it was easy to believe that he had once been a doctor.

'How did you do that?' asked Liz. 'How did you change without the power of the moon?' Liz had sometimes felt the stirring of her blood when danger threatened, but she had never transformed fully into vampire form without a full moon above her.

'Vampire blood,' said Eric, a proper smile settling on his lips at last. 'It's a trick we learned. By drinking from each other's wrists, we have the power to change whenever we want.'

Liz had tasted vampire blood herself once, up on the rooftops above Gatwick Airport, fighting Major Hall and his fellow officers. Thick, dark liquid as cold as ice, like a Bloody Mary on the rocks. It was the best damn cocktail she had ever drunk.

The vampires numbered a dozen in total. Men and women. Now they had changed back, Liz sensed no further threat. She looked into Eric's clear eyes and decided to trust him. But as for his proposal – to march into battle – that was another matter entirely.

'A dozen soldiers isn't a lot to take on an entire werewolf army,' she said. 'Are there any more of you?'

Eric shook his head. 'Only what you see here. Before we met you and the boy we hadn't encountered any other vampires since leaving the north. I daresay there are a few more out there, but we appear to be a rare breed. Perhaps one vampire for every hundred werewolves. Maybe not even as many as that.'

Liz nodded. At first she'd imagined herself to be alone in the world – just her, and the vampire who had gifted her this curse back in London. Then she had encountered Major Hall and his fellow vampires back at Gatwick. But they had been a small, isolated group. 'Why so few, do you think?'

'You're looking for an explanation?' Eric chuckled. 'I suppose it's only natural, we all are. But take a look around, Liz. Nothing makes sense anymore. What makes you think I can explain it?'

'Just you being a doctor, I suppose.'

His mouth curled up at the ends and the creases around his eyes deepened. 'Speaking as a doctor, I would probably say something about viruses mutating into different strains, or perhaps genetic factors causing infected people to respond to the virus in different ways. But medical science can't really explain what happened to the world. One day, perhaps we'll be able to pin down exactly what caused all this and rewrite the textbooks. Assuming that anyone ever writes a textbook again. But it might never be possible to arrive at a satisfactory explanation. It'll take decades to get civilization back to anything like it was, if we even manage to survive that long.' He stopped, aware from the look on her face that this wasn't what she wanted to hear. 'People will look back at this catastrophe and ask why we weren't better prepared. But how could we have been? We knew all about pandemics, of course. And we understood viruses – or thought we did. DNA sequencing, gene therapy, synthetic biology – we thought we knew it all. But this? How can you prepare for an event that scientists would have dismissed as preposterous? Not even an outlier, but simply impossible.'

'I suppose.'

Eric seemed to be warming to his subject. Perhaps Liz ought to have known better than to ask a doctor for a diagnosis. 'If there's a bright side to any of this, it's that one day in the future, we might be able to use what we learn to make new advances in medical science. Nature clearly has a few surprises up its sleeve, and if we can discover exactly how the virus that mediates lycanthropy operates, perhaps we can harness it for good.'

It seemed astonishing to Liz that Eric was looking forward to a day when hospitals and laboratories would exist once more, and when doctors and scientists would be able to resume their work. 'You don't think we should leave it well alone?'

'Turn our backs on science altogether? Perhaps. Some people probably think so. But if this event has taught us anything, it's that the world we inhabit is a dangerous place. There are a hundred different ways that natural disasters can kill us. Flood, famine, earthquakes, volcanic eruptions, asteroid strikes, solar flares. Ninety-nine per cent of all species that lived on this planet are now extinct, and humans weren't responsible for most of those extinctions. Without technology to protect us, we're doomed to go the same way.'

Liz smiled at him. 'You really like to look on the bright side.'

'When you're a blood-sucking fiend from beyond the grave, I find that a dose of realism helps to get you through the day.' Eric looked at her hopefully. 'So what do you say to my proposal?'

In a strange way, the conversation with Eric had put Liz at ease. By talking freely he had shown his vulnerable side, with all the flaws and doubts and misgivings of any other human being. He was not so very different from her. But it had also helped her make up her mind about what to do next. 'I am responsible for the safety of these children,' she told him. 'I won't lead them into any kind of danger.'

'No,' said Eric. 'But perhaps you could let them decide for themselves if they want to join us.'

'They're just kids,' said Liz. 'They're too young. We even have a baby with us, just a few months old. So, I'm sorry, but what you are asking is impossible.'

'I understand,' said Eric sadly. 'Then perhaps it is best that we take our leave.' He offered his hand for her to shake.

'Hey, chief.' It was Alfie who had spoken up. 'We ain't gonna run away, are we?'

'We ain't afraid of no wolves, innit,' said Leah, brandishing her spear. A chorus of agreement went up from the kids.

'They seem quite keen to stay,' observed Eric. 'What do you think?' His hand was still outstretched, inviting her to take it. But now she wasn't sure what shaking it might mean.

The kids looked at her expectantly.

Liz turned away to gather her thoughts. The rusting hulks of the ships lay before her in the dry dock like remnants of another age. Trapped by the wall of the harbour, they would never sail the seas again. The world they represented was gone, and nobody could know what the future might bring. But one thing she knew for certain was that these children would have no future unless they claimed one for themselves.

Still, it wasn't just the kids from London she had to worry about. She had made a promise to protect Samantha and her children. There was simply no way that Samantha could be expected to march into battle, and neither could Lily or Leo.

'I know what you're thinking,' said Samantha.

Liz turned to face her. 'I swore to Dean that I would do everything I could to protect you.'

'And you have,' said Samantha. 'You've kept your promise. But Dean would never have wanted you to run from your duty.'

Duty. It was the one thing Liz had never been able to escape from. She had never wanted to. Duty was her lifeline, the only part of her world that had ever made any sense. It was the reason she was here now, and the reason all these people were still alive and with her.

But if anyone had the right to put a stop to this, it was Samantha.

'I won't leave you behind,' said Liz, 'so if you have the slightest concern about joining these people, just say so. There's no shame in refusing. We can go somewhere else, and keep Lily and Leo safe. That would be the smart move.'

Samantha smiled. 'You knew my husband as well as I did, Liz. And we both know that Dean never made the smart move, but he always made the right one. It's time for you to make the right move now, and I won't stop you.' She held her baby tight against her chest, and Lily clutched her leg, the girl's fingers wrapped as always around her toy elephant. 'We'll follow you into this battle, Liz. Me, Lily, Leo and even Ellie. We may not be able to help very much, but we won't stand in your way, and we'll do our best not to slow you down. You know that's what Dean would have wanted.'

Chapter Sixty-Seven

The Pilgrims' Way

Warg Daddy didn't understand how it had happened, but somehow he had regained his self-belief. The kids had done it, he supposed, although by what means remained a mystery. By rights the opposite should have happened. They had stolen his shotgun, tied him to a tree, fed him snacks and humiliated him. Yet somehow, as a result, he had rediscovered hope. Not optimism exactly – he had never been an optimist – but the courage to face the future.

Freedom, you might call it. Freedom from the prison of fate. He was no longer ruled by the cold indifference of the gods. Or at the very least, he had gained the power to look the gods directly in the eye and tell them to go screw themselves.

But with that freedom came responsibility. Warg Daddy wasn't sure he was ready to deal with that just yet. For now, it was enough simply to savour his liberty and the giddy release it gave him.

His strength had returned, and with it his desire to walk. Walking was good. Each step was an adventure, and every mile a milestone. He had nowhere particular to go, but the simple pleasure of the action was its own reward. It was funny. As Leader of the Pack, he would never have dreamed of walking any distance. Why would he, with his bike at his disposal, and the thrill of speed and noise so much a part of the journey? He had covered so many miles on two wheels that to walk on foot seemed, well, pedestrian.

And yet he saw so much more while walking. Not just the blur of tarmac beneath him, as his greedy bike swallowed up the road, white dash after white dash, one town following another, each indistinguishable in a haze of bars, booze and fights. Now he noticed every passing tree, every blade of grass, every flower. He heard the bird calls, the buzzing of the hoverflies as they whirled around his ears, the distant barking of deer at dusk. Life was … what was the word? Beautiful. Divine. Sublime.

That was pushing it, maybe. But pretty damn fucking good, at any rate.

Living in the moment. That's what they called this. But how long could a perfect moment last? Eventually the bubble must burst, and he would have to face the future. Already that future was reaching out to him, trying to drag him out of the endless present like a gentle alarm seeking to rouse a sleeper from a dreamless sleep. Not blind destiny or cruel fate this time, but a future shaped by his own thoughts and desires. A life of his own, determined by conscious choice.

This great reset of his life was now his greatest opportunity. The past was behind him, the present slipping slowly out of reach. Soon only the future would remain. It was there, tantalizingly close, just waiting for him to claim it.

It all came down to the questions.

Moon Child

Now that he was able to make choices again, the number of questions pressing in on him seemed to be multiplying. *Where to go, what to do, how to live?* And they were just for starters. Finding answers to them all was one hell of a job. It had been so much easier relying on the coin. Although, as with any addiction, there had been a heavy price to pay. Indecision had cost him his arm, his friends, his girl and his self-respect. It had very nearly cost him his life.

So he had better start answering some fucking questions soon.

There were so many for him to ponder, yet there was no need to answer them all at once. Better to think a little longer and get the answers right. And so he walked, turning them over and over in his mind, feeling their shape, seeking one path out of infinite possibilities.

He walked at night and slept during the heat of the day, but so far he hadn't travelled very far. Without the coin to guide him, all directions seemed the same. He walked in circles, returning at the end of every night to the same tree the kids had tied him to. The kids were gone, but the tree remained. One fixed point in his new, fluid universe.

As he walked, he gazed up at the starry sky, seeing what had changed since last he'd looked. Some said the stars were eternal, but they were wrong. Comets and meteors tracked across the heavens like beetles tip-toeing across the still surface of a pond. Even the stars themselves moved if you watched them long enough, though what animated them remained a mystery to him. Where were they going, and what would happen when they got there? He couldn't say.

But everyone and everything was on a journey of some kind. So here was the question that mattered most: where to go?

He wondered if the ghosts would voice an opinion, but they kept mostly silent these days.

Subdued. Humbled. Maybe just bored.

He would have to consider the matter alone.

It took him many nights to work it out, but when he finally made his choice, it seemed inevitable.

He would return to Leanna. She was the one thing in this world he still wanted.

Vixen had been a fling; just a passing fancy, no different to a dozen other chicks. He saw that now. When the time had come for her to leave, they had parted without bitterness. Even though the bitch had taken his bike.

The Brothers had been with him far longer. Once, he had defined himself as their leader. But they were dead now, or gone, and no longer needed him. He didn't need them either. He had found contentment in his own company. The lure of power that had once fed his ego meant nothing now.

His bike had been his first love, but that was gone too, and in its place he had discovered the simple joy of walking.

None of those things mattered anymore. There was only Leanna. She was the pole star. She had made him what he was.

It was true that she'd tried to kill him last time he had seen her, but Warg Daddy wasn't a man to hold grudges. If she wanted to kill him all over again, then he wouldn't try to stop her. But there was always a chance she would take him back.

You had to have hope. Or courage, at least.

Chapter Sixty-Eight

Winchester, Hampshire

'So,' said Griffin, from behind his desk. 'Tell me exactly what you were doing when you were caught.'

He would have preferred to be up on his feet, pacing before his prisoners in what might be construed as a threatening manner, but the effort required, and the pain involved, ruled out such theatrics. He hoped he could nonetheless adopt an intimidating stance from a seated position.

Certainly the two men who had been brought before him looked frightened. Perhaps they expected to be tortured until they spilled their secrets. If so, he would do nothing to reassure them. This was the first time any of Leanna's scouts had been captured alive, and any information they might reveal could be of immense value at this late stage. The pace of events was picking up. The endgame was within sight, and there could be no mistakes now. After many weeks of cat and mouse, his ground forces were closing in on the enemy, herding them ever nearer to the coast where the fleet was waiting to surprise them. Perez's men had moved to the offensive, proving their worth in initial skirmishes and raids designed to keep the enemy on the move. And now Perez had delivered these two scouts directly into his hands. If they talked, the rogue would have earned his gold already.

'We meant no harm.' It was the older of the pair who replied to his question. A tall, good-looking man, aged around thirty, he was well-spoken and sounded educated. Griffin wondered what kind of life this man had lived before becoming a werewolf, but it was hard to think of the enemy as real people with homes and families. They were monsters now, nothing more.

The first step in war was always to dehumanize the other side. But in this conflict, the enemy was quite literally a different subspecies. Griffin had lived alongside them while he had been running the quarantine hospital, and knew that these creatures had long since set aside their humanity. They were no longer human; but neither were they animals. They were devious and cunning manipulators, and could not be trusted. It was important to keep that in mind when dealing with them. The two before him now were firmly bound with their hands tied behind their backs and wire muzzles fixed to their faces to prevent them from biting. The tiniest scratch or bite would be fatal.

'We were just observing,' continued the prisoner. 'We were trying to work out which side you were on. We didn't know if you were human or werewolf.'

'You expect me to believe that?' snapped Griffin. 'Let's try a different question, then. What information were you trying to determine?'

This time the younger man answered. He was little more than a teenager, perhaps eighteen or nineteen years of age. He was of a similar height to his older companion, with tanned skin and long blond hair hanging loose over his bearded face. His features held a rare beauty, although his blue eyes seemed haunted by horrors only he could see. He, too, spoke with a refined, articulate voice. There was a quiet authority to the way he talked, as if he expected to be believed at face value, however absurd his claim. 'It's like Ben told you. We wanted to find out if you were human or werewolf. That's all.'

'I would have thought that was obvious,' said Griffin, 'since you had just travelled here from the werewolf camp.'

'No,' said the blond boy. 'We were travelling in search of the Wolf Army. We need to reach them urgently. It's a matter of great importance.'

'Is it, now?' Griffin gathered his brows into a frown. Could these really just be a couple of lone werewolves travelling to join their compatriots? If that were true, then they had no intelligence value and he was wasting his time. But it was just as likely to be a ruse. 'You expect me to believe that you are fresh recruits for the Wolf Army?'

The boy looked offended at the suggestion. 'No!' he protested indignantly.

'Then are you spies or not?'

'We aren't spies,' he declared. 'And we aren't recruits for Leanna's army either.'

'You try my patience,' said Griffin. 'May I remind you that you were in wolf form when my men found you.'

'It's quicker for us to travel like that,' said the older man. 'Four legs are faster than two.'

'Indeed.' Was the man trying to make a joke? Griffin detected only good-natured humour. There was no trace of mockery in his words.

His puzzlement deepened with every reply this odd pair made. He took a moment to reassess them. There was no doubting that they were werewolves, and yet they didn't look like combatants. But Griffin had seen action in Afghanistan and knew that enemy soldiers could look just like civilians when they wanted to. If you could tell the bad guys from the good guys just by looking at them, life would be a whole lot easier.

'And we aren't going to fight,' added the man. 'We're going to stop the fighting.'

'To stop the fighting,' repeated Griffin sceptically. 'Really? Forgive me if I find that hard to swallow.'

'It's true,' said the boy, so earnestly that Griffin almost believed him. 'You have to release us immediately.'

Griffin felt his gaze drawn again to the boy's face. There was something about it that entranced him. Was it the clear blue eyes? Was it the look of innocence in those fine, youthful features? Whatever it was, it was mesmerizing. He pulled away, angry with himself for being so easily seduced, and addressed the older man instead.

'So let's get this straight. You claim that you were on a peace mission. You intended to go to the Wolf Army and ask them to surrender. And I need to release you so that you can continue on your quest. Is that right?'

'I know that it sounds –'

'Do I look like an idiot?' shouted Griffin. 'You're going nowhere, except to a prison cell for the rest of your lives. And once you're out of my sight, I wouldn't be at all surprised if one of my men were to decide that prison is more than you deserve. Not everyone shares my belief in fair treatment for enemy combatants.' He dropped his voice. 'Talk to me, and I can guarantee your safety. But if I send you away, don't be surprised if someone takes the law into their own hands and you end up with a bullet in the back of the head.'

'But we've already told you the truth!' said the boy.

Griffin closed his eyes and rubbed his forehead with both hands. He had no time for this. So many urgent demands pressed in on him. If the prisoners wouldn't talk, they would have to suffer the consequences. He should get his sergeant to remove this pair at once. But something kept him from giving the command.

'You know what?' he said. 'I'm tired. I'm so very tired.

My leg aches like the devil, and you have completely exhausted my patience. But I'm going to give you one final opportunity to save yourselves. So, start telling me what I want to hear.'

Chapter Sixty-Nine

Petersfield, East Hampshire

They came for him at night. Will Hunter and four of his strongest henchmen. Huge figures looming menacingly in the dark, their faces grim, their muscles tensed, looking like they meant business.

'What is the meaning of this?' bellowed Canning as they burst into his tent unannounced, but already the answer was abundantly clear. When armed thugs came for you in the darkest hours, you should expect to be dragged away kicking and screaming.

Unless they have something less pleasant in mind.

Two of the gruff northerners seized him by the arms. They pulled him from his bed and hauled him roughly to his feet in front of Hunter. He didn't even have time to grab hold of his eye patch.

The wolfman's face was a sneering mask of triumph. 'Lord General Canning,' he intoned, injecting the honorifics with a hefty dollop of scorn. He proceeded as if reading from an official arrest warrant, although he carried no such document. 'You are hereby arrested on suspicion of treason. You will be taken into custody until such time as the queen is ready to grant you a hearing. Then, if found guilty of your crimes, you will be publicly executed.'

Panicked thoughts flashed through Canning's mind as he struggled to make connections. Was this a desperate ruse on Hunter's part? A bluff? Or had he truly discovered something incriminating? If one of Canning's spies or assassins had talked…

'What is the nature of this so-called treason?' he demanded. 'What evidence do you have of any crimes?'

Hunter smiled a cold smile, and pushed his face up close to Canning's. 'Oh, there is plenty of evidence. More than enough to see you hung, drawn and quartered. You have enjoyed the queen's favour far too long. And all this time you have been plotting against her. Do you deny it?'

'Of course I deny it!' said Canning, mustering as much outrage as he could manage.

A fist struck him in the stomach, emptying him of breath. He folded in half, and a second blow caught the back of his head. A rough hand grabbed him by the hair and hauled him upright.

'You are scum, Canning. A worthless traitor. And you know what the queen thinks of traitors …' Hunter left the sentence unfinished, but seemed to be enjoying the moment too much to let it end. 'Shall I tell you what we found? A turncoat, paid by you to carry out your treacherous work. He was caught spying on the queen.'

'A turncoat? What is his name?' Canning wracked his brains, trying to work out which of his fools was most likely to have been caught.

'Why?' asked Hunter. 'How many of them do you have working for you?'

'Well, none, obviously. I deny all knowledge of a spy.'

Canning ought to have known better. Trust no one, that was his motto. And yet he had put his trust in a lowly collection of ne'er-do-wells. Spies and conspirators, paid to betray confidences and to hand over secrets. A most untrustworthy set of wretches. And by the sound of it, an incompetent bunch.

'Consider yourself lucky,' continued Hunter. 'If it were up to me, you would already be dead. Thank the queen for preserving your wretched life. But remember, Leanna never forgives. Once she has all the facts at her disposal, you will be a dead man.'

Canning recalled the merciless way Leanna had dealt with Vixen. And he was no well-oiled fighting machine like the Wolf Sister. He depended on others to do his dirty work for him. What could he do to save himself? His only hope now was to lie, and to lie well. To tell the biggest gobsmacking untruth of his entire life. 'What facts?' he blustered. 'The talk of some scoundrel. Their word against mine? I demand that you take me to Leanna right now. Once she hears the flimsy substance of your case against me, she will order my immediate release.' He lifted his shoulders as best he could. 'It is you, William Hunter, who will then face the queen's wrath. You have acted recklessly in coming to arrest me. I suggest that you are the traitor here. I insist that you take me to the queen at once!'

Hunter held his gaze for a while, his expression giving nothing away. Canning smelled a desperate fear in the air, but knew it was his own. When Hunter spoke again, all his hope died.

'I am here on the queen's orders,' said the wolfman. 'It was she who discovered the spy at work. It was she who personally extracted his confession. Leanna summoned me to her tent this very hour and ordered me to come here and make your arrest.'

Canning felt the words like another punch. He knew full well what would come next. Imprisonment. Interrogation. Torture. He had inflicted the same treatment on others often enough.

I fear it may be less pleasurable the other way around.

'You will come with me now,' said Hunter. 'Your prison is ready and waiting. You will be questioned, and then you will be sentenced.'

'What if I refuse to answer your questions?'

An evil grin split the wolfman's lips. 'Then you will be encouraged to speak. By whatever means necessary.'

'A man may admit to anything under duress,' protested Canning.

'Yes, indeed. I'm sure that no one knows that better than you, General.'

Chapter Seventy

Royal Portbury Dock, Avonmouth

It was dark inside the warehouse, but Mihai could trace the outline of its walls and roof, and sense the vast emptiness that it contained. The building was huge, like the belly of an enormous whale, long and wide and tall enough to swallow whole streets of houses and everyone who lived in them. All that space lay empty now, and useless, but once it must have been full. He let his mind wander, trying to guess what kinds of marvellous things had been stored here. Goods from across the wide oceans. Cars, perhaps. And fridge-freezers, big enough for all your ice-cream, burgers, pizzas and bottles of fizzy drinks. TVs, like the ones he had seen in store windows, so huge that when you stood in front of them the people on the TV were bigger than you. Or perhaps pirate treasure. Barrels of rum, and chests stuffed full of silver coins. Maybe even a dragon's hoard of gold and jewels. The bedtime stories his mother had read to him when he was small were full of treasure – and magic – and always had happy endings, but remembering those stories now made him sad. It wasn't just his mother – his first mother, his real mother – who was dead. All his dreams were gone too. He was no longer a kid who believed in fairy-tales. He was eleven now, almost a teenager. He knew that there were no dragons in the world, or fairies or dwarves. But there were far worse things. The nice stories had all been make-believe, but the scariest ones were true.

A faint glimmer of light drew a line around the square of the big warehouse door. Moonlight. He could feel it as much as see it, and with each passing day the blood lust was getting harder to ignore.

At first, the meals that Liz brought him had been enough to satisfy his cravings. Mice, squirrels, voles and other small creatures. Bite-sized snacks to help him regain his strength after the damage that had been dealt out to his body.

I was shot. Killed. Brought back to life.

He could remember the bullets biting into his flesh like teeth. After that, not so much. Darkness. Fear. A sense of ending. And then horror as alien life invaded his body. Liz's blood; the blood of the *vampir*. Cold it came, when blood ought to be hot. Dark and deadly, when it should have been red and filled with life. His own blood had fought to hold it back, but the flood was unstoppable, rising through every vein, artery and capillary like molten ice until he thought he would explode. It stopped his heart.

I died. Her blood was poison to me.

And then he had burst back to life, or some kind of strange unlife. The darkness surged through his body, becoming blinding light.

A life-giving force. Mother's milk.

The slow creep of ice had turned to fire, igniting him from within. He was reborn, but he was no longer Mihai, the boy who had listened to fairy-tales. Now he was a vampire's child. He was a character in his own fairy-tale.

He smiled. Never before had he felt so alive. But never had he been so hungry. The snacks of small living creatures, and the plates of sausages and dead meat that Kevin cooked for him could never be enough now that he was *nosferatu*.

He stirred, picking himself from the warehouse floor. Stealthy as a snake, he slid upright. He sensed the others around him. Dark shapes in the darkness. Liz, Kevin, Alfie, Leah and the kids. And the new vampires too. All asleep. He moved without sound until he was at Alfie's side.

The kid was younger than him. Only nine. Still a baby. Curled up in his sleeping bag with the sword clutched to his side, making soft snuffling sounds in his sleep. Leah lay beside him, older, with a watchful air about her even while asleep. She was too dangerous to touch. Mihai switched his attention back to Alfie.

The air inside the warehouse was full of smells. Salt from the sea, oil from machinery. The smell of packaging, and of old exhaust fumes, and the stale sweat of the people who had once worked here. The sweat was thick on Alfie too, mingled with the honey of his hair, the mud on his shoes, and the iron in his blood.

Mihai drew the scent into his lungs, savouring the flavour. He reached out and brushed Alfie's blond hair, falling long and dirty over his face. The boy was fast asleep and didn't stir apart from the regular rise and fall of his chest. Mihai lowered his face to the boy's neck. He wouldn't take a lot of blood. Just a few drops to quench his thirst. A short suck. A mouthful. Not enough to kill. Alfie was his friend. The throbbing of the pulse in the boy's neck drew him closer. He parted his lips and closed his eyes, ready to bite and sup.

A hand seized him from behind, closing around his shoulder like a band of iron. Mihai's teeth closed on air, and he felt himself being hauled upright. He turned and saw Eric's face staring back at him through the blackness.

A white finger went to the man's lips. *Silence!*

He resisted the urge to cry out. He struggled briefly but the man's arms were so much stronger than his. It wasn't fair. He glanced back at Alfie, feeling the agony of getting so close to his meal, only to be snatched away at the last moment.

Eric marched him away from the others, gripping him tight so he couldn't run off. He led him toward the warehouse door – not the huge door outlined by moonlight, but a smaller door to one side. He swung it open and pushed Mihai out.

Outside the warehouse, the moon was bright and Mihai felt its tug even more than he had inside. A raging thirst surged within him, and he opened his mouth, desperate to feed. If not Alfie, then this man. He would bite the hand that held him.

Eric's other hand shot out and gripped his jaw, locking it shut. No matter how hard he tried to shake himself free, he was caught. He punched and lashed out, but the man's broad chest absorbed every blow that he aimed. Eventually, exhausted, he calmed a little and felt himself being released.

'Don't try to escape from me,' warned Eric. 'I am faster than you, and stronger. If you run, I will catch you. Do you understand me?'

Mihai nodded, scowling at his captor. 'Is not fair. Was only going to drink a little blood. Was not going to hurt Alfie.'

Eric regarded him for a while before he spoke. 'It is never easy to become a vampire,' he said at last. 'Not as an adult. Perhaps especially as a child. You are not yet formed. You do not know yourself.'

Is not kid, Mihai was about to protest, but something made him hold his tongue. He wanted to hear what Eric had to say. There was something about the way the man spoke, as if he saw things others did not. The words came from someplace deep inside him, like cool water brought up from a well on a summer's night. His eyes sparkled silver in the moonlight.

'Your parents are dead?' asked Eric. 'Your real mother and father, I mean.'

Mihai didn't answer. He didn't want to tell this man his secrets. When you gave away your secrets, you gave other people power over you. He had learned that lesson quickly enough after his parents died.

Eric nodded, as if he had answered anyway. 'Liz told me that her husband was also killed. That must have been hard for you. A new father is never as good as the first, but perhaps better than none.'

Still Mihai said nothing. He didn't want to talk about Llewelyn. He had briefly allowed himself to believe that Liz and Llewelyn could become his new mum and dad. But that hope had been quickly crushed. He wouldn't allow himself to hope that way again. Hope was the enemy. It would betray you if you let it.

'I had a son once, older than you,' said Eric. 'But he's dead. He died in the madness that swept the world when news first began to spread of the werewolf plague. I was working at the hospital at the time, doing my best to save the lives of strangers. But I couldn't save the life of my own son. By the time I heard that he'd been caught up in the violence, he was already dead. Killed randomly, for no reason.'

Mihai said nothing, just watched, afraid of a trap. Why was this man telling him his secrets? Didn't he know to keep his secrets to himself?

'I had a wife too,' Eric continued. 'So dear and precious to me. But she was killed by a monster. A blood-sucking monster that drained the very life out of her.'

Eric turned the full force of his gaze on Mihai then, and the strength of that penetrating stare was like a lighthouse. Mihai knew that his silence had not protected him. All his secrets were as plain as day to this man who saw everything.

'I don't want to be monster,' he said. 'But am so hungry.'

Eric placed his hands on Mihai's shoulders. They rested firmly, but didn't squeeze like before. 'Listen to me, Mihai. You are not a monster. But you have needs. Needs that cannot easily be met. I understand that. I have cravings too.' He glanced up. 'Especially on a night like this when the moon is almost full. I am a grown man, and a man can control his urges more easily than a boy. But it was not always this way. When I first turned, I gave into my darkest desires. I told you what happened to my wife. But I only told you half the story. You see, the monster that stole her life was me. When the blood lust first came upon me, I couldn't stop myself. I drank the blood of the woman I loved more than any other, who had borne my son. And I didn't take just a little to quench my thirst. I drank her dry.'

Mihai stared up into Eric's eyes. They glittered yellow, but he felt no fear. So this man was a true monster, worse even than Liz, far worse than himself. But he was also a friend.

'I will carry the shame of what I did that night for the rest of my life,' Eric concluded.

Mihai nodded. He realised how close he had come to killing Alfie. One mouthful of blood would never have been enough to satisfy his need. He would have drunk until there was no more left to drink. 'What can I do?' he whispered.

Eric released his shoulders and rolled up the sleeve of one arm, exposing the white skin beneath. 'Take what you need from me.'

'I can feed?'

'As much as you need. I won't tell Liz about it. It will be our secret.'

Mihai regarded the bare flesh uncertainly. Was this a trick? He didn't think so. The man was not the tricky kind. A test, then, to see how he would react? He found that he didn't care. The scent of blood flowing beneath thin skin was overwhelming. His lips parted, and sharpened teeth thrust through his gums. Pain and pleasure combined. The taste of his own blood in his mouth overcame any last resistance and he sank his fangs into the man's wrist. Eric gasped but didn't pull back. Mihai sucked greedily, cramming the blood into his mouth, swallowing it as fast as it would come. Red trickled down his chin, and he sucked harder, not wanting to spill a drop. The blood was cold, just like Liz's. It was cold and dark and dangerous, and he felt its power flush through him. The world grew brighter, the night sounds louder, his sense of touch, of taste and smell turned richer and multi-layered. His lungs expanded as he drew in more of the lifegiving force. And the more he drank, the more he desired.

'Enough!' Eric drew his arm away.

Mihai clung on, but strong fingers prised his jaw open and the flow of liquid ceased. He snarled, angry at being denied his feast, but the hand that gripped him was too powerful to resist. He licked the last of the blood from his chin and felt the hunger slowly ebb.

Eric was breathing as hard as he was. A slow smile spread over his face and reached his eyes. 'You have a fine appetite, my young friend. But you must learn to control it.' He released Mihai from his grip and rolled his sleeve back into place, covering the two deep wounds at his wrist. 'That is enough for one night. Tomorrow, if you cannot control the urge, come and see me again. But remember this – never take blood unless it is given freely. Otherwise you truly will become a monster. And once you have set off down that dark path, there is no way back.'

Chapter Seventy-One

Christmas Common, Oxfordshire

Chanita heard the sound first. Felt it in the pit of her stomach. A low vibration in the glass of the windows. 'Do you hear that?' she asked.

'What?' Melanie was reclining on her bed, resting as Chanita took her blood pressure. The pregnancy was rapidly reaching its conclusion, and the relentless speed of it was exacting a heavy toll. Chanita wondered whether even Melanie's lusty constitution could withstand such a headlong rush toward new life.

'A noise. Like an engine. A car, maybe, or…' It wasn't a car. There was a juddering, vibrating quality to the sound that Chanita hadn't heard for a long, long time, but that had once been so familiar. 'It's a helicopter.'

The noise was growing louder now, taking on a distinct "thud-thud" as the chopper approached.

Another sound came to her. A door opening downstairs, and footsteps as Sarah came running up. She burst breathlessly into Melanie's room. 'Do you hear it?'

'Yes. Ssh!'

The three women listened together as the sound grew louder, closer. More ominous.

'It's probably just flying over,' said Sarah. 'Why would it be coming here? No one knows about us.'

'I expect you're right,' said Chanita, although her gut told her otherwise.

'No,' said Melanie, pushing herself up from the bed. 'Get the guns. We have to be ready.'

Chanita helped her climb out of the bed, supporting her weight as she hauled herself to her feet. Melanie winced with the effort, but didn't pause. 'Come on. Let's get into position.'

They had planned for this. Or rather, Melanie had made plans and had drilled them regularly. They all knew what to do. Rifles first, to keep the intruders away from the house. Then switch to handguns if they managed to gain entry.

They had planned. They had practised. But Chanita had never expected it to happen.

Melanie was already handing out guns and boxes of ammunition. Chanita accepted a rifle reluctantly and went to take up position at an open window. The chopper was almost overhead now, its rotor blades beating ferociously, the roar of its engine deafening. She watched as its grey underbelly passed directly over the house at a height of no more than a hundred feet. Its landing lights flashed bright in the darkened sky as it came in low, swinging around to begin its final descent. There could be no doubt now. It was coming in to land in a field just behind the house.

It wasn't a type that she recognized. Bigger than the Westland Lynx that had been a regular visitor to the evacuation camp at Stoke Park, ferrying supplies and personnel in and out, but smaller than the huge twin-rotor Chinook transport helicopters used by the military to carry heavy cargoes.

There was no time to wonder what it was doing here. She knew what she had to do. Take the lid off the box holding the magazines. Pull out a magazine and push it into its housing. Pull back the cocking handle and then release it. Flip the safety off. It was just like she had practised time and time again. Except this time, the thudding in her chest told her that it was for real.

She rested the butt of the rifle against her shoulder and braced herself ready to fire. Her aim wasn't quite up to Melanie's standards, but at a range of a hundred metres she could find her target at least half the time, and she hoped that would be good enough.

Melanie's words of caution ran through her mind. *We have friends, and we have enemies. If in doubt, assume the latter.* Her finger rested against the trigger, ready to squeeze as soon as a target came into range.

The helicopter had dipped out of view now, but she could tell from the change in pitch that its engine was slowing, the blades winding down. She scanned the line of trees at the back of the house for movement.

Sarah was crouched at the next window, her own rifle trained out across the dark fields and trees. 'Do you see anything?' she asked.

'Not yet.'

Yet even as she spoke, Chanita's eyes caught something. A figure, dressed in combat gear, advancing straight for the house. Then a second, and a third. Her finger was sweaty, her breath ragged. It was one thing to shoot at a target, quite another to shoot at a person. She held the trigger, unable to pull it. The men came on.

Then a shot rang out. And another. It was Melanie, firing from the next room.

The men ducked back, behind trees. The shooting paused.

Chanita waited, not breathing, hoping the men would turn and leave, and that she wouldn't have to shoot.

Then a voice rang out across the night air, loud and

clear above the drone of the copter. 'Hold your fire! We come in peace!'

Chanita gasped. She would have known that voice anywhere. Griffin. Her finger left the trigger and she lowered her rifle.

Then the sound of nearby gunfire began again.

Chanita's throat caught as she struggled to find her voice. 'Stop!' she shrieked. 'Melanie! Stop shooting!' She threw her rifle to the floor, heedless of whether it might go off, and rushed into the next room. Melanie was taking aim through the open window. Chanita dashed over, her eyes blurred by tears, and grabbed the barrel of the gun, snatching it out of her hands. 'Stop it!'

Melanie glared at her. 'What are you doing? This might be a trick. Get away from the window, you're an easy target standing there.'

'They haven't come to kill us, Melanie. They're friends, not enemies.'

'How do you know?'

'It's Griffin! He's come to rescue us.' She leaned out of the window, waving her arms into the night. 'Michael!' she called. 'Oh, Michael, it's Chanita! It's me!'

Chapter Seventy-Two

In flight

There was zero privacy in the back of a Merlin helicopter, and it was impossible for Chanita to speak to Griffin above the noise of the engine except through a headset and microphone that broadcast her words to Melanie and Sarah seated opposite. Not to mention the crew. But she had been separated from Griffin far too long to care about that.

'What happened to your leg?' she asked him. The Colonel was using crutches, leaning heavily against them when he walked, and one leg was clearly badly injured. He had tried to hide the pain, but she knew him too well for him to conceal his feelings from her.

'Oh, that,' he said. 'It's not very serious.'

'It looks serious to me. Let me see.'

'Really,' he said, brushing her hand away, 'it's nothing. Enjoy the ride.'

She could scarcely believe that she was leaving

Christmas Common. It had all happened so quickly. At first, she had been reluctant to go with Griffin, knowing that Melanie would refuse to come with her while Ben and James were still away. If the two men returned to the village and found the house empty, how would they ever be reunited?

'I can't abandon Melanie and Sarah,' she'd told the Colonel, and had been surprised at his amused response.

'No one has to be abandoned. How do you think I knew where to find you? Ben and James are safe and sound. We picked them up yesterday, spying on us. They told me the most unlikely tale I've ever heard, and just when they had stretched my credulity to breaking point, they finally told me the piece of news I most longed to hear, but never thought I would. That you were still alive.'

It didn't seem possible that he was alive too. Yet this was no dream. It was far too uncomfortable for her to be asleep. She was sitting next to him on a bucket seat bolted directly onto the fuselage of the Merlin, facing ninety degrees to the direction of travel. There were no first-class seats in the military, and the comfort levels made even the most basic of budget airlines look like luxury.

'I pulled out all the stops to reach you,' said Griffin with a grin. 'It's not so easy for a guy to rustle up a private flight just to come and pick up his girlfriend, you know.'

Chanita felt a rush of emotion at the word "girlfriend", but she didn't allow that to deflect her. She knew Griffin well enough to know when he was trying to avoid a serious talk.

'I thought you were dead,' she told him. 'When I heard that your flight had gone missing, I feared the worst. All communications were down. There was no news of what had happened to you.'

His expression grew serious. 'I was on my way to meet you at Stoke Park when my helicopter went down. I crash-landed in the Surrey Hills. The pilot and co-pilot were both killed outright. I was lucky to survive, but I was injured and couldn't walk for a long time. I finally made it to the western camp, but I was too late to find you. It was already burned to the ground when I got there. There were corpses everywhere. I assumed …' His voice cracked, but he shook his head and carried on. 'I must have just missed you by a day.'

'What happened next?' she asked. 'How did you end up in charge of the army?'

'The Prime Minister recruited me. I said no to her at first. I wanted to carry on searching for you. But she wouldn't give up. In the end, I agreed. So here I am, trying to fight a war.'

Chanita fell silent, brooding over what he had told her.

'What's wrong?' he asked.

'The Prime Minister. What was she doing all that time? The evacuation camp was cut off from the rest of the world. We didn't know if the government was still in place. We didn't know if anyone else was still alive. We needed help, but nothing came. It was a struggle just to survive from one day to the next.'

'But you did survive. I knew you would.'

'We managed until the werewolves came. Then everything went wrong. We fled. At least, the lucky ones did.' She hung her head, too ashamed to tell him the rest – that she had abandoned her post, the position that Griffin had appointed her to, leaving people in the camp to die.

He lifted her chin gently. 'Don't blame yourself. None of that was your fault. It's a miracle you kept people alive for as long as you did. Only the werewolves can be blamed for the killing. And it wasn't the PM's fault either,' he added. 'She was trapped underground in London for a month, sheltering after the nuclear attack. It wasn't until later that she took charge. If you want to blame someone for the lack of action, blame the rest of the government. They were hiding behind a barbed wire fence, protected by what remained of the army.'

'So now the Prime Minister's back in control?'

'No,' said Griffin. 'There is no Prime Minister anymore. And no government either. Only me and a few trusted military advisers. But as soon as this last battle is over, I'll be standing down. Someone else can take over, if there's any country still left to run. I have other plans.'

His eyes went to hers, and she held his gaze, trying to give him a reassuring smile. There were gaps in his story and she sensed there was a lot he wasn't telling her, just as she had not yet told him everything. But that could wait until they were alone together, or perhaps until this war was finally over. She knew that when they landed, he would be swept away once more in a frenzied rush of activity. Reports to receive. Decisions to make. Orders to give. The unrelenting burden of command.

She studied his face, noting the deepened lines that crossed his brow, the silvery hair that had always made him look much older than his years, now completely devoid of colour. The wry smile that used to animate his wide mouth was absent, but his eyes were the same. Cornflower blue. It was what had bewitched her when she'd first encountered him, and they still had the power to mesmerize her now. She gripped his hand tightly in hers.

Chapter Seventy-Three

Near Salisbury, Wiltshire

Canning stumbled along the road, one slow step after another, his wrists and ankles chafed raw from the iron rings that bound them. Hunter had chained him to the front of a tank. Not so much a prison; more a kind of open-air theatre, designed to inflict maximum humiliation on him.

I have become a common prisoner, the lowest of the low. A show, put on for everyone to see. Once I led this army as general. Now I lead it with shackles around my legs.

The humiliation wasn't the worst of it, however. Worse was the relentless rumbling of the tank's 12-cylinder diesel engine. Worse was the unstoppable choke of its exhaust. Worse was the constant possibility that if he stumbled he would fall beneath its enormous tracks and be crushed to death like a wriggling worm. What a horrible creation a tank was. Fine and mighty from a distance, especially when viewed from the safe vantage of his command vehicle. Up close, a monstrous beast, belching out dragon smoke and roaring like a lion. He could only imagine how terrifying it might be to face it bearing down on you in the thick of battle.

But I have endured worse.

There was that time he had lived in the sewers beneath London, creeping through the dark, cold and wet labyrinth, the stink of shit filling his nostrils, and nothing to eat but the rats.

I survived that ordeal, and rose from it greater than ever.

But at least he'd had friends to talk to then. The sewer rats. Now he had not a single friend in all the world.

Since his arrest, his only visitors had been Hunter and his bully boys. They had come to see him the previous two nights, when the tanks rested. Only Hunter had spoken to him, and the talk had been the same each time. *Why did you send your spies to watch the queen? How did you plan to kill her? Sign this confession!*

Then, after he had refused to cooperate, the beatings had come. Blows rained down on him from all sides. Punches. Kicks. Bites. Hammers.

Did they expect him to sign his own death warrant? If so, they misjudged him badly. After an hour or so of futility, even Hunter seemed to lose heart.

I give them nothing in return for their hard efforts. Is it a surprise they grow bored?

When the beatings ended, he snatched a few hours of sleep before the sun rose and the convoy moved off again.

Rumble, choke, chafe. Step after endless step. I hate the days and I hate the nights.

Leanna hadn't visited him once since his arrest. She was obviously waiting for Hunter to break him, so that she could come and crow over him. But perhaps even she was beginning to harbour doubts. Who would break first? The mad queen or her disgraced general?

Each day he hoped to see her, but each day he was disappointed. At least the monotony was broken by the changing landscape. They were approaching Salisbury from the east along the A30. A Roman road, arrow straight in its passage, although it rose and fell with the rolling hills. All around, the countryside was a luscious green with trees perched on hilltops and farmland to either side. When the land dipped, he could see for perhaps two miles.

A sign came into view by the roadside. *Salisbury*. One of many such signs they had passed. So the convoy was still continuing to its intended destination. Hunter hadn't changed the plan.

He lacks the wit to change it.

And yet with Will Hunter in command, everything had changed.

All my careful planning, so meticulously detailed, all gone to waste. Now we are led by a donkey. We are led to our deaths. And I fear that mine may come first.

At the very head of the convoy, he would certainly get a fine view of the battle when the fighting broke out. The chains around his legs and wrists would ensure that he remained in full view of the enemy too. He had 75 tons of armoured tank at his back, yet that would offer scant protection when the bullets began flying. And that was assuming he survived long enough to see the conflict begin.

I am just as likely to be crushed to death by this tank before we reach our destination. Or succumb at last to the nightly beatings and confess to my crimes. So many ways to die. It's a wonder I've made it this far.

The tank juddered to a sudden stop and he leant gratefully against it to rest. Behind him the rest of the convoy was also drawing to a halt. Tanks, tracked and wheeled vehicles, war machines of all kinds, followed by rank upon rank of infantry, stretching back along the road as far as his one eye could see.

Up ahead, a single spire was just visible, rising above the farmland. A thin, grey spindle reaching into the sky. The spire of Salisbury Cathedral, presumably. So they had almost reached the end of the road.

Soon the final battle will begin, and I find myself in the worst possible position.

He waited, wondering why they had stopped here. Was something happening? He strained to peer around the mass of the tank, but was unable to discern the reason for the unexpected halt. Without his network of spies available to inform him, he was entirely ignorant of everything that went on.

And ignorance, as he had repeatedly impressed upon his young charges back in his days as headmaster, was the very worst crime a person could be guilty of.

Chapter Seventy-Four

'Why aren't you dead?' hissed the queen.

It had taken Warg Daddy a long time to decide to return to Leanna, and even longer to find her. He had eventually tracked down the Wolf Army, easily giving the slip to the government forces that were closing in on it from the east and the north.

The humans numbered more than a thousand armed fighting men and women, with tanks and an array of other armoured vehicles at their disposal, all going in search of trouble, and the Wolf Army was much larger in size, with perhaps twice the number of soldiers. When these two forces collided there was going to be the motherfucker of all battles.

But that was nothing to Warg Daddy. He hadn't returned for war and glory. He had come to claim his girl.

Now he was beginning to doubt the wisdom of that decision.

Leanna sat astride a throne, a crown resting on her head. She had granted him an audience inside her royal tent, but she didn't seem very keen to see him. Her attendants crowded in around him, hissing as he entered, jostling him as he made his way up to the throne and bowed his head before his queen. He had tried to tell her why he had come back to her, to set out the right words in the right order, and to make sense of his tangled thoughts and feelings, but so far the meeting was not going well.

'You tried to kill me,' he said. 'And I'm cool with that. You're not the first girl who's tried to kill me.'

Leanna's face was hard and unforgiving. 'You betrayed me!' she shrieked. 'With that little slut! Well, she's dead now. I killed her.'

'Vixen?' Somehow Warg Daddy wasn't too surprised to learn of the Wolf Sister's demise. He felt nothing at hearing the news. 'She betrayed me too. So I reckon we're equal now.'

'You and I will never be equals,' sneered Leanna.

Warg Daddy knew it. How could he compare himself with a woman like Leanna? While he had made himself Leader of the Pack, she had declared herself to be Queen of the Werewolves. While he had cruised around with the Brothers, playing at being a boss, she had brought ruin to the world and raised a new world order from its ashes. They weren't playing by the same rules. They weren't even playing the same game.

But none of that mattered. He had no desire to compete with Leanna. That wasn't why he'd returned.

'I still feel it,' he said. 'Tell me you don't feel it too.'

'What?'

He placed a meaty fist against his chest. 'The thrill. The desire. Bubbling up from below like a volcano. Storming across the skies like thunder. Flashing down your spine like a lightning bolt.' He stumbled to a halt, all out of metaphors. No matter, he had made his point. It wasn't exactly love that he was declaring, but it was more than he had ever felt for any other woman. 'Look at me straight with those blue eyes of yours and tell me you can't feel the passion.'

Her blue orbs remained as cold as ever, yet he thought he could see through their hard exterior. Past the curtain of ice-blonde hair, beyond the scar that marred her perfect face. Beneath his gaze, the mask she wore peeled away and he caught a glimpse of the woman hiding behind it. Needful. Vulnerable. Full of desperate, unfulfilled desire.

Her ruby lips parted, but no words emerged.

'Leanna,' he said. 'You can't deny it. We were made for each other. Like black and white, hot and cold, order and chaos. I can't live with you, but I can't live without you. Now I'm back. What are you going to do about it?'

She still said nothing, but he could feel the need in her, beating as strongly as it did in his own heart. Words didn't matter. He knew what he knew.

It was the wolfman who broke the silence. Warg Daddy had never seen a man like that before, but the strange creatures seemed common enough amongst Leanna's new followers. Wolfmen and wolfwomen, walking around in broad daylight with the heads or legs or arms of beasts. Warg Daddy guessed that this one, who bore the head of a wolf and called himself Will Hunter, was Leanna's latest lover.

'Let's end this nonsense,' snarled the wolfman. 'We'll settle it once and for all. The way men do.'

Warg Daddy nodded his assent. That was all he had ever really wanted. To be a man, and when the time came, to die like a man. He had tried to be Leader once, had thought he wanted it, but leading hadn't agreed with him. It had made a monster of him, sent him down the path to madness, foisted the curse of responsibility onto his shoulders. In the movies the leaders always swaggered around, dressed in black, rocking cool shades, dishing out commands to their minions. No one saw the heavy burden they carried, like a deadweight slung across their back, like a dripping corpse carried in their arms. Warg Daddy never wanted to be a leader again. But to be a man, that was something he could grasp hold of. To be a man, to fight another man and claim his woman as his right. There was nothing hard to understand about that.

'Let's settle it, then,' he said. 'Like men.'

'Like men,' agreed Hunter. 'With or without weapons?'

Warg Daddy considered the matter. He had won his duel against Slasher unarmed. But he had been in wolf form then, and had still been in possession of all four of his limbs. Unarmed and one-armed was no way to win a fight against a man with the head of a wolf. His choice now was obvious – to fight with knives.

But before he could answer, Leanna beat him to it. 'Why don't you flip a coin to decide?'

Warg Daddy's mouth twitched. 'A coin?'

'It's the only fair way.'

He wanted to protest and tell her that life wasn't fair, and that he never wanted to flip a coin again, but that was the way of a coward. Instead he reached deep into his pocket and pulled out the brightly-polished disk he had carried for so long. He fingered it awkwardly, turning it over. Heads, tails, heads, tails. The coin weighed heavy in his hand.

'What are you waiting for?' sneered Hunter. 'Are you afraid?'

'Toss it,' commanded Leanna.

Reluctantly he flipped it, and it was suddenly aflame, catching the light as it turned over and over, spitting bright sparks from burnished metal. Heads, tails, heads, tails, as the gods pondered his future. Or as blind chance determined his destiny.

Luck. How bad could it be?

'Heads we fight with weapons; tails we fight unarmed,' he said. He snatched the spinning coin from the air and turned his palm up to reveal his fate.

'Shit.'

That was what happened when you defied the gods. It looked like the cold-hearted bastards were going to have the last laugh after all.

Chapter Seventy-Five

Winchester, Hampshire

It was the strangest of meetings. But a necessary one, and an urgent one.

At Griffin's side sat Group Captain Bampton, twirling his moustaches awkwardly, discomfort writ large in his embarrassed expression.

You find yourself in strange company, my friend. As do I.

Griffin's leg had flared up worse than ever, the mad dash out to rescue Chanita having taken its toll.

I am no longer built for heroics.

He winced, and shifted in his seat, but the new position was even worse than the previous.

Better just to keep still. There is nothing I can do to make this leg better.

No number of morphine tablets could quench the pain anymore, and he had moved to daily injections. The infection was spreading and he knew that soon his leg would be lost. But he couldn't spare the time to worry about that now.

Lose a leg, or lose a war.

He had already made that choice.

Opposite him sat Chanita, rested and showered and with a fresh change of clothes. He could scarcely bear to draw his eyes from her, but she smiled bashfully beneath his gaze, and dipped her head away.

I must try to focus on this meeting. Too much is at stake for distraction.

Next to Chanita sat a heavily pregnant woman, the one who had opened fire on him with an automatic rifle. Melanie. Her belly was so huge she could scarcely sit at the table, and she was accompanied by her sister, Sarah, for no good reason that Griffin could understand.

Yet Chanita had explained to him that she owed her life to these two women, and that he was obliged to overlook the fact that one of them had nearly shot him.

Next came the two lycanthropes – Ben Harvey, a former teacher, and James Beaumont, still a schoolboy when the contagion of lycanthropy had first swept across the nation and infected him. Both possessed some special ability, apparently, although the nature of that was yet to be explained. And finally, for some reason Griffin had been unable to fathom, Perez had returned from the front line and wormed his way into the meeting. Though how he had found out about it, yet alone persuaded Bampton to allow him to attend was a complete mystery.

A necessary meeting, but a strange one nonetheless.

'So,' said Bampton, 'to business. There is much to discuss and little time. The next full moon is in just three days, and it will be a supermoon. The clock is against us and there are important decisions to be made. Choices that may determine the very survival of the human race.'

Perez leaned forward eagerly, no doubt sensing an opportunity for further profit. Bampton blushed, perhaps conscious of the portentous tone of his opening words.

'Let's hear from James first,' said Griffin. 'I'd like him

to explain why he believes he can persuade the Wolf Army to declare a truce.'

Everyone turned expectantly to the youngest face at the table, but before he could respond, Chanita spoke. 'I think I should first explain why James is so special. Then you'll be able to understand why he is uniquely positioned to act as a bridge between humans and werewolves.'

'Go on,' said Griffin.

She brushed her black hair aside, a gesture that he knew all too well.

She is composing her thoughts. She expects me to disbelieve what she has to say.

But after everything that had happened these past days, he was ready to believe almost anything.

I robbed the Bank of England, found the woman I spent months searching for, and now I'm sitting down for a civilized discussion with a pair of werewolves. What could be more astonishing than that?

'Normal lycanthropes remain in human form most of the time,' began Chanita. 'They change into wolf form once a month, under the influence of the full moon. And the change is involuntary.'

'Yes,' said Griffin. 'This is well known.' He hoped he didn't sound too brusque. Months of military command had starved him of the niceties of normal conversation.

Chanita showed no sign of taking offence. 'James is different. He can change at any time of his choosing. And anyone he turns lycanthropic possesses the same ability. Ben, for example.'

Griffin looked again at the man and boy seated opposite.

Of course. They were in wolf form when captured!

How could he have failed to realize the implication of that fact? He had been so tired, he supposed. So weighed down with other concerns. 'You can control the transformation?' he said to James. 'Can you demonstrate?' He was eager to view this for himself. The precise nature of the transformation was still a mystery to him, and as a doctor he longed to make sense of its mechanism.

'No,' said Chanita. 'James and Ben are not performing animals. You can take my word for it.'

'All right,' said Griffin with some disappointment. He glanced at Bampton, who nodded his bemused agreement. 'Let's take it as a fact. How does this move us forward?'

'First, it means that James can act as a go-between. He has a foot in both camps, if you like. He can be wolf or human. It is his choice which form he assumes.'

'I can see that might be helpful,' said Griffin. 'Is there anything else?'

'We have a bargaining chip. Wolfsbane.'

'You'd better explain.'

It was Ben who offered an explanation. 'Wolfsbane is a herb that can be used to control a werewolf's urges. It can be made into a tea and drunk. Regular doses suppress the desire to kill. It means that werewolves can be rehabilitated, like me and James.'

'It means that we can offer Leanna and her followers a way to step back from the brink,' said Chanita.

Bampton cleared his throat. 'Is there any indication that the lycanthropes want to be rehabilitated, as you put it?'

'As far as I know,' said Chanita, 'no one has ever asked them.'

'Well, I guess that's true.' The group captain turned back to Griffin. 'What do you think?'

'It's an option.' Griffin was wary of killing the idea too quickly. But it seemed a slender rope to be grasping hold of at this late stage.

Perez had no such qualms. 'What happens if our furry friends are less than excited about the prospect of becoming tame poodles? What if they say *muchas gracias, amigos*, but no thank you? What if we send this boy, James, to Leanna, and she kills him? Where does that leave us?'

'It's a risk I must take,' said James, speaking for the first time.

'With respect,' said Griffin. 'There is more at stake than

just your own life. The lives of all surviving humans depend on what we decide here today.' He shuffled the papers in front of him. 'Under normal circumstances, I would never discuss an impending military operation with civilians. But there is nothing normal about the situation we find ourselves in. We are in final preparation for an all-out attack against the Wolf Army. In fact, our planning is already complete. All that is required is for me to give the command.'

'No!' said James. 'You can't.'

'If there's a chance for peace, however slim, we must take it,' urged Chanita. 'We have to try and avoid an all-out war.'

Perez shook his head. 'We can't negotiate with these creatures. They desire only one thing – to kill us all.'

The pregnant woman, Melanie, shot Perez a dirty look. 'Not all of them are evil,' she said. 'Look at Ben, look at James. There's always hope. There has to be.'

'Unfortunately hope is not enough.' Griffin raised his hand to bring the debate to an end. 'What I must do as military commander is assess the available options and make the decision most likely to ensure our survival. There are two ways that can be achieved. Firstly, a decisive victory that will eradicate the werewolf threat once and for all. Secondly, the possibility that James might somehow be able to negotiate a truce that leads to a lasting peace. I have to say, at this point I am inclined to choose the first option.'

'Why not give peace a chance first?' said Ben. 'Send James, and if his mission fails, then do it your way.'

'Because time is against us,' said Griffin. 'To ensure victory, we will need to deploy every one of our military assets – ground, sea and air, not to mention the use of unconventional forces.' He inclined his head in Perez's direction, who smiled graciously at his mention. 'Our air and sea power has limited availability, and depends on favourable weather conditions. Those conditions exist right now. I don't need to remind any of you how quickly the weather can turn against us, even in August.'

A stony silence greeted his words, even Chanita offering no protest.

Melanie glared at him angrily from across the table. 'There is a third option.'

'And what is that?'

'Tell him, Sarah.'

The woman's sister looked startled to be addressed, and bowed her head anxiously. She wasn't half as fierce as Melanie, and Griffin wondered if she would be too shy to say anything, but after a moment she spoke softly. 'Chanita has natural immunity. So do I.'

'Immunity?'

'To lycanthropy. A scientist at the camp, Doctor Helen Eastgate, developed a method for using antitoxins as a kind of vaccine against the disease. Chanita's blood contains naturally-occurring antitoxins. Helen injected them into my bloodstream, and now I'm immune too.'

Chanita took up the argument. 'We could use this to carry out a mass vaccination programme. That would stop the spread of the disease in its tracks. We started to implement a programme in the camp, but we were overtaken by events.'

'A vaccine?' said Bampton, fresh hope apparent in his tone. 'Could that be the solution? Where is this Doctor Helen Eastgate now?'

'Dead,' said Sarah. 'But I worked as her assistant. I know what to do. With the help of Chanita and the medical staff here, I'm sure we could make it work.'

Bampton was looking more dubious now. 'But how long would such a mass vaccination programme take?'

Sarah turned to Chanita, who shrugged. 'I don't know. A few months? A year?'

Griffin's eyes slid up to meet Chanita's. He could tell how much she wanted a peaceful solution, and he shared her longing – to end this bloody conflict not by taking more lives, but by saving them. But it was necessary to be realistic. He had hesitated before, at Gatwick, when he had a chance to bomb the Wolf Army into the ground, and the consequences had been disastrous. The Prime Minister had been right, and perhaps even General Ney too. Ruthlessness was the quality required of a leader, and it was past time he learned his lesson.

'We don't have a year,' he said flatly. 'Not even a month. And even if the entire population could be vaccinated, the military threat from the Wolf Army wouldn't go away. There are thousands of werewolves, perhaps tens of thousands. Can they be changed back? Does this antitoxin work against people who are already infected?'

'No,' admitted Chanita.

'Then we have no choice. Leanna's forces must be defeated militarily. The battle must be fought and won. And we must begin without delay.'

He began the laborious process of rising from his chair, grabbing hold of his crutches and lifting his weight onto one foot, the other dangling uselessly at its side. Every move was excruciating, but Chanita's desperate look hurt even more.

'Michael,' she pleaded. 'At least allow James a chance to try.'

'I'm sorry,' he said as Bampton helped him to his feet. 'My mind is made up.'

Chapter Seventy-Six

Old Sarum, Wiltshire

More people were coming through the gates of the citadel each day. Alone, in families, and sometimes in larger groups. Old and young; fit and injured. Chris had been suspicious of the newcomers at first, and had argued in favour of barricading the gates and turning them away. But Rose had welcomed them and he had come to realize that there was strength in numbers. These people were not simply refugees. They could be trained and turned into farmers, herders, butchers, beekeepers, carpenters, builders and weavers. Not to mention warriors. The list of professions needed to turn the wheels of even a primitive civilization was mind-blowing. But under Chris' guidance, the pieces of the jigsaw were slowly slotting into place. Long-term sustainability was within reach.

Not all was smooth-going. Some of the people stubbornly refused to be categorized in neat ways. One of the dog owners, for instance, had claimed knowledge of carpentry skills and also proficiency in motorcycle maintenance. Chris wasn't happy about that. He preferred his resources to be simple and clearly delineated. Multifunctionality was good in tools, but not so much in workers. In the human arena, specialization was more efficient and much easier to manage. Chris had informed the would-be carpenter/mechanic in no uncertain terms that he was henceforth a designated shepherd, and that he and his dog (canine operative #3) would just have to get used to it.

He watched from the outer bailey as the wooden gates opened to admit fresh people into the safety of the fortress. A mother with her two young children led the way, hand in hand. They were followed by a man with his arm in a sling, and an older woman hobbling along on a stick. Chris wondered where they had come from, and how they had managed to survive in the wilderness for so long. He doubted whether these people would add much to the growing community within the citadel, other than hungry bellies to feed. Reluctantly, he mentally assigned them to the substantial and growing group he had designated as non-producers.

The number of people living within the fortress had doubled, and then doubled again. The inner bailey was long since full, and newcomers were obliged to set up their tents in the much larger outer bailey, which had capacity for thousands if necessary. Chris had recruited a number of experienced builders and set them to work making proper houses to replace the tents. Accommodation wasn't an issue, and neither was food, thanks to the fertile farmland on their doorstep. It wasn't just barley stew that they were eating now. All kinds of vegetables had been found and Chris had worked out a system to harvest them, and to plant more in their place. He already had a team of farmers working steadily at the task.

As for drinking water, Chris had known that a large

floodplain like Salisbury Plain must have a proper river draining it, and he had located it at last. The Avon looped in a wide arc around the base of the citadel as it prepared to mingle its waters with three more rivers on its way to the sea. Its water was clean and plentiful, and he had organized water bearers to bring up fresh supplies each day. If the fortress ever came under siege, an alternative system would need to be worked out, and he already had ideas for a fully-automated rainwater collection system. Sanitation wasn't a problem either, as the original latrines of the castle provided a ready solution for waste.

Even the sheep were working out. The shepherds and their dogs had rounded up far more animals than he had expected, despite the grumblings of shepherd #3 and had brought them back to the safety of nearby pastures. Now the fields closest to the fortress were packed with sheep, and Chris was beginning to think that they might even be able to eat a few of them soon. After all, there were only so many woolly jumpers you could knit from a sheep, and sheep's milk tasted gross. It was possible that the utility of sheep was over-rated and he would have to recalibrate his plans.

The last to walk through the open gates were three teenagers. A tall, muscular boy dressed in jeans and a T-shirt led the group, cradling a black cat in his arms. Good. The boy looked like a strong worker, and cats were useful animals. They could be employed to catch vermin and keep food stocks safe. Behind him walked a thin, brown-skinned boy wearing glasses, with a turban on his head. Not much muscle on this one, but perhaps he had other skills. The boy had an intelligent air about him. Beside him came an older girl with long black hair tumbling over her shoulders. She carried herself with a fierce defiance. This one might spell trouble, or she might prove to be a good warrior. All three might be of use, and the cat too.

The new arrivals gazed in awe as they took in the sight of the city concealed within the earthen ramparts. The girl with the black hair protested when the guards at the gate tried to remove a metal hook she was carrying, but she eventually agreed to relinquish it. A sniffer dog gave them a good once-over, and the guards removed the rest of the teenagers' weapons – a hand axe, a knife and a pitchfork – before directing them to triage.

That seemed to be all for today and Chris found himself feeling disappointed at the small number. Waiting to see how many people would arrive each day and trying to assess their likely uses had become a key part of his morning routine. Once, he would have cringed at the sight of strangers being welcomed into the heart of their defences. Now, he looked forward to the occasion, hoping for a good catch. But each day now the numbers were dwindling.

He turned to leave, but a voice called out to him. 'Hey! I know you!'

It was the turban-wearing boy with the glasses. Chris scurried away, hoping to escape, but the three teenagers caught up with him, the black cat running alongside. The warrior girl blocked his path and he came to a halt, hoping that the guards had done their job properly and she didn't have any concealed weapons on her.

'I know you,' repeated the boy. 'Don't you remember me?'

The boy clearly wasn't as intelligent as he looked. Perhaps his glasses were faulty. Chris spoke slowly to make sure that he could be understood. 'How could I possibly remember you? You've only just arrived. I saw you come through the gate a minute ago.' He pointed to the entrance to the hill fort, so that there could be no misunderstanding.

'No,' said the boy, shaking his head. 'I remember you from before. You were our tech support guy at Manor Road School. I used to come to you for help whenever the printer got jammed or we needed a new ink cartridge.'

'Oh,' said Chris. He stared at the boy, trying to place

him. He had never really paid any attention to the kids at school. He'd been far more interested in the computers and the other hardware he'd been responsible for. 'I have more important matters to deal with these days,' he said.

'Are you in charge of this place?'

Now that was a much better question. Maybe this boy really was smart. And in a way, Chris was in charge, more or less. People might not always carry out his orders directly, but they did what Rose told them to do, and Chris was Rose's top adviser. 'In a manner of speaking. You could say that.'

The other boy spoke then, the tall one with the cat. 'Mr Johnson the sports teacher didn't like you very much. He said you deleted the stuff he downloaded from the internet.'

Chris had almost completely erased Mr Johnson the sports teacher from his memory, and wasn't best pleased to have him thrust back to centre stage again. The man was a bully, and a lazy one, and had caused Chris no end of problems in his job. 'People like Mr Johnson need to be more careful what they download,' he said. 'What people need to understand is that on a school network, unauthorized software is a serious breach of security. It only takes –'

'Can you help us?' interrupted the boy with the turban.

Chris turned back to him with consternation. He had only just begun to express his views on Mr Johnson, and while he might not possess advanced-level *people skills*, even he knew that it was rude to interrupt. 'I really don't have time,' he said. 'I'm a very busy person, you know.' He tried to push his way past, but again the warrior chick moved to block him.

'It's very important,' said turban boy. 'We've travelled hundreds of miles to find this place.'

'Yes, well, everyone travelled a long way to get here. I walked all the way from London. Why did you come here, anyway?'

Lycanthropic

'We heard that people were gathering from all over England,' explained cat boy. 'Because of the priestess.'

'Ah.' Now Chris understood. These kids were superstitious simpletons who had swallowed the whole virgin priestess story and had come expecting visions and prophecies. This cult that Rowan had started was really getting out of hand. 'Well,' he said, 'I'm sure you'll be able to see the priestess for yourself later. Perhaps there will be a feast or something. For now, I suggest you go and get settled in.'

He was already striding away when he heard the words that brought him up short.

'Actually we're looking for a girl from school,' called turban boy. 'Her name is Rose Hallibury. Do you know her?'

Chapter Seventy-Seven

Near Salisbury, Wiltshire

The crowd made a space for the fight, a wide circle carved out of men and women. Outside the ring, the mob throbbed and surged, hungry for excitement and for blood. Inside, the two opponents faced each other, ready to kill or be killed. At the edge of the circle, men stood linking arms, holding back the heaving horde, keeping in the assailants. No way out, except by winning, or by dying. Two had entered the space within: only one would leave with his life.

Warg Daddy recognised a few familiar faces in the crowd – Bloodbath and two surviving Wolf Brothers. Once they had been twelve. Now they were three. He guessed he was mostly to blame for that. He had cast aside his followers as he carved his bloody way through the world, carelessly and without regret. But now, as he gazed into the eyes of the three men he saw not blame or hatred there, but shame. Shame that they lived on, perhaps, while their comrades had perished. Or shame that they had turned their backs on him at his hour of need.

But they had done what they needed in order to survive. There was no shame in living. The shame was his as Leader, in allowing his Brothers to die.

No matter. Regret was a burden too heavy to carry for long. He was no longer Leader of the Pack. Now there was no Pack. They were all just minions of Leanna. He couldn't be blamed for anything now.

'Lift your eyes, Brothers,' he said to them beneath the din of the crowd. 'Do not turn away. Watch instead.'

He turned his own eyes then to Will Hunter. The wolfman was strutting around the edge of the circle like a gladiator in an arena, calling to his followers to cheer him on. They eagerly obliged, raising a chorus of approval, as if he had already won the contest. But Will Hunter was no gladiator, just one more pawn in Leanna's cruel game. He simply hadn't realized it yet.

Warg Daddy weighed his adversary. The wolfman cut an impressive figure. Tall, broad, with muscle-bound arms. He was stripped to the waist, all the better to show off his ripped torso. But looks counted for nothing in a duel.

He puts on this show to impress Leanna. He is a fool for her, just as I am.

Will was as tall as Warg Daddy and just as strong. He was younger and faster, and had both his arms. That was an advantage, Warg Daddy couldn't deny it. The fight would have been more evenly matched if the coin had granted him a weapon. But perhaps his adversary's greatest asset was his wolf head. It was outsized even for his huge body, with a short neck as stout as a tree trunk and a long snout thrusting forward, keen nostrils ranged to either side. Ranks of teeth lined his jaw like sharpened stakes, drool dripping from his mouth as his tongue slid in and out. His eyes were small but bright, like yellow marbles set deep in his skull, and his ears stood proud, twitching and alert to every cheer and shout from his supporters.

He plays the crowd. He sees this fight as a chance to advance his cause, to win favour with Leanna. He does not believe he may lose his life in this ring. He does not perceive the threat.

Warg Daddy nodded, knowing that he had found his opponent's flaw. *Arrogance.* Arrogance in a man was an easy flaw to fight. *A proud man can be goaded. A proud man hates to lose face. Let me feed his pride.*

Warg Daddy cast off his leather jacket, throwing the white wolf aside. It was caught by Bloodbath, who folded it in his arms. *I still have one supporter here, then.* He slipped off his Ray-Bans and passed them to Bloodbath for safekeeping. The sunlight stung his eyes, but the sun wasn't his greatest enemy today.

Then he tried to pull off his shirt, to strip to the waist like his opponent, but with one arm it wasn't so easy. The shirt caught over his head and he found himself stuck in a state of limbo, wrapped in a tangle of black cotton.

What a humiliating death this would make – stuck fast in my own clothing.

A roar went up from the crowd – laughter and jeers. He struggled to pull the shirt all the way, then settled for tearing it off, ripping the fabric into two jagged halves. He threw the rags to the ground.

Will tossed back his head with glee, and the crowd began to hurl their own shirts at him in mockery.

But Warg Daddy cared nothing for the crowd. Only one opinion mattered here. He sought out Leanna's face and found it unreadable, her blue eyes crystal cold, her blonde hair hiding the red scars on her cheek. She looked neither at Will nor at Warg Daddy, but at some distant point that only she could see. *She has no favourite, but waits to see the outcome of this contest. Whoever wins, wins her.* It was faint encouragement, to be sure, but enough to steel Warg Daddy's resolve for the battle ahead.

There was nothing now, save death or glory, and that was not for him to decide. Luck – his old friend, his old enemy – would make the decision for him. But Warg

Lycanthropic

Daddy would do what he could to nudge the odds in his favour. His days of trusting to fate were long gone.

The wolfman was busy rallying the crowd to his cause. He lifted his arms high, showing off, raising ever louder cheers from his followers and basking in their adulation. He turned his back on Warg Daddy, displaying his contempt, and the crowd roared their approval. 'Will! Will!' they chanted. Their voices rose to a crescendo.

Warg Daddy crossed the circle and delivered a single blow to his enemy's back, right in the kidneys. He watched as Will folded in half, wheezing with pain, spluttering with surprise. The crowd's cheers turned to a boo of outrage.

Dirty fighting. But it was better to win a dirty fight than to lose a fair one. Warg Daddy kicked his opponent hard in the ribcage while he still had the advantage. Once Will was back up, the wolfman would be in command. With two arms at his disposal and a wolf's head fixed to his shoulders, he had all the cards to play.

Once, twice, three times Warg Daddy kicked him.

Will roared with pain and anger and rolled on the ground, twisting himself back onto his feet and straightening up to his full height before Warg Daddy could land another kick. 'You cheating bastard!' He curled his fingers into a meaty fist. 'This is for you.'

The giant hand flew at Warg Daddy and met his jaw. There was an almighty crunch and the fist withdrew. A fresh surge of cheers went up from the crowd.

Warg Daddy reeled back, startled by the rapid return of violence. The wolfman was as strong as a bear and even faster on his feet than he looked.

Warg Daddy's skull rang like a bell and his vision turned a blurry red. He tasted salt and probed the bloody cavern of his mouth, his tongue exploring the farthest corners. No teeth remained; only rubble. He spat it out and returned to the fight.

Chapter Seventy-Eight

The crowd cheered loudly after Will's first punch, but Warg Daddy shut out the noise, steeling himself for a second round of fist work, as dark blood and spittle oozed from the empty hollow of his mouth. He spat out the last of his teeth and aimed a jab at Will's ugly face.

The wolfman dodged aside and swung an arm to catch Warg Daddy a smack on his shoulder. The blow was glancing, but was followed up by a second from the other direction. Warg Daddy moved to block it, but with only one arm, he stood no chance.

Two fists against one. The odds were stacked high against him.

He roared and ducked his head down low, charging his opponent like a battering ram and forcing him back. But Will grabbed hold of his head, wrapping one thick arm around his neck and pushing the other into his face. Warg Daddy brought his knee up into the man's groin, but the bastard clung on regardless.

Now punches began to rain down on Warg Daddy, striking him again and again in quick succession. He winced as the first drove into his stomach, forcing the air and the hope from his lungs with a great wheeze. He coughed and tried to pull away, but the arm that gripped his neck was tight as an iron band. The second blow caught the stump of his arm, fingers jabbing into the tender place where his limb had once been. Pain shot down his side like fire and he roared in reply like a helpless beast caught in a trap.

The third chopped at his neck, striking the nerve there and leaving him almost paralysed with agony. He had just regained some feeling when the fourth blow struck him square in the face. He heard his nose crunch flat as bones cracked open.

Warg Daddy hit back, punching desperately, and felt the arm that gripped him ease its pressure. Will thrust him away, and he stumbled back, tripping over his own feet and landing flat on his arse in the dirt. He puffed and panted, his chest heaving, trying to regain some breath before the torment began again. High above, the clouds drifted over – slowly, gracefully, serenely, and utterly indifferent to Warg Daddy's suffering.

Just as the world has always been.

But this was not the time for self-pity. The crowd jeered loudly, shouting themselves hoarse in their eagerness to heap scorn on his misery. He had no allies here, save for Bloodbath and the other Brothers, and what use were three against so many? If he wanted to live to see another day, he would have to get himself out of this fix himself. He blinked tears from his eyes and scrambled to his feet, just as Will came at him again.

This time it was the wolf's head that made the attack, sinking sharpened teeth into his armless shoulder. He cried in outrage and tried to haul himself away, but the harder he pulled, the deeper the teeth drove. Will gripped his chest and hugged him tight, and though he struggled to hit back, his arm was pinned to his side.

The teeth burrowed ever deeper and Will rolled his head from side to side, tearing flesh and sinews with each new twist. Warg Daddy aimed a kick at his opponent's knees, but he dodged aside and returned the blow with a sharp kick of his own.

Just when he thought he was done for, Warg Daddy felt the pressure ease. The great jaws snapped open and Will pulled back, giving Warg Daddy a shove that sent him spinning wildly across the circle. He fell to his knees at the edge of the crowd.

But there was no safety there. A hand reached out and whacked his broken nose. A booted foot struck him in the ribs. A thumb drove into his eye socket, pitching him over onto his side. Each man and woman in the crowd strained and clamoured to give him a taste of their own punishment.

He crawled away from them on his knees.

Back in the ring, Will was preparing another move. As Warg Daddy struggled back to his feet, the wolfman came whirling toward him and left the ground, one leg coming up to meet Warg Daddy's battered face. The heel of Will's foot connected with his jaw, making a deafening crack and shattering another bone. Warg Daddy's face became pulp, his jowls transforming into jelly, fragments of bone and cartilage flying off in all directions.

He lurched back and collapsed to the ground, a bloody wreck.

From the very beginning the fight had been unfair. A one-armed ruin of a man against an able-bodied opponent with the head of a fucking wolf. The blows continued to fall on Warg Daddy like hail, smashing into his face, turning his ugly mug into raw steak. They broke like waves against his stomach, crashed like piledrivers into his skull and pummelled the side of his head like pistons.

Every bone in his body felt broken. Every scrap of

flesh was bruised. If there was a piece of him that had not been punched or kicked, then it had surely been scratched or bitten.

But he was not yet defeated.

He pulled himself from the ground for the tenth time, or perhaps the twentieth, and staggered once more to his bloody feet.

Will Hunter watched him rise, ready to strike him down again, knowing that victory was already his. Warg Daddy was a puppet in his hands, beaten to a purple pulp on the outside, pulverised on the inside, and smashed to smithereens all over. Only stubbornness held him together. A wilful refusal to lie down and die.

But what do I keep living for? Have I grown so fond of suffering that I want it never to stop?

He looked for Leanna's face once more among the baying mob, but when he found it, it was as cold as ever, staring back disdainfully, no hint of emotion playing out there. No regret; no pity.

She feels nothing for me. I have been a fool for her, twice over.

It was late in the day to learn that hard lesson. Late in the day, and his story was almost told. Only one last page remained, and then the words would stop, and the book that was his sorry life would close, once and for all. A story was supposed to mean something, but from Warg Daddy's current vantage point, faced with an unbeatable opponent and waiting for the blow that would finally put an end to his torment, his own life made little sense to him. He had returned from the dead for Leanna's sake, but if she didn't want him, what was the point in continuing?

Was obstinacy a good enough reason? He decided it was not. It was time to die, then, at last.

He looked around for Death, searching the faces of the crowd for that hooded visage, listening for the tell-tale swish of a robe, or the clip-clop of a skeletal horse in the distance, and hoping there might be time for another round of chess before the curtains finally fell, but the trickster was nowhere to be found. Perhaps he too had grown weary of Warg Daddy's endless tribulations.

Across the circle, Will drew a knife from a hidden sheath strapped to his leg and held it aloft. The wolfman was a dirty cheat, no better than Death himself.

The blade caught the sun, flashing bright as a mirror, and as it blazed, a hush fell upon the roaring horde of spectators. Like the crowd at a gladiatorial contest, they turned as one in Leanna's direction, seeking her verdict. A nod or a shake of her head could decide Warg Daddy's fate in an instant. But the queen's face remained impassive, revealing a desire neither for death nor mercy.

Hunter made his own decision. He advanced across the circle, the knife in his hand.

Warg Daddy retreated, backing away with one shambling step for each of his opponent's strides. But the circle was only so large and now his back was pressed against the arms of the men who kept the mob at bay and the circle clear. His eyes flicked from left to right, but there was nowhere to run. Will kept on coming, no hurry in his measured stride, knowing he had all the time in the world. Warg Daddy closed his eyes.

A voice whispered in his ear. Bloodbath's. 'Take this.'

The hilt of a knife slid into his palm, unseen and silent, and he gripped it like a drowning man catches hold of a reed. His eyes opened again.

Will closed in on him, confidence writ in every move, ready to deliver the killing blow.

Warg Daddy waited until his enemy stood right before him. Then he lunged forward, the blade in his hand, its tip bright as diamond. It sank into the wolfman's chest, striking him in the heart. Warg Daddy shoved with all the strength in his one broken arm, burying the knife all the way up to the hilt.

Blood spurted from the wolfman's chest and his eyes grew wide with confusion. His own knife slipped from his hand, dropping harmlessly into the ground. Warg Daddy held his breath, waiting for some famous last words, but his opponent fell to his knees and toppled face down into the dirt, leaving only a surprised gurgle for posterity.

Death had been here all along. Watching and waiting. But it wasn't Warg Daddy he had been waiting for.

Chapter Seventy-Nine

Old Sarum, Wiltshire

They met atop the wind-blown hill. Rose heard her name being called and spun around, unwilling to believe the evidence of her own ears. But her eyes told her the same story.

Vijay. He was alive, and he was here.

'Rose!' He came running toward her, with Drake Cooper and Aasha trailing in his wake. He had grown a little taller since she had last seen him, and his face was gaunter. But it was the same Vijay. The sun glinted on his glasses as he crossed the grassy slope, rushing up to meet her.

'Vijay!'

He stopped a few paces from her, suddenly bashful and uncertain. She kept her distance too, not knowing what to do. She had thought of him often since leaving London, but had never dared to imagine that she would see him again. She recalled the manner of their parting – him, declaring his love for her, and she turning him away, knowing that everyone she loved was doomed to die.

But that was before. That was when her dreams had tormented her each night, showing her the future, revealing horror heaped upon horror. Everything she had seen in those dreams had come to pass – her parents dead, her brother, Oscar, dead, London burning. She had spurned Vijay so that he would live.

Now the dreams had ended and there was no longer anything to fear. She closed the gap that separated them and threw her arms around him.

He seemed startled by her reaction, but overcame his surprise quickly, embracing her in his own arms. They were stronger than she remembered. He was no longer the skinny boy she had known at school. He was becoming a man.

'Rose. I looked everywhere for you. I never stopped looking. I never gave up. I knew you were out there somewhere.'

'I'm here,' she said. 'You found me.'

After a moment they separated. Drake approached awkwardly and gave her a quick hug too, then Aasha came and kissed her cheek.

Chris looked on, apparently baffled by the turn of events. 'You all know each other?' he asked.

'We were at school together,' said Rose. 'Don't you remember?'

Chris shook his head.

'So,' said Rose, 'what have you guys been up to?' It had been January when she had left London, stumbling away from her burning house in the middle of the night, as the cruel wolf moon gazed down. Now it was August. Seven months. A lifetime.

Drake shrugged. 'All kinds of stuff. After we left London, we stayed in the southern evacuation camp for a while. That's where I found Shadow.' He bent down and scooped up a black cat that was curling its tail around his ankles. 'Shadow's good at finding vampires.'

'Vampires?' Rose arched her eyebrows. 'That's a joke, right?' Drake had always played the fool at school, cracking silly jokes and pranking people.

'No,' said Vijay. 'Vampires are real. PC Liz Bailey turned into one, but it's okay, she's a good vampire. Most of them are evil though. They're even worse than the werewolves. Haven't you seen any?'

Rose shook her head. She had thought she had witnessed enough madness in the world, but it seemed there was even more out there. She felt very glad of the wooden gates and fortifications that encircled the citadel.

'Vijay made us save a werewolf,' said Aasha, her dark eyes rolling.

'You saved one?' said Rose.

'He needed our help,' said Vijay, looking embarrassed.

'He was horrible,' said Aasha. 'A big ugly guy with a bald head, all dressed in biker's gear. He said he'd seen you at Glastonbury.'

'He did,' said Rose in amazement. 'He saved my life.'

'That's what he told us,' said Vijay. 'That's how I knew you were still alive.'

It seemed like they would have a lot of news to catch up on. 'What about the rest of your family?' Rose asked.

Vijay's face fell.

'They're all dead,' said Aasha. 'Our parents and our grandmother. They were killed by werewolves.'

'I'm so sorry,' said Rose. She knew first-hand how it felt to lose your entire family.

'What about all this virgin priestess business?' asked Drake. 'We heard people were gathering near Salisbury and thought you might have come here too. Now it turns out you are the priestess.'

'It's a long story,' said Rose, 'but I saw this place in a vision. That's what brought me here. I don't understand how I can have seen it. I'd never been here before. Even Chris can't explain it.'

'But that's easy,' said Vijay, a smile brightening his face again. 'We learned about Old Sarum in history lessons at school. Don't you remember?'

Rose cast her mind back, struggling to recall the lesson Vijay was talking about. Perhaps he was right. Perhaps she had learned about the place at school.

Chris was listening in to the conversation. Now he folded his arms in triumph. 'I knew there had to be a rational explanation,' he said. 'Prophetic vision! There's no such thing.'

Rose found that she really didn't care one way or another. But there was one thing she knew for certain. 'You must keep this to yourselves,' she said. 'It doesn't matter whether this was a vision or a memory, but what does matter is that the people here continue to have faith in me as their leader.'

'So you really are the boss?' said Drake. 'They all do what you tell them?'

'They need a leader,' said Rose. 'For now, that leader is me.'

Chapter Eighty

Near Salisbury, Wiltshire

Warg Daddy returned the knife to its sheath, wiping Will Hunter's blood from its blade. His body had been battered to breaking point and beyond. Not only had he lost an arm, he was now missing a set of teeth too. The number of his bones that were broken outnumbered those that were whole. It was an agony to remain standing, yet he dreaded trying to sit in case that was worse. Every muscle in his body twitched in torment. Every patch of his skin was raw. Every breath he sucked into his battered lungs tasted like fire.

He had won the fight by a hair's breadth, but if Leanna felt any pleasure over the outcome she was very good at hiding it. She cast a brief sidelong glance at the crumpled corpse of Will Hunter as she came over to meet him.

'So, you're still alive,' said the queen, her voice full of scorn.

She had always been distant, even when she and Warg

Daddy had been lovers. Even during their most intimate moments, when he had lost himself in her embrace, she had been elsewhere. Now the gulf between them felt like a chasm.

'I'm alive,' he agreed.

'I never asked you to come back.'

'No. You sent me away with a handful of poisoned pills as a parting gift. But I came back anyway.'

'Why?'

He knitted his brow into a frown, then instantly regretted it. It was far too painful to move his face. 'For you.'

Leanna's blue eyes narrowed. 'I don't want you.'

Her words hurt as much as one of Will Hunter's kicks. 'Then I wasted my time.'

'Did you expect me to swoon into your arms like a lovesick girl?'

'I expected nothing. But I –'

'What?'

'I hoped for something. Anything.'

'Only fools hope,' she sneered.

'I was always a fool for you, Leanna.' It wasn't the best answer, but it was the truth, and that must count for something.

They stood apart, silent resentment filling the space between them.

'So you came back,' she said at last, 'and you killed.' But he detected little bitterness in the accusation. It was more a statement of fact. No doubt she felt as little for Hunter as she did for him. They were both just tools that she had used then cast aside.

'I didn't ask to kill,' he said.

'And yet you killed the commander of my forces on the brink of battle. So now you must lead in Hunter's place.'

'Lead?' He tried to frown again but gave up when it hurt too much. 'You want me to command the Wolf Army again?'

'Someone has to.'

Will's bloody body was still lying where he had fallen, seeming to accuse them both, even in death. 'Take that thing away,' snapped Leanna at two of her assistants. 'I never want to see it again.' They scurried off to do her bidding.

She glared at him, her eyes as cold as ice. 'If you came back for me, then you must serve me. I am your queen. You will do as I say.'

Warg Daddy shook his head, even though the movement set his neck on fire. 'I will serve you as best I can. But I will not lead your army to war. My days as leader are done.'

He had freed himself from the merciless rule of the gods, and would not subject himself to the tyranny of giving orders. Not even for Leanna's sake.

He thought that she would fly at him in rage, but she maintained her icy composure. 'Then you leave me no choice.' She turned to another of her attendants. 'Release the prisoner!'

'At once, your majesty.'

Warg Daddy waited as the aide scuttled away to do her bidding. Before long, a man was brought to her in chains. He was old, in the winter of his years, with weak and spindly arms and a pronounced pot belly. Silvery hair was plastered to one side of his forehead. His clothing was tattered and mud-stained, and one of his eyes remained permanently shut. His face bore the dark bruises of a thorough beating, and he walked as if half the bones in his body were broken. Warg Daddy knew how that felt.

Another of Leanna's attendants freed the man's chains from around his wrists, and he rubbed them gratefully.

'This is General Canning,' said Leanna.

'General.' Warg Daddy offered his hand to the newcomer. This General Canning was a stranger to him, and he wondered where he had come from. If he had earned the title of General, he must have infiltrated himself into the queen's inner circle. Leanna didn't give her trust lightly. Judging from the man's battered appearance, it seemed as if he had lost that trust.

Canning took Warg Daddy's hand and shook it eagerly, making him wince with pain. 'Greetings to you. And congratulations on your victory. It was well fought, if you don't mind me saying.'

Warg Daddy tilted his head to one side, trying to work out if he was being mocked. 'I almost lost my life in that ring,' he said. 'Will Hunter was stronger, faster and more agile than me. He only lost because of his arrogance.'

A smile slithered across Canning's bruised face, and he opened his mouth to reveal a gap between his front teeth. 'And the help of a secret knife.'

'Two secret knives,' said Warg Daddy. 'That makes a fair fight by my reckoning.'

'Mine too,' agreed Canning.

'I see that you two will make a good team,' said Leanna, a scowl on her face. 'It is just as well. Warg Daddy, you will report directly to General Canning from now on.'

'No,' said Warg Daddy. 'I take orders from no man.'

Not once in his life had he obeyed the command of another, and it was far too late in the day to begin now. He turned his pummelled face toward the old man. 'I already killed one man who stood in my way today. I don't mind killing another.'

If there was one thing Warg Daddy had been good at in this life, it was killing. There was no point denying it. Better to embrace the fact and go along with the ride. If you were good at something, do it more. Now there was a motto he could live by. He could slip his blade between the ribs of this General Canning just as easily as continuing to discuss the matter. Better to act quickly than to give the other guy a chance to get his own strike in first. His hand moved to the hilt of his knife.

A broad smile spread across Canning's face. 'There is no need for killing,' he said. 'Not between friends at any rate. Save your killing for when the battle begins. Your majesty, Warg Daddy need not take my orders. I'm sure that he and I can come to a perfectly amicable agreement. A one-eyed man and a man with one arm are well matched.'

'Yes,' said Leanna. 'You two were made for each other.'

Warg Daddy eyed his new acquaintance suspiciously. He had heard only a few words from this general, and already he trusted none of them. Yet what options did he have? If he refused to give orders and refused to accept them, then he must try to find a way to work in partnership with this man.

Canning clearly felt no such misgivings. He rubbed his hands together with glee. 'Then I do believe it is time we got started, your majesty. Come, Warg Daddy, we have a battle to fight, and a war to be won. Our numbers are strong on the ground, but our enemy has air and sea power at its disposal. We will need an exceptionally cunning plan to avoid a crushing defeat.' He winked at Warg Daddy and slapped him on the back. 'Fortunately, I have such a scheme, all ready to put into action. So if someone would oblige me by fetching my eye patch, we can get this fighting started.'

Chapter Eighty-One

Winchester, Hampshire

Night had come and James was ready. He had enjoyed a final meal with his friends – he and Ben eating freshly-killed venison, provided by one of Griffin's men. Now he slipped from his tent already in wolf form, leaving his clothes and his few other possessions behind. He needed nothing now, just his faith.

It was all he had ever needed.

The camp was bustling, and overhead floodlights picked out soldiers, tents, tanks and trucks. But ink-dark shadows flowed around them, weaving a path for him to follow unseen. He set his paw to the ground, ready to go.

A whisper called him back. 'James!'

Ben stood in the open doorway of the tent, beckoning to him. James cursed, then turned around, ducking back inside the safety of the tent.

'Don't try to persuade me to stay,' he said. 'My mind's made up.'

'I know,' said Ben.

'That Colonel Griffin doesn't understand. He thinks he's doing the right thing going into battle, but he's about to make a terrible mistake. This war can be stopped. I can end it.'

'I know,' said Ben.

'You do?'

'Yes.' Ben grinned, his teeth white in the darkness. 'I don't know how you're going to convince Leanna to stop fighting, but I know that you believe you can. And that's good enough for me.'

'It is?'

'I know you, James, and I trust you. Where would we be without trust?'

James bowed his head. Ben's talk of trust was painful to him. His friend had no idea just how much he had been deceived. He really believed that James was going to Leanna to discuss some kind of truce.

My friend, I go to her so that she may kill me. I go in search of sacrifice, and redemption.

'Good,' he said. 'Then it's time for us to say goodbye.'

'I'm coming with you.'

'No.' James swung his wolf's head from side to side. 'You can't. It's too dangerous.'

'I'll be the judge of that.'

'But Leanna might kill me.' Even now he couldn't tell Ben the truth. That death was his goal. 'She might kill you too,' he added.

'True,' admitted Ben. 'But you stand a better chance of succeeding if I'm at your side. We've come so far together, you and I. Do you really think I'm going to leave you now?'

Ben seemed adamant, but James was equally determined. 'No, Ben. I won't let you. You're about to become a father. You must stay here with Melanie.'

'It was Melanie who asked me to come with you,' he said, but James knew that his words had struck home. Ben

Lycanthropic

would always put others before himself. Now he was caught between two conflicting responsibilities – to his friend, and to his unborn child.

'For the sake of the child, you must stay,' insisted James. 'It's your duty.'

Ben's face finally crumpled. 'I know,' he murmured. 'But I don't want you to do this alone.'

'I have to,' said James. 'It has to be this way.'

'All right, then.' Ben crouched down and embraced him, throwing his arms around James' hairy neck. James placed a paw against Ben's chest and licked his face. They shared a moment, wolf and man, together. Then James drew away, and stole off into the night.

Chapter Eighty-Two

Warminster, Wiltshire

The journey inland took Liz back along roads she had already travelled, but now she was heading east instead of west. She drove toward the rising sun and went to war instead of running from defeat, and she was glad to have purpose in her life again, even though it meant danger.

There's always danger, Liz. You should know that now. Sometimes we hide from it, other times we go in search of it.

You're the one who always went in search of danger, Llewelyn Jones, and look where that got you.

They drove in convoy, Eric's car – a seven-seater Land Rover Discovery – leading the way, followed by the other vampires in a range of vehicles. Kevin had swapped his smashed-up Renault for an Isuzu Trooper, and Samantha had upgraded her old Volvo to a VW van. Liz brought up the rear of the group in the Foxhound. The windscreen still bore scratch marks from Eric's claws, but the armoured truck had proved its worth many times and Liz wasn't giving it up now for anything.

Take good care of her, Liz. She's all that's left to remind you of me.

Apart from your incessant voice inside my head.

The A roads were still the best way to travel quickly, despite the pile-ups that blocked some sections. Even where lorries had overturned and spilled their loads across the carriageway it was usually still possible to pick a path through the debris. And in the one case where they found the way impassable, it didn't take long to make a detour along minor roads and re-join the trunk road a few miles further along. Now that they had purpose, the miles passed quickly. Soon they would be close to the enemy's camp.

Liz felt a curious mix of fear and anticipation. Her fear was not for herself, but for those travelling with her: Mihai, just a boy; Samantha and her children; and the kids from London. A motley collection of orphans, widows and refugees. She wondered where the sense of it was. She had collected this rag-tag group on her travels, saving them from danger, only to bring them with her to the most dangerous place of all. Some way up ahead, the werewolf army was massing in preparation for what might prove to be the decisive battle that would bring this crisis to an end, one way or another.

I should be running away, yet here I am, heading into the heart of darkness, babes and children at my side. What am I doing?

We've talked this through already, Liz. You've got to do what you've got to do. Now just get on with it and quit whining.

They stopped for the night at a service station off the A36. The place had been looted and ransacked, just like every other petrol station Liz had encountered. The fuel pumps were dry and the shelves inside the shop were empty. But there was space for them to park off-road, and a picnic area where they could sit and eat as the heat of the day began to fade, and twilight settled in. They would have to sleep inside their vehicles that night, but Liz hardly slept these days anyway. What did it matter where she lay awake, staring into the darkness?

The air was warm, but they lit a fire for light and comfort, and sat around it to talk of what had passed and what was yet to come.

Eric was in good spirits. 'We may be few, but we have an important role to play in the coming fight,' he declared, as they ate and drank beneath the first twinkling stars. The moon had risen, and Liz could feel its pull, even with her back to its silver eye. She tried to ignore it, concentrating instead on what Eric had to say.

'Government forces are closing in on the Wolf Army from the east, and the battle looks set to unfold on Salisbury Plain. We will approach from the west, with the objective of killing any werewolves as they flee the fighting. Our job is to make sure that none get away.'

'That's right,' said Kevin, his fist banging the wooden table. 'We'll smash the buggers. Grind them into the dust. Every damn one.'

Liz found herself less enthusiastic about the prospect of wholesale slaughter. 'Why?' she asked. 'Why kill them all? The ones who are fleeing the battle aren't the most dangerous. Why not let them go? Or take them prisoner?'

'Because we must eradicate this disease once and for all,' said Eric. 'Not a single werewolf must be allowed to escape. Each one is a seed for a whole new wave of destruction.'

There was logic in his words, but a fanaticism in his voice that Liz didn't care for. 'Why do you hate the werewolves so much? I know we all have good reasons for hating them, but the way you talk makes you sound like a zealot.'

Shadows crept into Eric's brow. 'A zealot? I don't think I'm being unreasonable, Liz. This has got to come to an end. It's us or them. Surely you can see that?'

Mihai nodded eagerly, the light from the fire making his

eyes sparkle. 'Always, *vampir* hates *strigoi*. For a thousand years it is so. All the stories say it.'

'All I can see,' said Liz, 'is that hate leads to misery. And if werewolves have to be killed, then what about vampires? Werewolves eat flesh; vampires suck blood. The same evil lives in both species.'

The fire crackled, spitting sparks into the night like starfire. Eric leaned forward. 'If you don't mind me saying, Liz, it's too simplistic to think of good versus evil. Werewolves are not all evil, and vampires are not all good. Far from it. Humans too – there is good and evil in everyone. Perhaps the reason we hate the werewolves is because they're so much like us. They hold up a mirror showing our worst failings, our biggest faults. They make us face up to what we have become. If we don't fight against them, we are choosing to side with them. We are condoning everything that is wrong with ourselves. We all have choices to make. The werewolves who joined the Wolf Army made the wrong choice. They must pay the price. They must bear the responsibility.'

'But if there is choice,' persisted Liz, 'then we have choice too. We can choose to kill, or choose to forgive and make peace.'

Eric looked pained. 'One day there will come a time for peace and reconciliation, but it is not now. Peace will come when war has run its course. When it does, I want to be able to look back and be certain I was on the right side.'

'That's right,' said Kevin. 'You gotta choose your side, whether it's family, friends or whoever, and then you stick with it. Doesn't matter if it's right; doesn't matter if it's wrong. Usually no way of telling anyhow. Just stick with it.'

'Come what may?' said Liz.

'Exactly,' said Kevin.

Eric's frown deepened and he cast a sideways glance at Kevin. 'Something like that, I guess. Although I would argue that we are definitely on the right side.'

'I hope so,' said Liz. 'I hope that humans come out on

top, and when they do, they'll realize that we were fighting on their side.'

'We'll deal with that when the time comes,' said Eric. 'In the meantime, there are things you need to know about the Wolf Army. Have you ever encountered a wolfman?'

Liz wondered what he meant. 'A wolfman? Of course.'

'I don't mean the normal werewolves. I'm talking about mutants. Strange creatures that are part human, part animal. They come in a variety of forms, but what they have in common is that they are fixed in wolf form all the time – they don't need the moon to change them.'

'Is *moroi*,' said Mihai excitedly. '*Moroi* is very bad monster.'

'You know of these creatures?' asked Eric.

Mihai nodded. 'In Romania, is many, many monsters. Mostly *strigoi*. Is person who can be animal. Demon lives inside them. Werewolf is called *vârcolac*. But *moroi* is animal all the time. Can be bear or bird or rabbit. It depends.'

'I've only seen the wolves. What else do you know of these *moroi*?'

'Is very strong and fast. Likes to eat people. Grr!' he lurched forward, making Lily cry out. 'Sorry,' he said, bashfully.

'You also told me some facts about vampires,' Liz prompted.

'*Vampir*, yes. Is dead person, killed by other *vampir*. Comes back to life. Makes more *vampiri*.'

'If they choose to,' said Liz. 'I made you a vampire because it was the only way to save your life, you know that.'

Mihai didn't seem concerned by Liz's reservations. '*Vampir* is very powerful monster. Is stronger and faster than *vârcolac*. Fire does not hurt *vampir*.' He glanced at the orange flames of the fire, burning brightly and chasing black spirals of smoke into the night sky, but made no move to test his claim. Liz knew, however, that in vampire form she had been able to walk through fire without harm.

'And can be invisible too,' said Mihai.

Eric laughed. 'Invisible? I don't think so, my young friend.'

'Is true,' insisted the boy. 'Is in many, many old stories in Romania.'

'Some of what those stories said wasn't true, though, was it?' said Liz. 'Like vampires being afraid of the cross, and being poisoned by garlic.'

'Well,' said Mihai, folding his arms firmly across his chest. 'Is still invisible.'

'Invisibility would be a useful ability to have,' said Eric, 'but I think we might have to make use of more conventional skills. When we go into battle in vampire form, we'll be formidable, but not invincible. We must work together as a team, and we'll be relying on Kevin here to provide covering fire.'

Kevin beamed. 'I'll be ready with the machine gun, don't you worry.'

'We'll be ready too,' declared Leah, raising her spear.

'And me!' cried Alfie, his huge sword in his hands.

Liz sighed. Eric's talk appeared to have succeeded in raising everyone's morale except for hers.

Don't worry about it, Liz. When you go into battle, Kevin and the kids will be right behind you.

That, Llewelyn Jones, is what worries me most.

Chapter Eighty-Three

Old Sarum, full moon

Morning came, and Chris was appalled by the sight that greeted him. Today the gates had not been opened, and now it was clear why the number of new arrivals to the fortress had been dwindling over the previous few days. Overnight, an army had appeared beyond the ramparts of the outer bailey.

He stood on the walkway above the gates, looking out across the plain toward the encroaching forces. They were little more than a mile away, crawling across the landscape in a wide column, tanks and other military vehicles at the front, followed by more vehicles behind, and a huge number of foot soldiers walking alongside. They were too far away for him to tell with any certainty which side they were on, but everything about the approaching army made him shiver.

He was glad of the ditch that encircled the lower ramparts, and glad too of the stout wooden doors that sealed the only entrance to the iron age fortress. But it would be foolish to imagine that these primitive defences would offer much resistance to a determined push by a well-equipped modern army. One well-aimed shell from a tank would split the gates apart, and the fortress would fall. He began to question the wisdom of taking refuge inside what now looked like a thoroughly ill-defended encampment.

At his side, Seth was clearly having similar thoughts. 'Is it too late to run?' he asked, stroking his smooth chin.

'Far too late.' The inhabitants of Old Sarum were in no fit state to run anywhere. While many were young and strong, others were older and weaker. There were children among them, and the sick and injured. Non-productive units, to Chris' way of thinking, yet even he had no intention of running away and leaving them to be eaten by werewolves. He had invested too much time and energy in building a sustainable future here. Besides, running was no longer a sensible option. As he watched, the invaders split into two, crawling like ants around each side of the fortress, surrounding Old Sarum in a neat pincer movement. Now there could be no doubt about which side the army was on. While many were in human form, strange mutants walked among them, with the heads, legs or arms of wolves. Chris stared at the new arrivals, his mind churning, but unable to grasp what he was seeing.

The sight was enough to render Seth dumb.

Other folk joined them on the ramparts to watch as the citadel was steadily encircled. Families, with frightened children gathered into their parents' arms. Groups of friends, huddled together for comfort. There were murmurings as they discussed what was happening, but the atmosphere was subdued, and their voices were soon drowned by the wind that gusted across the open plain.

'It's not all bad,' said Chris at last. 'We have advantages. Height, for one thing.' It was true that their vantage point from the earthworks gave them full visibility over the enemy troops. It would be impossible for them to do anything without being seen. 'And the ditch and embankment will stop any vehicles from entering.'

'That's true,' said Seth, sounding reassured. 'So you think we're safe?'

'No,' admitted Chris. 'If the tanks open fire on us, we'll be done for. And if the soldiers are determined to scale the ramparts, there's no way we can hold them back.'

'So we're doomed,' said Seth, his face crumbling into despondency.

'Probably,' said Chris. 'But let's not give up yet. Perhaps the werewolves will move on.'

'Perhaps.'

But any hopes Chris may have entertained in that regard were quickly dashed. The advancing army ground to a halt, the lead vehicles shuddering to a standstill and the rest fanning out to ensure that the citadel was completely surrounded. Enemy soldiers emerged from the vehicles to join the infantry walking alongside and began setting up camp. They unloaded equipment from the backs of trucks and erected tents and portable shelters. Soon, a temporary base had been installed in the fields around Old Sarum.

'What do you think they're going to do?' asked Seth.

'What do *you* think?' asked Chris.

'I think they're going to kill us all.'

Chris nodded glumly. He hated to admit it, but for the first time in his life, Seth was probably right.

Chapter Eighty-Four

Winchester

There was nothing left to be done but to give the order. Yet Griffin held back, waiting.

At his field command post, his officers waited for him. And at sea, Bampton and FitzHerbert were waiting too.

Months of planning had led to this moment. Everything was in place, and the attack must begin. The human shield was gone. The fleet was waiting in the English Channel. Perez's men were in place, reporting back from the frontline. Just that morning, Griffin had learned that the Wolf Army had surrounded the camp of human refugees located at the edge of Salisbury. The time to strike was now. Yet still he hesitated.

'Please,' Chanita had begged him the previous night after it had become clear that James had defied Griffin's command and left the camp without authorization. 'Give James time to complete his mission. There's still a chance for peace. Take it.'

'I have already made my decision,' he told her. 'James shouldn't have gone. He disobeyed my direct order.'

'What difference will another day make? A few more hours?'

'They may make all the difference. The weather may turn against us. The Wolf Army may do something unexpected. If I delay, any number of things could go wrong. In war, time is critical. We must not lose the initiative.'

'But isn't it worth waiting just a little longer, in case James succeeds?'

The disagreement had ended in an acrimonious row, with Chanita uncharacteristically storming off, leaving him feeling doubly ineffectual. He had failed to pacify the woman he loved and yet he had also failed to take the decisive action he knew he must.

To delay, risks catastrophe. I must not fail again.

Yet here he was, doing nothing, when all around him men and women waited for him to act. He could see it on their faces, each one silently accusing him of timidity, just as Chanita had accused him of recklessness.

He had lain awake all night, unable to sleep after the argument, and with his leg full of fire. No matter which way he turned in his bed, the pain grew steadily, until it was all he could do not to scream. Even the morphine couldn't help him now.

Fever had set in, and he would lose the leg. He was certain of that, just as he was certain he must give the order.

Yet still he waited.

What if James succeeds? What if, against all the odds, he can bring peace? Isn't that worth waiting for?

But where was James? He ought to have arrived at Leanna's camp already. The fact that nothing had been heard from him indicated that his mission had failed.

And if I wait, my mission, too, will fail.

'Sir?' A young communications officer from the Royal Corps of Signals held the field radio for him. 'Group Captain Bampton is on the line. He wants to know if the attack should go ahead as planned.'

Griffin took the radio from him and switched on the speaker.

'Griffin? We're ready to proceed. The weather is clear. Flying conditions are perfect. And FitzHerbert is grumbling, saying storms may move in. Shall we go?'

Every face was watching him, willing him to give the go-ahead. He thought of Chanita, pleading with him to give peace a chance. He thought of James, out there somewhere – who knew where? And he thought of the consequences of failure.

He knew what he had to do. He had always known it. And he felt anger at himself for delaying so long.

'Griffin, what shall I do?' asked Bampton.

'Proceed with the operation,' he said. 'Begin the attack.'

Chapter Eighty-Five

Salisbury Plain

James crouched low in the lee of the thicket, waiting for his breath to return. His journey between the two armies, which ought to have taken just hours, had been brought to an abrupt halt when a huge thorn became impaled in his paw. A blackthorn bush was the culprit, the evil thorn more than three inches long and as thick as a branch at its base. It had snapped off, leaving the tip of its sharp spear embedded in his flesh, and try as he might he had been unable to remove it. His paw was agony, and to put any pressure on it was impossible. And so he had hobbled, three-legged and clumsy across the landscape, slowed to the pace of a snail, as dawn swallowed night and the day grew hot.

If Ben had been with him, perhaps he could have helped. But it was better he was alone. If Ben had discovered the true nature of his plan, he would have tried to stop him. A rational man like Ben would never be persuaded by words like *faith* or *penitence* or *sacrifice*. No amount of persuasion would have convinced him of the rightness of what James intended to do when he reached Leanna. The lie he had told Ben and the others about negotiating a peace deal had been necessary.

He half expected to hear the roar of jets in the sky overhead as the RAF began its air assault, or the boom of explosions as tanks and artillery opened fire on the Wolf Army. He waited for the sounds of battle that would tell him that he was too late; that his mission had failed. Yet all he could hear was the murmur of the wind and the chatter of birds. The quiet voice of the natural world, calm and serene. The sun shone down from clear blue skies – English summer in all its finery – and it was easy to imagine that the world was at peace and all was well.

Please, God, let it always be like this. When I am done and gone, and my sacrifice has been made, let it be like this.

He cowered, picturing brimstone and earthquakes as the seventh seal opened. In his imagination he had watched it many times. An angel with a golden censer, burning incense at the altar and offering prayers to God. Seven angels with seven trumpets standing poised to sound. The first angel filling the censer with fire from the altar and casting it to the ground. Noise, thunder and lightning, earthquakes...

The spread of lycanthropy across the world, that had at first seemed so random and incomprehensible, had been inevitable from the beginning, the events foretold two thousand years ago in Revelation. Had it somehow been James' fault? He had played his part certainly. He recalled with shame the lust to taste human flesh that had filled him when he first became infected, lying in his hospital bed under Chanita's watchful gaze, not knowing what had happened to him except that a madman had bitten his arm and that he was changed. He had gone on to kill. First the priest, Father Mulcahy. Then, with Samuel at his side, he had embarked on a killing spree across London before finally bringing his shameful desire under control.

Oh, Samuel. If only you were still alive and by my side.

But Samuel was dead, and soon the first trumpet would sound.

Hail and fire, mingled with blood, would fall from the sky. A third of the trees and a third of the grass would burn.

And then the second trumpet…

It must not happen.

Only he could prevent it. And only through the ultimate sacrifice.

So why had God sought to stop him by setting a thorn in his paw?

It is a test.

He had been tested from the beginning and often found wanting. He had lost his faith, and turned to wickedness, before finding the right path again. Yet still God's voice was silent.

Another test.

He could expect no better. At the very end, God had turned His back on His own Son.

He took the sins of the world on his shoulders. I must do the same.

The second trumpet sounded in his mind, and an image of a burning mountain crashing into the sea came unbidden. Helplessly, he watched as a third of the sea became blood, destroying all the ships that sailed on it and the living creatures that swam in it.

I will not allow it.

He rose once more, curling his injured paw beneath him and limped forward, slowly and painfully, yet with steady purpose. After a while he crested a low rise, and before him appeared a great plain spreading out for miles across the low countryside.

The plain of Armageddon.

At its centre rose a series of concentric hills. Circular earthworks, built by men long ago as defence against their foes. Now it was peopled once more and surrounded by the Wolf Army.

He took one look at the vast array of soldiers and machines of war arrayed before him, and set off down the hill.

Chapter Eighty-Six

The Solent

From the slim expanse of sea that separated the Isle of Wight from the British mainland, nothing was visible of Portsmouth harbour except for its open mouth. During his long naval career, Commodore Francis Maynard FitzHerbert had watched that welcoming haven drawing close more times than he cared to recall. But this time the sight stirred up bittersweet memories.

Both *Queen Elizabeth* and *Prince of Wales* had operated out of Portsmouth Naval Base, and the city of Portsmouth had been his own home too. But he was not returning home this time – he was sailing to war. His home on the island of Portsea no longer existed, and his family, too, had perished.

During most of his adult life, his greatest fear had always been that his wife, Anne, might someday receive a visit by a senior officer, his face grave, who would deliver those terrible words, "killed in action", or worse, "lost at sea". He had never once thought that he might instead lose her.

Queen Elizabeth was away at sea when the fighting broke out in Portsmouth, but he had seen its aftermath at first hand. Ransacked buildings; whole swathes of the docks and city burned to the ground; bodies of civilians strewn in the streets or murdered in their own homes.

His wife, children and grandchildren were all gone without a trace, presumed dead. Everyone he had loved. Even little Keira, just three months old when news of the attack had reached him, and who he had only ever seen by video link. But he couldn't be certain what had happened to any of them. There was always a slim possibility that they may have escaped. But instead of offering hope, that uncertainty made his grief ten times worse.

There was nothing he could do but resign himself to the worst and face his loss with stoicism.

As his ship sailed steadily past the remains of the once-proud naval base and on into the tidal estuary of Southampton Water, he dragged his thoughts out of the past and turned instead to face what was coming. The final battle. The moment he had spent his whole life preparing for. He could never have imagined it playing out quite like this. But now that it had come, he was more than ready, and so were his crew.

The carrier strike group would have presented a formidable sight to anyone watching from the shore. Two huge carriers rising to a height of fifty metres above the sea, together with their attendant frigates and destroyers, cruising along the narrow strait of the Solent just two and a half miles wide. It would narrow even further as the fleet approached Southampton docks, and they would have to sail all the way to the mouth of the River Itchen in order to guarantee being within range of the enemy. The destroyers' 4.5 inch guns had a firing range of 27.5 kilometres – just enough to reach the Wolf Army's position near Salisbury.

Now that Griffin had given clearance to unleash the

full capabilities of the carriers, the enemy forces would stand no chance. Right now the carrier's flight deck was clear, all planes safely stowed below. When the initial shelling had finished and the next stage of the battle was in full swing the deck would be full of planes and their handlers, affectionately known as "chockheads". The roar of jet engines would drown out all other sounds, as planes manoeuvred into position before taking off into the air to deliver their deadly cargo of armaments. At the same time the marines would disembark and begin their advance to join up with Griffin's ground forces. Two hundred and fifty elite troops from 42 Commando would spearhead the assault from the south, cutting off the Wolf Army from every direction and ensuring their elimination. But first, a concentrated bombardment from the large-calibre guns of the destroyers would degrade the enemy defences, ensuring safe flight for the F-35 Lightnings.

Now, as the convoy neared its destination, every seat on the bridge was taken by the men and women who controlled the *Queen Elizabeth*. All were calm, assigned to specific duties, fully trained for what was to come.

'Radar reports all clear, Commodore,' called the Principal Warfare Officer.

The long-range radar mounted above the carrier's forward island was capable of tracking air and sea targets within a radius of 250 miles. They were not expecting any enemy activity, but FitzHerbert was taking no chances. As far as he was concerned, this operation was no different from any other. The nature of the enemy might have changed, but his response would not.

The full height of the windows in the bridge gave an unimpeded view of the land to either side. There was no movement visible there. No sign of anything untoward. There was no reason for concern. The weather was fair, the sea calm. Yet as the port of Southampton drew nearer, a tingling sensation ran up FitzHerbert's spine.

No doubt it was simply the heightened sense of

anticipation. Already the destroyers had moved to the front of the convoy, ready to open fire with their guns and guided missiles. The frigates were at the rear, tasked with defending the fleet against possible submarine attack. The carriers themselves were equipped with a wide range of defensive weaponry, from 30mm guns to anti-aircraft and anti-missile systems.

Not that any kind of attack was likely. To FitzHerbert's knowledge, he commanded the only significant naval force in the entire world. There was really no need for him to be concerned.

'Depth 21.4 metres,' called the Pilot.

'Maintain course,' ordered the Navigation Officer.

To port side, the golden sands of Calshot Beach reached out to welcome them. To starboard, *Prince of Wales* slid majestically through calm waters beneath untroubled skies. Conditions were perfect. Fortune was on their side.

Yet still FitzHerbert couldn't shake off the vague sense of undefined menace.

Chapter Eighty-Seven

Old Sarum

'What are they?' asked Rose, her voice sounding small on the wind-blasted walkway above the gates of Old Sarum.

She had woken at first light, Nutmeg's wet nose against her face, a familiar comfort in strange times. She had hugged the dog close, enjoying her smell and warmth. But there had been precious little comfort for her again that day. Ryan had come to fetch her, his face clouded with concern. 'What's wrong?' she asked.

'Come and see.'

The sight that greeted her as she climbed the steep slope of the lower rampart was worse than she had dared imagine. A great army encircled the city. And no normal army, but a menagerie of strange beasts.

Even from this distance it was possible to make out the wolfmen with their mismatched body parts. Fur and claws and fangs. She had seen nothing like them before, not even in her worst nightmares and visions. They were like fiends escaped from the underworld.

Chris, who was also watching from the gates, Seth at his side, had a more rational explanation. 'They're mutants,' he pronounced confidently. 'Every virus mutates into new forms. We should expect the virus that caused lycanthropy to do the same. This is the result.'

The wolfmen were going about their business in full daylight, with no moon in the sky. Men and women in human form worked alongside them, but Rose had no doubt that all of these creatures were werewolves of some kind or another. She had never seen so many together at one time. This must be the Wolf Army she had heard so much about. 'What are they doing?' she asked.

'It looks like they're setting up camp,' said Ryan. 'I guess they plan to be here for a while. They've completely surrounded us, but so far they've made no move to attack.' He paused. 'But we have to assume that's their intention.'

'Can we hold out if they do attack?'

Ryan answered her with a shrug. 'We'll do our best. But realistically?' He left his question unanswered.

Rose cast her gaze across the menacing forces arrayed before her. She wondered how many other leaders had stood in her shoes, surveying an invading power and deciding how to respond. Those who had shown fortitude and courage were the ones that history had recorded as victors. Those who had doubted themselves or given in to their adversaries had been forgotten.

'Start making preparations,' she told Ryan. 'Gather all men and women fit enough to fight. Organize lookouts so that we can keep watch day and night.'

Ryan nodded. 'I've already arranged for a team of lookouts. And I've picked out the strongest fighters. With Chris' help we've been arming them with axes, spears and bows and arrows.'

'I didn't know about that,' she said. 'You didn't tell me.'

'I didn't want to worry you with talk of fighting.'

Rose sighed. Despite everything they had been through, Ryan obviously still thought of her as a weak girl in need of protection. But she was no longer a girl, she was ruler of her tribe. 'Is there anything else you haven't told me?' she demanded, her voice a challenge.

He shook his head, contrite.

She placed a hand on his broad shoulder. 'In future, spare me nothing. If I am to save my people, I must know everything, however hard the news.'

A group of people were making their way along the stony path that led up to the gate top. Vijay, Drake and Aasha. 'We heard you were here,' said Vijay.

'You've seen the Wolf Army?' asked Rose.

Vijay shuddered. 'Yes. We were here when they first arrived. What are you going to do?'

Rose looked out across the grassy plain at the new terror that had engulfed her world. 'Defend the fortress at all costs.'

'We'll need fighters,' said Ryan. 'Can you three fight?'

'Totally,' said Aasha.

'We'll need our weapons back,' said Drake.

'That won't be a problem,' said Ryan.

'What about you, Vijay?' asked Rose. 'Can you fight?'

He nodded his head vigorously. 'Of course. You know I can.'

'Good.' The boy she had known at school had never been a fighter. But this new Vijay was almost a grown man. Taller, stronger, and with a look of determination on his face that gave weight to his words. She had no doubt he would fight to protect the citadel.

She hoped it may never come to that. The enemy that encircled the fortress numbered as many as them, and was armed with modern weapons, not primitive spears and axes. And they were beasts and trained soldiers, not ordinary men and women with families to protect. Fighting must be the very last resort. A final act of desperation.

A sudden roar made Rose look up. A shadow passed across her face and the noise grew in intensity as a dark shape split the air, travelling at tremendous speed. There was no time to react, except to duck low as the missile plummeted to earth. It struck the ground a half mile beyond the rampart, burying its nose in an armoured personnel carrier that was stationed at the perimeter of the enemy camp.

The vehicle erupted in flames.

A deafening thundercrack followed and black smoke spewed from the explosion, rising high into the blue sky. A great cloud of dust rolled out across the plain, and at its heart, red tongues of flame flickered through the dark mass.

Immediately the Wolf Army began to react – soldiers running for cover, scurrying into action, looking to the sky for more threats, and rushing to their vehicles. But there was no enemy for them to fight. The missile had come from out of nowhere.

A minute later a second explosion rocked the camp on the other side.

'It's the army, come to save us!' yelled Seth triumphantly. 'Everything's going to be all right!'

Rose felt her spirits rise, but Ryan's face remained gloomy. 'Those missiles could land anywhere. We need to get everyone under cover.'

'Come on, then,' she said. 'Let's start moving.'

Chapter Eighty-Eight

Salisbury Plain

So this was Ragnarök, the day of doom. The twilight of the gods. Two great hosts, armed with weapons of war. A tale foretold, now come to pass. And Warg Daddy was at the heart of it. Could any man ask for more?

And yet it was not like he had pictured – heroes locked together in close melee, sweat on their brow, blood on their blades. Battle axes and great longswords striking sparks from breastplates as Valkyries swooped low to scoop the bravely fallen off to Valhalla.

Where were the heroes?

There were none. Only men, dead and dying on the ground as exploding shells ripped their soft flesh to pieces.

Where was the enemy?

Miles away and out of sight. There was no chance to be a hero in this kind of war – only to await a futile end as distant forces rained down death upon the battlefield.

This was no battle. This was a massacre.

He strode across the ground as another blast ripped through the air, showering him with mud as an armoured troop carrier exploded in flames a short distance away. The force of the explosion almost stole the Ray-Bans from his face, but he grabbed at them, pushing the shades back into place to protect him from the burning sun.

Nearby, Canning stood grinning like a lunatic, watching as men staggered from the twisted metal, wreathed in flames and covered in blood. And they were the lucky ones. Their comrades lay still behind them, their bodies fuel for fire.

Warg Daddy reached for Canning's shoulder, twisting him round with his one arm to face him. The man was like a peacock in his ridiculous uniform, strutting around for all to see. It was a wonder he hadn't been the first to die. 'Have you lost all sense?' bellowed Warg Daddy into the general's face. 'We will be wiped from the face of the earth like this!'

Canning's grin stretched wider. 'Do not fear, my friend. All is in hand.'

'Nothing is in hand! Why are we not responding? We must fight back or take cover or we will be annihilated!'

Across the camp, another shell landed, spilling out sheets of flames with a deafening roar. Men screamed in agony. A tank rumbled past, tracks clanking, its gun barrel raised to the horizon ready to fire. Yet there were no targets for it to find and its gun remained silent. Canning watched it go, a look of detached curiosity on his face, as if he wondered what might happen next.

Despite everything Warg Daddy had said about not wanting responsibility, he had half a mind to choke the life out of Canning and take over command. Somebody had to, or they would all be dead.

Up on the ramparts of the nearby earthen fortress, tiny figures watched the battle unfold. Humans, weak and unarmed. It would be a simple matter to storm the citadel and take them hostage. A coward's way perhaps, but when the enemy was a coward, firing missiles and artillery from afar, what choice was left? It was better than standing around, waiting to see where the next shell would land.

'We should storm the citadel,' he said, shaking Canning to get his attention. 'Take the humans hostage.'

A single eye gazed back, revealing amusement. Was the man completely mad? 'We have no need for prisoners,' he said. 'The counter-attack has already begun.'

'I see no counter-attack, only defeat.'

'Be patient, my friend. I promise you that soon this short-lived offensive will end. The tide will turn in our favour. And then the real battle can begin.'

Warg Daddy looked around, but all he saw was chaos and destruction; burning vehicles and dying men.

So this was Ragnarök, the day of doom. There were no gods here, only madmen.

Chapter Eighty-Nine

The Solent

The bombardment had begun. The big guns of HMS *Dragon* and *Defender* were firing off their 46 pound high explosive rounds using targeting information reported from observers on the ground. Round after round after round, each accompanied by a deafening boom. After a brief interlude, a Harpoon guided missile took to flight and vanished quickly over the horizon, leaving a plume of white smoke in its wake, adding to the destructive power dished out by the destroyers.

The effects of the pounding on the enemy's defences were invisible to FitzHerbert. All he could hear was the commentary of his Principal Warfare Officer as she relayed the news from Salisbury. 'Confirmed. Target hit. Target destroyed. That's copied.'

Everything was going exactly as planned, and FitzHerbert kept his position on the bridge. There was no need for him to take any action or to give orders. The

Officer on the Watch had command of the ship, the Navigation Officer holding its position as the tide slowly rose.

Yet the tension was building inside him. The sense of threat was growing palpably. This was all too easy.

'Radar report?' he demanded.

'All clear, Commodore.'

'Sonar?'

'All clear, sir.'

Why was he worrying? Through the plate glass windows of the tower, all he could see was empty sky, calm seas, and low-lying land to either side. All clear of threats.

In the seat beside him, Group Captain Bampton appeared relaxed. His work, and the task of 617 Squadron would not begin until the following day.

The guns of *Dragon* began to fire again. *Boom. Boom. Boom.* A steady rhythm, regular as clockwork, as dependable as a heartbeat. Another missile launched, briefly filling the sky with fire and smoke, before disappearing again.

Two minutes later, the damage report was received. 'Target destroyed. That's copied.'

FitzHerbert began to pace the bridge. Bampton's eyes flicked in his direction.

Another minute passed.

'Commodore!' The sudden change in the PWO's voice was marked. 'Sonar reports incoming torpedoes.'

'Range?' he barked.

'3.2 nautical miles. Estimated speed eighty knots.'

'How many?'

'Two, sir.'

Incoming torpedoes could mean only one thing. A submarine in the water. Silent. Invisible. Deadly. It must have been tracking them this whole time. Only the firing of the torpedoes had betrayed its presence.

He'd thought that all the Navy's nuclear subs had been

Lycanthropic

destroyed in the fighting that followed the nuclear attacks. Was it possible that one had survived and fallen into the hands of the enemy?

The mood on the bridge had switched in an instant. Bampton was on his feet, but had the good sense to remain mute and let FitzHerbert do his job. 'Engage countermeasures,' he ordered.

'Aye, sir.' The PWO switched to giving commands. 'Control to Wildcat 1, Wildcat 2. Engage enemy torpedoes.'

The helicopters were already airborne and moved immediately to drop their air-launched Sting Ray torpedoes.

'Countermeasures deployed. Bears 2.7 nautical miles, incoming.'

A hush fell over the bridge and FitzHerbert waited with baited breath to find out which of the torpedoes would find their target: attacker or countermeasure. With both sets of weapons moving through water at high speed and reliant on sonar to guide them to their quarry, it could go either way. If the Sting Rays failed to intercept their targets …

It would take less than two minutes to find out.

'Bears 1.9 nautical miles, incoming.'

Across the water, the guns of HMS *Dragon* fired again, but the boom quickly died away, leaving silence as the seconds ticked on. Bampton returned to his seat, his hands gripping the leather armrests, knuckles white. FitzHerbert stayed still, listening, waiting.

'Sir.' The voice of the PWO broke the quiet. 'Bears destroyed.'

A murmur of relief travelled around the bridge. FitzHerbert exhaled, unaware that he had been holding his breath. His heart thumped loudly in his chest, each beat sounding louder to him than the guns of the destroyers.

It was twelve beats before the PWO spoke again. 'Sir, two more torpedoes detected. Range 3.1 nautical miles, incoming. Launching more Sting Rays.'

'Find that damn sub!' ordered FitzHerbert. 'I want all Wildcats in the air immediately!'

Chapter Ninety

Winchester

It began with a scream and then got worse. Nausea. Vomiting. The breaking of the waters. Ben didn't know much about childbirth, but he had never expected it to be this bad.

Melanie's back arched and she screamed again, clutching his arm like a vice and digging her fingernails so hard into his skin they drew blood. He wanted to cry out himself, but knew that would only earn him a slap. Melanie had already unleashed a torrent of cursing his way, and the look in her eye promised more of the same unless he gave her the support she needed.

'Is this normal?' he asked Chanita. 'Is something wrong?' They all knew that this was no ordinary pregnancy, that anything could happen. His mind was racing, conjuring all kinds of horrific scenarios and outcomes. The pregnancy had lasted just two months, and it was fair to say that they were in completely uncharted territory.

Here be monsters.

The thought would have made him chuckle if he hadn't felt so sick.

Chanita's gloved hands were smeared in blood and Ben had no desire to see where she was putting them. 'I'm no midwife, only a nurse, but I don't see any cause for concern.' She ran a cool gaze over Ben's sweaty face and clearly wasn't impressed by what she saw. 'It's time for you to man up, Ben. There's no room here for anyone who can't pull their weight. And I hope you're not a fainter.'

'Werewolves can't afford to be afraid of a little blood,' he offered, but he had to suppress a desire to gag as she wiped her fingers on a filthy towel. There was blood and there was …

Sarah re-entered the tent, carrying fresh towels and water. 'I hope this will do. These are the last of the towels, and I couldn't get hold of any hot water, only cold.'

Chanita took one of the towels and wiped Melanie's brow. 'We'll manage with what we've got. Plenty of women have given birth without the benefit of a modern hospital.'

No doctors were available to help them, and it was up to Chanita, Ben and Sarah to help get Melanie through her ordeal. No painkillers were on offer, nor any emergency backup if anything went wrong. There would be no Caesarean, no epidural, no senior consultant to step in and take over. Ben felt useless in his current role, but he guessed that by acting as an outlet for Melanie's pain, he was helping the process in some small way.

I am the painkiller, he thought grimly as Melanie screamed again, digging her nails deeper into his arm.

'Shush,' said Chanita. 'Save your energy. This will go on for a good while yet.'

'How long?' gasped Melanie.

'You've only just gone into labour. For a first baby, this can last hours, even a day or more.'

'Hours? You must be joking. How am I going to survive that long?'

'Try to stay calm. Breathe slowly and deeply. You might like to get up from the bed and walk around between contractions.'

'Get out of bed? I doubt I'll ever be able to walk again.'

'Honestly, Melanie, anyone would think you're the baby.'

Sarah looked on anxiously and Ben knew what she was thinking. *What happens when the baby is born?* But that wasn't a question he wanted to dwell on. He was glad when Melanie began to arch her back again, a fresh wail emerging from her lips and the fingers tightening around his once more. Pain kept the darkest thoughts at bay. And if Chanita was right, and this took hours or even days, then he wouldn't need to think at all for a long while yet.

Chapter Ninety-One

Salisbury Plain

So this was war. Funny.
Not funny hilarious, but funny strange. So far, war felt just like the rest of Kevin's life. Boring for the most part. Just a lot of hanging around, being told nothing, and waiting for something to turn up. Knowing that when it did, it would most probably be something bad. Grasping at opportunities, then seeing your luck turn to dust, running through your fingers and leaving you worse off than if you'd never bothered to try. Yeah, that was life for you. Kicking you when you were down, and then kicking you again for good measure, with a sneer thrown in for free. And still he never learnt the lesson, just kept hoping for something to change for the better. Idiot.

It was true that so far no one had actually kicked him.

He was slap in the middle of a war, but as yet he hadn't seen any fighting. The explosions were over the other side of the hill, the black smoke rising above the treeline, the bad things happening to some other poor bugger. But that didn't mean he was safe. This was how life was – it lulled you, making you hope that luck was on your side this time. Then, just when you thought that things might be looking up for a change, it came back to bite you on the arse good and proper. And give you another good kicking too, just to make sure you learned the lesson this time round.

But Kevin never did. He just kept hoping that this time would be different. Bloody fool. Yet how else could you go on? The alternative was worse – to roll over and die – and there was no way he was going to do that.

'Fight for what matters, son,' his old man had told him when he was a kid. 'Fight as if your life depends on it. Because it damn well does.' Sound advice that. His dad had been full of wise words. If only Kevin had bothered to pay attention to a few of them. But no kid ever listened to good advice, especially not from anyone old enough to have a bit of real wisdom to share.

No, we only ever listen to fools and fraudsters.

These vampires were no fools, but Kevin couldn't help wondering if they were fraudsters. Eric was giving them another pep talk right now, going on about noble causes and being on the right side of history. Fine words. This Eric could talk well enough, but Kevin didn't trust people who had so much to say. Doubly so if they were bloodsucking parasites. Kevin's old man would have had some wise words to say about that, he had no doubt.

I wish you were with me today, Dad.

Kevin had a funny feeling about today. Not funny hilarious, but funny bad. Like this was the day his luck might finally run out once and for all.

Run out? I never had any in the first place.

The day had the feeling of being his last. If so, he would make it count.

For Liz's sake. For Mihai's. And for his own.

He knew he'd messed up plenty of times. He'd been a bad husband. A bad father. And probably the world's worst father-in-law, getting Llewelyn killed and all that. No way he could ever make that up to Liz. But he was determined not to make things worse.

If I die today, I don't want it to be for nothing.

That would be the cruellest joke ever. To come all this way, only to get killed right at the start of the battle. Yet so far, it was other buggers doing the killing and getting killed. Maybe luck was with him after all.

Another explosion rumbled across the plain, more smoke billowing into the sky like black clouds. He was glad he couldn't see any more than that. He knew at first hand what a blast like that could do to a human body. He'd seen it for himself back in Northern Ireland. Roadside explosives. Semtex. Nail bombs. Mangled body parts strewn out across the pavement as rain washed blood into the gutter.

He didn't want to see it again, but it was stupid to pretend that he wouldn't. The explosions were on the other side of the hill for now, but Kevin wasn't daft enough to think that they would stay that way. Life was coming to get him. And death was following in its wake.

Chapter Ninety-Two

Salisbury Plain

He was too late. Too late by far. The first trumpet had sounded and the battle had begun. Falling stars were crashing to earth, bringing fiery death and destruction to the world.

James limped on, as fast as he could on three legs across the grassy plain, but knowing that time had already run out. For him, for everyone.

Ahead of him, men, wolves and machines milled about in confusion, the tanks gouging out deep furrows with their metal tracks. The air was filled with dust and noise and smoke. Beyond the mayhem rose the steep earthen banks of the citadel, crowned with men, women and children gathered as witnesses to the world's end. Silent watchers, gazing down on destruction.

An explosive blast went off in front of him, knocking him over with its brute force. He fell to the ground, his ears ringing, his limbs a tangle. Clumps of mud rained down on him and dust billowed out, enveloping him in a thick cloud of darkness. He coughed so much he thought he might die, but when it cleared he was still alive. He struggled back to his paws, then on he went, drawing ever closer to his journey's end.

The whole of the battlefield was in chaotic motion. Soldiers ran from one place to another, weapons cradled in their arms. Vehicles circled the camp, seeking to avoid the falling shells. Another enormous tank came his way, gathering speed as it approached. He stopped, his injured paw raised uselessly beneath him, staring as the behemoth grew larger and larger until it towered above him, its tracks churning death, ready to crush him.

It veered away to one side just before it reached him, and he set off again, heading toward the one still point at the heart of the chaos. A row of tents, one larger than all the others. If Leanna was anywhere, it was surely there.

His paw had grown ever more painful as he'd made his journey, the embedded thorn burrowing deep into soft flesh, but he swallowed the pain, putting it behind him. All that mattered now was the final few steps that would take him to his goal.

Leanna. The queen. Atonement.

Soldiers were everywhere, and he expected to be stopped at any moment. But he was wolf, just as some of them were part wolf, and he slipped among them unchallenged. When he reached the tent, he found it unguarded and went inside.

Three figures stood beneath the canvas – two he knew, one a stranger.

Leanna, the queen, was seated on a great throne. She was the first beast of Revelation, the beast from the sea with ten horns. Now, as her moment of triumph approached, she wore her horns openly upon her head as crests of a golden crown.

She was listening to the second beast, who was speaking of plans and ploys; of schemes and stratagems.

This beast had one eye, the other covered by a patch to hide his wickedness. He was tall, with silver hair, and spoke with the voice of a dragon, boasting of his great cunning at outwitting his enemies. 'Your majesty, I promise that this bombardment will shortly cease. I have arranged for a surprise attack that will bring the enemy to its knees.'

All Leanna's attention was fixed on her minion. 'You had better explain, Canning. And quickly, or my patience with you will finally come to an end.'

The one-eyed beast bowed low. 'Even as we speak, the enemy fleet is under attack from our forces. Some months ago, a report was delivered to me of an *Astute*-class submarine that had fallen under our control. It was seized during the fighting when the northern cities fell. I ordered it to remain hidden until needed. The vessel in question is aptly named HMS *Ambush*. It is right now engaged in a sea battle with government forces.'

Leanna lifted one hand to her chin and stroked it thoughtfully. 'But what use is one submarine against an entire fleet?'

The beast named Canning flashed a wicked grin at his queen. 'A submarine, by its nature, is impossible to detect until it reveals its location by launching a weapon. In the case of *Ambush*, the weapons at its disposal include torpedoes for sinking ships and missiles for bringing down helicopters. With the element of surprise, I doubt that it will have much difficulty sinking a small flotilla, especially one that has trapped itself by sailing into a narrow estuary.'

The third person in the tent was Warg Daddy. He had lost an arm and all his teeth since James had last seen him, but it was no surprise to find the third beast mentioned by St John in thrall to the first. 'Then why are we still under bombardment, Canning?' he snarled.

The one-eyed beast's thin mouth twisted into a grin, showing crooked teeth. He cocked his head to one side. 'Why, I do believe that it has already ceased.'

They all stopped to listen. It was true. The noise of explosions had come to a halt. Outside the tent, all was calm.

In the hush that followed, Leanna's gaze drifted in James' direction. She took in his wolf form, inspecting him from head to tail, seeing his fine sandy coat. Her eyes slowly widened with recognition. 'You!' she shrieked, rising from her throne in astonishment.

'Yes,' he answered. 'It's me, James.'

'How dare you come back to me!' Her eyes narrowed. 'Are you here to grovel and ask forgiveness? To beg for your life? To switch sides like that bitch, Vixen?'

'No,' he said. 'I've come to forgive you.'

Her cold eyes bored deep into his for a second. Then her voice erupted in rage. 'Forgive me? How dare you!'

Chapter Ninety-Three

The Solent

'Bears 1.7 nautical miles, incoming.' The voice of the PWO rang out clearly over the hush of the bridge.

Across the blue water, two more Wildcats struggled into the air, their rotors straining to lift them above the superstructure of HMS *Defender*. Another pair scrambled to take off from *Prince of Wales*, and soon there were six in flight, all armed with Sting Ray anti-submarine torpedoes. They moved to intercept the enemy threat.

'Bears 1.3 nautical miles, incoming. Countermeasures deployed.'

Seconds ticked past, each one an age. FitzHerbert paced the bridge, knowing that it would be better to stand still, but unable to contain his nervous energy. Eventually, after what seemed like minutes but must have been mere seconds, the PWO gave the report the commodore was waiting for.

'Bears destroyed.'

The release of tension from the officers present was tangible. FitzHerbert nodded briskly. 'Get a fix on the sub's location. Take it out.'

'Aye, sir.'

Bampton moved to his side, speaking for the first time since the start of the attack. 'We can destroy it, yes?'

FitzHerbert shook his head. 'The first thing you learn when you join the Navy is never to make promises. The sea makes its own rules.'

The group captain persisted. 'But with six choppers in the air, and a sonar fix?'

FitzHerbert swung his head angrily in Bampton's direction. 'We'll stand a much better chance if you let me do my job.'

'Of course, I'm sorry.' Bampton returned to his seat.

The exchange left FitzHerbert in a sour mood. It was unlike him to snap. He was unused to feeling nervous, even in the heat of battle. Yet with so much at stake, and faced with what was most likely an *Astute*-class submarine – the Royal Navy's newest and most deadly hunter-killer – he could be certain of nothing.

'Sir!' The PWO was looking out through the plate glass side window of the tower, her face white.

A low boom followed, coming from across the water. FitzHerbert turned to see fire in the sky. Two of the Wildcats had exploded into flames. One was already a blazing fireball, a smudge of black smoke streaming behind it. The other had been caught at the rear of the fuselage, fire burning hot in its engines, a boiling cauldron of red and yellow. As he watched, the flames took hold, creeping toward the cabin, the black skeleton of the aircraft outlined against the inferno.

There was nothing the pilot could do. The chopper began to tilt as it lost power, turning onto its side, then flipping upside down before beginning its final plummet from the sky. Two shapes appeared as the Wildcat corkscrewed downward – the pilot and co-pilot ejecting to safety. And then the craft split apart – the rotors, still slowly turning, going one way, the rest of the chopper plunging headlong into the sea.

The remaining Wildcats were taking evasive action, but they were too slow. The surface of the sea broke into white foam as another pair of missiles rose up from the deep. Quick as darts they found their targets and more explosions lit up the sky with bright flashes. Two more missiles followed in quick succession and it was all over. The last of the helicopters began their inevitable descent to their doom, black trails muddying the sky as they fought and failed to stay aloft. Mangled metal frames tumbled through the air, rotors twisting uselessly, flames fed by the choppers' own fuel. There were no survivors this time.

'All Wildcats down, sir. We have a position on the sub. Relaying to all units.'

'Give it everything we've got.' FitzHerbert cast a sad look across the gentle waves. The last debris from the Wildcats was still hitting the water, the fire quenched at last. In the green belly of the sea a deadly enemy was at large, and without the helicopters to defend the fleet, the sub now had the upper hand.

'*Northumberland* reports torpedoes fired. *Defender* turning its guns on enemy target.'

The first shell from the destroyer struck the surface of the water some two miles south of *Queen Elizabeth*, drawing a fountain from its depths. More followed and soon the quiet seas were a maelstrom. But even as the barrage continued, FitzHerbert knew that the battle was already lost.

The PWO's next report confirmed his worst fears. 'Bears 1.6 nautical miles, incoming.' Another pair of torpedoes in the water, and perhaps only minutes until they hit.

'Begin evacuation of all ships,' he ordered. 'Non-essential crew and auxiliary staff first.'

Bampton was at his side once more, a hand on his shoulder. 'FitzHerbert? Are you serious?'

'Never more so.'

'Then it's time to get the planes off too.' The group captain moved away to begin giving instructions to flying command.

On the bridge of the navigation tower, the various officers continued to perform their tasks with quiet assurance. Years of training kicked in, and they remained calm when it mattered most. On deck, aircraft handlers were scrambling into position, preparing to get the planes into the air, and the commodore knew that below deck a thousand other men and women would be going about their duties – pilots getting suited up, marines preparing to disembark along with their vehicles and equipment, the rest of the crew moving to evacuation positions. FitzHerbert's heart swelled with pride. He had given his orders and now it was down to others. There was little more he could do to change the course of events. A sense of tranquillity settled over him, even as half his mind remained at the highest alert, listening to every report.

'Bears 1.0 nautical miles, incoming.'

'42 Commando commencing evacuation.'

'Beginning deployment of evacuation slides. Crew to don life vests.'

The first pair of F-35s had already appeared on deck and the control tower was relaying its instructions to Bampton. 'FLYCO to flight deck. Begin take-off checks.' FitzHerbert watched the figures of men moving methodically about deck, signalling to the pilots in the cockpits. The first jets would be ready to take off within minutes, but no matter how quickly the crew went about their work, the task of raising, fuelling and prepping every one of the planes and getting them airborne would take the best part of an hour. An ice-cold dread gripped FitzHerbert's throat, filling him with a certainty that all was futile. He had been at sea for months, only for the mission to fail at the last moment. Just as he had raised a family, only to stand by as his children and grandchildren perished.

'Bears 0.5 nautical miles, incoming. Countermeasures deployed. Sir, more enemy torpedoes launched. Range 1.5 nautical miles. More countermeasures deployed.' A hint of desperation had entered the PWO's measured announcements. FitzHerbert could hardly blame her. She was young, barely in her thirties, and even he, a seasoned old-timer was beginning to crack under the pressure.

The reports and relayed orders continued to wash over him.

'Lightning 1, move to take-off position. Lightning 2, prepare to follow.'

Planes were rolling across the flight deck. Frigates turned, water churning at the bow. Marines had begun to disembark. The tankers were taking evasive action, moving away from the rest of the fleet. Meanwhile, the enemy remained invisible, detectable only by the sonar trace of its deadly weapons.

The first torpedo hit home, taking HMS *Northumberland* broadside on. A mighty explosion ripped through its steel hull beneath the waterline. A second followed moments later, leaving the frigate holed in two places. Immediately it began to list to starboard.

'Commence full-scale evacuation,' ordered FitzHerbert.

The first of the F-35s was in take-off position, its jet roaring. Its handlers retreated to a safe distance on deck. It was a race now to get the planes aloft before disaster struck.

'Bears 0.2 nautical miles, incoming. Phalanx close-defence system engaged.'

The Phalanx was the carrier's last line of defence. An automated radar-controlled close-range gun, designed to take out surface-to-surface missiles, fast attack boats and near-surface torpedoes. The 20mm rotary cannon swung into operation, directing its fire at the sea to starboard.

Rapid-fire rounds traced a line of white across the water's surface as the torpedoes sped ever closer.

FitzHerbert braced himself. The impact came seconds later as the enemy weapon struck the bow of the carrier. A massive explosion followed as the warhead detonated, rocking the huge ship from side to side. Water rose a hundred feet into the air, breaking over the windows of the forward island and washing the deck. It was followed by another explosion, halfway along the ship's length and beneath the keel. More water flooded the deck, leaving a cloud of sea mist in its wake.

'Damage report.'

'Hull breached, Commodore,' reported the Officer of the Watch. 'Fires reported in two places. Ship taking in water.'

Queen Elizabeth had shifted, listing to port. On the flight deck, the first of the Lightnings was attempting take-off, but with the deck covered in water and sloping to one side, it immediately began to slide.

'Abort take-off! Abort take-off!' Bampton was screaming into his mike, but the plane had lost control. Its wheels skidded, losing grip, turning the huge power of its jet engine in the wrong direction. The pilot struggled to right it, but the thrust from the turbine was too much. The plane accelerated sideways across the deck before plunging off the edge.

'Lightning 2, shut down engine.'

The second plane managed to avoid the same fate as its predecessor, but the attempt to get the F-35s into the air was over. Now the only task remaining was to ensure the safety of all crew.

The commodore could see for himself that the evacuation was well underway. The first of the life rafts was already making its way to shore. FitzHerbert walked the bridge, shaking hands with each of his officers in turn and relieving them of their command. The last man remaining was Bampton.

'Group Captain, it has been an honour to serve with you.'

'Likewise, Commodore.' Bampton gripped his hand tightly. Disappointment was written large on the group captain's face, but he bore it stoically.

'I will make my final report to Griffin,' said FitzHerbert. 'Get yourself onto one of the boats. As quick as you can. There's no telling how fast the ship will go down.'

Bampton's grip on his arm tightened. 'I'll wait while you make your report. We can leave together.'

'No, my friend. I shan't be leaving my ship. I will stay until the end.'

'Don't be a fool, man. This is no time for stupid heroics.'

FitzHerbert shook his head. 'I assure you I have nothing heroic in mind. This is a coward's way out.' He could see that Bampton didn't understand. 'I've spent my entire life at sea. As a boy sailing yachts, as a man commanding warships. It's all I know. The idea of living out the rest of my days on land and in disgrace terrifies me.'

'There is no disgrace in defeat, FitzHerbert. You did your best. No one could have done more.'

The commodore allowed a sad smile to twitch his lips. 'Ah, that's where you're wrong, Bampton. I could have done a lot more. And not just today. Now go.'

Bampton hesitated a moment longer and then came forward, the two men embracing, clasping each other tight. It was the closest contact FitzHerbert had experienced since he had bidden his last farewells to his wife. 'Goodbye, my friend,' said the RAF man. 'You will not be forgotten, I promise.' He left without looking back.

FitzHerbert returned his attention to the ongoing sea battle. The destroyers were moving to the attack, pummelling the sea with the full force of their cannon, but *Prince of Wales* had been hit too and was holed below deck.

Even if the destroyers managed to sink the sub, the fleet was useless now. With no air power, Griffin would have to face the final battle alone.

FitzHerbert's thoughts drifted finally back to his family. Once, they had been real flesh and blood, more precious to him than anything in the world. Now they were memories, but no less dear to him. If he had been a religious man, he might have hoped to be with them again soon, but the commodore had never been a believer in anything but the fearsome power and beauty of the sea.

Soon he would be nothing more than a memory in the minds of those men and women he had known and served alongside. That was the only legacy anyone could leave behind. He hoped, as Bampton had sworn, that his memory would endure. For a while, at least.

Chapter Ninety-Four

Salisbury Plain

'I understand, really I do,' said James. 'I know that you didn't intend to do evil. You were following a dream. Evil often starts with the best of intentions. People set out to do good, but they lose their way. We all end up in sin. But it's all right now. I forgive you.'

Leanna could barely contain her rage at his presumption. 'You? Forgive me? How dare you!'

For months she had sought out the arch-traitor, tasking Canning with the goal of finding him and bringing him to her alive. But Canning had failed her, over and over again. Now James had turned up out of his own volition. But instead of begging for mercy, he deigned to forgive her. Forgive her? For what? He was the one who ought to be seeking forgiveness. He was the one who had sided with humans. He was the one who had fought her. He was the traitor!

She would make him beg. She would make him grovel.

By the time she had finished with him, he would be crawling on the ground, begging for his death. A snarl escaped her lips, but instead of fear in his eyes, she saw only a deep well of compassion.

He smiled sadly. 'Samuel told me about your dream. He said you wanted to bring an end to human suffering. You hoped to cure disease, perhaps even to stop old age from sending us to our graves. But the truth is that only God can save us.'

He had changed since their last encounter, grown into a man. Even in wolf form she could see the difference. His golden glossy coat had thickened and become sandy. His shoulders were broad, his limbs well-muscled. But he was still a fool, speaking of sin and evil. Still clutching at his non-existent God.

'What has your God ever done for us?' she demanded.

'He gave His Son so we might live.'

'Enough of this nonsense!' she screeched. She had already allowed him to speak too long. There must be no more words from him, only screams. She bared her teeth, wishing she could be in wolf form like him, so that she could rend him limb from limb. But the moon had not yet risen, and she must face him in human form.

'Samuel had a dream too,' said James. 'His dream was different to yours, but just as grand. He dreamed that men and women would live in peace. Black and white, gay and straight, people of all nations, all together in harmony, celebrating their differences instead of fearing them.'

Leanna knew she should end this now, but she couldn't stop sneering at him. 'And what happened to Samuel's grand dream? Where is this peace and harmony?'

'Still a dream.'

'A pipe dream! Humans can never live in peace and harmony. They were born weak, cursed to suffer. Only the strong can be truly happy. That's what werewolves are. Predators. Hunters. We take what we will. None can refuse us. A new age has begun, and you and Samuel and all your pathetic friends are doomed to die.'

Leanna's fury continued to grow, her anger burning ever hotter. She lashed out at James, drawing blood from his cheek with her nail.

But he refused to meet her attack with violence of his own. 'A new age is about to begin,' he conceded. 'But neither you nor I will live to see it.'

'Liar!' She whipped his face with her other hand. But all he did was turn back to look at her. He almost seemed to take satisfaction from the blow.

She recalled the final look on Professor Wiseman's face as he sat trapped in his overturned Land Rover, deep in the Romanian mountains, his blood splashing scarlet against the snow that blanketed the narrow forest track. Just before she killed him, he had offered her a smile and some final words of reconciliation. *I forgive you. This was all my fault.* Words of weakness.

She had spilled Wiseman's life all over the crisp white blanket. She had gorged on his body, ridding herself of the rage that his forgiveness had provoked. Now she found herself with another fool offering forgiveness.

Stupidity! There was nothing to forgive. History would prove her right.

A sound to her left disrupted her thoughts. A clearing of the throat. *Canning.* What was that one-eyed idiot about to say?

'Might we return to this fascinating debate at another time?' he suggested. 'There is still the inconvenient matter of a battle to be fought. My plan to destroy the fleet appears to have been a success, but the war is not yet done. Perhaps ...'

He tailed off as she turned her gaze in his direction. 'Did I invite you to speak?'

'No, but ...' Still he blundered on. 'The fact of the matter is that James is not our greatest enemy. The land forces of –'

'I decide who is the enemy!' she screeched. 'I see

enemies everywhere! You, for one. I have set you simple tasks, to bring the traitors to me – James, Warg Daddy, Vixen. How many of them did you bring?'

'Well, I –'

'None, Canning! They came to me of their own accord. Vixen, I slew. Warg Daddy, I gave a second chance. But there will be no second chance for James, and there will be no more chances for you, so hold your tongue, unless you wish to lose it!'

He cowered back, alarmed, bowing and grovelling before her. He had the good sense not to speak again.

James had also fallen to his knees. 'Kill me, then, if you will. I am ready to die.'

She lashed out again, striking first one cheek, and then the next, drawing fresh blood. But each time he turned his face back to hers.

'Fight me!' she yelled.

'Kill me,' he said.

She struck him again, but there was no satisfaction in pummelling an opponent who didn't fight back. It was like eating dead meat out of a can.

At her side, Warg Daddy shifted, his combat shotgun in his hand, looking uneasy. 'This is wrong,' he muttered.

Leanna ignored him. She kneeled down, so that she was the same height as James, and gripped his chin in her hands. 'I will kill you,' she said. 'And I will kill your friends too. Melanie, Ben, and anyone else who helped you. But I won't kill them quickly. Their deaths will be painful and slow, and I will keep you alive long enough to watch them.'

'No,' he begged.

'Oh, yes,' she said, knowing that she had finally found a way to make him fear her. 'Canning, bring me some chains. I will keep James here until the battle is won, and then I will take my revenge at my leisure. It will be sweeter that way.'

'No,' repeated James. 'You must kill me now, before

the battle begins.'

'That's what you want isn't it?' She rose to her full height again, towering over him. 'Soon this battle will be won, and the age of humans will be over. They will be nothing but food and slaves. A new age will begin, when wolves rule the world under my command. We will do as we please, hunting and killing, and for humans there shall be nothing but terror and suffering!' She laughed in triumph. 'It is what they were made for!'

Chapter Ninety-Five

Winchester

'Goodbye, my friend. Goodbye.'
Griffin listened as the radio crackled into static followed by deathly silence. He had kept FitzHerbert talking, trying to persuade him to save himself, but the commodore had stayed resolute, determined to remain onboard his ship until the end. A pig-headed man, but a heroic one. There were few like him left in the world. Now he was gone, along with *Queen Elizabeth* and Griffin's hopes for a quick and decisive victory.

So it had come to this. Facing the final battle alone. No ships, no planes, no reinforcements. Only a scant company of ground troops, together with the ragged band of rogues under Perez' command. Every battle eventually came down to the same thing – boots on the ground, men with guns, infantry closing in for the kill. But without air and sea support behind them, their chance of success was slim. And soon the full moon would rise, transforming the enemy into ravening beasts, and who knew what might happen?

Griffin handed the radio back to the communications officer, feeling weak. The burning in his leg had reached an apex of torment, impervious to any amount of morphine, and it was spreading throughout his body. Fever. And with it, infection.

Lose a leg, or lose a war. A choice long since made. Now both might be lost.

This was no time for self-pity or introspection or even for mourning. The other commanders in the tent were looking to him for direction. Perhaps for hope itself. Yet he could offer them little of that. The burden of command grew heavier at every step. Only defeat or victory would release him of its crushing weight.

'What now, Colonel?' asked Lieutenant Hastings.

'We have no choice,' he answered. 'We must begin the ground offensive without air support.'

'Any changes to the plan, sir?'

According to the plan, the enemy's forces should have been decimated by the opening barrage and air attack before the ground assault began. But the bombardment had been cut short and the air attack stopped before it had even started. Griffin could do nothing about that. Wishful thinking never changed anything.

'There are none we can make,' he told Hastings. 'Proceed as planned.'

'Very good, sir.'

He watched helplessly from his chair as the others in the command tent began issuing orders. Instructions went out to the various units – infantry, armour, field artillery. They were outnumbered, and he could only hope that their training and experience would count. Not to mention the desperation of soldiers facing certain death if they failed.

He wanted to join his forces on the battlefield, but with the infection spreading through his body, he feared he would be a deadweight on his troops – just one more load slowing them down. And with the odds now stacked against them, his presence might tip the balance to defeat.

This is what I have become. A liability to my own side.

He wished that Chanita could be with him, but the thought brought him only more misery. They hadn't spoken since the meeting with James. There was still no word of the boy, no news from the front. Another hope dashed.

Suddenly the interior of the command tent felt stifling. His head burned with fever, matching the heat in his thigh. A new emotion surged through him – anger. He yearned to be away from this claustrophobic tent, striding across the field at the head of his army. Like FitzHerbert, he longed to command from the front. Liability or not, it would surely boost morale if he could be among his men as they faced this most deadly of foes. He had no fear of death.

'Take me to the battlefield,' he blurted. 'I want to see it for myself.' He gripped the edge of the table and hauled himself to his feet, grabbing at a crutch for support.

Lieutenant Hastings looked up, his features shifting first to concern, then to alarm. 'Sir?'

'I said, take me to the front.' He reached a standing position before the room began to spin. 'I'll be all right,' he muttered. 'I just need some fresh air.'

He took a step forward, but somehow his foot missed the floor. The canvas of the tent swirled overhead, like carrion birds swooping down to feed. He lifted an arm to shield himself from the dark shapes, but the flapping wings multiplied and the world came tumbling down around him.

When the ground stopped moving, he was lying on his back, wondering how he had got there. Hastings was at his side, kneeling down to tend to him. The lieutenant's mouth opened and closed, but all Griffin could hear was the raucous cry of crows. The birds had become a mass of dark wings, beating at his head in a roar of confusion. 'The crows,' he mumbled. 'Don't let them get me.'

He battered the creatures away with his hands until Hastings grabbed his wrists to stop him. 'Lie still, sir,' he said. 'There are no crows. The medic's on his way.'

'Don't let them get me,' whimpered Griffin again. 'Don't let them eat my leg.'

Chapter Ninety-Six

Salisbury Plain

James bowed his head and closed his eyes, knowing that everything he had done had come to nought. He had felt no fear when offering himself up to Leanna, only a calm desire to make the sacrifice that was required. One life given so that the world could be saved. Now he was filled with an ice-cold dread.

Was Leanna right? Had he filled his head with nonsense? It had seemed so right. Sin, evil, redemption, sacrifice. A simple story, with him at its heart, laying down his life for the sake of humanity. But that had been arrogance. A terrible pride. And he was being rightly punished for it.

My God, forgive me. I have sinned again.

Yet still God kept silent, offering no clue what he should do.

Do You even exist?

There was no voice in his head. Nothing to guide him.

I am alone, and in darkness.

Canning had gone to fetch the chains, and he returned with them now. Heavy metal links, clanking ominously.

Leanna eyed them gleefully. 'Bind him! Make it secure. He might change back into human form to try to escape.'

Canning leaned over him, his one eye staring, breathing heavily from the exertion of carrying the chains. He began wrapping the chain around James' body, tying his legs together so that he couldn't move.

'Tighter!' urged Leanna.

Canning heaved the chains, pulling until they squeezed James' ribs.

'Pull harder!' shouted Leanna. 'Make it hurt!'

Canning sighed yet did as she ordered, drawing the loops of metal even more closely together.

Warg Daddy stood watching, the shotgun in his hands, a heavy frown over his features. He said nothing as the steel chain bit into James' flesh, making him whimper in pain.

Leanna crouched low. Despite what she had said about taking her revenge later, it seemed that her desire to punish him was too great. She took the chains in her own hands, pulling them ever tighter until they drew blood.

James panted, almost unable to breathe. His lungs hungered for oxygen, but were unable to fill. 'It's too tight!' he gasped.

'No,' said Leanna, 'it's not tight enough.' She wrenched the chains another notch closer, the cold links sliding across each other like metal snakes. A mad gleam entered her eyes. 'I want to see you suffer. I want to hear you beg.'

James closed his eyes, seeking solace in darkness. All the air was gone from his lungs. Perhaps the end had come at last. Soon it would be over. A new sense of elation filled him, even as the last breath in his body was squeezed out. He felt no fear now that the final hour had come – only a calm desire to make the sacrifice that was required.

Leanna continued to draw the chain tighter, her

strength an unstoppable force, and as she pulled, her rage rose higher, her mouth frothing as the hate and bile poured out. James shut her out, closing in on himself as the final seconds ticked by. His thoughts began to drift, and he knew that he would be with Samuel very soon. A faint light appeared in his mind's eye, a glimmer in the darkness. It grew steadily, ushering in the new age. The sacrifice was nearly done.

A huge blast sounded and the light went out. His eyes flicked open and he saw Leanna's face before him. But there was no more madness in those cold blue eyes. All hate had been erased. Her body crumpled to the ground, peppered with gunshot, blood oozing from a hundred wounds.

Warg Daddy stood behind her, the shotgun cradled in his arm like a baby. 'A little kindness never hurt anybody,' he said. 'Canning, unbind him.'

Canning's mouth had dropped open in astonishment, but he quickly gathered his wits and came to James' aid.

James' lungs opened wide as he drew in a life-giving breath. But that was the last thing he wanted. 'No!' he cried. 'You must kill me too!'

Warg Daddy shrugged. 'You just can't please some people.' He lowered the shotgun to the ground. 'There's going to be more than enough killing here already.'

Chapter Ninety-Seven

Salisbury Plain

Johnny Perez chuckled to himself, picturing the riches that awaited him when all this was done. Always eager for gold, he had driven a hard bargain with Griffin. And to his surprise the Colonel had come up trumps, procuring more of the precious metal than he could possibly have imagined. Well, now was the time to earn that gold.

It was possible that a few of his men would die in the coming battle. More than possible, and more than a few in all likelihood. But that meant more gold for the rest of them. A grin crept slowly across his face, until he was beaming with pleasure. More gold was always a cheering prospect.

In truth he was enjoying himself immensely. He had never worked alongside the good guys before. He had always been the bad guy, revelling in lawbreaking and pulling stunts that left the authorities looking dumb. *Naturalmente*, a few of his men had paid the price for those adventures, serving time behind bars. But there were always casualties in war. Perez had managed to keep himself out of jail throughout his long and distinguished career as a rogue by making sure that there was always someone else to take the blame.

But times changed, and the successful businessman changed with them. So here he was, ready to do battle with a band of werewolves, to do his duty and save the human race, et cetera, et cetera. All fine and dandy with him, as long as he received his payment, and he had seen the gold with his own eyes and had no doubt that Griffin was a man of his word.

A principled man, the Colonel. Definitely one of the good guys. Not the kind of man Perez was used to dealing with, but an easy one to negotiate with. Perez' previous business associates had been just as likely to cut off his hand as to shake it. His grin grew even broader. He didn't anticipate doing any repeat business with Griffin. Saving the world once was enough for any man, especially one as reprehensible as himself. And with all that gold in his filthy hands, he would never need to work again.

There was just one thing. A battle to be fought. His side of the bargain to be kept.

The shelling had stopped, and there was no sign of the promised air assault that was supposed to bomb the enemy into the mud. Yet Griffin had given the order to begin the ground offensive.

A flicker of doubt crossed Perez' mind. Was the Colonel truly a man to be trusted? He had certainly been reluctant to release that gold in advance of the fighting. But that was only to be expected. Payment on delivery were the usual terms. If the gold had changed hands in advance, Perez would already be very far from here, leaving some other fool to save the world.

No, the Colonel could be relied upon, Perez was certain of that. And the rest of the government forces would be joining him in battle very soon, if not immediately.

He lifted his field binoculars to his eyes and scanned the battlefield. A small amount of damage had been inflicted on the enemy forces. A burning tank. A blasted anti-aircraft gun. A handful of bodies. Not exactly the devastation he had been told to expect. And where was the rest of the army?

His second-in-command was waiting idly at his side, chewing tobacco, his jaw chomping carelessly away. A nasty habit, to be sure, and one that would no doubt reward him handsomely with some form of unpleasant cancer, if he managed to live that long. But not as disgusting as his previous deputy, who had liked to pick the dirt from his fingernails with a flick-knife. 'Are we waiting?' the man drawled. 'Or are we going to do something?'

Perez lowered the field glasses and flashed him a grin. Smiles cost nothing, after all. 'You are eager to play the hero, yes? You yearn for a good story to tell your grandchildren one day?'

The man spat a gobful of tobacco onto the ground and wiped drool from his chin. 'I'd rather die fighting than die of boredom.'

'Wise words, my friend,' agreed Perez, slapping him merrily on the back. 'No one should ever have to die of boredom.' He scanned the ground once more with the glasses. The werewolves were starting to reorganize themselves now that the artillery fire had ceased. There wouldn't be a better time for the attack to begin. Griffin's forces were still nowhere to be seen, but with a little luck perhaps the battle could be won before they even entered the field.

Perez made the sign of the cross and muttered a quick prayer, just like his *mamá* had taught him. He had no idea if it would help – you never knew with prayers – but it certainly couldn't hurt.

He treated his deputy to another grin. 'Let's go and

earn that gold, then.'

Chapter Ninety-Eight

Salisbury Plain

The battle was underway at last. Noisy, violent and bloody. A real battle this time, not the shadow fighting of the past day, when shells had rained down on Canning's forces from distant warships. Now those ships were scrap metal rusting on the sea bed, and the war had shifted to the land.

An incoming shell exploded before him in a starburst of red and orange fire, showering him with dust and debris, but Canning didn't flinch. What reason did he have to fear anyone or anything? He was invincible.

His meteoric turn of fortune would one day be the stuff of legend. It was scarcely days since he had been reviled as a traitor, chained to that loathsome tank and paraded before his own troops as a prisoner, no better than the human slaves he had once gathered as hostages. Now everything had changed.

Will Hunter dead. Leanna dead, and him finally wearing

the crown. Literally. He had plucked Leanna's golden coronet from her head just as soon as he had convinced himself that the gunshot blast really had finished her off. He had caressed her face briefly, seeing how the cold light from those ice-blue eyes had at last been extinguished, how that blonde hair fell limp across her ruined features. No matter how important she had believed herself to be, her soft flesh had been easily pulped by the lead shot of Warg Daddy's combat shotgun.

Warg Daddy. That enormous, leather-clad, one-armed brute had rapidly become Canning's favourite person in the entire world. Especially since he had shown no interest in taking charge in Leanna's place. Instead, the man who had once claimed the title of Leader of the Pack had vanished into the melee, keen to taste more violence and to kill, or be killed – he didn't seem to care which. Canning had gladly watched him depart. Warg Daddy had been a useful weapon, striking Leanna when she least expected it, but a weapon like that was dangerous to hold. When asked why he had blasted his queen and former lover to death, he had shrugged, saying only, 'I shut her up. Someone had to.'

Canning had shaken his hand and waved him off to battle. He hoped he would never see him again.

James, meanwhile, had been left tied up with the chains that until quite recently had held Canning captive. The young man seemed quite unable to understand what had happened, and had expressed only a desire to be killed. By someone. By anyone. Sacrifice, he wanted. Well, Canning had no time for that kind of nonsense. He would deal with James later. Right now, the battle clamoured for his attention.

All around him, men, women and half-wolves were moving into action, small arms in their hands, rocket launchers on their shoulders. Tanks churned the mud, Land Rovers darted ahead, bouncing over the rough ground, and all kinds of wheeled and tracked vehicles advanced toward the enemy. The roar of guns filled the air, and in the distance, smoke rose from the enemy lines as the first of the government forces showed their positions and moved to the offensive.

This was the kind of warfare Canning knew best from his history lessons and his wargames. Infantry on the ground. Battalions, divisions, brigades. Units for him to move around the board. Who might he best compare himself with? George Washington at Yorktown? William the Conqueror at Hastings? Napoleon at the Battle of Ulm?

Yes, Napoleon Bonaparte was the commander he felt most kinship with now. A military leader *par excellence*. An emperor who had seized power through a *coup d'état*. A ruler who had lifted his nation from the ruins of revolution to European dominance. A strategic mastermind, well-suited as a model for Lord General Canning.

He corrected himself. *King* Canning.

It was still early days, but so far the ground campaign was running smoothly. More than smoothly. Like a rolling juggernaut crushing everything in its path. But there was little *finesse* in the *blitzkrieg* approach. His plan was more subtle than that.

Napoleon had pioneered the manoeuvre he had in mind. The *Ulm Manoeuvre*, historians named it. Soon the world would witness its evolution – the *Canning Bluff*. Oh yes. History in the making, and him at its very heart. He inhaled deeply, savouring the rich scent of explosive residue drifting on the breeze. Did life ever taste sweeter than this?

Chapter Ninety-Nine
Salisbury Plain

Warg Daddy's thumb squeaked against his bald crown as he bounced across the ragged terrain. He and half a dozen others were crammed into the back of an open-top Land Rover, rifles and other small arms bristling and ready for the kill. It was more cattle truck than combat vehicle, but Warg Daddy didn't care. He was on his way at last, racing into battle, the blood of the first kill already drifting like nectar on the breeze.

He would have preferred the feel of a bike between his thighs – a steel stallion to ride to war – but with only one arm, that was now an impossibility. He would never know that feeling again.

No matter. He didn't expect to return from this battle. This journey would be his last, in this world at least. Afterward, he yearned only to be taken to Valhalla a hero, there to join his fallen comrades.

Bloodbath was with him in the back of the truck, along

with the two remaining Brothers. With luck on their side, they would go with him to death, and onward to the great hall of the slain where the feasting would begin.

Right now they were heading straight into the heart of the enemy's position on raised ground. A steep hill rose up from the plain, providing good cover for ground troops. Warg Daddy lifted his nose and sniffed for prey, but all he could smell was the stink of exhaust and the drifting smoke of fire. The enemy was close though, and he raised his shotgun, ready for action. Bloodbath and the others had assault rifles in their hands. Better weapons for range, but Warg Daddy was happy to wait until the enemy was right before him before unloading its barrel into their brains.

Soon he was in the thick of it. Sniper fire opened up from a nearby ridge, and the Land Rover turned toward it, engine screaming, tyres spinning as they sought to grip the path. The Brothers returned fire, silencing the enemy. Another Land Rover joined the sortie, and together they roared up the slope, pummelling the defending position with fire as they went.

When they crested the ridge the fighting began in earnest. A squad of enemy troops waited to surprise them, under cover of trees. They opened fire as the Land Rover came to a halt. Warg Daddy's finger closed around his trigger and the shotgun roared in his hand. A man's body heaved and crumpled, falling backward to the ground. The shotgun thundered again, and a second man fell face first, his chest riddled with shot. The drumming of automatic fire reverberated all around, and men screamed and died on both sides. Offerings to the gods of war.

Warg Daddy smelled blood and felt its intoxicating power. He advanced toward the trees, indifferent to danger. Only the thick leather of his jacket shielded him from the enemy's bullets. He let off shots as he went, closing in on the opposing infantry, unleashing one deadly blast after another. *Boom, boom, boom*, like the beat of a drum. Returning fire went wide over his head and all around him, enveloping him in a hail of lead, but still he marched on, blasting his way to victory or death, it made no difference.

Shouts came to him from behind. Warnings. An armoured combat vehicle struggled up out of the mud, turning its machine gun in his direction. And now he came under heavy fire. Automatic gunfire rang out, deafening and brutal, filling the air with death.

The Land Rover barrelled in his direction, men returning fire and giving him cover. It slid past him and a hand reached down to grasp his arm. *Bloodbath*.

'Fall back!' came the command. He shook his head, eager to continue the assault, but more hands grabbed him and hauled him into the Land Rover. Wheels spun, splattering mud, and they skidded off down the hill again, beating a quick retreat. Warg Daddy roared his frustration, but all around, more enemy vehicles were in pursuit, coming down the hill.

'We have to fall back,' said Bloodbath. 'Don't worry, it's all part of the plan.'

'Wait, there's a plan?' It was the first Warg Daddy had heard about it.

Chapter One Hundred

Salisbury Plain

The full moon had risen, pale and ghostlike in daylight, but huge. Liz already felt its strength, even though that power would not reach its zenith until darkness fell. Beside her, Eric clearly sensed it too.

'It's a supermoon,' he explained. 'Larger and brighter than a normal moon. It occurs when the moon's orbit brings it closest to Earth. The gravitational attraction makes tides rise higher than normal. Some say that supermoons cause disasters like earthquakes and volcanic eruptions.'

'I wonder what effect it has on vampires,' said Liz.

'You feel it?' said Eric. 'I do too. A tingling in the arms. A quivering of the heart.'

'A hunger,' concluded Liz. 'A thirst for blood.'

'You must resist the urge,' cautioned Eric. 'Don't let the moon control you.'

'Perhaps we can use it to our advantage.'

Eric shook his head. 'Giving into temptation makes us into our own worst enemies. Cool heads are needed now, not hot hearts.'

Liz nodded. She knew full well how dangerous a hot heart could be.

That was always the source of your troubles, wasn't it, Llewelyn? That passionate Welsh heart beating in your chest. Without that, you'd probably still be alive today.

I'm no doctor, Liz, but I'm pretty certain that without a beating heart, I'd definitely be dead. Besides, don't give passion a hard time. Without a heart you'd never have agreed to marry me. I wouldn't even have asked you to.

She hated it when he was right.

'What about the effect on the werewolves?' she asked Eric.

'I can only imagine that they feel its power too.'

'That can't be good, can it?'

'Nothing good will happen today, Liz. If we're both still alive at the end of it, that will be a great outcome.'

'Nothing like setting your expectations low, right?' But Eric was right. It would be a mistake to go into battle expecting glory. She had done her best to dampen down the enthusiasm of Mihai, Alfie, and the other kids, not to mention Kevin. But her words had done little to quench their eagerness to go to war. They were frightened too, of course, terribly frightened. They had seen enough death to know how swiftly and unexpectedly it could fall. She hoped that fear would temper their bravery and stop them doing anything too reckless. 'Remember,' she'd cautioned them, 'our task is to capture or kill any escaping werewolves. Don't go charging off into danger. Leave the real fighting for the soldiers.'

'Don't worry, love,' Kevin had reassured her. 'You can count on us not to do anything daft.'

'No, Dad, I can't. That's why I'm telling you this again.'

They'd arrived at the edge of the battlefield an hour earlier, creeping cautiously over the ring of hills once the opening artillery bombardment had come to an end. Now they were observing the situation from a safe distance. Before them, a giant natural amphitheatre was laid out, almost as if it had been created precisely to stage the great spectacle that was unfolding. The plain stretched out for miles, with a circle of hills all around and another hill at its centre, and an ancient walled fortress on top. The hillfort was occupied by hundreds of people, civilians trapped in the middle of the fighting. To the south lay the city of Salisbury, although it looked as deserted as any of the towns Liz had passed through since leaving the safety of the hotel.

The Wolf Army was camped around the hillfort, but had now begun to move, engaging government forces positioned on a distant hilltop. The humans had initiated the offensive, using the strategic advantage of high ground to launch an attack. But the werewolves had been quick to respond. With her acute vision, Liz could see what the human soldiers were perhaps unable to perceive – that the Wolf Army had split into three groups, one making a frontal attack from the south, the other two circling east and west to surround their adversaries.

'It's going to be a massacre,' she said. 'We need to help them.'

'Is that your cool head or your hot heart speaking, Liz?' asked Eric.

'It's the voice of compassion. We can't just stand here and watch people die.'

Eric shook his head gravely. 'Remember what you told the boys about charging into the fray. We are outnumbered a hundred to one, Liz. There's nothing we can do to help those soldiers.'

Liz stared out across the windswept plain. Everything Eric said was true. But that didn't make him right.

Chapter One Hundred and One

Old Sarum

'Notch. Draw. Loose.'

The werewolves were dispersing, moving out across the plain in the direction of distant hills. Gunfire and explosions peppered the horizon as humans and werewolves clashed. But that didn't mean Old Sarum was safe. The Wolf Army would be back, Ryan was sure of it, and when they returned, the city must be ready to defend itself.

Rose had assigned him the task of protecting the fortress. But she'd spoken only of posting sentries and lookouts. Raising an army had been far from her thoughts.

But not from Ryan's. He had no military training or experience of any kind, but it had been obvious from the beginning that one day they might have to face a full-on attack from armed werewolves. He had begun to make preparations, fashioning a civil defence force from the people at his disposal.

The population of Old Sarum now ran to a thousand or more, but only a fraction of its inhabitants showed the necessary inclination and aptitude for fighting. He had picked out the most promising, and trained them as well as he knew how, teaching basic combat skills and organizing them into units. When numbers and equipment were inadequate, tactical capability must make up for the shortfall. Each unit of ten defenders was capable of working autonomously, defending a portion of the perimeter embankment, falling back if overwhelmed, or thrusting forward to take advantage of any breach in the enemy ranks.

Where his knowledge came from, he couldn't say. Instinct, you might call it, or perhaps it was nothing more than the accumulation of years spent watching action movies and playing video games. Perhaps he was simply fooling himself that he knew the first thing about how to defend a city. If so, Old Sarum would fall at the first engagement.

The men and women who made up his rag-tag army were armed with little more than the weapons that Chris had devised. Axes, spears and bows and arrows. They wore no armour other than vests sown with thick hinds of boiled leather, studded with metal rings and bands. Head protection was provided by an assortment of motorcycle crash helmets, cycling helmets and in a few cases saucepans fitted with rubber inserts to make them wearable. Part of their training had been convincing them that the defensive value of their outfits outweighed their ridiculous appearance. Once the Wolf Army had made its terrifying appearance, all talk of style and fashion disasters had quickly stopped, and the faces of the city's defenders had grown hard and determined.

'Notch. Draw. Loose.'

Ryan was using the hours still remaining to prepare for

battle. The arrows that Chris had devised, made from flintheads bound to sticks, were fired from homemade longbows fashioned from limbs of yew wood tied with scavenged string from nearby Salisbury. A manufacturing team under Chris' command was attempting to produce more, but supplies and time were both desperately short. Every arrow used for practice had to be retrieved and reused. When actual fighting began, every shot must count.

'Remember,' called Ryan, 'only release the arrow when the target is clearly in sight and well within range. If you miss, you may be dead before you have time to reload.' Grim talk, but this was no time for glib reassurance. Each man and woman here must understand what it would take to win, and what would lead to defeat.

He watched a while longer, before calling an end to the practice. Firing arrows was tiring, and he needed his archers to be rested when the invasion came.

He moved on to the next group, occupied in throwing spears. The spears were easier to make and more numerous, but less accurate and with shorter range. They could be used to drive forward an attack if the opportunity arose, and could also be used by untrained civilians if necessary. Ryan watched them hurl their weapons at practice dummies, scoring hits about three times out of four. It was better than the previous day, but still not good enough.

Finally he turned to the few equipped with what Chris referred to as battle axes. In reality they were simple stone axe heads fitted onto short wooden shafts. Heavy to lift and difficult to wield. Only the strongest men were able to handle them, and it seemed a waste to deploy his best fighters in this way. But if the archers failed and the werewolves broke through the ranks of spears, it would be the axemen who presented the final defence. He watched as thickset men heaved and groaned, slashing the air with their crude weapons.

'All right,' he called, after witnessing a few more

minutes of sweat and grunts. 'Enough. Go back and rest, but be ready for anything.'

His units would come if the alarm was sounded – a blast from a set of trumpets they had found in a nearby music shop. Each unit would self-organize into a mix of archers, spear-throwers and axemen, and would move to its designated location on the outer rampart. They would fight to the best of their ability, knowing that if they fell, so would the city.

But Ryan wasn't kidding himself for a moment. His stone-age forces would offer little resistance to soldiers equipped with guns, mortar and vehicles. If the citadel came under attack, it might all be over in minutes.

Chapter One Hundred and Two

Salisbury Plain

Gold. Just when you thought you had it in your hands, it ran through your fingers like liquid. Perez acknowledged the grim reality of his situation with a shrug. He had won and lost fortunes before. The winning and the losing was easy, it was the holding on that was hard. This time it was his life he was struggling to hold on to.

'It was a trick,' declared his deputy, spitting tobacco on the ground in disgust. 'A dirty werewolf trick.'

'It was, my friend, it was.' Perez was no fonder of being tricked than the next man, but in this case he had to hand it to the wolves. They had used a classic feint, deploying a weak invasion force to lure him out of a strong defensive position. Meanwhile, enemy soldiers had moved undercover to attack Perez' men from behind.

Now they were surrounded and cut off from the main body of the army, which had still not made an appearance. The fighting was growing increasingly intense and desperate. At least, he consoled himself, none of his men would be tempted to turn tails and flee. There was nowhere to run.

'We were tricked, but we are not yet beaten,' he declared. 'Now is the time for us to dig deep and earn our gold.'

He had no idea what impression his words might make on his men, but words were the best he had to offer them now. That, and his trademark smile. He flashed it wide as men rushed past, assault rifles in hand, running to join the front line. 'That's good. Don't let them beat us,' he called, but his words were drowned by an exploding mortar bomb.

The enemy was closing in, and the conflict was heating up.

Perez ducked as fragments of shrapnel flew through the air. He wasn't *too* worried about the possibility of death. He had faced it before and had always managed to escape unharmed at the last minute, so had no reason to believe that this time would be any different. And yet. The bombs and the bullets were getting closer all the time. He raised his own rifle as one of the wolfmen appeared from behind a vehicle. Holding the trigger down in a burst of rapid fire he planted a row of bullets in the man's chest. Blood sprouted from the holes like seeds. '*Estupendo*,' he cried.

But another wolfman appeared behind his fallen comrade and unleashed a hail of bullets in return. Perez crouched low. In the sky above, the moon was climbing, growing brighter in the heat of the late afternoon. Despite the strength of the August sun, the moon cast a sinister shimmer over the battlefield. He had rarely seen the heavenly sphere so large and dazzling. The patchwork of light and shade that made up its wrinkled surface was visible even to his naked eye. It wasn't a reassuring sign, and the wolves appeared to be drawing comfort from it. Perhaps they were even drinking its power in some diabolical fashion. As the sun slid steadily toward the horizon, Perez felt his hope slip away with it.

'*Santa María, Madre de Dios.*' He had offered his best prayers before battle, and felt let down. What had he done to deserve this fate? A thousand misdemeanours, no doubt, some worse than others. Most of them worse, come to think of it. But still. He had finally chosen to perform a selfless and heroic deed for the good of all, et cetera, et cetera, yet God had chosen this occasion to punish him for his sins. There was no sense in it. All he could do was soldier on.

An RPG flew out of nowhere and blasted the wolfman to pieces, and Perez leapt to the attack once more. 'With me!' he cried, and three men were at his side in an instant. He turned to seek his second-in-command, but his deputy was sprawled on the ground, a fragment of shining metal impaled in his forehead. Very bad luck indeed. But that fragment must have sailed past Perez by a whisker. His prayer had worked, after all.

Well, now was the moment to give thanks, and to use the time he had been granted. Raising his rifle once more, and leading his men from the front, he charged off down the hillside, blasting at the enemy for all he was worth.

Gold. If he ever got his hands on any, he would have earned every ounce.

Chapter One Hundred and Three

Salisbury Plain

Few things in life were as satisfying as a duplicitous scheme coming to fruition, and the *Canning Bluff* was no exception. The enemy's advance guard had fallen for the ruse and were being eradicated as he watched. The sound of gunfire and small arms punctuated by cries and screams grew steadily louder as the slaughter intensified. Surrounded on all sides, all escape routes cut off, the humans continued to put up a desperate struggle, but it was only a matter of time now, and time was definitely on Canning's side. Tonight, the full moon would work its dark magic, transforming him and his soldiers into wolves, but by then this first ground battle would be over and victory would be his.

Even though sunset was some way off, the supermoon ruled the sky. It was almost as bright in the eastern hemisphere as the sun in the west, and bigger than any moon Canning could recall. As the sun's rays weakened, the moon grew stronger. He felt a tingle in his hands as moonbeams brushed his skin. Turning his face to the heavens, he allowed silver light to caress his face. It was too bright for him to hold directly in his gaze, and he turned his eye away, dazzled by its beauty.

His skin began to itch.

He rubbed at it with one hand, scratching his arm, but the itching continued. A heat spread throughout his limbs, like tinder catching fire. Soon his skin was ablaze all over. What was happening? Without warning, ashen hairs began to force their way through his pores, crowding together over hands, arms and face, knitting themselves into a thick and shaggy cloth of silver. Soon it covered him from head to foot.

Fire filled his limbs as the muscles grew strong, pumping up until he had the physique of a younger, stronger man. His chest grew broad, and his legs long, making him a foot or more taller.

Lastly came his teeth, twisting through gums in the familiar way of the time of the moon. They closed in ranks, as sharp as knives, and with them came the hunger. Yet this wasn't the change he had grown accustomed to whenever the moon was full. This was new, and different. He had become no wolf, but a wolfman. And no common wolfman like Will Hunter and his ilk, but larger and stronger and far more powerful.

He turned his head from left to right, gazing with keen sight. Every blade of grass arrayed before him made a crisp impression, standing tall and filled with seed, waving gently in the summer breeze. Insects clung to the swaying stems – beetles, grasshoppers, flies of infinite variety and form. He narrowed his field of view to home in on one of the tiny creatures, and found its miniature eyes staring back. The glassy circles made a myriad shimmering surfaces, mesmerising in complexity. The fly spread its intricately-patterned wings and took to flight, skimming away into the distance. Canning followed it with his telescopic vision to take in the great sweep of the plain.

The fighting had paused, as the rest of his company also transformed beneath the moon. Those who had been human had become wolfmen, and those who had been half wolf already had grown into giants – bearlike creatures loping across the grassy battlefield with hands as huge as hams, and jaws the size of tigers'.

A sense of elation ripped through him. The moment had come, just as Leanna had promised. The time when a new breed of men and women would inherit the earth. Not the meek, but the mighty, and he the mightiest of all.

He opened his mouth to shout, and out came a roar, the roar of a lion.

When he was done, a new sound clamoured for his attention. He cocked his head to listen. A distant noise, of metal and men, of mighty engines and turning wheels. The main body of the government forces was on the march, coming to battle from the east. Although they were some miles off, his ears twitched, picking out the trundle of tanks, the drumming of tyres over tarmac as heavy vehicles rolled along the road in convoy. They were still out of sight, beyond the nearby rise of land, but they would be here soon.

And further to the south, another army was coming. Lighter vehicles, fewer but faster, and with them the faint *thud-thud* of helicopters. The entirety of the government's surviving forces, converging for a final showdown.

A grin spread across Canning's face as moonlight glinted down. *Let it begin.* He was ready. He was more than ready.

Chapter One Hundred and Four

Winchester

A crow descended, wearing Chanita's face, its wings a black flurry. 'I'm sorry,' murmured Griffin. 'I'm so very sorry.' But the crow pecked at his hand, merciless in its anger. He let it feed, knowing that he deserved every thrust and stab of its sharpened beak. 'Go on, then,' he urged it. 'Take me. I'm ready to die.'

'No one expects you to die, Colonel,' said the crow. 'Least of all me.'

Griffin opened his eyes and saw a man standing where the crow should have been. He was dressed in green operating scrubs and wore a facemask. There was no bird's beak stripping skin from his body, only the smooth steel of a needle sticking into the radial artery in the back of his hand. A canvas roof stretched overhead, and for a moment he thought he was back in Afghanistan. He struggled to remember what he was doing. 'I am a colonel in the Royal Army Medical Corps,' he muttered. 'I command a field hospital in Helmand Province.'

But that wasn't right. And where was Chanita?

The surgeon frowned at his words, and Griffin realized that he was lying in bed and no longer in command of anything, not even his own faculties.

Chanita wasn't here, only the medical team assigned to take care of him. The surgeon dabbed the back of his hand with surgical gauze, fixing the needle in place and attaching it to a long plastic tube. 'This won't hurt,' he said. 'In a minute I'm going to give you general anaesthetic, and then we'll take care of your leg. I'm afraid it will have to go. The infection has spread too far. You really should have had it seen to sooner, Colonel.'

Griffin tried to rise from the mattress, but his limbs refused to respond. He shook his head. 'The campaign … the battle …'

'Is safely in the hands of others.'

'But I am the commanding officer.'

'You don't need to know what's happening right now.'

'I do. Tell me. That's an order.'

The surgeon furrowed his brow in a show of displeasure, but stepped aside and another face loomed into view. Griffin struggled to bring its features into focus. Eventually they coalesced into the watery form of Lieutenant Hastings.

'Sir.' The word was crisp and precise, but the lieutenant seemed reluctant to add to it.

'Tell me everything,' said Griffin.

After a moment's hesitation, Hastings continued. 'The ground troops are in theatre. Our forces have engaged with the enemy as planned. But they are outnumbered.'

Griffin struggled to remember the rest of the plan. He recalled that the fleet had come under attack and that both carriers had gone down, their planes lost, but there was more to the plan than just the air assault.

'The marines are moving up from the south coast,' said Hastings. 'They should be engaging any minute.'

Yes, that was it. The Royal Marines, with Bampton leading them. They had helicopters, armoured amphibious vehicles and other specialized equipment. The elite battalion of commandos would bolster the regular ground forces and turn the battle around. 'Any news from Perez?' he asked.

Hastings exchanged a glance with the surgeon, who was hovering around, his gloved hands clasping and unclasping. 'Sir, we've lost contact with Perez. His men were surrounded and overwhelmed. And besides …' He stalled.

'I think that's enough,' concluded the surgeon. 'It's time for me to put you under, Colonel.' He approached the bed, inspecting the intravenous tube trailing from Griffin's hand.

'Tell me,' insisted Griffin. 'I want to hear it all.'

Hastings' face wavered back into focus. 'It's the werewolves, sir. They've changed form – even in daylight. We think it's the supermoon enhancing the usual effect of the full moon.'

Griffin allowed himself a small smile. 'But that's good news. If they turn into wolves, they won't be able to operate their vehicles or use their weapons. It will be an easy victory for us.'

The lines on Hastings' face seemed to deepen beneath the harsh light of the operating theatre. 'I don't think so, sir. They seem not to have changed into wolves this time, but into … some kind of superhuman.'

'Superhuman?' Griffin faltered, confusion creeping back into his thoughts. Was he lapsing once more into a fever dream? He thought he saw the eyes of a crow perched on Hastings' shoulder. It watched him, mocking.

'That's quite enough,' snapped the surgeon. He moved Hastings aside and leaned over the bed. 'I'm starting the anaesthetic. I want you to count backward for me from ten.'

Griffin felt the fight go out of him. The surgeon was right. This was someone else's problem now, and there was nothing he could do. He began to count, just as he'd been instructed. 'Ten ... nine ... eight ...' And then there was nothing, not even the crows.

Chapter One Hundred and Five

Salisbury Plain

Gunfire roared to his left, tanks raced past him to his right, and in the darkened sky ahead a helicopter gunship swooped in at speed, its blades flickering beneath the shimmering moon, the angry clatter of its chain gun raining down fire on the ground below.

Warg Daddy pounded forward, oblivious to danger, his combat shotgun clutched in his hairy fist, his legs pumping like pistons, all traces of fatigue banished from his body. His heart beat as smoothly as the engine of any bike he had ever ridden, pushing limitless energy to his limbs. He could run for miles if he had to. He could run all night. He could run until every single one of his foes had perished.

The helicopter veered off to the left and an enemy vehicle drew to a halt before him, disgorging the troops it carried. They dropped to the ground and took up position ready to fire, each of their faces picked out in black and white against the night. Frightened eyes stared back at him. Human eyes, weak now that the sun had set, even though the moon was strong, casting a silver sheen as bright as day over man and machine alike and lending both a metal lustre.

A beautiful sight. A magical light. A night for killing.

Shots rang out as the first of the soldiers loosed some rounds at him. He let them sail past, no more bothersome than the buzz of flies. The eyes of his enemy widened. Fear turned to terror. More shots came, and now all the soldiers were discharging their weapons at once, fear engraved on their silver faces.

A bullet entered his flesh, burrowing into his shoulder and out again the other side. It sliced through skin and tore through muscle, cleaving bone and shearing ligament.

He opened his mouth and let out a roar.

The wound burned, fire coursing in the bullet's wake. But it was healing fire, burning away the pain, knitting together torn muscle and stitching broken skin back together. In seconds he was whole again, or as whole as he would ever be with one arm long gone, not to mention the teeth that Will Hunter had scattered to the ground. Old injuries would never heal, but fresh wounds he had no need to fear.

Not this night. Not while the mighty moon held sway and all the power of creation flowed through his veins.

He sped up, the turf hurtling beneath him with ever greater haste, the clamour of battle now drowned by the beats of his heart. The taste of his enemy's fear sweetened his tongue. The shotgun lurched in his hand, its bass voice crooning its song of destruction, and the first soldier went down, the shot drawing a fine lattice of blood over his face and chest. The shotgun sang again, and another life was taken. Death would have his work cut out tonight.

The last two soldiers cracked. One rose to his feet and spun, making his escape. The shotgun took him in the back, teaching him that running away was futile. When the full moon wore its silver crown there was but one choice – to fight or die. He pitched forward, rolling to a lifeless heap.

The other threw his weapon to the ground and raised his hands in surrender. Warg Daddy savoured the moment. The man was young, his skin only lightly bearded. 'Don't kill me,' he begged. 'Make me one of your own. I want to be like you.'

Warg Daddy nodded his understanding. He recalled a night like this on Clapham Common. He had sought out a werewolf, thinking to capture one and bend it to his will. What folly. The werewolf had caught him, but instead of killing him had granted him the gift of her own blood. Wolf blood. Now Leanna was dead, but her gift and her legacy lived on. It was Warg Daddy's turn to grant the same to those worthy.

'Only the strong may become wolf,' he warned the soldier. 'The weak will perish.'

'Please,' begged the man. He rolled up his sleeve and offered his forearm. 'Bite me.'

Warg Daddy grasped the arm and held it firmly. The arm was frail. So breakable. And the man's pleading was pitiful. Warg Daddy had seen far stronger men beaten by lycanthropy. The gift of wolf blood had proved the kiss of death even for some of his own Brothers. This arm would never be strong enough to hold the gift that was his to give. It would be cruel even to try. Instead he twisted it and broke it from its socket. It was like pulling the wing from a barbequed chicken.

The man let out a scream of agony.

Warg Daddy snapped the arm in two, shearing bone from bone, and watching as blood splashed out of the rendered arteries. He supped from it, letting hot nectar flow down his throat. The beating of his heart was more than enough to drown the soldier's screams. When his thirst was sated, he cast the limb aside, as its dying owner slumped into unconsciousness.

A blessing. A kindness. Warg Daddy knew that he was benevolence itself.

He turned his attention to the vehicle that had disgorged the four infantrymen. A British Army Panther. He had used one himself at the Battle of Heathrow, when he had been commander-in-chief of Leanna's forces. He had won that battle, but had played no part in the fighting other than to give out orders. The blood had been on the hands of others. Now they were on his own. He liked it better that way.

The hulk of the armoured troop carrier stood tall against the sky. Inside he spied another soldier. A coward, more craven even than the ones who had run or surrendered. *A big candy-ass pussy.* The man was watching from the driver's seat of the vehicle, his eyes wide and staring. He seemed frozen in position, unable to handle what he had just seen.

That was just a taster. Hors d'oeuvres. An appetizer before the main course.

Warg Daddy shouldered his shotgun and gripped the Panther's door with his one hand. It was solid steel and locked from within. A gentle tug did nothing, so he pulled harder. Moonlight bathed him, lending him its strength. White light flowed through his veins. The door began to yield, creaking gently, rivets popping one by one.

The driver came to his senses, seeming to shake himself from his stupor. His hands gripped the wheel knuckle-tight, and the Panther's engine coughed into life, revving urgently as he pushed his foot to the floor.

Warg Daddy drove his fist through the side window, turning the reinforced glass into a spider's web of milky white. His fingers groped around inside for a lever to open the door, but he found none. Instead he curled his hand around the sheet of crumpled glass and tore it away like linen, casting it to the ground.

The vehicle began to move off. Warg Daddy stepped

onto its running board and leaned inside, pulling harder on the door. The full power of the moon flowed through his fingers, and metal squealed beneath his touch. Hardened steel offered little resistance to him now. It screamed as he peeled it away, layer by layer like the skin of an orange. First the window frame. Then the door. Then the roof. He swung himself inside the cab and took a seat next to the driver. The man's mouth fell open in horror.

Warg Daddy pushed his fist through the front windscreen and laughed as it filled with white cloud as thick as any fog. The driver stamped on the brakes, bringing them to a sudden halt. Warg Daddy reached across and turned off the ignition. 'Going somewhere?' he enquired.

The man was shaking in his seat. Warg Daddy reached over again and pulled the steering wheel from its fitting with a loud crack. He tossed it aside. The soldier continued to flutter like a leaf.

'One of your friends tried to flee,' Warg Daddy told him. 'I shot him in the back. One gave himself up to me. I tore off his arm and let him bleed to death. Two fought bravely and died like real men, while you sat in your seat and did nothing. What do you think I should do to you?'

The man voiced no opinion on the matter, so Warg Daddy gave the question some consideration himself. 'I think,' he suggested, 'that you should die a horrible death.' He nodded to himself, knowing the rightness of his words. 'Yes,' he concluded. 'I think it should be most horrible.'

It was a beautiful night for killing. Far above, a trillion stars glittered and sang while he set about his work.

Chapter One Hundred and Six

Salisbury Plain

Liz darted forward, sprinting across the open ground so quickly she almost outran her own shadow. The supermoon had changed her, granting her powers she could never have imagined. She flew down the grassy slope, taking two wolfmen unaware from behind. Steel-sharp claws severed their necks, cutting through fur and flesh and bone. They died before they even knew she was there.

It was just like Mihai had said. She had become invisible, moving so fast that none could see her except for the other vampires. Eric and the others had spread out across the battlefield, making lightning strikes against the werewolves, taking them down one by one, then moving on to strike again.

Samantha and her children were safe inside the

Foxhound. Liz had told her to lock the doors and not to open them for anyone, and to stay there until the fighting was over. But Kevin, Mihai and the kids from London were out there fighting. Nothing she could say had been able to dissuade them. If anything happened to them, she knew she would never forgive herself.

A shell fell from the sky and exploded nearby. Fire flashed, but Liz ran through it, impermeable to heat, her blood a supercooled, supercharged, superstrong source of dark power. She leapt and landed on a moving vehicle, some kind of armoured truck a bit like a Foxhound, but larger and clad in metal grilles on top of its regular armour. She swung from the armoured panels, using them like ladders to clamber on top of the moving vehicle. A roof-mounted gun began to blast at her, but she snatched it away, tearing it from its mounting and tossing it over the side.

The vehicle lurched, turning sharply to throw her off but her feet held her fast. She tore at the steel panels along its side, ripping them from their holdings and hurling them away, but that achieved little. The driver and crew remained safe inside. Instead, she slid down onto the front of the truck, standing atop the engine hood. The driver bucked and swayed to each side, but her feet gripped the metal with iron strength and she rode each roll like a surfer on a swelling sea.

She plunged one fist through the front of the engine cover, breaking metal struts apart like thin plywood. The panel came loose, exposing the beating heart of the vehicle to her. The engine roared its protest. Liz knew little about car maintenance. When Llewelyn had talked with Kevin about cylinder heads, gaskets and pistons, she had paid no attention. But she knew how to find the weak points in a machine. Rubber hose. Wires. Pipes. They were all very breakable.

She ripped out the hoses first, releasing steam and hot oil. Then came the wires, sparking with fury as they flew.

The pipes she crushed between thumb and fingers, as easy as squashing ripe fruits.

The engine died quickly, and the truck lumbered to a halt. Liz flew to the door and tried to pull it open, but it was too strong for her even in vampire form. That didn't matter. She had taken out an enemy unit. One more blow against the Wolf Army. But how many blows would be needed to turn the tide of battle?

Despite her daring, despite the best efforts of Eric and Kevin and Leah and Alfie, the enemy was just too numerous for them to make a real difference. The first attack by government forces had ended in crushing defeat. The main thrust that followed had been a rout, with human forces massively outnumbered and outmanoeuvred by the half-wolf beasts that swarmed across the battlefield, heavily armed and possessing superhuman strength. Even the reinforcements that arrived from the south with helicopters and other heavy weapons had been cut off by the Wolf Army and outgunned. Liz had watched with dismay as copter after copter had been taken down by ground-to-air missiles.

Now the remaining humans were fighting to stay alive. Divided and surrounded, small groups were making their last stand. Liz might take out a few wolves here, or knock out an armoured unit there, but she couldn't hope to win this war.

This can't be the whole of the army, Liz. There must be more in reserve. Perhaps they'll be here soon.

Even Llewelyn's voice of encouragement had lost its power to raise her spirits. Whatever hope the Welsh dragon offered, she knew the truth. There was no army waiting in the wings, no hope of rescue, no prospect of humans winning this war. The final battle had become a crushing defeat, and she was on the losing side.

'Liz, pull back!' It was Eric's voice, loud in her ear. The other vampires were with him, clustered together in defensive formation. Some had fallen; others were injured beyond the power of the moon to heal them. 'We are losing this fight. We must withdraw.'

Liz looked around the battlefield in desperation. The wolf-men and the other mutants were everywhere and had the upper hand. The human forces were in disarray – running, hiding, dying. 'If we pull back now, it's all over,' she protested.

'It's over anyway. This battle is lost.'

He's right love, you know he is. You have to save the others. Kevin, Samantha, the children ...

'All right,' shouted Liz, angry that her dead husband needed to remind her of her responsibilities. The bloodlust hadn't completely taken over her mind, but even so ... in the heat of the moment it was hard to remember that there was more to life than killing. She cast one last look over the corpses and the burning wrecks that covered the ground. She had done her best, and there was nothing more she could do here.

'Pull back!' called Eric again, and this time Liz did as he commanded.

Chapter One Hundred and Seven

Winchester

'Push!' said Chanita, and Melanie pushed like she didn't know she could. 'Good, now breathe.'

Melanie screamed, digging her nails ever deeper into Ben's arm. Sharing the pain helped a little, but she had so much of it that a hundred Bens wouldn't have been enough. This couldn't be normal. This couldn't be what millions of women had endured since forever. She knew that childbirth was painful, but she could never have imagined it was like *this*. Yet Chanita didn't seem worried. She remained calm, as if she had seen far worse. But nothing could be worse. Nothing.

'Now push again,' said Chanita.

Push. Breathe. Push. Breathe. Melanie didn't know what she hated most. Chanita's nannying instructions, Ben's hurt puppy-dog eyes, or the pain of the contractions.

Contractions. A word entirely unable to convey the agony of labour. These were not "contractions" – they were waves of pure pain, as her uterus curled tight as a fist and made her want to die.

'Push!' said Chanita, and Melanie pushed. She hardly needed telling. Every muscle in her body strained to get this thing out of her. Whatever kind of creature Ben had put inside her, she wanted it gone. She pushed with all her might, but still the damn thing clung on, unwilling to leave the safety of its cocoon.

Sarah mopped her brow with a cold cloth, but the relief was short-lived. Pain swallowed everything. She had been going for hours like this, maybe days. Time meant nothing now. Only the pain had meaning.

'I can see the head,' said Chanita. 'Not much further now.'

Yet Melanie was already beyond exhausted. She had no strength to push again. The baby could stay where it was for all she cared, trapped in an endless wave of contractions. She wished she could simply pass out and become insensible to it all. She longed for the darkness to take her, and to feel nothing. To feel nothing ever again.

'Push!' said Chanita. 'One last time.'

Melanie pushed, or at least her body pushed for her. She was no longer in control of anything. She had lost her dignity, lost her strength, lost her desire to even breathe. She only wanted one thing – for it to stop.

She felt a movement. Different to the contractions. A sliding, slithering, squeezing as the baby left her. The pain heightened to an impossible peak, and then it was done. Relief flooded her. The worst was over. She eased her grip on Ben's arm.

More movement flashed at the limits of her vision. Chanita was busy with a knife. Ben gasped. Sarah froze, the damp towel falling from her hands. Melanie tried to look, but whatever they were staring at was out of her view. She tried to sit up, but her muscles rebelled, too weak to lift her even one inch.

'What is it?' she croaked. The screaming had left her voice half broken.

No one spoke, but after a moment, a tentative cry emerged from the other end of the bed. A keening sound, like the wailing for the dead. Hardly a human voice, it grew slowly in strength, rising piercingly to a crescendo, before beginning again.

Ben and Sarah stood motionless, and even Chanita had backed away from the bed, her hands bathed to the elbows in blood, her face masked with horror. Now there was only Melanie and the *thing*.

She felt it move.

A shudder passed through her. Then a hand pressed against her abdomen. A human hand, scrabbling for purchase. Tiny fingers, rippling against her skin. They gripped her, creeping along her belly, setting off fresh spasms in her exhausted muscles. A second hand grasped her, and then the creature was climbing slowly up her body. She tilted her head and took her first glimpse of her baby.

A face held hers. A child's face, but like no other. Huge yellow eyes, open wide, gazed into her own. Below them a nose, broad and long. More snout than nose. It quivered gently. The child's mouth opened and it cried again, a mournful sound. The mouth was filled with tiny teeth, each a perfect pearl, glinting softly. A long pink tongue slid out. Wet, probing, strong.

It is tasting my skin.

The creature seemed to like what it found and crawled toward her, one small hand after another. This was a new horror, worse even than the contractions. Melanie tried to push herself away, but she had no strength to move. She tried to scream, but all her screaming was done.

The creature made its slow and steady way up her body. Now it was fully in view. Part-human, part-monster, it had the look of a devil. Coated black from head to toe with thick, matted fur, it was covered in blood and all manner of slime. It slithered ever closer, its head bobbing along her chest like a blind worm. When it reached her breast, it stopped.

Melanie found her voice at last. 'Take it away!' she yelled. 'Get it off me!'

But the others seemed unable to react. Only the creature had the power of movement. It lifted its head, its lips parting wide to let the flickering tongue emerge once more like a snake. It licked her nipple, delicately at first, questioningly. Then it clamped down hard and began to suckle.

Chapter One Hundred and Eight

Old Sarum

'The werewolves are winning,' said Ryan. 'Nothing can stop them.'

Rose nodded, knowing that it was true. The human army had attacked the werewolves from three sides, throwing all the destructive power of tanks, artillery, rockets, helicopters and small arms at their foe, but there was nothing they could do to overcome the superior force ranged against them. The werewolves had fought back with the might of modern weaponry, but also harnessing a strange and ancient power, turning them into nightmare shades from the darkest crevices of the human imagination. The creatures that swarmed beyond the earthworks of Old Sarum were more like apes or bears than wolves, standing tall on two legs, and with the heads of giant beasts. Tattered uniforms still clung to some of them; others went naked apart from the thick fur that covered their bodies.

Sounds of gunfire rattled in the distance and shells continued to fall as the night wore on. The fight had become a massacre. Desperate troops, hemmed in and backed into isolated clusters, continued to resist the inhuman enemy, but one by one they fell. Moonlight glittered, brushing both the dead and the living with its silvery touch. The battlefield was a maelstrom of movement. Humans and monsters criss-crossed the plain, advancing and retreating in a chaotic dance. Fires burned, bathing all in a red glow, and dark smoke stood in columns in the still air. Nutmeg watched, the fires reflected in her warm eyes.

'We must protect the citadel at all costs,' said Rose. But she knew that she was asking Ryan to do the impossible. If the werewolves could defeat well-armed soldiers, how could a civilian militia armed only with handmade spears and axes hope to achieve victory?

The gates to Old Sarum had been sealed at the first sign of danger, and the outer earthworks had been abandoned. The inner wall was thirty or forty feet higher than the outer rampart. Rose had ordered everyone to gather within the inner bailey where they could watch and prepare a last defence of the citadel. A few stray shells had fallen in the outer bailey, gouging ragged craters in the earth, but mercifully there had been no casualties. But once the battle outside ended, the victors would turn their attention to Rose and her people.

'We'll put up a good fight,' said Ryan. 'But you know we can't hope to win. Perhaps it would be better to surrender.'

'If we surrender, they will kill us.' Rose had witnessed for herself the unrelenting savagery of the enemy.

'Then we'll fight, and hold out for as long as we can,' said Ryan.

Rose walked the battlements, Nutmeg trotting

alongside as she observed the grim events below. She needed to be visible, to show her people that she was not afraid. But inside she felt sick. One way or another, her people would perish, either in battle or as captives. The werewolves spared no one.

A woman tugged at her sleeve, pleading. 'Save us from those beasts! Don't let them inside, whatever happens!'

'I won't,' Rose assured her. But a man armed with a bow and a quiver of arrows regarded her through eyes already defeated. He said nothing, yet his thoughts were plain enough – what was the point of such an empty promise? What hope could there be against such insurmountable odds? 'Be brave,' she said to him, but her voice sounded weak and pitiful, even to her own ears.

At every step the same question haunted her. What was worse – to die fighting, or to live as a slave enduring untold cruelties before being eaten or slain or starved? It was an impossible question to answer, yet the choice was clear enough. Those who had the strength and the desire to wield a weapon must be given the chance to defend their families. She would not simply open the gates and allow the slaughter of the innocent.

Vijay was among those watching from the inner rampart. The distant fires and explosions warmed his cocoa-coloured skin. She gave him a hug, taking comfort from his embrace. She wished she could stay in his arms forever and never be called on again, but she pulled away, fearing to lose herself if she stayed too long.

Drake and Aasha were at his side. 'Any news?' asked Aasha hopefully.

'Only what you can see.' Rose wouldn't spell out the truth for all to hear. They could see for themselves what was happening.

'You think the werewolves are going to come for us next?' asked Drake, his fair hair bleached white in the moonlight. The black cat curled around his legs, its eyes bright and sparkling. It regarded Nutmeg with a look of haughty indifference.

'Maybe they'll leave us alone,' said Rose. 'Or perhaps the army will beat them.' Other people had gathered to listen to her, and she would not let them hear any words of defeat.

'Maybe,' said Drake doubtfully. 'But if they do come, we're gonna fight them yeah?' He held a pitchfork in his hand, its four metal prongs dull but sharp.

'Only if they try to enter the citadel. The fortress is strong. We can defend it.'

'Yeah,' said Drake, lifting the pitchfork aloft. But he couldn't hide the tremble in his hand.

Aasha held a metal hook and a net in a steady hand. Her dark eyes radiated defiance. 'Why wait? We know they're going to come for us sooner or later. Why not go out and fight them now?'

Rose glared at her angrily. 'I will not lead my people into danger.' Since becoming leader she had faced untold doubts and uncertainties and had been required to make many difficult choices. But one certainty remained constant. She must do everything to ensure the safety of her followers.

Her words did nothing to quell Aasha's boldness. 'Don't they deserve to make up their own minds? They're already in danger.'

Rose refused to give ground. 'They are safe inside these walls. From here we can hurl spears and rain down arrows on any attackers.' When Aasha said nothing she filled the silence with more justification. 'Anyway, they chose me as their leader.'

'Did they?' challenged Aasha. 'Or did they simply believe your dreams and visions? Did you trick them with your lies?'

The crowd that had gathered stirred uneasily, men and women shifting and muttering. 'Be quiet,' hissed Rose. 'These people are terrified. Think what effect your words will have on them.'

But the words had stung Rose herself more deeply than anyone. She had never intended to trick anyone. She was not deceitful like Rowan. But she had employed the same methods as him, peddling a fantasy fuelled by superstition, hallucinogenic herbs and the after-effects of her own trauma. Had her people truly chosen her, or had she knowingly deceived them, using fake mystical powers to lead them to this place? 'I will not choose danger,' she repeated coldly.

'The longer we do nothing, the less chance we have of winning,' argued Aasha. 'The soldiers are being killed right now. Soon they'll all be dead, and then the werewolves will come for us.'

Rose turned to Vijay, confident that he would back her. He had always counselled caution and preached the virtues of peace. Perhaps he could find the right words to reassure her. 'What do you think, Vijay?'

He looked smaller than ever standing next to the others. Drake had grown almost into a man since Rose had last seen him, and Aasha too was taller. Vijay had hardly altered. His face still had the smoothness of a boy's. Yet even though his body hadn't changed, his spirit seemed to have grown stronger. His eyes displayed a calm fearlessness. He had seen things and done things that Rose couldn't even guess at. He possessed a quiet power of command.

He smiled at her gently. 'I know what you expect me to say, Rose. You think I will argue for peace. For forgiveness of our enemies. Peace and forgiveness are always the best outcome. But sometimes a time comes to make a stand.' He reached out and took her hand. 'A long time ago, when we were still at school, you told me that there are many ways to be strong.'

'I remember.'

'And one of them is to fight.' His hand was soft, but his eyes were as unyielding as granite. 'My grandmother died so that Aasha, Drake and I could live. She didn't lay down her life as a victim, but fought for what she believed in. Now is the time for us to do the same. Otherwise we will all die as victims. You know we will.'

'But how?' whispered Rose. 'We are surrounded. Outnumbered. Overwhelmed.' She felt all eyes on her and knew that what she said next would determine the fate of everyone in the citadel, perhaps the whole of humanity. Yet the words she clung to were those of others. 'Chris says that to go into battle with primitive weapons would be suicidal. Ryan says we must stay behind our defences, where we hold the advantage.'

'I'm sure they're both right,' said Vijay. 'I know nothing about wars and battles. All I know is that we must stand up for what we believe in. We must pick up the sword for the sake of righteousness and justice.' He held no sword, only a small hand axe, the kind used for chopping wood. 'If we fight we may all die very quickly, but if we do nothing we will surely die anyway. I would rather do something and hope that my actions can succeed.'

'Most of the people here don't even have axes like yours,' she said. 'They have only the stone weapons that Chris made. Most of them have never even fought.'

'It's your choice, Rose,' he said. 'The people picked you to lead them. They placed their trust in you, not because of fanciful dreams and empty promises, but because you are wise. They knew that when the time came you would choose the right path.' He looked around at the crowd that had gathered and smiled again. 'Now is the time for you to decide.'

Chapter One Hundred and Nine

Salisbury Plain

The voice of God had returned at last and James knew that he had never truly been alone. All those months of unanswered prayer. All that time spent doubting and losing his faith. It was not God's silence he had endured, but God's stillness. He had simply lacked the wisdom to know it.

God had been guiding him throughout, not through words, but through the events he had experienced. Many of those had been traumatic, but after each one he had grown and become closer to the person God wanted him to be. Jesus himself had endured untold trials and suffering at the hands of the Father. It had been necessary. His life on Earth had ended with the ultimate agony and sacrifice.

But James had not been called upon to make the same sacrifice. After all, what good could it have achieved?

None. Instead, a miracle had saved him from his own folly. A miracle in the shape of Warg Daddy. How else could James explain how he had been spared?

Now, although he was bound with iron chains, he was free. He did not need to be a martyr. He could return to his life, and be with his friends once more.

But first he had to find a way to escape. The metal chains bit hard into his flesh. Yet the moon still shone, and its power moved within him.

Not the moon's power, he reminded himself. *God's power*. God made the moon, and his ways were always mysterious. The power of the moon could be used for good or for evil, and what was moonlight anyway but a reflection of the sun, hidden but always present? Leanna had chosen the wrong path, but others could choose the path of righteousness. James knew now why God had chosen him for his task. Not to lay down his life in a futile gesture, but to use his experience to persuade others. To show them the right way to use the gift of wolf blood.

The fighting continued, and the killing too, but the worst was surely over. James didn't know which side was winning, but that didn't matter. His own mission was clear – to walk among the moon-touched and show them how to use their power for good.

But he could do nothing while he remained bound. The chains had bitten deep, wounding him badly, yet the moon had kissed his flesh, making it whole once more. He flexed his muscles, gently at first, feeling the strength of the iron, then probing its weakness. He tightened his arms. The metal cut him afresh, but he pushed harder still, until one link of the chain broke apart. With all his might he forced it open, unlocking the shackles that held him. And then he was free. He shrugged the chain to the ground and rose tentatively, rubbing his limbs where they had lost all feeling. It took him a few minutes before he could move again, but then he was on his feet.

A voice seemed to come to him. A voice beneath the

roar of guns and the clash of stone and steel. Samuel's voice calling to him, leading him onward. *Keep going, James. Don't give up. Remember that dreams can never be killed, only forgotten or abandoned.*

Chapter One Hundred and Ten

Old Sarum

Y ou could walk both the inner and outer ramparts of Old Sarum, but the inner rampart was the natural place to stand and defend. It was shorter in length and taller in height. From here a defender could meet an approaching enemy from a position of strength. Chris had explained the logic to Ryan, who had agreed, and Rose had accepted their plan.

Yet now something incomprehensible had happened. Something perplexing and illogical that made Chris' head ache.

He stood in dumb silence as Rose urged her followers to take up arms and go out to meet the enemy on the plain, making some ridiculous speech about freedom and righteousness and justice. 'It makes no sense,' he said to Seth, as Rose herself was handed a flint axe by Ryan and the people cheered as she led them into battle like some modern-day Boudica.

'None,' agreed Seth. 'It's like, literally senseless.'

They watched together from the top of the inner rampart, spears in hand, as Rose ran down the slope toward the enemy, Ryan at her side, followed closely by turban boy, cat boy and warrior girl, all of them whooping and screaming as if that might somehow frighten away the werewolves.

Out on the surrounding plain, the last of the government forces were fighting to the death with the surviving werewolves. Heavy weapons met armoured combat vehicles. Well-trained troops sprayed overgrown gorilla-like creatures with automatic rifles and in turn were blasted by shotguns and punched to the ground by gigantic fists. The casualties on both sides were horrific. It was a place of slaughter, the ground thick with the dead.

'So,' said Seth, 'should we go with them?'

'No,' said Chris. 'That would be incredibly stupid. I can't fight. I don't know how.'

'Nor me,' said Seth, fingering his spear uselessly.

They watched in amazement as people continued to flood past, surging over the top of the rampart and down the other side to engage the enemy. They were ordinary men and women, strangers to combat, flocking to their deaths. All they had to defend themselves were the crude stone weapons that Chris himself had designed. 'They're all going to die,' he said.

'Probably,' agreed Seth. 'So what should we do, then?'

Chris looked sideways at his oldest friend. 'We should stay here where it's safe and watch what happens.'

'Yeah. Totally. That would be smart.'

They had been through a lot, him and Seth. Good times. Bad times. In recent times, mostly bad. But whatever they had done, they had always done it together.

Seth stroked his beardless chin. 'It would definitely be smart to stay here and watch. But somehow I think it might be better if we joined in.'

Seth had said a lot of dumb things in his life. So many that Chris had given up counting years ago. Suggesting they go into battle against overwhelming numbers of werewolves armed only with stone weapons must surely rank as one of the dumbest ever. It was quite possibly one of the most idiotic things anyone had said in the whole of human history.

'You think we should join in,' said Chris.

'Yeah,' said Seth.

Chris nodded. 'Let's fight, then. Together.'

'Together,' said Seth.

They brandished their spears and shouted, 'For victory!' Illogical actions, that accomplished nothing. But God, they made Chris feel good.

Then they ran off down the slope, shrieking mad battle cries, waving their spears aloft; two old friends, side by side in battle.

Chapter One Hundred and Eleven

Winchester

'It's a girl,' said Chanita. 'You were right after all.'

'Look at her,' said Ben encouragingly. 'She's ours. She's our baby.'

Melanie sat up in bed, fresh sheets covering her nakedness. She held the baby in her arms against her chest. Chanita and Ben were right. The baby was a girl, and she was beautiful.

The child was looking up at her with an unfaltering gaze. A burning, intelligent, questioning look. She had ceased her crying, and was now quiet and calm. A smile came to her rosy lips, and Melanie's heart flipped over. All memory of pain was gone. The dark horror had passed too, and in its place, love burned strong and bright.

The creature had changed. Perhaps it was mother's milk that had wrought the transformation, or perhaps it was the child's will. Either way, a miracle had occurred. After a few minutes of suckling, the creature had paused its feed and the black fur that covered it had vanished, drawing back like an ebbing tide, leaving only pink skin in its place. The animal snout shrank to a button nose, and that horrible tongue that pressed and probed and *violated*, withdrew from sight. Only the yellow eyes marked the child out as different. Together with her smile.

'How is it possible?' asked Sarah with wonder. 'Babies don't smile until they're several weeks old at least.'

'How is any of this possible?' said Chanita. 'She was born just two months after conception. And she has the power to change her form.'

'But what is she?' asked Sarah. 'Is she a werewolf? Is she like Ben?'

'She's mine,' said Melanie. 'That's all that matters. She's my baby girl.'

Ben laid a hand on hers. 'She's ours,' he corrected. 'And she's perfect.'

'What will you call her?' asked Chanita. 'Have you thought of a name?'

Melanie didn't need to think. The answer was obvious. Her daughter had been conceived beneath the glittering moon, and had been born by the light of the supermoon. 'Her name is Moon Child.'

Chapter One Hundred and Twelve

Salisbury Plain

Kevin looked around and found himself alone. Liz and Mihai had long since vanished, blurring into thin air with some new vampire trick. Now Alfie and the mental kids had gone too, swept away in the swirling crowds that mingled and clashed together before breaking apart to form new patterns.

Madness.

Don't go charging off into danger, Liz had warned him. *Leave the real fighting for the soldiers.*

But they were all soldiers now. And danger was everywhere. Total war. Men, women, monsters, all fighting for survival.

A hairy giant lumbered out of the chaos, coming straight for him. Kevin waited until he could see its yellow eyes glowing like headlights. Then he raised his arm and shot the bastard in the middle of the forehead. The beast toppled to the ground, face-down in the dirt. Kevin gave it a good hard kicking to make sure it wasn't getting up again. You never could tell with werewolves.

That was his last bullet. He shouldered the rifle, unwilling to toss it away. They had been through a lot together, him and that gun. A good weapon was like an old friend. Trusted. Comfortable. You knew you could always depend on it in a tight corner. Except he couldn't anymore.

He pulled his knife out of its sheath and readied himself for the next confrontation. With burning vehicles and thick smoke all around, the enemy could come out of nowhere. A sudden noise made him spin round, the blade ready to kill.

'Oi, chief, take it easy, blud.' It was Alfie, the great sword raised before him, slick with dark liquid. Leah came next, her spear in her hand, and then the rest, bristling with knives, baseball bats, crossbows and half a dozen scavenged firearms. They stuck together, pointing weapons in every direction.

'You lot all right?' asked Kevin. They were too many to count and Kevin still couldn't remember half their names.

Leah nodded. 'All good. You seen Liz?'

'Can't see none of them vampires,' moaned Kevin. 'I just hope they're safe.' But he could have kicked himself at his own words. When had hoping ever done the slightest good?

Leah pointed to the east with her spear. 'Look. It'll be sunrise soon.'

The sky was turning salmon pink as the first blush of a new day crested the hills. The moon, meanwhile, was sinking ever lower, its power waning. 'Yeah, that's got to be good,' said Kevin. Even if the sun had no effect on the werewolves, it would at least make it easier to see the hairy buggers. With only a knife to keep him alive, daylight couldn't come quick enough.

Lycanthropic

'Come on, then,' he said to the kids. 'Let's see if we can find one more to kill before tomorrow comes.'

Chapter One Hundred and Thirteen

Salisbury Plain

Warg Daddy's ammo was gone but the fight went on, though the dead now outnumbered the living. The heavy weapons that had opened the night's hostilities had long since fallen mute, the big guns destroyed or their shells all spent. Occasional gunshots still peppered the night, but long bursts of automatic fire had ceased. Now the sounds were of grunts and moans; of metal striking stone as the two sides came together to engage in close combat.

Warg Daddy's shotgun made a good club if he held it by the barrel. He swung the butt at an approaching target and was rewarded by the sound of a skull being smashed, the brainy pulp spilling out like so much juice from an overripe melon. It was one of the hilltop hippies who had run down from the mound, whooping battle cries to mask her terror as she met her doom. Easy pickings.

He was growing weaker though. It wasn't just fatigue from fighting for so many hours. The moon itself grew duller as it slid toward the horizon. Soon it would pass from view and he would be back to his usual self. Not quite man, but no longer wolfman. But until then the fight continued, and he set about it with glee. Bloodbath and his two other Brothers had joined him, and they fought together, bringing death to all in their path.

It wasn't all easy killings, though. There were strange creatures out there. He didn't know what they were, but they came from nowhere, dealing death with tooth and claw before vanishing into the night. A man could lose his life that way and not even know it.

Many of his own side had fallen and more would perish before the sun reclaimed the sky. But however and whenever it came, he was ready to face his own end. To fight alongside his Brothers and die a warrior was all he wanted.

'To the right,' yelled Bloodbath, and he turned to see one of the phantoms incoming. It was only a blur, scarcely a shadow, but the blows it dealt were solid enough. One Brother fell and then another, their necks ripped open in red chasms. The attacker blurred again, darting away before coming in for a fresh attack. The creature was silent, but its stink washed over him – the stench of corruption, as stomach-churning as a freshly-opened tomb.

Bloodbath's knife flashed in his hand, cutting left, right, up, down. He spun, drawing sharp lines as his blade cut the air. But the ghost danced around him, dodging each thrust with ease.

Warg Daddy swung the shotgun, swiping at the blurred shape. But wherever he turned, the ghostly figure had already moved on, leaving only a memory in its wake.

'Back to back!' he cried, and he and Bloodbath faced their foe together, slashing, clubbing, hacking as sweat poured off their arms. The blade winked; the club drove.

Moon Child

But their speed was no match for their opponent. A single claw as sharp as a rapier plunged through Bloodbath's neck, skewering him like a raw steak. His knife fell to the ground and his head slumped forward.

Warg Daddy swung the butt, connecting with the invisible assassin. The shotgun stock brought the attacker to a violent halt. It froze in time, unmoving at last, and Warg Daddy saw it for what it truly was – a grinning corpse, animated from the grave, a flesh-rotten hideous revenant come to deliver some strange retribution.

'Eat butt, motherfucker!' he yelled and drove the heavy stump of the shotgun into the white skull of its face.

The creature crumpled, screaming like a devil, and he battered it again. One, two, three heavy blows, until its head caved in, oozing thick grey sludge. A fresh wave of nausea broke over him and he turned away to gag.

The sight of so much carnage filled him with disgust. Three fallen Brothers, the last of their kind, and the ghoulish fiend that had claimed them, all heaped together like so much meat. There was no dignity in death, just as there was so little in life. Even the mightiest king would be back in the dirt one day, however bright their crown might shine.

When the next assassin came, he didn't even hear it until it was too late. He smelled the stink of rotten flesh just as he felt the teeth against his neck. By the time the blood began to flow, the deed was done. He raised a hand to stem the wound, but the crimson fountain was unstoppable. It was all he could do to lift his gaze to see what manner of spirit had done this to him.

A woman stood gasping before him, breathless from her exertion. A dead woman walking. Her face was bone, her lips blood-red. Her arms were sheathed in a skeletal shell and her hands bore twisted knives in place of fingers. Her breast dripped red with the blood of her enemies. When she opened her mouth, only a cold hissing sound emerged as she sucked in air. 'You killed my friend,' she said at last, the words like icy wind against his skin.

'Your friend killed mine,' he answered.

'Then we are equal.' She turned and was gone, just a trick of the light as the first rays of the sun touched the ground, turning silver into gold. A dream? Perhaps. A nightmare? Certainly.

Warg Daddy sank to his knees, the blood flowing freely now, despite his best endeavours to stop it. The moment had come at last, the time for songs to be written about his passing. Except that he was all alone, his Brothers gone before him, and no one would write a single word to mark his death. He would lie here until some poor soul came to shovel his remains into a dark hole, or burn them on a funeral pyre. There was no song in that. None worth singing at any rate.

Still, it had been a good life, a damn good one, and he gave thanks to the gods for all he had been given.

The noise of battle grew soft and distant as the sun continued on its journey. To rise and then to fall, that was the way of the world. All things must pass. He could no longer move his head, and could see only what lay before his eyes. Mostly mud and grass.

Soon there will be nothing.

The air grew still and a deep shadow fell across him. A horse's hoof came into view, and a heavy cloak swished softly. Bony fingers reached out to him and twisted his face to the sky. A skull stared down at him, but not the skull of the creature that had bitten him. The hooded skull of a rider beside a pale horse. Stars spiralled endlessly within its empty eye sockets.

'You came back for me, then,' said Warg Daddy. 'You didn't forget.'

'My friend,' said Death, 'I come for all at the appointed hour. You know that.'

'So this really is the end?'

The skull's jaw cracked open in what might have been the ghost of a smile. 'This time I will take you with me. We shall go on a journey together, although we must part before we reach the final destination. The last steps must be yours alone.'

Warg Daddy understood. There would be no trickery this time. No games of chess. No banter to pass the time. Only acceptance. The world darkened and he rose to his feet, going willingly with Death toward the final curtain. It was not so far to walk. The curtain had been there all along, just a breath away. Just one final beat of the heart. With a last flourish of his skeletal hand, Death twitched the heavy velvet fabric aside to let him glimpse what lay beyond.

A smile came to Warg Daddy's face at the sight. There were his friends, waiting to greet him. They sat at a long bench at an oak table, just one of many in a hall so vast he could see neither its end nor its beginning. Dead heroes of Valhalla feasted at every table, drinking and making merry. There was Snakebite, the fallen Brother grinning in welcome through the red forest of his beard. His face bore no trace of anger or resentment at the way Warg Daddy had betrayed him. All that was in the past and long forgotten. Beside him sat Slasher and Wombat. All the Brothers were there. Meathook, Bloodbath; even Weasel and a few of his gambling cronies from The Tarnished Spoon. They were all friends now, and all debts were paid.

They raised their horns of ale and he stepped through to embrace them.

Chapter One Hundred and Fourteen

Salisbury Plain, waning moon

Wisps of smoke lingered like early morning mist, but even through the haze it was clear that the *Canning Bluff* had not been sufficient to secure victory. Now, as the sun rose higher and the moon hid its face, Canning judged that neither side could win.

He had been king for less than a day, but it would be futile to battle on in a bid to lengthen his reign by a few more hours. This had always been Leanna's war, not his. He was no fanatic, nor was he driven by the lust for revenge that had consumed her. He cared nothing for slogans, grand causes or loyalties. He cared for his own skin. *Live to fight another day*, that was the smart move now. Melt away in the chaos. There was certainly no shortage of that.

Now that the moon had set and he had returned to

human form, he could easily pass for one of the refugees roaming around the battlefield in stunned silence. Especially with his eye patch. That was a nice touch. People would look on him with pity. He could slip away before anyone noticed or started to ask awkward questions.

He disrobed quickly, casting aside his fancy clothing, and hid his golden crown beneath it. There were corpses aplenty willing to offer their own clothes to him, and he stripped two before finding a new outfit that fitted. A bloodied shirt and jacket and muddy trousers. Not quite the style he was used to, but he had worn far filthier rags during his days in the sewers. In any case, the stink would conceal any trace of wolf he might be carrying. Not that humans could smell such things. Their noses were poor organs, scarcely fit for purpose.

A ragged group of survivors wandered into view. Two men and two women, their eyes hollow, their faces blighted by what they had witnessed this past night. One of the women was wounded, and limped along, supported by the two men. The other woman still carried a stone-headed spear, although she appeared barely capable of lifting it. All of them looked utterly exhausted.

He approached them slowly, affecting a limp of his own, and an air of helpless bewilderment. 'Help me,' he pleaded. 'Oh please help me.'

Pitiful eyes turned his way. One of the men offered him an arm to lean on. 'Can you walk?' he asked.

'I think so,' bleated Canning. 'My leg was hurt during the fighting.' He indicated the blood on his shirt, wishing now that he had selected a pair of blood-soaked trousers to go with them. But it was too late to change his story. An injured leg it would have to be.

'Have you come from Old Sarum?' asked the spear woman.

Canning hesitated. He had indeed intended to pass himself off as one of the Stone Age folk, but perhaps that was unwise. His eye patch was a memorable detail. These people might wonder why they hadn't seen him before. 'No,' he answered. 'I was one of the werewolves' slaves. They chained me to a tank and made me into a human shield. If I complained they beat me.' That was at least half true. His face was still marked from the beatings Will Hunter had given him. At this rate he would end up believing his own story. He lifted his eye patch, treating them to a close-up look at his hollow socket. 'See what they did to me!'

The woman averted her gaze. 'Such evil,' she muttered. 'But you are free from them now. We are all free at last.'

Canning was grateful to her for bringing up the topic of freedom. The sooner he got away from this place the better. 'Where are you going?' he enquired. 'Not back to Old Sarum?'

'There is nothing for us there,' said the man who was helping him. 'We just want to get away and put all this behind us.'

'Me too,' said Canning. 'Do you have a destination in mind?'

'West,' said the woman. 'I had a cottage by the sea in Devon. I want to go back there.'

'Excellent,' said Canning. 'A cottage by the sea, how lovely. My dear, would you mind very much if I came with you?'

Chapter One Hundred and Fifteen

Salisbury Plain

The survivors drifted aimlessly amid the devastation. Humans or werewolves, it no longer seemed to matter. There had been no victors in this war. Both sides had lost. Now they came together to save themselves, and perhaps each other. Now that the moon had gone, the madness of the night seemed no more real than a nightmare dissolving in the light of day. Dead and wounded lay everywhere, and the able-bodied went from one to another, comforting or tending, or simply covering those who were past help.

James walked among them, wondering how to begin. His task seemed insurmountable but he had to start somewhere. The first step was always the hardest. He found a place and began to speak.

'Friends,' he said. 'This war is over. But peace will not

be easy.' No one was listening to him, but he ploughed on regardless. 'A great divide has come between us. Some of you have been changed, through no fault of your own. You are victims. We are all victims. You cannot change back to how you were before. Instead we must move forward, together. You may think this is impossible, but I can show you the way.'

A few people began to gather around him, stopping to listen. He guessed they had nothing better to do with their lives. They looked miserable and defeated, but they were listening, and that was all that mattered. He carried on.

'Our societies have always been divided. Nations have fought each other since the beginning of recorded history. Different races, different creeds, different political beliefs – there is no limit to the number of ways we can divide ourselves. We are all different, yet we have more in common than separates us. The truth is that we are stronger together. And we need each other in order to survive. Even now. Especially now.'

The crowd was growing, even though the reception to his words was lukewarm at best. He knew that his message would be hard for some people to accept. He didn't even know if it was possible to bridge the great divide between human and lycanthrope, but he had to try. Those who had lost the most would be the hardest to win over. But the opportunity to sow the seeds of peace had never been so great; the alternative never so bleak. He would do whatever it took to make people realize the truth.

He was about to go on when he caught sight of a familiar face among the onlookers. It took him a moment to place her. So much time had passed and so much had happened since they had last met. But yes, it was her. He beckoned, and was pleased to see her come to him. 'Liz,' he said. 'Police Constable Liz Bailey.'

She offered him a weak smile. 'I'm Mrs Liz Jones now.'

There was no sign of any husband, but she had acquired a motley collection of children, and they flocked around her, each one holding a weapon of some kind. James saw the trauma in their eyes and could only guess how deep the damage went. This was the raw material he must work with – a broken generation in desperate need of repair. But that was why his mission was needed.

Liz was broken too, he could see it. 'Is your husband here?' he asked.

She shook her head sadly; no words were necessary.

'I'm sorry.' He guessed he would be using those words a lot in the days to come.

'What are you doing, James?' she asked.

'Sowing the seeds of peace and reconciliation.'

'You've taken on a big challenge. A lot of people don't want reconciliation. They want to see the last werewolves rounded up and killed.'

'I know. But werewolves aren't all evil. It's the moon that makes them act the way they do. The moon has always driven people mad. I have a solution to that.' He reached into his pocket and pulled out a bag of herbs.

'What's that?'

'Wolfsbane. It makes a nice cup of tea. And taken regularly, it can help even the worst werewolf control their urges. I should know – it worked for me.' He dropped his voice to a whisper. 'What about you? You're no longer … human. I can tell.'

'No. But I'm not a werewolf. I'm a vampire.'

He grinned. 'I'm not exactly a regular werewolf either. Perhaps there's no such thing. We're all unique.'

She took the bag and gave it a tentative sniff. 'I wonder if this stuff works for vampires too?'

'Try it,' he urged.

A small group of refugees trundled past – three men and two women. Two of them were struggling to walk and were being helped by the others. James looked hard. One of the men stood out. He was taller than the rest, despite stooping forward as he stumbled along. His thin hair was silver and he wore a black patch over one eye. A distinctive look, and one that James would never forget. He was Leanna's deputy, now seeking to slink away in the guise of an injured human.

Liz followed the direction of James' gaze and her eyes grew wide. 'Canning,' she hissed. 'It's Canning!'

'You know him?'

'I know him from London. He was the headmaster of a local school. He killed some of his students and teachers and ate them in his office.' She paused and turned to James. 'It was Canning who infected the teacher who bit you and turned you into a werewolf.'

'Was it?' James wondered what he was supposed to feel at this bombshell. Shock? Anger? A thirst for revenge? He felt none of those. Liz's news was a fact, nothing more. Just another part of his life story. A piece of the jigsaw that explained who he was and how he had become that way. If it hadn't been Canning, it might easily have been another. Canning hadn't committed the foul deed on purpose – lycanthropy had twisted him and made him a monster.

'He was one of the ringleaders,' continued Liz. 'Look at him now, trying to make his escape. He can't be allowed simply to get away with it!'

'Liz,' said James, reaching for her, but she was already striding across the field.

'Canning!' she bellowed. 'Don't make another move!'

The grey-haired man affected a look of surprise. 'Canning?' he stammered. 'You must be mistaken. My name is Heathcote. I'm Mr Heathcote and I come from Swindon. I used to work in insurance.'

'Liar!' Liz reached him and took up position in front of him, her arms folded across her chest. 'I bet that limp's a fake too,' she snarled.

Liz's band of kids fanned out around her, their weapons turned on the rogue headmaster. One of them, a tiny kid with a huge sword, asked, 'So, you gonna kill him, chief?'

'Yes,' said Liz. 'I think I am.'

Chapter One Hundred and Sixteen

Salisbury Plain

Liz's anger bubbled up until she could contain it no more. Everything bad that had happened seemed to crystallize in one instant. Dean's death in London, leaving Samantha a widow and her children orphans. The cold-blooded murder of Gary the butcher by Serbian gangsters. Llewelyn's death at the hands of werewolf bikers. And just last night, Eric's death in battle, killed by the leader of the werewolf gang. Quite how they all connected to Canning wasn't clear, except that he was part of the pattern, a step on the path that had led Liz from normality to the destruction of her world.

The kids had surrounded Canning, but she knew it would be a mistake to underestimate him. Besides, she didn't want the kids involved. If one of them got hurt, she would never forgive herself.

Mihai stood beside her, but she wasn't certain she had the right to ask for his help. If she had to do this deed alone, then she would. But she didn't need to ask. Mihai rolled up his sleeve and offered her his arm. 'Liz, is time to take bite. Is time to drink blood of *vampir*.'

She accepted his gift gratefully, grazing his thin arm with her teeth and taking just enough of his blood to precipitate the change. It happened just like Eric had promised. Just a tingling to start, but soon a rushing and surging of cold blood through her veins. The change took her back to vampire form and in an instant she was ready.

Canning's one eye narrowed. He shoved aside the man who had been helping him walk and straightened to his full height, his limp forgotten. Reaching inside his jacket he produced a pistol. 'I hoped I wouldn't have to use this,' he drawled. 'But it's just as well I kept hold of it. You could call it my insurance policy. Perhaps I wasn't lying when I told you that I worked in insurance.'

Liz advanced on him. 'Your pistol doesn't frighten me, Canning. Vampires aren't really afraid of anything.'

'A vampire?' he said. 'I always wondered what you were.' He sniffed the air. 'I knew you weren't a normal werewolf.' He rolled up one trouser leg and withdrew a knife strapped to his calf. 'Ah, this must be what was making me limp. Are you sure you want to get into a fight with a man armed with a gun and a knife?'

'Oh yes, Canning,' she said. 'That's exactly what I want.' She knew that she could slit his throat from ear to ear before he even managed to pull the trigger.

She was about to lunge for him when she felt a hand on her shoulder. It was James. 'Liz, stop. Don't do this.'

She shook him off. 'I have to. For the sake of everyone he killed.'

'But there's something bigger at stake now. Peace and reconciliation.'

'I can never be reconciled with this man. Why should he live when so many others have died?'

James sighed. 'I can't give you a reason, Liz, except that if the killing doesn't end now, when will it? When everyone who committed a crime is dead? There is evil in all of us, but we must learn to live together: humans, werewolves and vampires. This is the moment to start over again.'

Liz's chest rose and fell. The energy building inside her needed an outlet. If not violence, then what?

Just chill, Liz. Take it easy. Do nothing for a change. Llewelyn's voice again. Always so damn annoying.

Easy for you to say, dead guy.

Yeah, I know. But James is right. Killing Canning won't fix anything. And even if it did, people would want to kill you next. Especially once they find out how bloody dangerous you are. So just leave it. Walk away.

And then what?

Just keep walking. It's a beautiful day for a stroll.

Slowly, she felt the ice that filled her blood begin to melt. In its place came a mellow warmth. She knew from the look on James' face that she was returning to her normal self.

'Good, Liz,' he said. 'I know how hard it was to stop yourself. But you showed strength. You did something that Leanna never could. You mastered your emotions.'

Canning let out a loud sigh of relief. 'Well, now I feel rather foolish,' he declared. 'This gun isn't even loaded.' He tossed it aside.

Liz found that her cheeks were coursing with hot tears of relief. Violence hadn't been necessary. Acceptance had been just as powerful in quenching her need. 'So, is it finally over?' she asked.

'No,' said James, 'this battle is over, and the war too. But the fight against evil goes on, for darkness is all around us, and within us. But so is good. Good is everywhere too.'

'And what about Canning? Does he just walk free?'

'He will never be free of what he has done.'

'Maybe,' said Liz, 'but if we're going to start putting

this world back together, we have to build it on the right principles, and that includes justice.' She grabbed Canning's arm and twisted it behind his back. 'I am arresting you on suspicion of murder. You will be given a fair trial and allowed to defend yourself. Witnesses will be called to give evidence, and a jury will decide if you are guilty.'

Still a cop, then, Liz?

Yes. But this was my final arrest. Now I'm officially retired.

She handed him over to two of Eric's vampires who had gathered to watch. Canning struggled briefly, but their grip was unyielding. They led him away, his head bowed.

Chapter One Hundred and Seventeen

Old Sarum

Rose just wanted to go to sleep and not wake up for a day or more. She had never felt so tired in her life. But she had to keep going just a little longer before she could rest.

'You did it, Rose,' said Ryan. 'You led your people to victory. You defeated the werewolves.'

Rose shrugged. 'I just let people do what they wanted to, that's all.'

She and Ryan were back in Old Sarum, the gates of the fortress now open wide to welcome all who wanted to enter. Some of the people had already come inside, but others would never return. They lay where they had fallen in the fields beyond the protective circles of the earthworks. A light breeze stirred the grass, and smoke still rose from the blighted tanks and other vehicles that had met their end on Salisbury Plain. She wondered what would happen to all that dead military hardware. It would rust, like the tanks she had seen at Imber village, and over time it might be stripped for scrap. But she hoped that some of it might remain as a memorial to the fallen. It would surely never endure as long as the stones of Stonehenge, however, still standing so many millennia after anyone could remember why they were there in the first place.

'Anyway,' said Rose, 'it was Vijay who persuaded me.'

'Okay,' said Ryan, 'but take some credit. Without you, the werewolves would have won. You basically saved the world.'

She shook her head. 'I tried my best to be a leader. But I was a fool even to try. People should make their own choices, not follow others.'

Ryan wasn't giving up that easily. 'Don't say that, Rose. They still need you now that the battle is over.' He gestured at the stone walls and earthen ramparts that surrounded them. 'How else are we going to get this place up and running again?'

'I don't know. But it's not up to me. I'm stepping down.'

She had made her decision back in the heat of battle, when the fighting had been at its fiercest. The brutality she had witnessed was only possible when groups of people let others make decisions on their behalf, allowing themselves to be seduced by promises of a better future. She would make no such promises again. She was done with dreams.

'What will happen to this place, then?' asked Ryan.

'People can stay if they want to,' said Rose, 'but I think most of them will choose to leave. No one wants to live next to a mass graveyard.'

The work on burying or burning the dead had already begun. The August heat would turn the bodies into nests for flies and maggots in no time if they were simply left. But Rose wanted no part in it. She was ready to move on.

Where she would go, she wasn't sure. The city where she had grown up was gone. And she had developed a liking for the countryside. Perhaps she would find a little cottage for herself and Nutmeg, and they would live out their days alone and in peace. Unless…

She spied Vijay coming back over the bridge that spanned the outer ditch of the fortress. He had gone into battle at her side, but the chaos had quickly separated them and she had heard no news of him. Now she found herself breathing more easily, knowing that he was safe. Aasha was with him, and Drake too. Drake was limping a little, but otherwise the three of them appeared unharmed.

She and Ryan stood together as the three small figures slowly crossed the great expanse of the outer bailey. As they came closer, Vijay spotted her and quickened his pace. Soon he was running, leaving Drake stumbling in his wake. He didn't slow down until he had crossed the inner bridge and reached her. But he stopped a little way off, eyeing Ryan nervously.

'I'll catch up with you later, Rose,' said Ryan and moved off into the crowd.

It was only when he was gone that Vijay came to her. Again he stopped before he reached her. 'You're safe,' he said.

'And you too.'

He glanced nervously over his shoulder, but Drake and Aasha were still some way off. 'We beat them, Rose. We brought the war to an end.'

'Maybe,' she said. 'Although I think that in the end, both sides were beaten.'

'Yes. Fighting is harder than it looks. And nasty too. I didn't think I would be able to do it.'

'But you did. You fought for what you believed in.'

'So what happens now?' he asked.

'I don't know. What do you mean?'

'Do you plan to stay here?'

'Would you like to?'

'I'd like to go wherever you go,' he said. 'But I thought that perhaps…'

'What?'

Vijay looked around the faces of the crowd before turning back to her. 'I wondered if you and Ryan…'

Rose stared at him, then laughed. It was the first time she had laughed in a long time. 'Me and Ryan? You think we're together?'

'I don't know. I just thought…'

'Ryan's a great guy. I couldn't have done this without him. But we were never… I mean, he's too old for me for one thing. You weren't jealous, were you?'

'Jealous?' Vijay dropped his gaze to the ground. 'Jealousy brings pain to all it touches. It is to be avoided at all costs. I would never…' He looked up. 'Yes, I was a little bit jealous.'

She grinned. 'There was no need to be.'

'I see that now. I was weak. And foolish. Again.'

'So let's find somewhere we can go together. You, me, Nutmeg, Aasha, Drake and Shadow. We can go anywhere now. We can do whatever we like.'

'Yes,' he said, taking her hands in his at last and giving her a kiss on the lips. 'Whatever we like.'

Chapter One Hundred and Eighteen

Salisbury Plain

'Hi there,' said Chris. 'My name's Chris. Chris Crohn.'

The woman gave him a shy smile in return. 'Sarah,' she said. 'Sarah Margolis.'

They lapsed into silence.

Chris studied the woman a little more closely. She was quite pretty, maybe a year or two older than him. Long dark hair tumbled over her shoulders. She had nice eyes. Kind eyes. Thoughtful eyes.

She lowered her gaze and Chris knew that he had been staring too much. Some people said it was rude to stare, even though it was a perfectly natural function that was in fact essential for survival. 'I'm sorry,' he said.

'What for?'

'I'm no good at conversations, so I don't know what to

say next. I don't have *people skills.*'

That drew another smile from her. 'Nor me. Not really.'

'You don't?' said Chris.

'No, although I'm much better than I was. I used to suffer from a condition called *anthropophobia*. It means –'

'Fear of people,' said Chris. 'Wow, awesome.'

Sarah tucked a loose strand of hair behind one ear. 'Not many people have heard of it. It's a very rare condition.'

'I know,' said Chris. 'I've never met anyone with it before.'

'I don't really have it anymore,' said Sarah.

'You don't?' said Chris, disappointed. 'Oh well, never mind.'

Sarah turned away from him, and he sensed that he may have said something awkward. He wondered if he might make up for it by paying her a compliment. He could, for instance, tell her that she was pretty. But he knew from prior experience that such behaviour could easily backfire. The Human Resources manager at Manor Road school had made that crystal clear to him that time he had been called into her office.

'So, where are you from?' asked Sarah after the awkward moment had passed.

'Old Sarum. I'm one of the Stone Age people.'

'You saved the day,' said Sarah, grinning.

'Do you think so?'

'Yes. Everyone says you're heroes.'

Chris felt a stirring in his heart. Sarah was right, he supposed. He *was* a hero. He had already told Seth the same thing. He puffed his chest out with pride. 'In fact,' he said, 'I was the one who invented the Stone Age. Or reinvented it.'

'Impressive,' said Sarah.

'So, did you take part in the battle yourself?'

'No, I've only just arrived. I'm here to meet my friend,

James.'

'Okay.' Chris scoured his brain for more words to say. This was the best conversation he'd had in a long time, and he didn't want it to stop. 'Where are you from?' he asked.

'Christmas Common. It's a little village in Oxfordshire. My sister and I have been living in an old house there. But I'm from London originally.'

'Me too,' said Chris. 'I haven't always lived in the Stone Age.'

Sarah laughed. 'You're very funny, Chris.'

'Am I?' Nobody had ever told him that before. Especially not a pretty woman. A feeling rose up inside him. He didn't know what it was exactly, but it was a good one. Even better than when he'd charged down the hillside waving his spear and shouting. And a lot less dangerous.

Sarah turned her thoughtful eyes on him. 'So where will you be going next, Chris?'

He hadn't really had a lot of time to consider his next move. He'd assumed that he'd be staying on at Old Sarum, but already people were beginning to drift away, packing up their tents and moving on. It seemed that now the battle was over, there was nothing to hold them together. 'I was planning to go to Hereford,' he said. 'I thought it would be a safe place to escape from the werewolves. But I don't suppose I need to do that now.'

'No,' said Sarah.

'So I might just hang out with my friend, Seth. He's my best friend. We've known each other forever.'

He and Seth had handled themselves pretty well during the final battle. The flint weapons had been surprisingly effective, although that was probably because the enemy's ammunition had run out and both sides were reduced to hand-to-hand combat. Not that Chris or Seth had fought any actual werewolves themselves. They had arrived too late to encounter any real danger. But he still felt as much a hero as if he had single-handedly defeated the enemy.

Sarah nodded.

'What about you?' he asked.

'I'll be staying with my sister. She's just given birth to a … a daughter.'

'A baby?' said Chris, unable to keep an edge of alarm from his voice.

'Yes. A baby girl. So she needs my support right now. It's up to Melanie where we go, but I'd like to return to Christmas Common. It would be a good place to raise a child.'

'Good,' said Chris. He wondered again what he and Seth would do next. Stay at Old Sarum? There was nowhere else for them to go.

'There'd be room for you and your friend at Christmas Common,' said Sarah. 'And anyone else who wanted to come. The village has plenty of empty houses, and it's very nice there.'

'Christmas Common?' said Chris agog. This conversation was moving so rapidly he could barely keep up. 'Wait, can I clarify exactly what you're proposing? Are you inviting me to come and live with you in your village?'

'Yes,' said Sarah with a giggle. 'I think I am. I think I'd like that very much. So what do you say, Chris?'

Chapter One Hundred and Nineteen

Winchester, quarter moon

It was easy to forgive Griffin now that he had lost a leg. Now that the war was over. Now that James had returned from his mission and the world was at peace. Chanita's biggest regret was that she had been unable to forgive him before, when he had needed her most. She dipped a cloth into a cool bucket of water and placed it over his forehead. This was how it would be in the future, now that medical supplies were almost exhausted. Analgesics, antibiotics, anticonvulsants, antidepressants. Funny how all the most common drugs began with the letter "a". Soon even anaesthetics would be gone and they would be back to the days of Florence Nightingale, when the only pain relief available during an amputation like the one that had taken Griffin's leg was half a bottle of whisky.

'Chanita,' he murmured. 'Are you still there?'

'I'm here, Michael,' she answered softly. 'Don't worry. I'm never going to leave you again.' She had stayed with him since the battle, sitting at his bedside or sleeping on a camp bed next to his.

'I'm sorry,' he muttered. If he had spoken the words once since regaining consciousness, he had said them a hundred times. 'I should have listened to you.'

'Shh,' she soothed. 'There's no need to apologize for anything. You did what was right. If you had waited for James, the werewolves might have won the war.'

'We can never know what might have happened.'

'No.' However many possible roads lay ahead, only one could ever be taken. The others would remain forever unexplored, and it was necessary to forget their tantalizing possibilities, else you would lose yourself in the tangle of paths and find yourself stranded amid the what-ifs and if-onlys. The future was all that mattered now. A shared future – hers and Griffin's intertwined.

'The surgeon thinks you might be able to try sitting up soon,' she told him. It was agony to see him so weakened, but thankfully the infection that had almost claimed him was gradually receding. His temperature was back to normal and he had begun to eat tiny morsels of food. If he continued on the road to recovery, he might even be able to walk again one day – with the aid of crutches, of course. And her help too.

'I would like that,' he said. 'I would like to sit up, and rise from this bed, and see the world for myself.'

'All in good time. There's no hurry.'

'No.'

'Johnny Perez came to see you,' she said.

'The mercenary? When?'

'While you were asleep. Everyone thought he'd been killed, but it seems that he was just drunk. He popped up again without so much as a scratch, to claim his gold. For all the good it will do him.'

Griffin smiled. 'He was the most underserving man on

the battlefield. But without him and his men, we would never have prevailed. Where is he now?'

'Trying to figure out a way to move his gold.'

'I'm sure he'll work something out. He always seems to land on his feet.' Griffin lapsed into a brooding silence then. 'I wish Bampton had survived instead of him. Or FitzHerbert. Or any of the men or women who served with them.'

Chanita removed the cloth from his forehead and cooled it in the water again. The fever had abated, but the simple act of tending to him soothed her just as much as him. They needed each other, just as James had convinced her that humans and werewolves needed each other to survive.

'We are two species now, but we will merge again and become one,' James had told her.

'I don't understand.'

'Don't you? Yet you were the one who delivered Melanie's daughter. The Moon Child.'

Chanita still couldn't entirely grasp the nature of the baby she had helped to birth. Not girl, not wolf, nor even a hybrid like James or Ben. She was a changeling; a fairy creature, almost magical. Sometimes she took on human form, sometimes animal. At other times she was half and half. Chanita could only guess at what she might become.

'She is our future,' James had said. 'In a sense, she is Leanna's child.'

Again, Chanita had found herself unable to follow James' logic.

'Leanna wanted to harness the healing powers of lycanthropy to end human suffering. But the path she chose was the wrong one. It brought fresh suffering to all. Moon Child shows us another way. A way that brings both sides together in lasting peace.'

James had gone with Melanie, Ben and the girl to live in Christmas Common. Sarah, too, had returned to the village, along with a group of survivors she had befriended at Old Sarum. Some were human, others were werewolves. Chanita had worried whether old enemies would be able to live together, or if segregation might be necessary to ensure peace.

'Aren't you worried about having them alongside you?' she'd asked James.

'I would be worried if we lived apart. We need more diversity, not less. Division was at the heart of Leanna's dream, but Samuel's was always about togetherness. Now it's coming true at last.'

It certainly seemed that with the help of wolfsbane, and under Ben's guidance, the werewolves were learning how to control their murderous instincts. They would never be vegans, but seemed happy enough to live off animal meat and to stay indoors on the night of the full moon.

But Chanita was in no hurry to return to Christmas Common. Griffin would need more time to recover before he could be moved. And it wouldn't do any harm to wait and see just how well James' experiment in human-lycanthrope relations went.

It seemed that Griffin was following the same train of thought as her. 'Any news from Ben?' he asked.

'He and Melanie have settled in well. They've repaired the house and turned one of the bedrooms into a nursery. Melanie has taken up gardening.'

Griffin smiled. 'Is she filling her garden with death traps?'

'Vegetables this time.'

'I'm surprised she has the time with a newborn on her hands.'

'Melanie never was much good at sitting around.'

'And you? How do you enjoy sitting around, doing nothing but look after me?'

She gripped his hand and held it tight. 'I'm a nurse, Michael. Looking after people is what I do.'

'You're a nurse,' he agreed, 'but I'm not anything anymore. Not a soldier; not a doctor.'

'You're a patient,' she told him. 'Not a very *patient* patient. But you're *my* patient, and you're all I want.'

Chapter One Hundred and Twenty

Midhurst, West Sussex, new moon

The neatly tended borders of the hotel gardens were becoming overgrown. Brambles, nettles and weeds of all kinds were encroaching, but Liz didn't mind. She'd found a corner where blackberries grew and had sent Alfie out to pick some for breakfast. He'd returned empty-handed but with purple juice all over his face. 'Yeah, I ate them,' he admitted. 'Gonna cuff me, chief?' The boy was so cheeky and cheerful that Liz found it hard to be cross with him.

The sun-ripened berries were attractive to birds and insects as well as to small children, and the grounds of the hotel were filling up with all kinds of wildlife. Squirrels, hedgehogs, badgers, rabbits; several species of deer.

Alfie isn't the only one with juice running down his chin, eh, Liz?

Better to catch rabbits for breakfast than to take a bite out of Dad's arm.

Yuck. Don't even think about that.

There was more than enough food to keep Liz and Mihai from growing hungry, and with some work the gardens could easily become a sufficient source of food for all of them – Kevin, Samantha, plus all the children. The kids weren't afraid of getting stuck in to some hard digging and weeding, at least for the moment. Growing vegetables was still a novelty, she supposed. She wondered if the younger ones would keep working through the winter.

'When they're hungry, they'll work,' said Kevin darkly. 'Anyway, if we plan ahead, we can bottle and preserve plenty to keep us going.'

'What do you know about planning?' Liz asked him.

'Not so much. But I know a thing or two about bottling. My old man used to pickle his own onions. A nice bit of chutney too.'

'See if you can pass your skills on to the next generation, then,' said Liz. 'Just keep that stuff well away from me. My nose is sensitive.'

If I was still around, I'd be looking into brewing some beer.

It's just as well you're not, then. We have bigger priorities now.

Yeah, I guess so. Still… a world without beer. Perhaps it's best I'm out of it.

I wish you weren't. I miss you every day.

Llewelyn's grave was becoming a little wild too. Liz was reluctant to clear away the plants that were slowly covering it. One day she supposed the space would become completely hidden beneath roses, thistles and maybe even trees. In a way, Llewelyn would live on through the plants. Cutting them back would be like killing him all over again.

You're getting sentimental, Mrs Jones. You need to watch that.

Call me a realist. I don't have time to clear gravesides. There's real work to be done. It would have been handy to have a big, strong man like you around.

Liz had wondered what Samantha would do after the

war, but she seemed happy enough to stay on in the hotel. 'I feel very safe here with you, Liz,' she said. 'And Lily adores living here. When Leo is old enough to walk, he's going to love it too.'

'I'm sure he will,' said Liz. 'So, it's happy ever after, eh?'

Samantha reached out and held her hand. 'Not quite. We paid a heavy price. Both of us.'

'We did.' Two husbands lost. It would take a long time for Liz to make sense of it, if she ever could. Perhaps there was no sense.

There never was any sense in the world, Liz. I told you that when I was alive.

There was never much sense in some of the things you said, Llewelyn Jones.

You say that, Liz, but then again, a cup of tea saved the world. So go figure.

The wolfsbane tea, he meant. She had kept the dried herbs that James had given her and used it to brew a pot of tea. She and Mihai had drunk it together one night.

The Romanian boy had sniffed at it suspiciously. 'Is just for wolves?' he asked.

'Who knows? Maybe it will work for vampires too.'

'And will do what to us?'

'Keep us healthy.'

'Not kill us?'

'Certainly not.'

He wrinkled his nose at the smell. 'You go first.'

She took a sip and tried not to let her face show how bitter it tasted.

Mihai wasn't fooled. 'Is gross?'

'Gross,' she agreed. 'Try some yourself.'

It took some coaxing, but eventually he managed the cup. Liz forced herself to drink another. It definitely had a soothing effect on her. 'Do you feel better?' she asked Mihai.

'Better that it is all gone. Do we have to drink it again?'

'Once a week, I think. Just to be safe. We'll have to look for more in the garden.'

She found some now, peeping up next to the small rock that was Llewelyn's headstone. Coincidence? She didn't think so.

You think I had something to do with this, Liz?

Well, did you?

I just lie here in the ground all day and night, doing nothing. You can't pin this on me.

She picked some leaves from the herb, leaving the rest growing. She had no idea how to cultivate wolfsbane, but it was yet another skill she would need to master.

The sun was moving around from behind the hotel, and the shadows that covered the lawn and the gravestone slowly slid away. It was good to feel sunlight warming her face. Just for a short while.

Careful you don't burn, Liz. I don't want to see you go up in flames. Not after all you've been through.

I'll try not to let that happen.

She had walked a long, dark path, never alone but often lonely. Now, at last, it was time to turn and face the light.

With a pair of sunglasses on, naturally.

Epilogue: Five Years Later

Christmas Common, Oxfordshire

Moon Child skipped along the grassy path, Uncle James following a few paces behind. When she'd been small, she and her uncle had often walked this route together hand-in-hand, skirting around the edge of the settlement. Now, she was almost as tall as him and too big to walk hand-in-hand like a toddler. She was only five, but growing much faster than the other children in the settlement.

She'd learned to walk when she was just three weeks old, and was speaking fluently by the age of six months. She had begun reading shortly afterwards, devouring book after book after book.

Her friends at school were all older than her. She'd skipped kindergarten, and spent only a few months at junior school before moving on to senior school. At first the children there had found her strange, and she'd struggled to find her place, but now she was one of the crowd, having fun and getting into trouble like the rest of them.

She was maturing much faster than her friends, however, and would leave them behind before too long. That made her sad, but they would still be her friends, and she was looking forward to making new friends. She was already well acquainted with all the adults in the settlement. Some of them had been a little afraid of her at first, but they knew her well now and understood that although she was different, she was one of them.

Uncle James had told her what life had been like before the Great War. He'd explained that he'd been bullied because he was gay. And that his friend, Samuel, had been hated by some people for no other reason than he had black skin.

At first, Moon Child thought he was teasing her. 'But that's silly. Aunt Chanita has black skin, and nobody hates her. Some people have black hair, and others have yellow or red or brown, and people have all kinds of different coloured eyes. Why does it matter? I don't understand.'

'It's hard to explain,' he'd conceded. 'Things were very different in the old days.'

They found a place to sit together on a big rock near the edge of the settlement. After the long summer's day, the rock was very warm from the heat of the sun. Moon Child drew her special power from the sun too. James and the others got their power from the moon. Moon Child could do that as well. But the sun's power was stronger. That's why she could do so much.

'I'm glad I grew up after the Great War ended,' she said. 'Now everybody is different to everyone else, and it doesn't matter. Luke at school is a werewolf but he can only change when the moon is full; you and Daddy can change whenever you like. And there are people like Mummy who are stuck in human form and can't be anything else, and others who are wolf or half-wolf all the time. But they're all still people, just like us.'

She stretched out her arm and watched as the back of her hand changed from pale pink to dark tan then ebony black before fading back to the creamy white that matched her mother's complexion. Moon Child could make her skin any colour she wanted, or wear different shades over different parts of her body, depending on how she felt. Her father had explained to her that she had the power to control her genetic expression at the cellular level. He had given her a book that explained all about cells and genes, so that she would understand what he meant.

'Yes,' agreed Uncle James. 'Things are better now than before. You know, Samuel had a dream…

'That dream's come true, hasn't it?'

'Yes, I think it finally has.'

Moon Child knew that she was the only one of her kind so far, at least in this settlement, but Daddy said that soon there would be more like her, and perhaps others who were different again. Nobody could guess what kind of powers they might have. That's why being different was so exciting.

'Everybody's unique,' she said. 'But deep down we're all the same.'

'You are very wise.'

'Now you're being patronising.'

'That's a long word.'

She stuck her tongue out at him. 'Just because I'm only five doesn't mean I don't know long words.'

'That,' he said, 'is indisputably true.'

'Are you teasing me again?' she asked.

'Yes, I like to tease you. I enjoy seeing you laugh.'

So she gave him a laugh then, because she liked to see him smile. Uncle James was often sad, and Mummy and Daddy said it was because he had been through so much change. But Moon Child didn't understand that. Change was good. Change was thrilling.

'When I'm old enough to finish school, I want to learn to be a doctor,' she told him. 'Aunt Chanita's already showing me how to be a nurse, and Uncle Griffin promised to teach me about medicine when I'm a bit older.'

'I'm sure you'll make an excellent doctor,' said Uncle James. 'We're going to need more doctors. And nurses too. And all kinds of people to replace the ones who were lost.'

Moon Child grew sad then, thinking of the billions who had perished during the Great War. But that was why she wanted to become a doctor. She wanted to use her special powers for good.

She looked back at the settlement she called home. Just like her, it was growing and changing rapidly. New houses were being built and roads upgraded and repaired. Work had started on a larger school to accommodate all the children who had been born since the Great War, and those who were yet to be born. In her books, she had seen photographs of vast cities, filled with people and cars and great glass towers that reached into the sky. The cities were all gone now, but Moon Child wondered if one day her own settlement might grow to be as large as the cities of old. She hoped it would.

She looked ahead and saw that the sun was setting. 'Let's see if we can catch it before it goes down,' she said to Uncle James.

'We'll have to run really fast if we're going to do that.'

She sprang to her feet. 'Come on, then, let's go.'

Bounding forward, she plunged headlong through the air like a salmon leaping in a river. Her body was quicksilver, changing even without conscious thought. By the time she landed, her hands were paws, her fingers tipped with claws strong enough to grip the ground with ease. A coat of fine black hairs spread across her skin and she gave a yelp of pleasure through her long muzzle. She hit the ground running.

'Wait for me,' called Uncle James.

It took him much longer than her to make the change, but he managed it in the end. She waited patiently for him beneath a tree, licking her paws clean with her long pink tongue. The sun was just starting to sink beneath the horizon, like a great ball of fire kissing the distant hills. 'Come on,' she called. 'Be quick.'

'I'm coming.' He ran towards her and together they chased the sun until it had gone completely and the sky was filled with the purple flush of twilight. By the time they returned to the settlement, the moon hung bright above them. Moon Child looked up. Daddy had once told her a story about people who travelled to the moon in giant space rockets that roared like thunder and belched out fire. They had planted a flag on the moon, and it was still there today, although there was no wind on the moon to make it flap. She'd thought he was teasing her again, but Uncle Griffin said it was true. Moon Child hoped she could go to the moon one day. She would find out how to build a rocket. There was bound to be someone who remembered how to do it, or a book that explained how. And even if there wasn't, she would find a way herself.

After all, anything was possible.

Moon Child concludes the Lycanthropic series.

If you enjoyed this book, please leave a short review at Amazon. Thanks!

About the Author

Steve Morris has been a nuclear physicist, a dot com entrepreneur and a real estate investor, and is now the author of the Lycanthropic werewolf apocalypse series. He's a transhumanist and a practitioner of ashtanga yoga. He lives in Oxford, England.

Find out more at: stevemorrisbooks.com